The Gray

MW01133386

The Graymoor Mansion B&B
© 2008, 2013 Mark A. Roeder

Cover Photo Credit: Wisconsinart on Dreamstime.com.

Cover Design: Ken Clark

ISBN-13: 978-1482703320

ISBN-10: 1482703327

Printed in the United States of America

Acknowledgements

I'd like to thank Robbie Ellis-Cantwell, Ken Clark, and Kathy Staley for proofing the original version of this manuscript. I'd also like to think James Adkinson for proofing this revised edition and for correcting formatting errors. The efforts of these four have greatly improved this volume.

Dedication

This book is dedicated to the members of my Yahoo Fan Club. It's an honor to be associated with such a caring group of people.

In Memory of Denise Bromley
and her love of chocolate cake.

1966 – 2008

Sean—Graymoor Mansion Bed & Breakfast—Verona, Indiana—May 2004

I pulled my loaded-down Cavalier to a stop in front of Graymoor and looked through the windshield at my home.

"Wow."

I hadn't returned since Christmas, and I could see that even more work had been completed. At last, Graymoor looked as it must have on the day it was originally completed, at least on the outside. A professional-looking sign by the gate read:

Graymoor Mansion Bed & Breakfast
Opening Soon
Now Taking Reservations

Another sign near it read, "Beware of Ghosts." The transformation of the dilapidated old home into a B&B had taken five long years, but at last it was about to open.

I'd been away at college during most of the restoration—studying hotel management, believe it or not. While construction crews were swarming all over Graymoor, I'd learned the ins and outs of running a hotel. The Graymoor Mansion Bed & Breakfast was going to start out small, but my parents and their silent investor, none other than Jordan of *Phantom* fame, were hoping to turn Graymoor into a major hotel. Doing so would allow the renovations to continue. All of Graymoor might someday be restored to its former glory. From the outside it appeared that day had already come. My parents (and scores of workers) had performed a miracle.

I guess I should explain how my parents had managed to restore so much of Graymoor in such a short time; not that all of it was restored. Most of it was as yet untouched, but all the main rooms had been redone, as well as loads of bedrooms. I couldn't wait to get a look at the Natatorium and Solarium. They were unfinished when I left, but Mom had told me over the phone they would be completed by the time I came home. Anyway, the whole project started just before I graduated from good old Verona High School...

"I have a proposition for you," Jordan said, as he, Mom, Dad, my boyfriend Nick, my cousin Avery, Jordan's partner Ralph, and I sat around the kitchen table drinking coffee and tea after a tour of Graymoor.

"A proposition?" Dad said.

"I think Graymoor has the potential to eventually pay for its own restoration."

"How's that?" Avery asked.

"If you were to turn it into a hotel, paying guests could not only provide the funds for day-to-day expenses, but also to renovate the house."

"A hotel?" my mom asked. "That sounds far too ambitious."

"You could start it out as a Bed & Breakfast by renting out only a few rooms and then go from there, expanding as the opportunity presents itself."

"Even that would take a huge amount of capital, which we just don't have," Dad said.

"That's where I come in—as an investor."

"An investor?" I asked.

"Yes. This old house means a lot to me. You all know the connection between my dad and Graymoor. It was one of his dreams to restore it to its former grandeur. I'd like to help you realize that dream."

"Jordan, it would take a massive amount of money even to get started," Mom said.

"Money is not a problem. *Phantom's* CD sales are up, and our last tour was a great success. I've been investing most of the money I've made since the very beginning. I easily have enough to cover what I have in mind and then some."

"Whoa. You *are* rich," Avery said.

Jordan laughed.

"There's one huge problem with your plan," Avery said. "You're forgetting Graymoor has a notorious reputation. No one in Verona would *ever* spend the night here. The ax murders occurred over a hundred years ago, but no one around here has forgotten."

"On the contrary, the history of the house almost guarantees it will be a success. Perhaps the residents of Verona will be reluctant to stay here, but it isn't local residents who patronize hotels. It's travelers. A few may pass on Graymoor because of its reputation, but even more will come because of it. Hotels rumored to be haunted do quite well."

"Graymoor isn't just rumored to be haunted," I said. "Anyone staying here overnight will almost be guaranteed to see a ghost."

"Even better," Jordan said. "The ghosts will be a major selling point."

To make a long story short, after much discussion over a period of weeks, Mom and Dad took Jordan up on his offer. My parents remained the owners of Graymoor. They provided the house, and Jordan provided the funds to restore it. Jordan would likely never come out ahead on his investment and he knew it, but he didn't care. He loved that old home as much as we did. Not everything is about money.

Now, the renovations had been underway for years. I gazed at my old home once again. I could not get over the change. I grabbed my backpack and left the car. I walked through the massive iron gates and crossed the mowed lawn, admiring the roses, daisies, and black-eyed Susans. Dozens of other flower varieties peeked out from beds as well. I stopped for a moment, remembering the yard as it had been on the day we moved into Graymoor. Then, the grounds were overgrown and creepy, looking more than anything like an Addams Family movie set; now, they were beautiful. What a difference a few years could make.

I crossed the porch and opened the massive front door. A hint of varnish was in the air, and I could hear hammering in some distant part of the house. Construction had been going on continuously throughout my college years. It nearly drove me insane the first few weeks after I graduated from high school. My rowdy college dorm was quiet in comparison. Now, I'd just graduated from college and had returned home. It felt good to be back.

"Sean, hey bro, what's up?" Avery asked as he grabbed and hugged me.

"When did you get in?"

"Yesterday. I flew out here as soon as my last final was done. I couldn't be late for the massive graduation party. It's hard to imagine: you, Nick, Marshall, Skye and me all graduating at the same time."

"It's not that amazing. We all graduated from high school at the same time too. Remember?"

"Yeah, well, it's not as if we had the same courses. College isn't high school Sean."

"I guess you're right. I took some time to actually work in hotels to gain experience, and Nick took a lighter load since he knew it would take me an extra year to finish."

I frowned.

"What? Are you still upset Nick didn't finish up so he could move in with you the last year?"

"That's the past Avery."

"Uh-huh."

"Marshall's courses actually took five years to complete. Only you and Skye decided to take an *entire* year off in the middle of college."

"That trip to Europe was worth it. I had a blast! I have no idea why Skye chose to remain in California instead of coming with me."

"I've got a good idea. I hear California is filled with buff boys."

"Damn, those French babes were hot," Avery said.

"Yeah, I hear girls with hairy legs are a real turn-on."

"Like you know anything about girls."

"Ignorance is bliss. Speaking of girls, where's Nicole? Or has she dumped your sorry ass already?"

"Dump this fine bit of masculinity? Dream on! Nicole flew home to visit her parents. She's going to meet me at Phantom World."

"You're starting to sound like Skye."

"Me sound like Mr. Testosterone?"

"Yes, you."

"So when do Marshall and Nick get here?"

"Everyone is supposed to arrive by tomorrow. How many days do you have to stay?"

"Just four. The park doesn't open for almost three weeks, but we have orientation. I'm helping train some of the newbies since I worked there last summer."

"I wish you could stay longer. I haven't seen you since Christmas."

"In four days you'll be sick of me," Avery said.

"I doubt that."

It was hard to remember the Avery who had been such a total jerk when he was a teenager. Who would have guessed that I'd come to think of him as a brother? I suppose sharing life-threatening events had something to do with that.

Avery led me into the kitchen.

"Guess who's here?" he asked.

Mom turned away from the range and then ran toward me.

"Sean!"

She hugged me and kissed me as if I was thirteen instead of twenty-three.

"Oh my! You've grown."

"You saw me at Christmas, Mom."

"I still think you've grown. You boys have changed so much."

"Yeah," Avery said. "I keep getting more gorgeous, and Sean here isn't the pudgy little geek he used to be."

"I hate to be the one to give you the bad news, Avery, but you're not gorgeous, and I've only lost five pounds. I'm *still* pudgy." I sighed.

"You look fine, and I *am* gorgeous."

"You should not have lived with Skye this year. He's completely rubbed off on you," I said.

Avery gave me a look that indicated there was a story to tell, but not in front of Mom.

"I'm so glad to have you home," Mom said, hugging me again. "My son, a college graduate."

"Come on, Mr. Big Shot. I'll help you unload your car," Avery said, rescuing me from Mom.

I tossed my backpack on one of the kitchen chairs, and Avery and I walked out to the car to begin carrying in the many boxes that loaded down my Cavalier.

"So, you ready to put that expensive college education to work?" Avery asked.

"Definitely. I interned at an 800-room hotel. I'm sure I can handle a start-up bed & breakfast. We're just going to rent out eight rooms in the beginning."

"I don't envy you. I think working in an amusement park will be a breeze compared to what's ahead of you."

"I'm looking forward to it."

"You always were a little odd."

"So tell me about Skye," I said.

"Oh, man, that boy gets around. Every time I walked in our apartment there was a new guy with Skye, and he was out every night too. I seriously think he fucked every gay guy at the university and also several of the straight ones. And of

14

course, you know Skye; all the guys he hooked up with were gorgeous."

"How would you know who's gorgeous?"

"Hey, you don't have to be queer to know a good-looking guy when you see one—a point proven every morning as I look in the mirror."

I rolled my eyes.

"I suppose the love affair of the century is still going on?" Avery asked.

"Of course."

"Damn, I don't know how you and Nick handled that long-distance-relationship shit. Zoë and I tried my freshman year. What a disaster."

"Well, you're still friends."

"True, but I thought she was 'the one' at the time."

"How many girls have you thought that about since Zoë?"

"Just three, counting Nicole, but Bette turned out to be such a freak."

"Sounds like a perfect match to me."

"Screw you, Sean," Avery said, smiling.

"Oh, bisexual now, huh? I told you college would broaden your horizons. Did you do a little experimenting while you were in California?"

"Dream on, homo boy."

"This is sick," I said. "I actually missed you."

"Hey, I grow on you."

"Like fungus."

It was Avery's turn to roll his eyes. "You've got to get some new material, man. You are still such a geek."

I stuck out my tongue at him.

We had made our way to the third floor by then, with each of us toting a box in our arms. Just before we reached my room, a Gothic side chair slid across my path, nearly tripping me up. The disturbance was followed by a disembodied giggle. At one time such events freaked me out, but after years in Graymoor I was no longer troubled by furniture that seemed to move by itself.

"I see some things are still the same here," I said.

"Yeah, and I still think the ghosts will send whatever guests we get packing. Not everyone is accustomed to candles lighting themselves, disembodied moans and an organ that plays itself."

"People are going to love this place. You'll see."

"I hope you're right," Avery said.

We continued to catch up as we carried boxes up to my room. It was going to take a good deal of time to unpack. Who knew so much crap would fit in a tiny apartment?

The fact that I was back home for good hit me after Avery and I had unloaded the car and I was sitting alone in my old room. It felt strange to be there after all those years of living away from home. Sure, there had been visits, but it wasn't the same as living there full time. Now, I was back. Most kids went away to college to escape from home, but my college education led me right back to Graymoor. I wasn't one bit sorry. I knew this is where I belonged.

***

Avery knocked on my door just before six p.m., disturbing the end of a rather pleasant nap.

"Mom says supper will be ready soon."

Mom was technically Avery's aunt, but she was his mother in every way that mattered. He'd taken to calling her Mom about the time we graduated from high school. That was about the same time Avery and I began to think of each other as brothers, not cousins.

I stretched and yawned and followed Avery downstairs. Halfway across the parlor the aroma of something wonderful met my nostrils. Avery looked at me. He'd noticed it too.

"What is that?" I asked as we stepped into the massive kitchen.

"That is Martha's five-cheese lasagna," Mom said, nodding toward an older woman I'd never seen before. "Martha is going to be handling most of the cooking and baking for the B&B. She's our head chef. Well, currently our only chef."

"Hey, I'm Sean," I said as I stepped toward Martha. "I would have hired you with nothing more to go on than the scent of that lasagna. I wasn't even hungry when I walked downstairs, but now I'm starving."

"It's very nice to meet you, Sean. Your mother has told me a lot about you."

"If I know Mom, you're sick of hearing about me, I bet," I said.

"Not at all. Now sit down everyone. The garlic toast is nearly ready."

"Just wait until you taste Martha's blueberry muffins," Dad said. "And her pecan pancakes and—"

"We've been trying out dishes for the bed & breakfast," Mom said. "All these years I thought I knew how to cook, but Martha—"

"Oh, stop," Martha said. "If those caramel-pecan breakfast rolls are any indication of your baking abilities, you're an excellent cook, Kayla."

I could tell Mom and Martha got on well. I liked Martha already. She was kind of grandmotherly, although she probably wasn't over fifty and seemed full of energy.

Supper was superb. I had never tasted such lasagna, not even in the best Italian restaurants. It was beautifully seasoned and the cheeses... Mmmm. The garlic toast was equally delicious, as were the cooked apples and gourmet mashed potatoes which were seasoned with herbs and mixed with melted cheese. I could have made a meal out of the potatoes alone. Avery talked little during supper. He was too busy stuffing his face. Apparently, he shared my opinion of Martha's culinary skills.

"So when do you think we can open?" I asked as we were eating.

"We'll need to discuss that with you," Dad said. "We've begun taking reservations starting on June 14th."

"How's that going?"

"All eight rooms are booked for nearly all of June," Dad said. "The only advertising we've done was a small one-time ad in the *Verona Citizen*."

"Wow, that's great. So locals are booking rooms?"

"Yes."

"Hmm, I seem to remember someone saying that no locals would ever stay in Graymoor," I said, turning to Avery.

"Hey, can't a guy be wrong now and then?"

"You're wrong all the time Avery; that's what's so right about you."

"And you rip off lines from M*A*S*H far too frequently, Sean."

"Sometimes I can't help myself."

I turned my attention back to my parents. "Once we get going, I'll implement my advertising scheme. Ads are really expensive in most of the travel magazines, but I thought we'd try it on a limited scale. I thought we could focus on some smaller regional publications, web sites and so forth. If we can get a travel columnist to come, we can get a lot of advertising for the cost of a night's stay."

"See, Dear, I told you that the tuition money was well spent," Mom said to Dad.

"What I'm hoping to do is make use of word of mouth. If we can impress our first guests, hopefully they'll spread the word. I thought we might offer a discount for referrals."

"That sounds great," Dad said.

"I've been working up several ideas. I did a marketing plan for Graymoor as one of my class projects. I got an A, so at least Professor Coltrane thinks it's sound."

"I can't wait for you to see the Solarium," Mom said.

"So it's finished?"

"And beautiful," Mom said, "although beautiful isn't a strong enough word to describe it. Mr. Diggory has done an incredible job."

"Mr. Diggory? That sounds like the perfect name for a gardener," Avery said.

"He's a wizard with anything that grows," Dad said. "You won't recognize the Solarium when you enter it. You'll swear those plants have been growing in there for years."

"I can't wait to see it," I said. "Can we take a look after supper?"

"Of course," Mom said. "You will be amazed at the transformation. You should see what he's done with the Natatorium as well. It's a paradise."

"So the pool is finished?"

"It's ready for guests."

"Wow."

When I'd departed, most of the repairs and restoration in the Solarium and Natatorium had been completed, but the pool and massive planters were empty. Now, all was restored to what it once had been. I never thought I'd live to see the day. I felt as though I'd been waiting for this forever.

"Tomorrow, you can meet Mrs. Hawkins, our housekeeper."

"Why isn't she here now?" I asked. "Isn't the staff living in?"

"She's still in the process of moving in."

"Where's Mr. Diggory?"

"Out and about on the grounds most likely," Martha said. "We have a terrible time getting him to come in and eat. He just can't keep himself away from the gardens. I'll take a tray out to him later."

"He sounds very dedicated."

"More than you could believe," Dad said.

19

"Have you filled all the positions yet?" I asked. It was a task I would have liked to have had a hand in, but it was hardly possible, since I was away at school.

"We've completed the first round of hiring," Dad said. "We'll let you handle the rest of it. Once we get going, we'll need a larger staff. We already have a stack of applications for household staff, gardening assistants and so forth."

"Great. I'll want to consult with Mr. Diggory before we hire anyone to assist him. I think he should have the final say over any staff involved with his area. I'll be consulting you about kitchen staff as well, Martha. I'm sure you know best. One thing I want to avoid is micromanaging."

It was a bit surreal to be an adult sitting there with my parents. I was getting ready to take over the running of Graymoor—the bed & breakfast aspects of it, at least. Dad would be in charge of the restoration, of course. Who better to ensure it was restored properly than an archaeologist with a background in architecture?

I was hoping to see more of Dad now that I was back home. Mom said he'd been around more than usual during the restoration. His career often took him far from home. I guess we were just lucky he wasn't an Egyptologist. We might never see him then. Dad worked mainly with early Colonial American sites on the order of Jamestown or Williamsburg.

It seemed like just yesterday I was an insecure and uncertain teenager. Where had the time gone? I still felt very much like that teenage boy in some ways, but I knew I was up to the task at hand.

After supper, Avery and I offered to help Martha clean up, but she shooed us out of "her" kitchen. Mom and Dad took us on a little tour.

"We'll show you the Natatorium first," Mom said.

We walked through the winding hallways of Graymoor. I wondered how many of our guests would get lost while exploring. I'd already taken the original house plans and made maps that guests would be advised to carry with them.

Even so, maps couldn't possibly show everything. I'm sure they would be of assistance though.

As we neared the Natatorium, an unfamiliar smell wafted to my nostrils. I couldn't identify it at first, but then realization dawned on me: it was chlorine. Another scent mixed with it: floral. It was quite a pleasant combination. As we drew even closer, the aroma became stronger and the air more humid.

"Holy shit!" Avery said as we entered the Natatorium.

I gasped as I stood beside him. I was not prepared for the sight that met my eyes.

"It looks like something that belongs in a Roman Emperor's palace," Avery said.

I couldn't have agreed more. The Olympic-sized pool was filled with sparkling blue water for the first time since I'd lived in Graymoor. Large tropical trees grew from huge planters, and ferns and ivy trailed down columns and arches toward the pool. Purple and lavender water lilies grew in wide, shallow containers. With the life-sized statues of nude, athletic young men, it really did look like a scene from ancient Rome. The light was failing outside, but concealed lighting and lights in the pool itself beautifully illuminated the Natatorium.

"We have a surprise for you," Mom said, and she led us to the side of the Natatorium that connected with the house. A large doorway led from the Natatorium into what had been a huge room, empty except for abandoned planters and antique pool furniture. When I stepped inside, I gasped again.

"Skye will love this," Avery said. "When he comes for the party...I mean."

"A gym? You put in a gym?" I asked.

I couldn't believe it. All kinds of weight machines filled the room. It looked better-equipped than the university's weight room.

"We told Jordan it was unnecessary, but it's something he really wanted to do," Dad explained.

21

"With the pool and all this equipment, it's like a spa," I said. "All that's missing is a hot tub."

Dad pointed to one corner; sitting there was a sunken hot tub.

"I don't even want to think about what all this cost," I said.

"We're well into the millions," Dad said.

"There is no way Jordan will come out ahead on this," I said, "even if we open up a hundred rooms."

"As if he cares," Avery said. "He said himself that profit isn't the point."

"Yeah, but still. You know, we're going to need to hire someone to oversee the pool and gym."

"We're already ahead of you. He arrives tomorrow," Dad said.

"Let's take a look at the Solarium now," Mom said.

She took us the long way around, through the house instead of cutting across the yard. Every room we passed had been restored, looking as it must have on the night of the Graymoor murders. I wondered how our guests would react to the frequent ghostly re-enactment of *that* terrible event.

The Natatorium had made me gasp, but the Solarium absolutely took my breath away. Since the first day I'd wandered into the Solarium, I'd dreamed of seeing the vast space filled with life. Everywhere I turned there were trees, shrubs, flowers and vines of all descriptions. The Solarium no longer seemed like one huge open area, but like a series of beautiful living rooms decorated with statuary, columns and arches. I had the feeling fifty visitors could wander through the space at once and yet feel a sense of solitude.

The sun had gone down, but the Solarium was lit with subdued, hidden lighting. The stars blazed above as we wandered through a tropical paradise below. I knew then that I'd never want to leave home again. I breathed in the warm, moist air. The fragrance of Calla Lilies, Angel's Trumpet, roses and other blooming plants wafted around us. Some of the plants were potted, but most grew in the numerous beds throughout the Solarium. I could almost swear I was in a jungle instead of northern Indiana.

We tarried long in the Solarium. It was just too enchanting a place to leave. I found myself wishing I could sleep there. I couldn't believe my family actually owned such a thing. I couldn't believe any gardener could create it. As with the Natatorium, the plants in the Solarium looked as if they'd always been there. How Mr. Diggory was able to create such beauty in only a few months I'd never understand.

I returned to my room later simply astounded by what I'd seen. It isn't often that one's hopes and dreams are exceeded. Everything seemed so wonderful that it nearly made me fearful. I'd known so much tragedy and terror in my life that the present seemed unreal, like a dream.

Skye

I walked into the terminal and immediately spotted Sean and Nick. They smiled and waved. I gave Greg, a cute and built college boy I met during the flight, a wink and went to join my friends.

"Skye!" Sean said, hugging me.

Greg walked by and grinned. Nick didn't fail to notice.

"Who was that?" he asked.

"Just a friend I made on the flight. He's got the hottest ass."

"You guys didn't...on the plane?" Sean stammered.

"It's called the Mile High Club, Sean."

"Why am I not surprised?"

"Hey, I had some time to kill, and he was hot, so—"

"Spare us the details," Nick said. "Why didn't you fly in with Avery? Sean said he got in two days ago."

"I didn't want to rush off like he did. I had a few goodbyes to make."

"Don't you mean a few guys to make?" Sean asked.

"Hey, I was leaving forever. I had to say goodbye properly. Besides, I've spent more than enough time with Avery over the last year. So when did your flight get in, Nick?"

"About an hour ago."

"Good. You guys didn't have to wait too long for me, then. South Bend doesn't have the most exciting airport."

"I guess that's why Marshall is flying into Indy," Nick said.

"That, and there are no direct flights from London to South Bend," Sean said.

"Can you even get to Indiana from London?" I asked.

"I thought you said Marshall had a layover in Atlanta?" Nick said.

"Okay, his flight was almost direct. Damn, you realize we haven't seen Marshall in five years?" Sean said.

"I wonder how much stranger he's become," I said. "After five years in England at that school for psychos."

"Not psychos, psychics," Sean said. "He was studying psychology and parapsychology, Skye."

"Hey, I'm just practicing. I have to give him a hard time. He'll think I don't like him if I'm too nice to him."

"Now there is some screwed-up logic," Nick said.

"Did someone say screw?" I asked.

"So, I hear you got your degree," Sean said.

"Yep, sports fitness."

"You think you'll ever put that to use? I mean, what's a B.S. in dumb jock really worth?" Nick asked.

"I've already got a job waiting on me, smart ass."

"Really?" Sean asked. "Already? You just graduated. You didn't mention this in any of your e-mails."

"Yep. As for the e-mails, my life is far too full to mention everything."

"Is it near Verona? I hope you won't be moving off to New York or somewhere. I'd like to see you occasionally."

"Oh, you'll be seeing a lot of me."

"So your job is close then? Is it here in South Bend?"

"Notre Dame?" Nick asked.

"Nope."

"Who are you working for then?" Sean asked.

"You."

"Huh?"

I laughed. "I'm the new personal trainer and spa manager for the Graymoor Mansion Bed & Breakfast."

"What?" Sean asked, almost shouting. "My parents didn't tell me!"

"I asked them not to. I wanted to be the one to give you the news."

"Avery didn't say anything either."

"He doesn't know. Do you think I'd be stupid enough to entrust Avery with a secret? Shut up Nick."

Nick closed his mouth before he even had a chance to utter a comment on my intelligence.

"This is so awesome!"

"Just remember, if you try to make me call you boss, I will kick your ass. You're also going to start working on those abs," I said, looking down at Sean's midsection.

"Yes sir," Sean said, grinning.

Sean and Nick helped me find my luggage and load it onto a cart. I didn't see how it would all fit in Sean's Cavalier, which was already loaded with Nick's stuff, but my bags went in without a hitch. Soon, we were on our way to Verona.

"Whoa! You're really going to live in Graymoor?" Sean asked.

"Are you sure you're brave enough?" Nick asked.

"Don't make me pound you Nick. Of course, I'm going to live in Graymoor. It's not that scary. Besides, Marshall assured us years ago that the evil presence there is gone."

"Unless Devon comes back for a visit, which is a distinct possibility," Sean said.

"At least he's the devil I know, but anyway, moving to Graymoor is perfect. I wouldn't feel right about moving back in with my sister and Matt, especially now that Colin has a little brother. It would be too crowded, and I don't do diapers."

"Ah, I thought you weren't afraid of anything, Skye," Sean said as he drove.

"Have you ever smelled a dirty diaper? Be afraid; be very afraid."

"So I guess you don't want to move in with your mom and stepdad, either?" Nick asked.

I leaned up from the backseat and punched Nick hard in the shoulder.

"Owww!"

"That's what you get for calling Josh my stepdad."

"Well, it is true, you know."

"Don't remind me."

"Are you two still not getting along?" Sean asked.

"We do okay. He's no longer in danger of getting his face rearranged. He's been a good deal nicer to me since I saved his ass. I even kind of like him; just don't tell him that."

"How are things with your mom?" Nick asked.

"A little strained, but we get along. She's more or less comfortable with my sexual orientation now. I've forgiven her for abandoning me when I was kid. After all, she did come back, and what good does it do to hold onto a grudge? Things aren't entirely as they should be between us. Like I said, I've forgiven her, but forgetting is a whole other matter."

"Mom showed me the Natatorium and the new weight room," Sean said. "I guess you haven't seen them?"

"No, but I did work with your parents, advising them on what machines to order. I told them the basic machines that are a must and gave them a wish list of other equipment that isn't a necessity but would be great to have in the gym."

"From the looks of the gym, I think they ordered everything," Sean said.

"Sweet."

"I can't wait to see it," Nick said.

"You guys will not believe the change in the Natatorium and the Solarium," Sean said. "It will knock your socks off."

"How about my boxers?"

"You haven't changed Skye," Nick said.

"I can't wait to get started. I'm hoping that some guests will eventually come mainly to use the spa. I'm going to tailor fitness programs for them to use at Graymoor and when they get back home. I'm expecting things to be slow at first, but hopefully word will get out. I want to talk to you,

Sean, about advertising in some fitness publications. I really think the spa can draw in a lot of business."

"I have no idea what our advertising budget will be," Sean said. "I'll have to talk to Jordan about that. He's the one writing the checks."

"I was thinking we could offer some weekend fitness packages or something like that," I said. "We could include specially prepared meals for the fitness-minded, something a bit different from the usual menu."

"Whoa, Skye! You sound like a businessman," Nick said.

"Nah, not me. I just have a few ideas. Making them work is Sean's job."

"No pressure there," Sean said. "So when did Mom and Dad hire you?"

"About six months ago. I'd been talking to Gold's Gym and a couple of other fitness chains. I'd really planned to move to Chicago or maybe New York after graduation. I was considering staying in California even more. Your parents convinced me to return to Verona. I could make more in a big city, but at Graymoor I can manage the gym. The cost of living is far lower as well. I also get room and board, so I'll actually be making more working for your parents than I would elsewhere. Do you know what it costs for an apartment in Chicago? It's unbelievable. And L.A.? Forget it! Plus, I will be near my family this way."

"It's going to be great having you around," Sean said.

"I'm looking forward to it. The only thing I don't like about returning to Verona is the lack of gay guys. There's no way Verona can compete with Chicago or L.A. in that department. If the B&B really gets going, maybe some hotties will stay as guests."

"I knew you had an ulterior motive," Nick said.

"Hey, I've grown accustomed to having a whole university at my disposal. I can't go cold turkey."

"Cold turkey? Yeah, right!" Sean said. "If I know you, you'll get laid before dark."

"Nah, I may not even look for anyone until...tomorrow."

"You know, if you had a boyfriend, you wouldn't have to look for hook-ups," Nick said.

"Where's the fun in that? No offense, but be with the same guy all that time? Doesn't that get boring?"

Sean and Nick looked at each other. I couldn't be sure from the back seat, but I think they exchanged a grin.

"Not at all," Nick said. "Besides, Sean and I haven't seen each other since Christmas."

"Yeah, I know what you two will be doing as soon as we get to Verona."

"Don't you know it!" Sean said.

"Hmm, maybe I should look for someone tonight. I may have to set up my laptop and check out gay.com."

"Don't you mean slut.com?" Nick said.

"I'm gonna have to hurt you, boy."

I was amazed at the transformation of Graymoor when we arrived about an hour later. I had been back to Verona for Christmas, but I hadn't actually been inside Graymoor Mansion for some two years. Sean and Nick were far too eager to dash off and get naked together to show me around, but what I did see as Sean's mom led me to my room was impressive. The term mansion truly fit now. While Graymoor had always had a dilapidated edge before, now it was as good as new—at least the parts I glimpsed. I don't mean that it looked like a new home. Far from it. The whole place was undeniably old and filled with antiques. A sense of history permeated the air, yet all was fresh, sound and clean.

I was impressed with my room. It was rather large and seemed almost palatial compared to my apartment. The furniture was all antique, of course. I wasn't big on antiques, but they fit at Graymoor. The room was comfortable and had a decidedly masculine feel to it. Sean's mom had obviously picked it out just for me. The color scheme was hunter green and yellow. The yellow was pale, but not quite so pale as to be a pastel. The soft carpet, heavy drapes, bedspread and the tiny shamrock designs in the wallpaper were all hunter green. The wallpaper was predominantly yellow and the ceiling was gilded tin.

My bed was awesome! It was an antique, of course: a double with a high, carved headboard that reminded me of the bed in the Lincoln bedroom in the White House. I loved the large oval in the headboard and footboard. I plopped myself down on it, and it was so comfortable I could have lain right there and taken a nap. I moved around on it a bit, and there was not a squeak to be heard. That was a good thing because I intended to use the bed for far more than just sleeping.

My room also included a marble-top dresser that matched the bed and a huge wardrobe with a full-length mirror. There was an old roll-top desk and chair, a large table and a couple of comfortable chairs. There was a big, heavy-looking bookcase that would be perfect for my CDs, books and magazines.

I think the bathroom might have been my favorite part. The bathroom was a new addition. Even I knew indoor plumbing was virtually non-existent in rural areas in the Victorian age. The bathroom fit—so well I bet most people wouldn't have realized it wasn't an original part of the house. It was rather large, with gleaming brass hardware everywhere I looked. There was an old-fashioned claw-foot tub, big enough for two (which definitely gave me ideas), as well as a separate shower. The floor and the walls up to about ten feet were tiled, the floor in hunter green and the walls in pale yellow, except for a single row of tiles that matched the floor. Above the tile, the walls were painted yellow and the ceiling was gilded tin with fancy designs in it, just like in the main room. No expense had been spared. I knew right then and there that someday Graymoor would be a first-class hotel.

I walked back into my room and looked out one of the three large windows. I was located on the third floor and had a magnificent view out over the Natatorium and Solarium.

I was itching to see the gym, but wasn't quite sure how to get there. I found a pamphlet on my desk that folded out to become a map, however. I left my room behind and descended to the first floor. After that, I used the map to find my way to the Natatorium. I took a couple of wrong turns, but at last I managed to get there.

"Whoa!" I said out loud, even though I was quite alone.

I simply couldn't believe the sight before my eyes. I'd seen the Natatorium in its dilapidated state, but I wasn't prepared for the sight before me. The Natatorium was gorgeous. The crystal clear blue water looked so inviting I wanted to jump in right then. I couldn't wait another moment to get a look at the gym, so I quickly walked to the gymnasium.

"Wow!"

Sean was right. It looked like Jordan and Sean's parents had purchased every piece of equipment on my wish list. I felt as if I'd died and gone to heaven. Everything was gleaming and new. Most universities didn't even have a setup like this. Just getting to use the equipment would be a thrill. I almost couldn't believe I was going to be paid for managing the spa. There was even a hot tub!

I wanted to work out right then and there, but I was too fatigued by my flight. The last thing I needed was an injury because I was too tired to do my exercises properly. I yawned. I seriously needed a nap. There was so much I wanted to do, from working out to swimming to unpacking to checking out the local gay scene, but I opted to return to my room. Once there, I stripped naked and flopped down on the bed. I closed my eyes and was asleep in minutes.

The light was getting dim when I awakened from my nap. I needed a breath of fresh air, so I dressed and walked downstairs and out the front door. I found Sean and Nick roaming among the flower beds in the moonlight. No doubt they'd been making out. I could use some lip and tongue action myself.

I hadn't been there for two minutes when a large, black limo pulled up. I was more surprised by who climbed out of the back of the limo than by the car itself.

"Marshall!" Sean and Nick said, running toward him.

"Hello, mates!" Marshall said.

I walked over to join them. Marshall nodded at me.

"Hey Skye."

"You're taller," Sean said.

"You're a bit taller too," Marshall said.

"A limo?" Nick said. "Did you become rich and famous while you were gone?"

"I'm afraid not," Marshall said, "although I'm better off than I was. London is full of opportunities. The limo was actually cheaper than a taxi."

"Marshall, you have a British accent," I said, laughing.

"It will fade in time, unfortunately, now that I'll once again be under the influence of you bloody Yanks and your barbarian dialect."

We helped Marshall lug his bags upstairs to one of the rooms that had been renovated for guests.

"If the rest of the house looks anything like this, it must be incredible," Marshall said as we dumped his bags on the antique bed.

"Just wait until you see the Solarium and Natatorium," Sean said. "You won't believe it. The Dining Room has been restored, as well as several bedrooms, sitting rooms, studies and hallways. Of course, I'm sure you noticed the main stairway has been redone. Construction crews have been swarming all over the place for five years, and they're still going at it."

"I'm sure the construction has stirred up a lot of ghosts," Marshall said. "Changes always do that."

"I told you he wouldn't be here five minutes before he mentioned ghosts," I said.

"He is definitely correct," Sean said. "Mom and Dad have experienced sightings far more frequently since the restoration began. I've only been home for a few days now and then over the last five years, but even I've noticed an increase in supernatural activity."

"And here we thought you had rid Graymoor of ghosts," Nick said.

"Only of the evil presence and the trapped souls," Marshall said. "Believe me, there are plenty of ghosts left."

"You say that with such certainty," Nick said. "You just got here minutes ago!"

"Which is long enough for me to have already seen a few specters."

"So, you're still seeing dead people, huh?" I asked.

"Did you see *Sixth Sense*?" Nick asked. "I think it came out about a year or two after you left for England."

"Of course I saw it. I was living in London, not the Amazon. I found it quite accurate for a bloody Hollywood film."

"Come on, Nick," Sean said. "You know he watched it. It was probably required for his Ghost 101 course."

"Funny!" Marshall said.

"So did you learn anything useful at that school?" I asked.

"Loads," Marshall said. "It was a dream come true!"

"Can you use any of it to make a living?" I asked, "or will you be waiting tables at Café Moffatt?"

"There's a name I haven't heard in a while, but yes, I can use all of it to make a living. I've already been doing so. In fact, I'm planning on opening my own business right here in Verona."

"What kind of business?" Nick asked.

"Paranormal investigations for those troubled by ghosts, or what they believe are ghosts. Also, counseling for ghosts themselves. I'll likely be traveling a great deal, but I'm going to use Verona as my base of operation."

"What are you going to call it—Freaks 'R' Us?" I asked.

"You're still trying to be funny, aren't you Skye?"

"Screw you!"

"And still a slut, I see."

I grinned. I'd missed trading barbs with Marshall.

"Counseling for ghosts?" Sean asked, ignoring our exchange. "How can you make any money on that? It's not like the dead can pay."

"I'll be hired by the living who have contact with a troubled ghost."

"So, like a horse whisperer, only with ghosts?" Nick asked.

"More or less."

"So you, like, talk to ghosts through a séance?" Sean asked.

"A séance is no longer necessary for me," Marshall said. "I've sharpened my skills, although at the academy they determined that my psychic abilities were quickly increasing without training."

"You can't make our heads explode just by looking at us can you?" Nick asked, teasing.

"Let me see," Marshall said, staring hard at him for a few moments. "No, I guess not. What a pity."

"You are so not funny," Nick said.

"Well, at least he tries," I said.

"Let's let Marshall get some rest," Sean said. "We can pester him about his psychic abilities later. Besides, this is Marshall we're talking about. We'll never get him to shut up once he gets started."

"I am tired. It's about four a.m. London time, and it was a long flight."

"Have a good night then," Sean and Nick said.

"Yeah, good night, Marshall. It's good to have you back," I added.

"Good night, guys. It's good to be home."

***

I awakened just after seven the next morning. I showered in the impressive bathroom connected to my room and then dressed. I could remember when Graymoor didn't even have electricity. Now, my room was comparable to that in any luxury hotel in the U.S.

I stepped out of my room and walked down the hallway. I met Marshall as I reached the second-floor landing. Apparently he had just awakened as well. Together, we made our way to the kitchen. Sean's mom and Martha greeted us as we entered.

"Our first guinea pigs of the morning," Martha said.

"Good morning, boys," said Sean's mom, Kayla.

"Did you have a nice flight, Marshall?"

"It was long, but yes," he said.

"This is Martha Merlot, our head chef. Martha, this is Marshall, one of Sean's friends."

"Head chef. It makes me sound impressive, but it's really just a grand way of saying I'm the cook," Martha said, smiling. "We've just been concocting a Greek omelet. Would you boys like to try it?"

"I would love to," I said.

"Me too," Marshall said. "Martha Merlot? You wouldn't happen to be the Martha Merlot who wrote *Descent Into Darkness* would you?"

"As a matter of fact, yes."

"I read your book while I was at school. One of my professors raved about it in class, and everyone started reading it. It was brilliant!"

"You never told me you're a writer." Kayla looked at Martha in confusion.

"Oh, it's really only a hobby—something I do to keep myself occupied. I've only written one book."

"You could do it professionally," Marshall said.

"It would seem like work then. Where's the fun in that?"

I laughed. I'd met Martha only the night before when I was raiding the kitchen for a snack, but I liked her already.

"Marshall has been in England studying the paranormal," Sean's mom said.

"The paranormal? How fascinating," Martha said.

"Ghosts, psychic phenomena, et cetera," Marshall said.

"I grew up with a ghost," Martha said.

"The one you mentioned in your book?"

"Yes, but she's fictionalized in the book. My grandmother died when I was six. I was able to speak with her until I was about twelve or so. After that, I lost the ability, but I could still see her, and even the rest of the family could feel her presence. My mother didn't believe my stories for quite a while, but then I began to tell her too many things that grandmother had shared with me–things only she would know."

"That's something I loved about your book: the way the ghost interacted with the main character. Of course, I loved the whole book. It was right up my alley."

"Let's hope you like my Greek omelet, as well. It's almost ready."

"If it tastes anything like it smells, it will be delicious," I said.

The omelet was incredible. I especially liked the feta cheese. It had a pungent but delicious taste. Marshall and I both devoured our omelets while we talked with Martha and Sean's mom. There was no sign of Sean, Nick, or Avery at breakfast. Apparently, they were all still in college-boy mode—sleeping in as late as possible. I would have remained in bed myself, but I was too excited.

Marshall went off to explore, and I headed for the gym to prepare for our guests. There was a massive amount of work to be done, from checking over the equipment to creating signs to checking the chlorine content of the pool and more.

While standing near the pool, I caught sight of an attractive guy on the other side of the glass wall. He was conferring with a couple of men who were obviously construction workers. The one who caught my eye, however, was dressed casually in tan slacks and an attractive white, button-down shirt. He was black haired, tall and quite good looking, at least from a distance. Before I had a chance to truly check him out, he'd walked away. Perhaps Verona had more to offer in the way of men than it had when I'd departed five years before.

Before I knew it, it was time for lunch. Despite the delicious omelet I'd eaten that morning, I was ravenous. I arrived in the Dining Room as Martha and Mrs. Hilton were setting great covered platters upon the immense table. Sean and Nick were bringing in yet more platters and bowls, while Sean's dad, Avery, and Marshall were already seated at the table. There was also an older lady I didn't recognize, but she soon introduced herself as Matilda, the head housekeeper. She reminded me a bit of Gretchen, the head housekeeper from that old show *Benson*. There was an older man too: Basil Diggory, the head gardener. I told him what a fantastic job I thought he'd done in the Natatorium.

"Wow, I can't get over how much everyone has changed," Marshall said, looking around the table.

"That's what happens when you stay away for five years," I said,

"You know Skye, I didn't think you could get any more buff."

I laughed.

"Actually, for the last couple of years I'd just been working on definition. I don't want to get any bigger."

"Good, I was afraid you would turn into one of those body-building freaks. Those guys don't even look human."

"No, that's not for me. I don't like cosmetic muscles. I want them to serve a purpose."

"Still kicking ass?" Marshall asked.

"Whenever necessary."

Our conversation was interrupted by lunch, which didn't upset me in the least.

"We'll be trying out items for the menu for the next several days," Martha announced. "I hope you all like roast duck. If not, we also have herbed pork chops and baked salmon."

"I thought this was going to be a bed & breakfast. You'll be serving lunch and dinner too?" I asked.

"We're giving it serious consideration," Kayla said. "We're going to start with just breakfast, but we may expand later on. Martha thought now was a good time to experiment."

"After that omelet this morning, I'll be your guinea pig any day," I announced.

"Me too," Marshall said.

Martha smiled.

In addition to the selection of meats, there were twice-baked potatoes seasoned with rosemary, baby carrots that tasted so delicious they were like no carrots I'd ever eaten, corn with red peppers, freshly baked yeast rolls and German chocolate cake for dessert.

"There is no way I can eat like this every day," I said. "I would get so fat, but it's so good."

"Yeah, I'm going to have to work hard to practice moderation with Martha around. No offense, Mom," Sean said.

"Oh, none taken. Martha studied cooking in France."

"I can't say I'm surprised," Avery said.

"If you don't all stop complimenting me, it will be bread and water for the rest of the week," Martha said.

"If the bread tastes like these rolls, I wouldn't mind," Nick said.

"There is just no winning with you boys."

"They can be quite a handful," Kayla said.

Sean looked at Nick, grasped his hand and smiled.

"So, Nick," I said, "what are you doing with yourself now?"

"I'm going to help my dads, since I studied horticulture, farm management and botany at Purdue. I'm also seriously thinking about starting a business as a florist. Later on, I'm going to be helping Mr. Diggory take care of the Solarium and the grounds."

"So you studied more than just farming, huh?"

"Much more."

"I think botany is fascinating," Marshall said. "I'd like to know more about it, but I don't have the time. There were so many plants in the Solarium I couldn't recognize."

"We're planning to label them all and turn it into sort of a botanical garden," Nick said. "Right, Mr. Diggory?"

"I told you it's Basil, and yes." Basil smiled. I liked him.

"Excellent," Marshall said.

"We're all going to be very busy, I'm sure," Sean said. "Only poor Avery will miss out. He has to leave for Phantom World soon."

"Hey, I won't be on vacation. I'll be working!" Avery said.

"You call that work?" Sean asked. "Don't you just stand around and tan all day or something?"

"I didn't say it was difficult."

I looked around the table. I missed all the California boys, but it was good to be back with my friends.

Ralph—Fort Wayne, Indiana—May 2004

I gazed out the window of the room I shared with Jordan in the Hilton. By looking to the left, I could see the old Hotel Indiana and the adjoining Embassy Theatre. I could still remember the first time I watched *Phantom* perform there. Seeing my favorite group perform live was a dream come true, but what had happened afterwards was beyond my wildest dreams.

Jordan joined me, still stretching.

"It's about time you got up," I said.

"Hey, it's only a little past nine. Give me a break. I'm on vacation."

I leaned over and gave Jordan a quick peck on the lips. If people had told me six years ago that Jordan and I would get together, I would have thought they were out of their mind. The idea that Jordan Potter, the lead singer of the most popular band in the world, would date a guy like me—an Indiana farm boy—was just plain crazy, except for one thing: we'd been inseparable for the last six years.

I didn't think of Jordan as a rock star. I thought of him only as my boyfriend. Even in the beginning when I'd been completely star-struck, I wasn't attracted to him because of his fame. I loved his music, I idolized him and I thought he was beautiful, but I loved Jordan for himself. If it hadn't been that way, we wouldn't have lasted two weeks. As we grew to know each other and I learned that Jordan was a real live boy and not a god, we grew even closer. Jordan was a rock star; there was no denying that. Music was his life. I won't even say he's just an ordinary guy, because he's far from ordinary, but I will say that I love him for him, not because he's famous. In fact, I quite often wish he wasn't quite so famous so we could have a bit more freedom.

Jordan's eyes were drawn to the Embassy Theatre as we gazed out the window.

"Almost six years have passed since we first set eyes on each other," Jordan said. "I remember looking down at you from the stage and wishing I could talk to you. I never thought I'd see you again, but only a few hours later: bam!"

"I knocked you on your ass," I said, giggling.

"Literally."

Jordan and I had met after the concert at the nearby Holiday Inn. We were both coming around a corner from opposite directions when we collided. Fate brought us together, a bit violently.

"What's up for today?" I asked.

"Breakfast, general laziness and lounging about, and we also have that tour of the Embassy and Hotel Indiana. I can't wait to see inside the hotel. There's just something intriguing about an old empty hotel. I'm also eager to get a good look inside the Embassy," Jordan said. "I really didn't get to see much of it when we performed there. We're always so rushed."

"Well, there's no rush today Babe. I'm going to take a shower, then you can take me to breakfast."

A few minutes later, we were in the elevator descending to the second floor. We stepped through the doors, made a couple of right turns, walked down the wide hallway toward the sky bridge. We stopped for several moments to look over the balcony and down into the lobby of the Hilton. Jordan and I had stayed in some of the best hotels, but I think the Fort Wayne Hilton was my favorite. Of course, there were special memories attached to it. I remembered six years before when *Phantom's* tour bus was parked out front. I'd walked by the entrance to the hotel, hoping to catch a glimpse of Jordan, Kieran, or Ross. I'd glanced at the rich-red carpeting going up the wide stairway to the second floor and never dreamed that someday I would be inside—with Jordan himself. Now, Jordan and I were looking down upon that same stairway. Perhaps dreams did come true.

Two teenage girls spied us from below and quickly made their way up the stairway.

"I think you've been spotted," I said.

Jordan grinned.

The girls were upon us in seconds.

"It is you!" said the blonde girl, who was probably about fifteen. "I told you it was Jordan!" she said to her friend. "I can't believe it!"

"It's very nice to meet you," Jordan said, extending his hand.

Jordan was always very gracious to his fans. That's one of the things I loved about him.

"Oh, I wish we had a camera," said the other girl. "No one will believe we met you!" She was a real cutie, also about fifteen, with long wavy dark hair.

The blonde was already digging in her purse for a pen. "Will you give us an autograph?" she asked.

"Of course," Jordan said looking around for something to sign for them. I spotted some Hilton Honors pamphlets, grabbed a couple and handed them to Jordan.

"What are your names?" asked Jordan.

"Kara," said one.

"Kelsey," said the other.

Jordan took the pen and began autographing the pamphlets for the girls.

"Oh, I'm so stupid! My phone has a camera!" said Kelsey, the blonde. "Could you take a picture for us?" she asked me.

"Sure."

Kelsey quickly showed me how to take a photo with her phone. The girls stood on each side of Jordan and he put his arms over their shoulders. Kara looked as if she was ready to melt. I took three shots to make sure at least one would turn out well. I remembered what a thrill it was for me to meet Jordan the first time.

"Thank you so much," Kelsey said as I handed her camera back.

"No problem."

"You're Ralph, aren't you?"

"Yeah."

"You're sooo lucky!"

"Oh, I know," I said grinning.

"No, I'm the one who is lucky," Jordan said. His words filled me with happiness, because he meant them.

"We have to get going, but it was very nice to meet you," Jordan said.

"This is such a thrill for me!" Kara said. "You can't imagine! I listen to your music all the time!"

"I'm glad you enjoy it. Without people like you, I couldn't be a musician."

Jordan shook the girls' hands again, and then we departed. Jordan was rather talented at getting away from fans in a polite manner. Those girls would probably have stood there and talked to Jordan all day if they could have, but like most of *Phantom's* fans, they realized that Jordan was a busy guy.

"You think we'll be able to have breakfast without getting mobbed?" I asked. "I'm still a little leery about traveling without Mike." Mike was Jordan's bodyguard. While Jordan wasn't often in true danger, his fans could get out of hand at times.

"We'll be fine. No one even knows we're in Fort Wayne. It's not as though there's a concert tonight."

We were on the sky bridge by then. We stopped and looked down at the traffic on Calhoun Street.

"I just worry that someone will hurt you."

"Ralph, we've discussed this before. If it's going to happen, it's going to happen, and nothing can be done about it. You worry too much. A few years ago I was in serious danger, but that's over. Just relax, okay?"

"Yeah, I'm sorry. I just don't want to think about losing you."

"So don't."

We walked on toward the parking garage. Jordan was right. I overestimated the danger to his life, but I just couldn't help it sometimes. I willed myself to chill out as we walked toward the SUV we'd rented for our visit to northern Indiana.

"So where are you taking me?" I asked as Jordan drove down through the levels of the open garage.

"Chad told me about this great breakfast place called Omega. It's a café, but most of the locals go there for the breakfast menu."

"No Burger Dude this morning?"

Jordan laughed. "No, I'm in the mood for something bigger than French-toast squares and cinnamon minis."

We exited the garage onto Jefferson Boulevard, but soon turned north onto Lafayette.

"You seem to know your way around," I said.

"I memorized the directions Chad gave me. You seem to forget I also lived here for a while as a kid, although only for a few months. I used to dream about someday being in a band and performing in the Embassy."

"That dream came true."

"Yeah."

"I miss Chad," I said.

"Yeah, I haven't heard anyone say 'dude' for quite a while," Jordan said, laughing. Chad said 'dude' more than anyone else I'd ever met. He talked like a California surfer boy, but he wasn't from the West Coast, he was from Kentucky. Chad did sound for *Phantom* on tour and was an all-around technical whiz. He was also hilarious.

We drove north through Fort Wayne for several minutes, turning onto Coliseum before we made it to the café. I was a little concerned Jordan's presence would create a scene—it had happened many times before—but no one took notice of him as we walked into the café. If the waitress recognized him as she led us to a booth, she didn't say anything.

There were quite a few customers in Omega, but it wasn't crowded. Most of those dining there were older, which is probably the main reason Jordan went unrecognized. Most of *Phantom's* fans were under thirty. Jordan looked up from his menu and smiled at me. I could read his thoughts. He loved the attention of his fans, but he also loved to get out and just be like everyone else for a change. He wasn't able to do that often enough.

"Oh, I am so getting the Hawaiian Omelet," announced Jordan after a couple of minutes.

"Hawaiian?"

"Yeah, it has pineapple, onions, green peppers, mozzarella cheese and even cherries on top."

"That sounds truly horrible," I said.

Jordan threw the straw's paper wrapper at me.

"Well, you don't have to order it, wise guy."

"Don't worry! I'm ordering a banana-walnut Belgian waffle."

We sat, drank our ice tea and gazed around Omega after we'd ordered. Omega was well...café-looking, which made perfect sense. There was nothing extraordinary about it, but it was rather pleasant with its booths and tables. It was just a good old ordinary, locally owned café. It was clean and comfortable, and I was glad to be there with Jordan.

Our orders arrived shortly. Jordan's came with two sides, and he'd chosen pancakes and hash browns, with an additional side of bacon. I'd ordered bacon with my Belgian waffle as well, and I wondered about the wisdom of my choice. The waffle was so huge I doubted I could eat it all. It was completely covered with banana pieces and walnuts. Still, Jordan's breakfast dwarfed mine. It took up most of his side of the table.

"Are you sure you wouldn't like something else?" I asked Jordan. "Perhaps some scrambled eggs, toast and sausage?"

"Perhaps later."

"Yeah, right!"

"This is the best omelet ever," Jordan said.

"It's certainly the biggest. Did they use an entire dozen eggs to make it?"

"It's going to take me all morning to eat this."

"Well, we have the time."

"Yeah, and isn't it great?"

We sat and enjoyed a leisurely breakfast, uninterrupted by anyone except for our waitress bringing us more tea and asking if we needed anything.

After breakfast, we headed back downtown. We parked once more in the multi-story parking garage and walked back across the sky bridge. We didn't return to our room, but instead crossed the Hilton and walked into the convention center that adjoined it. We made our way to another sky bridge that led across Jefferson Boulevard to the Embassy Theatre. We stopped and gazed at the huge marquee for a few moments.

"I remember when that was lit up with *Phantom*," I said.

"And it probably will be again. I want to come back to Fort Wayne."

"Yeah, but if you're doing a concert, there's no way we'll be able to walk around like we are today."

"True, but I'm sure we can find something to do in the hotel room," Jordan said, wiggling his eyebrows.

"If you keep talking like that, we're going to have to go back there right now."

We continued on and descended a flight of stairs that led down to the street. We exited and turned not toward the theatre, but to the east and walked the short distance to the Foellinger-Freimann Botanical Conservatory.

"I came here the day we met—before the concert," I said as we pushed open the doors. "I dreamed about running into you or Kieran or Ross."

"Well, today you can give me a tour," Jordan said.

We walked to the counter, where we paid for admission and received a map. I'd only been to the botanical garden once before, but I remembered it well. I could already catch the scent of daffodils as we walked past several interactive displays created for kids. We went straight to the first of three massive glassed-in rooms.

"Wow, this is beautiful," Jordan said as we pushed open the glass doors. The fragrance of daffodils grew stronger and was joined by that of tulips.

"It was different when I was here last. They change the display in here every few months."

"I've never seen so many tulips," Jordan said.

They were everywhere. A wide path of stone circled the center of the room, while another meandered through it. On both sides of the paths were hundreds of tulips landscaped with other flowers, large stones and benches. There were red tulips and yellow, pink and lavender—every color of tulip I could imagine, in fact. The daffodils were huge. Many of them were the customary yellow, but others were peach-colored and some pinkish. I leaned over to smell one and drew in its heavenly scent. Jordan took a large breath.

"I love the smell in here."

We took a seat on a bench and just sat there gazing at all the flowers. There was a large tree at one end of the room, with smaller trees spaced about. It was like sitting in an indoor park.

"If I lived near here, I think I would come every day," I said.

"As beautiful as it is now, I bet it's really awesome in the winter," Jordan said. "Can you imagine the weather all cold and nasty outside, then you come inside and find a garden? I think I could just live in here."

"No, you couldn't. Where would you plug in your keyboard?"

"You know what I mean. When we settle down and get our own home some day, we should have some kind of greenhouse as a part of it. Nothing this big, of course, but a part of the house where we can grow plants all year long."

"We already have a home—the cabin," I pointed out.

"True, but I was speaking of a home with a bathroom and running water."

"Maybe we could build on."

"It's certainly a possibility. I have grown to love Phantom Farm."

Phantom Farm was the name we'd given to our little piece of property in southern Indiana. It wasn't truly a farm, just a little log cabin in the woods, but we had planted roses, lilacs, peonies, a snowball bush and had tried to raise a little garden in the clearing near the cabin.

"I don't think you'll ever settle down anyway, Jordan."

"Oh, I don't know. I don't plan to stop being a musician, but I can see the day when *Phantom* won't tour as often. Everyone is bound to get sick of hearing us sooner or later. According to the critics, we should have crashed and burned long ago."

"That just shows how much the critics know," I said.

Jordan and I admired the flowers for several minutes, then stood and hugged. I don't think I could have been happier than I was at that very moment. Taking our time, we walked among the tulips, hyacinths, and daffodils. Eventually we wandered through the next set of doors, stopped to admire a display of carnivorous plants and then passed some more displays for children on our way to the tropical room.

Unlike the previous greenhouse, the tropical room had changed little since I was there last. There were some different potted orchids here and there, but most of the trees and other plants were far too large to be removed. The room was built on two levels, and even on the upper level, some of the breadfruit and other trees towered over our heads. I was delighted to show Jordan my favorite part of the botanical garden—the waterfall. Although man-made, the waterfall looked completely natural. The stone path passed under a huge outcropping of rock, and water poured down on both sides of the path.

"Standing here, it almost seems as if it's raining," Jordan said.

The air was warm and moist and filled with the scent of vegetation. There were few flowers here except for the orchids and birds of paradise, but the scent in the air was no less pleasant. I pointed out all my favorite sights to Jordan as we followed the paved paths—the kumquat, orange, banana and coffee trees, the goldfish pond and, of course, the chocolate tree. It's just too bad it didn't have Hershey bars growing on it. After we'd climbed some steps from the lower level to look at the chocolate tree, we followed the path along the short remaining distance to a dead end. There sat a small bench. I took a seat and Jordan sat beside me.

"Here is where I sat the last time I was here—dreaming of meeting you. It's so incredible to come back here with you now. I used to fantasize that we'd meet, but...I never dreamed we would fall in love. It just doesn't seem possible."

"Well, it must be, since it happened."

"You could have had anyone you wanted, Jordan."

"I don't know about that. It doesn't matter. You're the one I want."

"I sometimes wonder why."

"That's because you underestimate yourself. You don't realize how wonderful you are. You don't understand that I want you because you're so incredible. You make me happy, and I love being with you. I feel like you're a part of me that I lost and then found again. You're everything I want, Ralph."

"It sounds like you're writing a song."

"Maybe I am," Jordan said, smiling, "but I mean every word. I love you, and I always will."

I leaned my head on his shoulder and practically cried tears of joy right then and there.

We wandered through the tropical room and then eventually found our way to the desert room, where all kinds of cacti and desert plants awaited us. For some reason, I was drawn to the creosote bush and its distinctive odor. It's not

50

what I'd call a pretty scent, but it was pleasant nonetheless, like the scent of melting tar on a country road on a hot summer day.

We went outside and followed the path that led through pines and other trees, admiring more daffodils and tulips. There were also long pools of water along a large paved area that was probably used for parties. We wandered all over the botanical gardens inside and out. We must have spent two hours there before returning to our room in the Hilton to rest.

True to our plans for the day, we took a long nap. Jordan set the alarm to prevent us from missing our tour of the Embassy Theatre and Hotel Indiana. After all that walking in the botanical garden, it was relaxing to lie back on the king-sized bed and snooze while curled up next to my boyfriend.

We awoke about a quarter past one and opted to eat at Desoto's, which is located within the Hilton. We'd eaten there when we stayed in the Hilton on our last tour. Desoto's was a wonderfully quiet little restaurant and sparsely populated since the lunch rush was over. I ordered the Hilton Burger with bacon, lettuce, tomato, onion and both cheddar and Swiss cheese. Jordan opted for the Desoto Dagwood, which came with ham, salami, turkey, pepperoni, lettuce, tomato, red onion and melted Swiss, cheddar and Monterey Jack cheeses. We both chose onion peels, which were a lot like onion rings, instead of fries.

We sat and talked about nothing in particular while we enjoyed the ambiance of Desoto's. It was elegant with cloth napkins and candles on the tables, but not overdone. Soft music played in the background, as it did in all the public areas of the Hilton. I found it soothing.

"It's sure a lot quieter than the last time we were here."

"That's because Ross, Cedi and the *Dragonfire* boys aren't with us," Jordan said.

"No kidding. Ross is a handful all by himself. He and Cedi together... Whoa, did I need a vacation from those two."

Jordan laughed.

"Did I tell you the label signed *Dragonfire*? They're working on their first CD. *Phantom* may be doing a song with them. We're still working out the details."

"Awesome! I'm sure you didn't have anything to do with that, did you Jordan?"

"Well, I did tell the pencil pushers they'd be crazy not to sign *Dragonfire*. Oh, and I pushed the idea of a joint *Phantom/Dragonfire* song. I think what really decided the label was greed. I told them how the crowds went nuts over the boys, and the execs saw dollar signs."

"I'm sure that got them."

"It's their weakness."

"This is great. Drake, Daniel and Drew are great kids."

"Yeah, although I had enough of Drew on the tour. He's way too much like Ross and Cedi. The terrible twins are enough. We don't need a terrible trio."

I laughed. "That's a good name for them."

When our orders arrived, I was amazed at the size of my Hilton burger. Jordan and I could have shared it and still have had plenty. The pile of onion peels looked like a mini-Mt. Everest.

"This is the best burger I've ever had in my entire life," I said after tasting it. "I think we should just live in the Hilton and eat here every day."

Jordan laughed.

"I think you might get tired of burgers after a while."

"Well, then I'd try a Dagwood. How's yours?"

"Excellent," Jordan grinned. "I think we picked the right spot for a vacation."

"You came to Fort Wayne for a vacation?" asked our waitress as she neared. "I didn't think there was anything to see in Fort Wayne."

"That's because you live here," Jordan said. "No one recognizes what their own hometown has to offer. We were just in the botanical garden this morning. It's incredible."

"You know I've never been," said the waitress.

"You work right across the street and you've never been?" I asked. "You've got to go! If I worked so close, I think I'd visit after work every day just to unwind."

"I might try that sometime. Do you boys need anything else?"

"No, thank you," I said. "Everything is great."

Our waitress smiled and departed, leaving Jordan and me to talk alone. Desoto's closed at 2 p.m., but I noted it reopened at 5 p.m. I wanted to eat there again, but I doubted I would be hungry again before the next day. I hadn't eaten all of my burger, but I was stuffed.

We departed at 2 p.m., although our waitress told us there was no rush. We were due at the Hotel Indiana at 2:30. We spent our time wandering around the Hilton, admiring the prints, paintings and other decorations. Like Desoto's, the Hilton had an elegant, but not overstated ambiance. Some hotels were overdone and just too fancy for comfort. The Hilton wasn't like that.

We headed for the Hotel Indiana a little before our appointment, once again walking over the enclosed sky bridge that crossed Jefferson Boulevard. It had begun to rain, and it was nice not to have to get out in the elements.

The lobby of the old Hotel Indiana had been redone and was used from time to time for receptions. Both Jordan and I were more eager to get a look at the upper floors, where the old rooms were left just as they were when the hotel closed in 1966. A charming lady named Dana acted as our guide and told us a bit about the history of the hotel as we made our way to the upper floors.

"The hotel and connected theatre were constructed in 1927," Dana explained. "The hotel had 250 rooms, each with its own tub and shower bath. Inside was the Café as well as the Cocktail Lounge and Circular Bar, famous for its food, beverages, music and entertainment. Later, Sam's Barbershop was located in the hotel basement, and the Indiana Drug Store and Dr. C.B. Parker's office were located on the first floor. We use much of the second floor as office space, but the floors above are just as they were when the hotel closed."

Dana ushered us into one of the old rooms, which was still furnished with a bed, dresser, nightstand and lamp, as well as a desk and chair. The room wasn't large, but still larger than I had expected. The floor was comfortably carpeted, and I wouldn't have minded staying there one bit, even though it wasn't nearly as nice as our room in the Hilton across the street.

"It's kind of freaky thinking of all these empty rooms," Jordan said. "Just think of how busy this place must have been at one time, and now most of it is abandoned."

"It almost feels haunted," I said. "I don't mean by ghosts, but it's as if a memory of all the guests that stayed here lingers still."

"Has any thought been given to reopening it?" Jordan asked.

"Yes, but the cost is prohibitive," Dana said. "The building really isn't up to modern codes and lacks handicap accessibility and a whole list of other things that would be required. It costs about $250,000 a year just to keep the hotel and theatre going as it is."

The rooms all looked pretty much alike, so soon Dana led us into the Embassy Theatre, which was actually part of the same building.

Just as on the night of the *Phantom* concert, my breath was taken away by the lobby, which soared to a grand height. The architecture of the Embassy was striking. Dana told us it was an old movie palace and that the ornate architectural details in the Egyptian motif were inspired by the discovery of Tutankhamun's tomb in 1922. The lobby featured beautiful sconces, glittering chandeliers, ornate columns and eye-catching decorative work.

"The Embassy and Hotel Indiana were originally constructed as the Fox Theatre and Hotel, and were built at the same time at a cost of one million dollars," said Dana, "and that was back in 1927. The theatre was quickly renamed the Emboyd, and it retained that name for most of its history. In 1952, the theatre was leased to an amusement company and the name changed to the Embassy Theatre. The Embassy operated primarily as a movie theatre until 1972, when the owners decided that it would be more profitable to demolish the theatre and create a parking lot. Fortunately, the loss of the old building was averted by the efforts of local citizens. In 1974, a group of local artists performed to kick off the Embassy Drive, which eventually raised the $250,000 needed to purchase the Embassy and the Indiana Hotel. As you can see, the Embassy has been beautifully restored."

"And to think this almost became a parking lot," Jordan said. "It's unthinkable."

"True," said Dana, "but most of the old movie palaces have been demolished, and many are now parking lots."

"We've played in a lot of grand old theatres on tour," Jordan said. "Have you ever been to the Murat in Indy?"

"Yes," said Dana. "I could wander around for hours in the Murat."

"We've done a couple of concerts in the Egyptian Room. It reminds me a bit of the Embassy."

"Me too," I said.

Dana next led us into the actual theatre. As we entered, my mind went back to the first time I was inside. I'd been there since that night, but it was surreal being there now with Jordan. The last six years seemed almost like a dream.

The auditorium was as beautiful as the lobby, with ornate decorations everywhere. I could tell just by looking at Jordan that he already missed performing, even though it hadn't been that long since he'd last appeared on stage.

"Now I'll show you one of the treasures of Embassy—the Grande Page Pipe Organ. It was installed in 1928. It was one of three of its size built and is one of two still in its original home."

Dana signaled an unseen someone, and the massive white organ with gold accents slowly rose up out of the orchestra pit. There were four levels on the keyboard, as well as all kinds of switches above. Under the bench were lots of pedals. I couldn't even imagine how difficult it must have been to play.

"It was built by the Page Organ Company of Lima, Ohio," Dana said. "The organ has over 1,100 pipes that fill the Main Pipe Chamber and Solo Pipe Chamber on either side of the stage; they range in size from 16 feet to only 7 inches. Its instruments include the marimba, harp, piano, glockenspiel, xylophone and the "toy counter," containing snare and bass drums, cymbals, Chinese gong, castanets, tambourines, tom-toms, triangle, wood block, steamboat and train whistles, sirens, fire gong, telephone, claxon, sleigh bells and chirping birds. Back in the days of silent films, all the instruments and sound effects helped organists convey the emotions, characters and story lines of the movies."

Dana allowed us to wander around by ourselves for a while. Jordan and I must have spent an hour in the auditorium and lobby. We stood on the stage for a while and looked out at all the seats.

"Sometimes I never realize just how many people are out there when I'm performing," Jordan said. "With all the lights, it's usually hard to see beyond the first few rows."

"I'm just glad you're the one who has to stand here," I said.

"Aw, don't you want to sing at a concert, Ralph? That can be arranged, you know."

"I would be so nervous I'd hurl," I said. "Besides, I don't sing that well."

"You sing beautifully," Jordan said.

"You are such a liar sometimes."

We returned to the lobby of the Hotel Indiana and thanked Dana for showing us around. Dana asked for Jordan's autograph, both for herself and her daughter, and Jordan signed one for each of them.

Since relaxing was our major plan for the day, we hit the hot tub in the spa area on the second floor of the Hilton after changing into our swimsuits in our room. We had the place to ourselves and sat side by side in the hot tub as we gazed out the large windows at the buildings of downtown Fort Wayne.

"It would be cool to soak in this tub in the winter when the snow was falling outside," I said.

"True, but I'm glad it's May. I love warmth."

"Then you should be truly happy right now."

"I'm always happy when I'm with you, Ralph."

"Aw," I said, putting my head on his shoulder.

That night we met Hunter, a long time *Phantom* fan who lived in Fort Wayne, for a late supper at a Mexican restaurant called Cebolla's, another of Chad's recommendations. Hunter was taller than I remembered, but then again he was seventeen-years old when I'd seen him last, and he was now twenty-three. He was just as thrilled to see Jordan as he had been all those years ago.

"I remember when I used to chat with you on the internet," Hunter told Jordan, "before I knew who I was really talking to."

"Yeah, and when I finally told you, you didn't believe me."

"Could you blame me?"

We got lost in talking about old times. I was truly glad to see Hunter doing so well.

Cebolla's had a fun atmosphere, with lots of bright colors and gaudy decorations. Our booth was located along one wall, and there was a sloped tile roof overhead that extended to the edge of our booth, making it seem as if we were eating on a veranda somewhere in Mexico.

Chad definitely knew what he was talking about, because as we soon discovered, Cebolla's served some of the best Mexican food ever. It was the real thing too, not Americanized. I was completely amazed at the speed of the service. Not five minutes passed from the time we ordered to the arrival of our dinners.

After supper, we bid goodbye to Hunter, returned to the Hilton, and ended our day as it had begun, by looking out the window at the skyline of downtown Fort Wayne. The Hotel Indiana stood dark and silent in a world of lights, and I imagined former guests settling in for the night.

Jordan and I undressed and climbed into our king-sized bed. We held each other and made out until we fell asleep.

I was sorry to leave Fort Wayne behind when we departed a few days later, but I was equally excited that our next stop was Verona. I couldn't wait to visit the Selby farm again, and I was even more eager to get a look at the renovations of Graymoor Mansion.

Sean

The combined graduation party of Nick, Skye, Marshall, Avery and me was held the day after my fellow graduates arrived.

Our party was a rather large affair, even though only friends and family were invited. My parents set it up in the ballroom, which was definitely the perfect location.

Graymoor's ballroom was the most ornate room in the whole house. The entire floor was a mirror, which had a rather disorienting effect at first, but beautifully reflected the stained-glass windows that occupied most of the walls as well as the entire ceiling. The gorgeous stained-glass windows were brilliantly backlit by sunlight, which is why the party was being held during the day. The entire ballroom had an Egyptian motif, with sphinxes, pyramids, mummies and scarabs in rich blues, greens, golds and reds.

Temporary help had brought in long tables, and Martha had set up an impressive buffet. How she had time to prepare everything after that magnificent lunch I'll never know, but I was quickly learning that Martha was a miracle worker.

"Congratulations," said my best friend, Zoë, as I greeted her at the door. "I'm jealous. I have two more years to go."

"Well, my degree isn't as advanced as yours," I said. Zoë was studying oceanography out in California. "So how are the dolphins and the whales?"

"Good, I hope."

Zoë hugged me. "Oh, how I've missed you!"

"Zoë!" Nick said, hugging her as soon as she released me.

There were hugs all around, as friends we hadn't seen— or had seen rarely since high school—arrived for the party.

"Whoa! Oliver! You stud, you," Skye said when he spotted the boy that most of us had once thought of as a pudgy Harry Potter. The pudginess was gone, and Oliver, now nineteen, had turned into quite an attractive young man. He still wore glasses, but now they made him look sexy instead of nerdy.

"Hey, Skye!"

"You've been working out!" Skye said. "Let me feel that bicep."

Oliver flexed his arm, and I was quite surprised by his solid muscles. Apparently, so was Skye.

"Damn boy, you're getting buff."

"I'm just trying to keep my gorgeous boyfriend."

Clay, who was standing beside Oliver, blushed.

"Keep me? I thought I was going to the gym to keep you."

"Uh-oh," I said, "I think they're about to go disgustingly mushy on us."

"You and Nick do enough of that yourselves," Skye said. "Sometimes you relationship-oriented guys are so sickeningly sweet you make me wanna hurl."

"Aww," Zoë said, "so you still haven't found anyone special?"

"All the guys I hook up with are special—and hot," Skye said.

Zoë rolled her eyes.

"You'll never change, Skye."

"You've got that right."

"Hey, Zoë."

Zoë turned around at the sound of Avery's voice. He gave her a hug.

"I've missed you," she said.

"How's my favorite ex?" Avery asked.

"I couldn't be better!"

Many couples don't get along well after a breakup, but Avery and Zoë had settled back into their old friendship roles quite nicely. Perhaps that's because geographical distance, not an argument, broke them up. They had both been in

California for the past few years, but California is a big state. Not everyone could make a long-distance relationship work. I was glad they still got on well. Things could have been rather awkward otherwise.

I mingled with the many guests, catching up with friends and family. I'd been home a few times in my college years, but never long enough to see everyone. Most of my friends had also been away to college, and our vacations often didn't occur at the same time. Marshall wasn't the only one I hadn't seen in years.

Marshall's parents couldn't come to the party. They had tired of the cold, northern-Indiana winters and moved to Florida. Marshall didn't seem distressed by their absence, perhaps because he was surrounded by friends.

My parents had hired a local band for the event. I didn't recognize any of the band members even though they looked to be about my age. They were surprisingly good, moving from covers to some of their own songs. The drummer was a real hottie with wild curly blond hair, but I did no more than take note of him. I was devoted to Nick.

Zoë and Avery began dancing. I briefly wondered if they would perhaps take a romantic interest in each other again, but then I came to my senses and remembered that Avery was dating Nicole. Avery was finished with school also, but Zoë was not, so distance would still be a problem even if Avery was single. Plus, there aren't many dolphins in Verona. Avery was soon to leave for his summer job at Phantom World, and Zoë would shortly be returning to California. Others joined Avery and Zoë on the dance floor, and soon most of us were dancing.

It felt so good to be with Nick again. Despite some problems, we'd actually managed to maintain a long-distance relationship. Throughout college, I'd seen him only on vacations and between semesters. Often we both returned to Verona for the few days so we could be together, but sometimes one of us traveled to the other or we met somewhere in between. Now, he would be only a few miles away, and we could see each other whenever we wanted. I knew both of us were going to be extremely busy, but even if we only had a couple of hours to spare here and there, we would have far more time together than we had had since high school. It was time to pick up our discussion about moving in together too. We'd talked it over some, but living together was an impossibility when we lived so far apart. The distance was gone, so perhaps it was time to take the next step in our relationship.

We talked and ate and danced the afternoon away. Slowly, the great stained-glass windows dimmed as evening came upon Verona until only the old gas lamps that had recently been converted to electricity lighted the vast ballroom. The lights reflecting off the floor gave the ballroom a magical quality. I felt as if I was wandering through a fairy tale. I don't think anyone wanted the night to end, but by 1 a.m. or so most of us were exhausted. I bid our guests goodbye as they departed, knowing I'd see most of them again soon. Nick was staying the night, so we retired to my room on the third floor. We'd planned to make wild, passionate love after the party, but we were both ready to drop. We settled for stripping, climbing into bed and giving each other one passionate kiss before we drifted off to sleep.

I awakened the next morning with Nick's arms wrapped around me. I just lay there, enjoying the sensation of being held for a while. It had been far too long. Being parted from Nick for weeks and sometimes months hadn't been easy. There had been temptations. I'd been surprised to find that other guys were interested in me—more than a few, actually. Remaining true to Nick was more difficult than I'd imagined, and at times I wondered if we were doing the right thing. Somehow, we had survived our separation, and we never need be parted from one another again.

I wanted to keep lying there, but I was in such desperate need of Nick that I couldn't remain still. I gently kissed my boyfriend on the lips until he began to stir and return my kiss. Our kiss deepened and our tongues entwined.

I wrapped my arms around him, and we devoured each other. I was aroused to a fever pitch even before I kissed him, and it took no time at all for Nick to reach the same state. We kissed each other's lips, neck and chest. Our lips sought our ear lobes, abs and nipples. I dove down and engulfed Nick, causing him to moan and groan as I worked feverishly to bring him to climax. His orgasm was not long in coming, and when he finished, he returned the favor. I don't think I'd experienced such a lack of control since my first time. The sensation of Nick's mouth and tongue made me lose it in seconds.

We still weren't finished yet. We had the entire morning to spend naked together, and we intended to make good use of it. I led Nick to the shower, and we bathed each other, getting our bodies all soapy and wet. We spent so much time making out and exploring each other's bodies that it's a wonder we didn't run out of hot water.

When we finally stepped out of the shower, it was only to dry off and return to the bed. We rolled over and over each other, hugging, kissing, feeling and fondling. Nick guided me onto my stomach and slowly entered me.

It had been so long since I'd bottomed that I hissed in pain, but I wanted it more than I'd ever wanted anything. Nick was a patient lover. He took it slowly, and I relaxed until I could take him inside me with ease. Once we were both ready, we went at it like wild boys. After Nick had groaned in ecstasy, I took my turn topping him.

We needed another shower by the time we were done, and we couldn't keep our hands off each other. We went for a third round while the hot water pounded down upon our writhing bodies. Even Skye would have been proud of us.

Spent at last, we dried off, dressed and headed downstairs. It was already 11 a.m. and we'd missed breakfast, but lunch wouldn't be long in coming. I wasn't hungry anyway. After the excellent and far-too-large meals of the day before, I felt like I wouldn't need another bite for a week.

"Where is everyone?" I asked Martha as we entered the kitchen.

"Your parents are in the old summer kitchen. They're getting ready to move things in from your mom's antique shop. They said they might bring over a couple of loads of antiques today. Skye is in the gymnasium, checking to see if the equipment is properly set up. I haven't seen your cousin since breakfast, and I haven't seen your friend Marshall at all."

"How about Mr. Diggory and, um...Mrs...um...the housekeeper."

"Mr. Diggory is in the Solarium, I believe, or out on the grounds. Mrs. Hawkins is in her office, trying to get things organized. Can I get you boys anything to eat?"

"No thank you," I said. "I'm sure we can wait for lunch." I looked to Nick for confirmation, even though I already knew the answer.

"So...what do you want to do with the rest of the morning?" Nick asked.

"I need to get my own office in order, but that can wait until the afternoon. Why don't we go for a swim? I'm dying to try out the pool."

"Yeah, maybe Skye will join us."

We bid Martha goodbye and headed back to my room.

"I think you want Skye to join us just so you can see him without a shirt," I said.

"Guilty as charged."

"You're wicked."

"That's why you love me."

"Well, that's one of the many reasons I love you," I said.

Marshall was just coming down the stairs as we neared the second-floor landing.

"Hey, we're going for a swim—want to come with?" I asked.

"Um, yeah, sure, sounds good!"

"Cool, we're going to change and then head for the pool. Want to meet us there?"

"Yeah, I'll dig my suit out of my bag and meet you there in a few," Marshall said.

Nick and I continued our ascent.

"Isn't it cool to have almost everyone under the same roof?" Nick said.

"Yeah, but it's only temporary. Avery will be leaving for *Phantom World* the day after tomorrow, and Marshall will only be here until he finds his own place."

"And I have to go home this afternoon. I've barely seen my dads."

"I'm just glad you'll be back soon," I said, stopping to give Nick a kiss on the lips.

We entered my room, and I rummaged through my dresser for swimsuits. I found a couple of pair and tossed one to Nick. We quickly changed and headed for the Natatorium.

"It's going to feel odd with Skye living here," I said. "Nice, but odd."

"It will be like having your own personal bodyguard," Nick said.

"True, although I don't think there's much need anymore."

"I, for one, am truly thankful for that," Nick said. "I had enough of living in fear during high school to last me for the rest of my life."

"No kidding. I wonder whatever happened to Ben Tyler, the sole survivor of the Evil Four."

"Who knows? He probably went off to college somewhere. Even if he comes back to Verona, I don't think he'll be any trouble," Nick said.

At the very end of high school, the worst of the gay bashers, known to my circle of friends as the Evil Four, were murdered one by one, until only Ben was left. He had actually come running to Skye for protection. Ben was a follower type, and I doubted he would initiate any trouble on his own. Besides, he owed Skye big time.

"It all seems so long ago now, doesn't it?" I said. "I know things are far from perfect here in good old Verona, but compared to what it used to be like..."

"We even have the Potter-Bailey Gay Youth Center now. We need to do some volunteer work there when we can. Maybe we could help with some of the meetings."

"You mean spread our wisdom to the next generation of gay youth?"

"We're not that old, Sean. There isn't a next generation yet. I'm sure some of the high-school boys could benefit from our experiences."

"I'm sure some of the high-school boys will benefit from Skye's sexual expertise," I said and laughed.

Before long, we had made our way to the Natatorium. The crystal-blue water looked warm and inviting. I leaned down and dipped my hand into it.

"Just right," I pronounced. "Let's go find Skye."

Skye was in the gym, carefully checking out one of the many machines. I wasn't exactly sure what he was doing, but he was looking the machine over and checking off something on a clipboard.

"Don't you look professional?" I said.

"I'm inspecting all the machines to make sure they were properly assembled. A loose nut can spell disaster."

"We're going to go for a swim. Want to join us?"

"Sure, I could use a break. This isn't the most exhilarating of pastimes. I can't believe this is my job, though. It's a dream come true."

"We'll see you in a bit," I said.

Nick and I walked back into the Natatorium, stripped off our shirts, pulled off our shoes and socks and dived into the pool. The sound of splashing water filled the Natatorium.

"Did you ever think you'd see the day when this pool would be filled with water?" Nick asked.

"Truthfully, no. I always dreamed about it. I thought that maybe it was something you and I might manage, but I seriously doubted we could ever swing it."

"Oh, this is wonderful," Nick said, flipping onto his back.

Nick and I swam back and forth in the pool until Skye arrived wearing a skimpy blue thong. Despite my devotion to Nick, I could feel myself becoming aroused. Skye had a beautiful body in his high-school years, but at twenty-three he was just incredible. Skye had muscles bulging out everywhere, yet he'd avoided the over-bulked, body-builder look. His body was strong, firm and graceful—a true work of art. Nick noticed me checking out Skye and grinned.

Marshall joined us soon after. When he pulled off his shirt, I noticed that he was a bit more muscular than he had been in high school. He wasn't what I'd call buff, but he was toned-up a bit more. He looked good.

"Damn, Marshall, doesn't the sun ever shine in England? You're as pale as a ghost," Skye said.

"It's rarely warm and clear enough there to get much sun," Marshall said, "Plus, I spent most of my time inside."

"Why am I not surprised?" Skye said.

We all swam for a quite a while without talking much. The sun was shining through the glass roof above, and I could see the trees outside gently swaying in the breeze. Inside the Natatorium were large trees in immense planters as well as numerous varieties of ferns, ivy and flowers. The smell of chlorine mixed with the scent of the roses, lilies and other fragrant blooms. I almost couldn't believe that this was Graymoor.

"So, did you date any hot English babes while you were across the pond?" Skye asked.

"I didn't do a lot of dating, but I went out a few times," Marshall said.

"There was a British dude at the university," Skye said. "I'd always heard British guys were kind of lackluster in bed, but Winston sure wasn't. Wow! And that accent...it freaking turned me on."

"Everything turns you on, Skye," Marshall said, laughing.

"Hey, I can't help it. A guy has needs, you know?"

"I'm sure yours never went unsatisfied, Skye," I said.

"Only occasionally. I did have to study now and then."

"Have you heard from Kate lately?" I asked. Kate was Marshall's girlfriend in high school, but they had broken it off when they left for college.

"We haven't e-mailed each other in over a year. You know how it is."

"You'll just have to find a new girlfriend now that you're back," Skye said. "Maybe you can land one before that British accent of yours wears off."

"Then it will have to be quickly," Marshall said. "It's going fast."

"I'll steer some babes your way. I did that a lot at school for my buds—those poor, pathetic straight boys."

"You're so gracious, Skye."

"I try!"

"When are you going to settle down and get yourself a boyfriend?" Marshall asked. "Don't you get tired of a different guy every night?"

"Hey, I didn't have a different guy *every* night. I invited the best ones back. I'm not that big of a slut, despite the rumors. The whole relationship thing isn't for me though. It's great for guys like Sean and Nick here, but that's just not me."

"So you're going to remain single forever?" Marshall asked.

"Damn straight! Well, you know what I mean."

"You'll never change, Skye," Nick said.

"Hey, why mess with perfection?"

We all groaned and splashed Skye with water. That started a water fight, and we played and laughed like kids.

Skye

I pulled up in front of my old boyhood home, now the home of my mother and her new husband, Josh. Actually, they had been married for a few years now, but I still thought of Josh as mom's new husband because he wasn't my dad. In fact, Josh had been my best friend since middle school. When I discovered his relationship with my mother during our high school years, a rift opened between us. When Josh discovered I was gay, the rift deepened. Things had changed, and a lot had happened since then. Josh and I would never recapture our friendship as it was, but I'd learned to accept his relationship with my mom. He made her happy, and in the end that's all that mattered. Josh was more at ease with my homosexuality as well. I think somewhere along the way he realized I was the same Skye he'd always known.

I got out of the Skyemobile and walked to the front door. I was still driving the same car I had in high school. It was almost completely worn out. Since I now had a job and no school expenses, I intended to look for a replacement.

Josh opened the door.

"Hey there, Son," he said, then laughed.

"Hi, *Dad*," I replied in my best smart-ass tone.

There was a time when I would have kicked Josh's ass for calling me Son, but it had become a joke with us. Josh was indeed my step-dad, but he was only a year older than I was. His relationship with my mom had created quite a scandal in Verona, especially when Josh's parents found out. I wasn't around for the excitement, but the warring parties had since all made peace.

"Skye!" Mom said, rushing toward me. "I haven't seen you for months!"

"You can see me far more often now. I'm only a few blocks away."

I'd told Mom all about my job at the B&B when I'd been hired.

"Come on into the kitchen. Lunch is ready."

It did feel rather good to be back in my old home, eating my mom's cooking. Sure things had changed drastically since I was a kid, but still much was the same. The three of us sat down at the old kitchen table and filled our plates.

"This fried chicken is excellent," I said. "I think you and Martha at the B&B are part of a conspiracy to make me put on weight."

"Martha is the cook there?"

"She's the head chef, although right now she's the only chef. She studied in Paris, and her dishes are incredible."

"I hear Graymoor is really something," Josh said. "A lot of people around here can't wait to get a look inside."

"Well, we'll be open soon. We're going to operate on a small scale at first. Sean and his parents intend to focus on quality, not quantity. I think we're starting out with eight rooms, and will expand from there. I believe that thirty guest rooms have already been renovated and there's plenty of room for expansion."

"How many rooms are there in Graymoor?" Mom asked.

"No one knows for sure, but over a hundred. There are at least seventy bedrooms."

"Why would any family need that many bedrooms?"

"Well, Mr. Graymoor was quite an eccentric, and apparently lots of family and visitors stayed there a great deal of the time. Graymoor was almost like a hotel back when the family owned it. There just weren't any paying guests."

"I don't know if I want to go inside or not," Josh said. "That place freaks me out."

"Well, without a doubt it *is* haunted," I said. "The idea of going inside used to intimidate me a bit, but it's not so bad, especially now."

"Have you...seen anything in there?" Josh asked.

"I've heard more than I've seen. Sometimes there are voices coming from empty rooms. Sometimes the organ in the parlor plays by itself. There are ghostly footsteps and knocks. I thought I caught a glimpse of a ghost floating down the hall, but I'm not sure. I may have been seeing things. I did see a chair slide across the floor all by itself, and I've seen the ghost cat a couple of times." I left out the most incredible stuff because it was truly unbelievable to anyone who hadn't witnessed it.

"Ghost cat?"

"Yeah, there's this cat that wanders around Graymoor, only the Hiltons don't have a cat. If you don't look closely, you can't tell the difference between a living cat and the ghost cat, which is kind of transparent. The first time I saw it, I thought it was a real, but then it disappeared right in the middle of the hallway."

"Whoa."

"Ah, come on over some time, Josh. It's not that bad inside. I'll hold your hand if it will make you feel any better."

Josh stuck out his tongue.

We turned our attention to the fried chicken, mashed potatoes and coleslaw, so our conversation slowed down considerably. I ate with moderation. I had no intention of putting on weight. I'd worked way too long and hard on my abs to see them disappear under a layer of fat.

I felt secure and content when I departed in the mid-afternoon. Things weren't perfect between Mom, Josh and me, but the dramatic scenes were over, and what issues we had weren't going to rip us apart. I was sure there would be times I'd want to punch Josh in the face, but I'd learned to be more tolerant of him, and he'd learned not to push me too far.

It was definitely good to be back. If I could only find a few hot guys to have fun with, my life would be complete.

***

The Grand Opening of the Graymoor Mansion Bed & Breakfast had finally arrived. The very first guests showed up just after noon. I knew I wouldn't be too busy in the

Natatorium and adjoining gym, but that would allow me to ease into things. After all, I'd never run what amounted to a health club before. Eight rooms were filled: six with couples and two with single occupants. Three of the couples had kids, so we had a total of twenty guests. I wondered how many guests we would have once we were operating at full capacity. That wouldn't happen for quite some time, however, so I wasn't concerned about it.

About half past one, a couple and their two kids wandered into the Natatorium wearing their swimsuits.

"Hi, I'm Skye. Let me know if you have any questions or need anything. The towels are by the entrance to the locker rooms."

"Thanks, Skye," said the dad, a reasonably attractive man who was probably in his late thirties.

I went into my little office, which had large windows that looked into both the Natatorium and the gym. I'd been busy creating forms to use in my capacity as a personal trainer. I wanted to be able to present guests with workouts tailored specifically to them, and by designing the forms myself, I could do so with greater ease. I'd also been creating a lot of info sheets on different exercises and diet plans.

A few guests dropped in throughout the afternoon, primarily to make use of the pool and hot tub. One couple did come into the gym, but they were only interested in the treadmills and stair-steppers. I didn't expect to get many serious weight-lifters in the gym, but I was eager to show someone the ropes.

The Natatorium and gym were empty most of the time, but that was no problem, as I had plenty of work to do. Despite the fact I'd been busily preparing for opening day, I still had several tasks to finish. Just keeping the pool and the weight equipment up required a lot more time than most would imagine. Nevertheless, my job was anything but boring. I loved it!

In the late afternoon, I used some of the down time to work out. I felt like a kid in a candy store. I almost couldn't decide what machine to use first. The university had had some kick-ass equipment, but the B&B's machines were even more advanced. The first time I saw Jordan I was going to kiss him on the lips! Actually, I would've liked kissing him in any case. Too bad he had a boyfriend.

A good-looking teenage boy ambled in about four p.m. He stood and watched as I finished my last set of lateral pull-downs. I could tell by the hungry expression on his face that he was attracted to me, but nothing was going to happen between us. The kid was cute—with shaggy black hair, a nice tan, and soulful brown eyes—but he was also about fifteen. I had a firm rule. I didn't get it on with anyone under eighteen no matter how cute he might be. I'd worked hard to help out other gay boys, and I wasn't about to do something that might harm one of them. I think most boys are ready for sex well before they're eighteen, but some aren't. Anyway, that was my rule. I even had a t-shirt that said, "You must be at least eighteen to ride this ride."

"Hey," I said as soon as I finished my set. "I'm Skye. Is there anything I can help you with?"

"Yeah, I wanted to work out a little, but I don't really know what I'm doing."

"All right! I've been waiting for someone like you all day!"

The boy grinned. He was way cute. If I was his age, I would've been making out with him for sure.

"I'm Kevin, but my friends call me Kev."

"Well Kev, what do you want to accomplish? I can show you a few exercises, give you some advice and even set you up with a workout program you can do at home."

"Cool. Well...I'd like to look like *you* someday."

I smiled. "Flattery will get you everywhere. I can help you get started. One cool thing about working out is that you can accomplish anything you want, as long as you stick with it."

"How long have you been working out?"

"Since I was younger than you. I got into weightlifting seriously when I was about fourteen."

"I'm fifteen, so I guess I'm getting a late start."

"No way. Most guys don't get into it until later. Of course, most guys give up and quit. That's why so many guys are out of shape."

"Is it hard?"

"No. It takes dedication and persistence, but it isn't difficult. The biggest misconception that most guys have is that you have to strain your guts out to get buff, but that's just not true. Let's start you out with a standard bench press—it's the best exercise for developing your chest. I'll give you some pointers as we go along. Before you leave, remind me to give you some info as well, so you can take it home."

"Okay, cool!"

I led Kev through several exercises, including bench presses, butterflies, lateral pull-downs, seated rows, curls, ab crunches, and more. He carefully watched as I demonstrated each exercise. I noticed that not all of his interest was based in a desire to get buff. I noticed a bulge forming in his shorts. There was no doubt that Kev was gay and attracted to me.

"Do you really think I can look like you someday?" he asked when I'd run him through an entire beginner's workout.

"Sure, if that's what you want. There are a lot of benefits to being in shape, Kev. Not only will you look good, but you'll feel great, and it will earn you a lot of respect. When I came out in high school, no one gave me much trouble, because they knew I could kick their ass.

"Came out? You mean you're..."

"I'm gay. Let me guess...you didn't know athletic guys could be gay."

"Well, no..."

"Let me tell you something, Kev. There are all kinds of gay guys, just like there are all kinds of guys. It's not something to be ashamed of."

"Um, do you tell everyone you're gay?"

"No. I don't keep it a secret, but I don't announce it any more than I do what kind of music I like best or what kind of car I drive. It's just a part of me. I only tell someone when I think they can benefit from knowing."

Kev peered at me.

"You know I'm gay, don't you?" he asked nervously.

"Yeah," I said.

"How?"

"By the way you look at me."

Kev blushed.

"It's okay. I'm flattered. Now let me get you some info sheets on the exercises I just showed you. I'll work up an exercise routine for you and slip it under your door before you check out. Do you have weights at home?"

"Yeah, free weights."

"Okay, I'll design a workout around free weights. That's a great place to start. Here, I'll give you this card too. This has nothing to do with weightlifting, but it might be of use." I handed Kev one of the business cards for the Potter-Bailey Gay Youth Center. I kept a stack on my desk just in case. "There's a toll-free number on there that is answered day and night in case you need someone to talk to."

"Thanks."

Kev stood there and gazed at me for a few moments. I could read the desire in his eyes. Luckily, he was too shy to make a move.

"Um, thanks again Skye—for everything."

"No problem and good luck."

"Bye."

"Bye."

Kev almost made me wish I was his age again, but guys my own age were much more fun. Guys under eighteen could be cute, but they didn't really have all that much going for them.

I needed to get out as soon as I could and find someone to play with. It was too bad Jarret wasn't in town. We'd had some hot times together before I left for college. I wondered if Thad still worked at The Park's Edge. He was another hottie who was usually up for a good time, but Thad had probably moved on. I doubted he'd made a career of waiting tables in Verona.

I picked up where I'd left off with the workout that Kev had interrupted, but was interrupted again several minutes later. Kev was back to use the pool, but with his parents this time. He smiled and waved before he jumped into the water. He seemed like a well-adjusted kid.

Another couple and their kids came in soon after. The Natatorium echoed with the sounds of splashing water and screams of delight and laughter. Graymoor had truly come alive again. I smiled and made my way to my office. I thought I might as well get started developing Kev's workout plan, since I didn't think it was proper to work out with guests around. I was pleased I'd found a job I truly enjoyed.

After work, I took a long walk in the evening shadows. I'd had mixed feelings about returning to the quiet of Verona, but there was no way I could turn down such a wonderful opportunity. If the bed & breakfast was a success, I was set for life. I could always move on to something different later on if I tired of managing the Natatorium and gym. I was doing what I loved, and I was getting paid for it. What could be better than that?

I'd been glad to escape Verona at the end of high school. At the time, I had no intention of returning for more than a visit. I'd set my sights on living in a big city, filled with excitement and hot guys. Now that I was back, I found I didn't mind the quiet, leisurely pace. If I yearned for excitement—of the sexual variety or otherwise—Chicago and Indianapolis weren't all that far away.

I was sure I could also find a little excitement closer to home. I'd done okay in that regard during high school. Of course, I had a regular thing going with Jarret back then. We'd lost touch during college, and I had no idea where he was now. It's too bad he hadn't returned to Verona too. Jarret was one talented boy in the sack, and he had the tightest... Well, I'd better not go into too much detail. I don't know how much you can handle.

As I neared the park, I heard angry voices. I quickened my pace out of habit. As I drew closer, I could make out three figures. Two of them were facing off against the third. I closed in to see what was up and speeded up even more when I heard the word "faggot."

"Come on. Hit me, queer. Do it," said one of the pair of bullies, shoving the third boy in the chest.

"Just get off me! I don't want to fight you!"

"Of course, you don't! You know you'll get your ass kicked, art fag!"

The three looked about high-school age, about my height, probably seniors. Hearing the angry voices took me back to my own high-school years.

"Should I hold him for you?" I asked, walking into the midst of the three. "Or do you think two on one is enough?"

"Fuck off, man!" one of the bullies said.

"Wrong answer," I said and decked him. He dropped to the ground. "Now, let's see if our next contestant does better." I stepped in front of the other boy.

"Uh, um," he said, looking down at his friend who was writhing in pain on the grass.

"You know the problem with being a bully, um...what's your name?"

"Uh, um, Kerr."

"Well, Kerr, the problem with being a bully is that there's always someone bigger and meaner just around the corner."

I grabbed the front of Kerr's shirt in my fist and lifted him off the ground with one arm. "Do you know what the world would be like if everyone picked on those who are weaker? It wouldn't be a very pleasant place now, would it?"

"Uh, no."

79

"Take now, for instance. Do you have any idea of what I could do to you? Do you have any idea of how I could make you scream and cry? You wouldn't like that, would you?"

"Uh...no, sir!"

"I didn't think so. And you know, this guy back here that you're picking on, I don't think he enjoys it too much either. Think about that the next time you decide to pick on him, because when I find out about it, I'll come looking for you and give you a little taste of what it's like to be on the receiving end."

I lowered Kerr to the ground. His buddy had crawled to his knees by then. Kerr helped him to stand and then led him away, looking back now and then in fear.

"I'm Skye," I said, turning to the boy standing behind me and extending my hand.

"Wow, I've heard of you. I thought you moved away. Oh, I'm Craig," he said, shaking my hand.

"Friends of yours?" I asked, nodding towards Kerr and his buddy.

"Hardly. They live to give me a rough time."

"Not anymore," I said.

Craig laughed.

"If they give you any trouble, just let me know. I'll convince them it's not in their best interest, health-wise, to continue."

"Thanks!"

"Don't mention it. I'm not very fond of bullies."

"I'm sure they'll think twice about giving me trouble. I think Kerr just about pissed his pants while you were holding him in the air. Damn, you're strong! Kerr has got to weigh 160 at least!"

"So, do those guys pick on you just for fun, or is there a reason?"

"Well, I'm gay. They don't know it for sure, but they suspect, and that's reason enough for them."

"I know the type. You're gay, huh? You're cute too. How old are you?"

"I'm seventeen."

"Great."

"Do you have a boyfriend, Skye?"

"No, I'm not the boyfriend type. Why don't I walk you home? Just to make sure you get there safely."

Craig grinned, and we were on our way. I know what you're thinking, but no, I didn't put the moves on him. Craig was kind of cute, but a bit too young for me.

Ralph

"It's been too long since our last visit to Verona," Jordan said as he parked our rented SUV in front of Graymoor Mansion.

We stepped out and looked at the massive old home.

"Wow," I said.

"Wow is right."

"It's...beautiful. It almost doesn't look like the same house."

"I can't wait to see inside," Jordan said.

We grabbed our bags and walked through the gates toward the Victorian home. It felt good to stretch my legs, even though it took a little less than two hours to drive from Fort Wayne. I opened the front door, and we walked into a massive parlor. A small front desk was located near the door. It matched so nicely with the rest of the room that it looked as if it had always been there. Jordan rang the bell sitting on the desk. In moments, Sean appeared from the kitchen.

"What does someone have to do to get some service around here?" Jordan asked with a grin.

"Jordan! Ralph!"

Nick came rushing up behind Sean. I had little doubt he would be present since he knew we were due to arrive. Nick was a major *Phantom* fan and had had a big crush on Jordan since he was a teenager.

"Hey, guys!" Nick said.

"What I've seen so far looks incredible," Jordan said, looking around at the vast parlor that acted as a lobby for the bed & breakfast.

"We just came from the Hilton in Fort Wayne," I said, "and as beautiful as it is, it's nothing compared to this."

"Your money is being put to good use," Sean said. "Restoration work has been going on continuously for more than four years now. If you listen carefully, you might hear a hammer or saw in the far distance."

"Let me help you with your bags," Nick said, approaching Jordan.

"Thanks."

Sean took one of my bags and led us to our room. I must say I was impressed with the room that awaited us.

"Would you guys like to rest, or are you ready for a tour?" Sean asked.

"There is no way I can rest before I see the house," Jordan said. "I've been dying to see what has been done with the place. I can't tell you how hard it has been to stay away, although being far too busy has helped."

Sean and Nick led us back downstairs. Our first stop was the kitchen, where Sean's mom joined our party. For the next two hours we toured Graymoor, starting with the parlor, the Dining Room, various sitting rooms and bedrooms and then onto the Ballroom, the Natatorium, the Solarium, the Tower Room and the Library. I'm not even going to try to describe what we saw. It was all too beautiful for words.

We ended up back in the Dining Room, where Martha, who was delightful, served tea. When I say tea I don't mean just a cup of tea, which would have been enjoyable enough, but an English high tea with crumpets, cucumber sandwiches and all sorts of little goodies. Martha served the tea out of a huge, silver teapot. The porcelain cups decorated with roses were so beautiful that I was nearly afraid to drink out of mine.

"I'm...astounded," Jordan said, when we were all seated. "I'm simply astounded. The photos you e-mailed me didn't even begin to do this place justice."

"So, you're going to film the video here?" Nick asked excitedly.

"Of course," Jordan said. "We already decided that based on the photos. Everything is set, and the crew is on its way."

"Excellent!" Nick said, beaming. "When do Ross, Kieran and Cedi arrive?"

"Ross, Kieran, Cedi should be in tomorrow, and the crew should get here the day after that."

"I'm so excited!" Nick said.

"Really?" Sean asked, as if he was shocked. "We couldn't tell."

Nick punched him in the shoulder, still grinning.

Jordan, Kieran, Ross, and Cedi had been scouting locations for a video. They had been considering some of the great old movie palaces like The Embassy in Fort Wayne, but after seeing the photos Sean's mom had e-mailed us, I had suggested they film right in Graymoor. There were several beautiful interiors, and the band and crew could stay right in the house for as long as the shoot lasted.

"This will be excellent publicity for Graymoor," Sean said. "If you guys don't mind, I'd like to get the *Verona Citizen* to do a piece on use of Graymoor as a location for your video, with the stipulation that it's printed *after* you've finished."

"That sounds like a great idea, especially the *after* part," Jordan said.

"Yeah, Graymoor would be flooded with onlookers if people knew *Phantom* was here," Nick said.

"Want them all to yourself, do you Nick?" Sean asked.

"You know it!"

"The film crew is also going to shoot footage for a 'making of' piece that we'll include on our next CD or DVD," Jordan said. "Some of the music programs may also want some of the footage. I've already instructed the crew to focus on Graymoor for the background pieces."

"Great," Sean said.

We sat and chatted and enjoyed our tea. Graymoor was so different than it had been when we'd toured it before. It had been transformed from a run-down old home into a thing of beauty. I could tell Jordan was well pleased.

After a nap in our room, Jordan and I changed into swimsuits and headed for the Natatorium. We had arranged to meet Nick there at four p.m. Sean couldn't come. He was too busy making arrangements for the arrival of our film crew and all the equipment.

Nick was already in the pool when we arrived. I noticed he devoured Jordan's bare chest with his eyes. He just couldn't help himself. I knew how he felt. I'd been the same way when I first met Jordan. Well, I still couldn't keep my eyes off him, but now I looked at him in a different way.

Skye, whom we'd met briefly on our tour, changed into a swimsuit and joined us in the pool as well. Both Jordan and I did our share of checking Skye out. He could have been a model for Abercrombie & Fitch or Calvin Klein. Skye didn't fail to check out Jordan either and even gave me a few looks.

We swam and played around in the water, then lounged about the Natatorium with Nick while Skye returned to his work. Nick asked Jordan all kinds of questions about *Phantom* and Phantom World. Skye joined in now and then as he moved about performing various tasks. He had a sweet job. I wouldn't have minded to spend my days by the sunny pool.

I couldn't believe all the projects Jordan had taken on. *Phantom* was a full-time job in itself, with performances, appearances, working on new songs, and so forth. On top of all that, there was Jordan's involvement with the Graymoor Bed & Breakfast and Phantom World. Of course, Jordan didn't have to do much besides write the checks for the restoration of Graymoor, but it still demanded some of his precious time. Kieran and Ross were equal partners with Jordan in Phantom World, and they'd hired talented individuals to run the park, but it was still a massive amount of work. There was also the Potter-Bailey Gay Youth Center in Verona, for which Jordan was ultimately responsible. Thank God Jordan knew how to surround himself with capable people. He ran what amounted to an empire.

I nearly laughed out loud when a couple of teenage girls entered the Natatorium and screamed when they spotted

Jordan. Skye, who had retreated to the gym came rushing in, but quickly figured out what had happened. It took the girls a good while to calm down, but they finally did so. The girls joined us, and Jordan sat and talked with them for a long time. The girls readily agreed not to tell anyone he was in Verona, and Jordan promised he would pose for a photo with them before they had to check out.

I noticed the girls devoured Jordan's smooth, naked chest just as Nick did. Even though Jordan was publicly out, he still had a tremendous number of female fans who drooled over him. They could be overly aggressive at times, but most were like these girls.

"Don't you get tired of that?" Nick asked when the girls departed. "I don't think I could take it, especially the screaming."

"Well, I'm not overly fond of the screaming either," Jordan said, "but I don't mind the attention. Sometimes, it's a lot of fun. Of course there are times when Ralph and I would rather just be left alone, but those girls and all the other fans make our lives possible. I couldn't do what I love to do without them, so I think I owe them a little time. I enjoy talking to the fans. They have such wonderful things to say, and they ask some very interesting questions. The only time the fans get to be a problem is when there's a large group of them somewhere like a mall."

"I bet you get mobbed."

"It's happened. That's why I usually travel with a bodyguard. Mobs can get dangerous."

"Yeah, I've been crushed a few times myself," I said. "It can get a little scary."

"I try to avoid situations that could get out of hand, but that means Ralph and I can't go a lot of places we would like to go. We did slip into Glenbrook Square Mall for some shopping while we were in Fort Wayne."

"Did you get recognized?"

"No, Ralph and I worked on my disguise quite a bit before we went. We hid my hair under a black bandanna and Ralph made me up so that I had a Goth look going."

"Oh, man, I wish I could have seen that!"

"Yeah, I had on black eyeliner, black lipstick, Goth-style clothes—the whole bit."

"He didn't look anything like himself," I said.

"No one bothered us. I think a couple of old ladies were actually afraid of me."

"You did smile at them," I said.

"Do fans ever ask you really personal stuff?" Nick asked.

"Sometimes, but that's the exception and not the rule."

"He gets hit on quite a bit," I said, laughing.

"Really? Even though they know you're taken?"

"Yeah, sometimes I get some...inappropriate offers."

Nick laughed.

"I think it would be really cool to be famous, but only for a little while. I wouldn't mind to be you for a couple of weeks, but after that, I would want to go back to being me."

"That's the problem with fame," Jordan said. "It can't be turned on and off."

We had a nice talk with Nick, then returned to our room where we lounged around and relaxed some more. I loved vacations!

***

We were just coming down the stairs when Ross descended upon Graymoor.

"Is this *MY* room?" Ross asked loudly as he stood in the huge parlor.

"No, Ross, although it would take a room this size to contain your ego," Jordan said.

"Hey! It's hard to be as wonderful as me!"

"And to think I actually missed him," Jordan said, turning to me.

"I heard that!"

"Service! Service!" Ross yelled as he rang the bell on the desk repeatedly.

"I knew it had to be you," Sean said as he came striding across the room.

"Sean!" Ross said, running at him and jumping into his arms. Sean stumbled, but managed not to drop Ross.

"You should have let him fall," Jordan said.

"And let me get hurt?" Ross asked loudly. "What would my billions of fans think?"

"Billions, Ross?" I asked.

"Yeah, the whole world loves me!"

Sean just shook his head.

Ross was already surrounded by bags, but Shawn, his bodyguard, kept carrying in more.

"Ross, you pack like a prissy girl!" I said. "You've got enough stuff for a month!"

"I only have the bare necessities."

"You're going to need an extra room just for your luggage," Jordan said.

"Come on," Ross said. You can all help carry it to my room."

"Gee, thanks," I said.

Jordan, Ross, Sean, Shawn, and I were all loaded down as we made our way up the grand staircase. Ross could have learned a thing or two about packing from Jordan and me. We traveled light. Of course, Ross seemed rather impervious to advice. He had his own way of doing things.

Mike, Jordan's bodyguard, arrived later in the day, and he was set up in the room next to ours. I always felt better when Mike was around. He took the job of guarding Jordan seriously. I was amazed he'd let Jordan and me travel to Fort Wayne alone. It had taken a good deal of convincing.

We all had supper that night in the Dining Room. Martha outdid herself with a New Orleans menu of Cajun shrimp, gumbo and just about everything else one would expect to find in a good New Orleans restaurant. Ross, of course, outdid himself at being obnoxious, but as always, in an entertaining way. Nick joined us for supper, and I noticed several looks exchanged between him and Ross.

Ross was flirting with Sean and Nick. The three of them had a bit of history. They had become—shall we say— intimate a few years before when Ross visited Verona. It had caused a temporary falling out between Jordan and Ross, but that was because of a misunderstanding that was soon cleared up. Even when he found out the truth, Jordan still didn't approve, but he figured what was between Ross, Sean and Nick was their business.

Ross also flirted with Skye, the incredible hunk in charge of the Natatorium. If I was single, I would have flirted with Skye too. Skye seemed quite interested in Ross, which didn't surprise me a great deal, because Sean had told us Skye was gay. After all, Ross was quite good-looking. Before I'd met and fallen for Jordan, I'd had some fantasies about Ross—and also Kieran for that matter. Once I'd met Jordan, I forgot about everyone else. I never had sexual thoughts about Ross or Kieran now. We were friends and more like brothers in a way. Besides, I knew way too much about Ross to be turned on by him. I nearly laughed out loud at the thought.

Ross flirted some with Marshall too, but he had no chance with him. He would probably have been eyeing Avery as well, but he had departed the previous day. Maybe he just wanted to avoid Ross.

Had there been any guests staying at the bed & breakfast, I'm sure Ross would have found others to flirt with as well. Ross was bisexual and was definitely a big flirt. Jordan considered him to be a bit slutty, and I can't say that I disagreed. Ross had hormones that worked overtime. I thought he might begin to slow down when he left his teen years behind, but at twenty-two he was wilder than ever. It was probably a good thing Sean hadn't booked any guests for the days we would be staying at Graymoor. There were only a few guests the day Jordan and I arrived, like the girls we'd met by the pool, but now Graymoor was empty except for the staff and those of us seated at the table.

Luckily, neither Jordan nor I was Ross's keeper, though we did worry that he'd get himself into trouble. He was a talented musician, but not overly blessed with good sense.

Jordan and I retired early to our comfortable room and spent the evening reading and talking while curled up next to each other. We treasured our quiet moments, because we had so few of them. It didn't matter what we were doing: I was happy as long as Jordan was at my side.

Sean

There was a light tap on my office door.

"Come in."

"Hey."

"Oh, hey, Nick."

"You sound surprised to see me."

"I was expecting someone else. I thought you had gone home already."

"No, after you headed back here, I showed Ross around."

"Oh."

"Sean, there's something I'd like to talk to you about." Nick's voice quavered slightly. I knew from experience it meant he was nervous.

"What?" I asked, closing down my Internet connection.

"About us and...Ross."

"Go on."

"Well, you remember four or five years ago when he visited the farm?"

"Of course, I do."

"Well," Nick said, swallowing hard, "I was wondering what you would think about getting together with Ross again."

"You mean having sex with him again?"

"Yeah."

"Nick, I...I really only did *that* because I knew it was something you really wanted. You know I wasn't entirely comfortable with it."

"You enjoyed it."

"Yes, physically I enjoyed it. Sexually it was new, exciting, and hot. It made me uncomfortable though. I don't like sharing you like that."

"I know, but...we did it before, and I know you really like Ross..."

"I like a lot of guys Nick, but that doesn't mean I want to sleep with them."

"You know it's hot with Ross," Nick said.

"I'm not questioning that. I just don't know if it's a good thing for our relationship."

"What would it hurt? We did it with him before..."

"I just...I just don't want to, Nick. What happened before was a one-time thing. I don't want Ross to become a permanent part of our relationship."

Nick's face fell, making me feel a bit guilty and then angry, because I shouldn't have been made to feel guilty for wanting to keep my boyfriend to myself. To me, sex was more than a physical act that gave pleasure. Sex was making love. Bringing a third party into it, no matter who, lessened it somehow. I'd gone along with it once, but I didn't want to repeat the experience.

"Well, I...okay," Nick said.

"Come here," I said. I met him half way, took him in my arms and kissed him. Our kiss deepened, and our hands began to roam. We were interrupted by a knock on my door.

"Duty calls," I said. "Let's finish this later."

"You can count on it," Nick said, kissing me once more on the lips.

I opened the door.

"Mr. Hilton?"

"Call me Sean, come in."

"Hi, I'm Kane. I'm here to talk to you about the assistant-gardening position."

"Have a seat."

"I'll see you later," Nick said. He nodded at Kane and departed.

I quickly gave Kane a once-over as I took my seat behind the desk. He was quite young, no older than I am. He wasn't especially good-looking, but he was nicely built, with bulging biceps and pecs that stretched his shirt to the ripping point. I wondered how long it would take Skye to seduce him. I didn't know if Kane was gay or not, but if there was any chance to get into his pants, I was sure Skye would manage.

I looked at Kane's application, skimming it over. What I paid the most attention to was a post-it-note attached by Mr. Diggory that simply said, "Yes."

"Your application says you have a background in gardening."

"Yes, I started mowing lawns when I was a kid and ran my own lawn service until college. I concentrated on courses related to professional gardening, landscaping and design in school. I've also volunteered extensively at the Foellinger-Freimann Botanical Conservatory in Fort Wayne."

"Sounds good. Tell me about yourself, Kane."

As Kane spoke, I began to get a feel for him. He was friendly, animated and obviously enthusiastic about his profession. Personality was as important as expertise, as Kane would be working around guests and would quite likely be giving tours of our own botanical garden.

"Well, Kane," I said after a short time, "I think I've heard enough. Mr. Diggory, our head gardener, has recommended you so you obviously impressed him. I see no reason not to hire you. Now, let's discuss salary, benefits, and so forth and see if you're interested."

I nearly laughed at myself as I sat there going over details with Kane. I sounded like a businessman when I sure didn't feel like one. Kane was so enthusiastic that it made even what could have been a boring task at least somewhat fun. It took him no time at all to accept my offer. I set him to work filling out the necessary paperwork.

After Kane departed, I walked to the window and looked over the grounds. Nick's suggestion that we get back together with Ross disturbed me. I knew Nick had a thing for Ross, but I thought his curiosity had been satisfied long ago. It seemed I'd been mistaken. The revelation made me ill at ease.

***

The following day was extra busy. Kieran and Cedi arrived mid-morning, and *Phantom's* road crew and the film crew for the video rolled in soon after. *Phantom's* instruments and sound equipment arrived in a large truck. The film equipment came in an even larger truck. Luckily, large trucks were a common sight at Graymoor due to the renovations, so they wouldn't attract unwanted attention.

With the arrival of two crews, our number of guests soared. My parents and I had thought ahead and not scheduled any regular guests for the days when *Phantom* would be filming in the house, but we still had a far greater number of people than we'd ever had before. We used nearly all of the guest rooms that had been renovated.

I had hired some temporary staff to help out in the kitchen and with housekeeping from the applicants who had applied for full-time positions. I asked Martha and Mrs. Hawkins to take notes on who they might want to hire for permanent positions. We would definitely be hiring both kitchen and household help in the near future.

I was amazed by the lights and cameras set up in the ballroom. It was like being on a movie set. Of course, I guess it *was* a movie set, only the movie being filmed was only about five minutes long. I wasn't sure Graymoor's power grid could handle the huge lights. The lights could best be described as miniature suns. I was relieved to discover the film company had brought along its own generators. Apparently, they were accustomed to working on location.

The actual filming wouldn't begin until the next day, but by mid-afternoon *Phantom's* music vibrated the walls of Graymoor. I could even hear the muffled beat from my bedroom on the third floor, and they were practicing on the first floor!

Nick was beside himself, of course. He was getting to see *Phantom* perform live in what amounted to a private concert. I hung around some, but I was far too busy to just stand and watch what was going on in the ballroom.

It was a good thing Graymoor had a cavernous kitchen. I'd always wondered why anyone would need a kitchen that vast, but Martha and her helpers put a good deal of it to use in preparing supper. Jordan had offered to bring in a caterer, but Martha wouldn't hear of it. She was even a bit insulted by the suggestion. When Jordan mentioned it, I thought she was going to scream at him.

I didn't expect Martha to prepare her usual gourmet cuisine, but even with unfamiliar help and an especially large number of guests, she pulled it off. She served Chicken Kiev, twice-baked potatoes, herbed rice, yeast rolls and a delectable collection of desserts, which included cherries Jubilee, blueberry cheesecake and carrot cake. I forced myself to eat moderately and it wasn't easy!

I tried to keep my work from creeping into the evening hours, but there were so many little details to handle that my day seemed practically endless. Not everything could be attended to during normal working hours either. On top of that, our entire staff was still settling in. Some, like Mrs. Hawkins, our head housekeeper and Martha, our head chef, were experienced, but others were quite new. Despite my degree and my internship, this was the first time I'd actually run a hotel on my own. True, I had my parents to help me, and we were operating on a very small scale, but it was still a whole new world to me. I thanked God we had the foresight to start out small, but I knew that we needed to grow rapidly to make Graymoor a going business.

So far, my days had been busier than anticipated, and I'd had little time to spend with Nick, but I was still happy and content. I was back home with my family. My friends were close at hand—some of them living in Graymoor itself. Best of all, Nick was never more than a few miles away, and often as not, he was no more than a few feet away. It almost seemed like he was living in Graymoor too.

I was finally finished with my work for the day about eight p.m. Since Jordan was currently residing in Graymoor, I wanted to drop off some advertising proposals so he could check them out. I thought I'd done a rather nice job of creating an advertising scheme that would get us maximum coverage for minimum cost, but I wanted a second opinion. Jordan was the one paying for the advertising, so I wanted his approval before I moved ahead.

I climbed the stairs to the second-floor landing and turned left toward the room Jordan shared with Ralph. I walked down the long hallway and made another turn. I stopped dead in my tracks, horrified by the scene before me. The papers in my hand fell to the floor.

"Sean!" Nick cried.

I just stood there while the color drained from my face and my eyes filled with tears. Pain and anger enveloped me.

"Oh, shit," Ross said.

"Sean, I can explain," Nick said.

"You don't need to explain anything to me Nick. I understand perfectly," I said.

I turned on my heel and quickly headed back the way I'd come. The image of my boyfriend making out with Ross was burned into my mind.

"Sean, wait!"

I could hear Nick running to catch up with me, but I didn't slow or look back.

"Sean!"

Nick grabbed my arm and twisted me around.

"Don't touch me!"

Nick stepped back.

"Sean, it's not what you think!"

"Isn't it? What are you going to tell me, Nick? Was Ross about to fall and you saved him by shoving your tongue in his mouth?"

"No, I just...we didn't mean for it to happen...we just..."

"I don't want to hear it, Nick. I just don't want to hear it! I thought you loved me. After all this time...after everything we've been through.... I don't care how it happened, Nick; the bottom line is I caught you kissing Ross. How could you Nick? How could you do that to me, to us?"

I turned and ran down the hallway, blinded by tears. I ran up the stairs and straight to my room. I slammed my door, locked myself in, threw myself on my bed and bawled my eyes out.

Later, I lay on my bed, staring at the ceiling. Finding Nick and Ross together felt so unreal. In all our time away from each other during college, I never doubted Nick's faithfulness for a moment. Not once did I fear that he might cheat on me. It was unthinkable. There were times I didn't think I could go on—being so far from Nick and needing him so badly. There were times when I'd thought that maybe we were making a mistake and that we should have allowed ourselves to date others, but I never really wanted anyone but Nick. Even when I was attracted to other guys, I thought of Nick, and suddenly no one else mattered. I thought Nick felt the same way about me. If Nick decided that our long-distance relationship wasn't working, he would have discussed it with me. He wouldn't just cheat on me, but now...here we were back together, and I'd caught him with another guy. I'd held him in my arms only the night before. We'd satisfied each other's desires. We could have been together again tonight, but he cheated on me. Nick chose to have Ross when he could have been with me. The pain of the rejection and betrayal tore my heart out.

Ross attempted to speak with me the next morning as I crossed the parlor. He was standing with Jordan, Ralph and Cedi, checking out the old pump organ when I came downstairs.

"Sean, I..."

"Don't talk to me!" I snapped and continued on to the kitchen without slowing down.

"What was that about?" Jordan asked Ross as I walked on. "What did you do this time, Ross?"

I heard Ross sputter and make some kind of gurgling noise. I wondered what Jordan would think when he found out the truth.

Nick was gone of course, and that was fine by me. I didn't want to see him, speak to him, or hear from him. I was so hurt and angry I knew I couldn't bear the sight of him or the sound of his voice. I had intentionally missed breakfast because I didn't want to deal with anyone. I grabbed a donut and a cup of tea and headed straight for my office. I buried myself in work so I wouldn't have to think about what had happened.

Nick made no attempt to contact me during the entire day. I was relieved, but also angered. If he called, I would have hung up on him, but the fact he didn't even try spoke volumes. He was the one who had done wrong. He was the one who cheated on me. He should have been on his knees begging for forgiveness, and he didn't even bother to try to explain.

I knew I wasn't being entirely fair. He had tried to explain the night before, but I was too angry to listen. What explanation could there possibly be? There was no mistaking what I'd seen with my own eyes. Nick and Ross were making out. It looked as if they were trying to swallow each other. They were all over each other, right there in the hallway. When Nick and I kissed like that, the next step was tearing each other's clothes off.

The best-case scenario I could come up with was that the kiss wasn't planned. It happened just as Nick said. He and Ross had given into temptation. If that was so, he had still cheated on me. The trust between us was broken. If I couldn't trust Nick, how could I continue my relationship with him?

The other possible scenarios were far worse. Was this the first time he cheated on me or merely the first time I'd caught him? Had Nick and Ross been fooling around earlier in the day while I was working? Had they been hooking up while Nick was in school? Had Nick slept around during our college years? I had always been so sure of Nick's faithfulness, but I could no longer be sure of anything. I couldn't decide if I was more hurt or angry.

I stayed away from the ballroom where *Phantom* was working on their video. I was curious to see what was going on, but I didn't want to see Ross, and I feared Nick might be there. I knew how hard it was for Nick to stay away from his idols, especially Ross.

Just before lunch was served, I stopped in the kitchen to grab something I could take back to my office. I wasn't in the mood to speak with anyone. All morning I had done a rather good job of distracting myself with the myriad of details that went along with running a bed & breakfast. I was still learning the ropes, so things didn't go all that smoothly. Getting the various computer programs I needed up and running took hours alone, and that was only the beginning. I thanked God for the courses I'd taken in college and for my internship. Without that preparation, I would have been completely overwhelmed.

I ate lunch at my desk while gazing out the windows. Fluffy clouds floated lazily in a blue sky. Everything had been going so well only the day before. Now, I felt lost and disoriented. I had waited so long to be back with Nick, and now I was so angry with him I didn't know if I ever wanted to see him again. If he wanted to break up with me, he should have done it when we went our separate ways to attend college. Instead, he'd waited until I was back in Verona, where my chances of finding someone to love were practically nil.

Finding someone to love—I didn't know if I even wanted that now. I'd always thought that once I found a boyfriend, my troubles would be over. Boy, was I wrong about that. The pain and the heartache weren't worth it. I didn't know if I'd ever date again.

I went right back to work after I finished eating, to avoid yet more unpleasant thoughts. I spent three busy hours at my computer dodging the topic of Nick. I desperately needed to stretch my legs after all that sitting, so I stood and took a walk through the hallways of the fourth floor.

I strolled around for several minutes—thinking of Nick, of course. The image of him kissing Ross was burned into my mind. How could he do that do me?

I heard footsteps behind me as I neared the Library. I thought perhaps it was one of the resident ghosts, but when I turned, I found it was a living being—the last one I desired to set eyes upon.

"Sean—"

"Save it, Ross!"

"I just want to explain."

"You want to explain making out with my boyfriend? Is that what you want to explain, Ross?"

"We didn't mean for it to happen."

"Yeah, that's what Nick said, but it did happen, didn't it?"

"Let's put things in perspective. It was just a kiss."

"Bullshit! I saw how the two of you were going at it! That wasn't just a kiss!"

"Sean, you're being unreasonable."

"*I'm* being unreasonable? You're the one who made out with *my* boyfriend, no—make that my *ex*-boyfriend. You think that just because you're a famous rock star you can have anyone you want, don't you? You think you can do anything you want and get away with it."

"That's not fair, Sean," Ross said, scowling.

"Well, stealing my boyfriend wasn't fair either Ross, but hey, why should *you* care? You've got what you want now. Nick has what he wants too. He's always wanted you. I was just someone to fill in until you came back into his life, or have you two been fucking behind my back all along?"

Ross began to speak, but I cut him off before he could get started.

"You know, don't tell me! I don't fucking care anymore. You and Nick can fuck each other all you want! I'm through with the pair of you."

I turned and began to walk away, but Ross grabbed my shoulder.

"Sean—"

"Don't touch me!"

Tears streamed from my eyes, and I trembled with anger.

"Sean—"

"I fucking hate you!" I screamed at Ross.

He reached out to me, and that's when I decked him. I clocked him right in the jaw. Ross staggered back, growled and flung himself at me. The next thing I knew, we were rolling around on the floor beating the shit out of each other. We scrambled to our feet and kept going at it. All the pent-up anger that had been boiling inside me spilled out, and I did my best to kick Ross's ass. I quickly discovered he was a good deal stronger than I was. Ross got in at least two good punches for every one of mine. He grunted as I punched him in the stomach. He came back at me with a blow to the chin that made me stagger, but I didn't back off an inch. I didn't care how much damage he did to me. All that mattered was hurting him for what he'd done.

Ross finally shoved me away, and we stood there panting and glaring at each other. I wanted to attack him again, but I was too exhausted and in too much pain.

"I hate you, Ross," I growled at him. "I fucking hate you. When you're finished with that video I *never* want to see you again!"

Grimacing in pain, I turned away from him. I did my best not to hobble down the hallway. I didn't want Ross to know how much he'd hurt me. I looked back when I heard Ross walk away. I grinned when I saw him stagger. He had a little trickle of blood flowing from the corner of his mouth. I only wished I could have hurt him worse.

I cleaned up in a restroom and returned to my office. Surprisingly, I felt a good deal better after beating the shit out of Ross. I guess it would be more accurate to say that we beat the crap out of each other, but the pain I'd suffered was well worth the damage I'd done to that asshole.

I next came across Ross at supper. *Phantom* would be filming in Graymoor for some days yet, and I wasn't about to hide out in my office forever. Our eyes met and narrowed as I entered the Dining Room, but we spoke not a word. Jordan scowled at Ross when he noticed the look that passed between us. Jordan obviously wasn't pleased with Ross at all.

I took a seat on the same side of the table as Ross but at the other end so I didn't have to look at him. I wanted more than anything to punch him in the face again and again for stealing my boyfriend, but my bruised and battered body couldn't take any more. Ross wasn't his usually zany self during supper. Perhaps getting his ass kicked had dampened his spirits. Cedi, whom I hadn't met before the previous day, joked and laughed. He reminded me a lot of Ross. At least, he reminded me of Ross's zany side. I sure hoped he wasn't like him in other ways. The world had enough assholes.

After supper, Jordan caught up with me in the hallway.

"Can we talk?" he asked.

"Sure."

We slipped into an empty sitting room and closed the door behind us. We took seats in tufted armchairs that faced each other.

"Ross told me what happened with Nick. I can't tell you how sorry I am, Sean."

"You don't have to be sorry, Jordan. What happened is not your fault."

"I know you're right, but I can't help but feel responsible. It was my idea to shoot the video in Graymoor, which is why Ross is here."

"If you think like that, you can make yourself feel responsible for just about anything," I said. "The idea to shoot the video here is awesome. It merely brought Ross and Nick together and provided the opportunity for what happened between them. It was Nick and Ross who made the choice."

"I'm so sorry this happened. You and Nick were so happy together. I don't know what goes through Ross's head sometimes. He can be so irresponsible."

"It's not just Ross," I said. "It takes two, you know? It's not as if Ross forced himself on Nick. There was something there or it wouldn't have happened. Five years ago, when Nick, Ross and I...well, you know..."

Jordan nodded.

"Well, the three-way with Ross was Nick's idea. I can't say I was completely against it, because Ross *is* extremely attractive. I only went along with it because I knew it was something Nick wanted badly. To be honest, it kind of hurt me. I knew Nick had a huge crush on Ross, and I didn't feel too good about that. He had—and has—a huge crush on you too, but you were already unobtainable. Ross wasn't. I thought that by agreeing to the three-way that Nick would get Ross out of his system, but I guess I was wrong. I guess I've been wrong about a lot of things."

I looked at Jordan.

"I guess Ross told you about our fight?"

"Yeah."

"I'm not usually that violent, but Ross just..." I growled in frustration.

Jordan gazed at me with compassion.

"Do you know what you're going to do about your relationship with Nick?"

"No, but I feel like it's over. This incident has raised a lot of doubts in my mind. You know, Nick and I kept our relationship going throughout college, even though we were far away from each other. I find myself wondering now how faithful he was to me. I passed up some really great guys because I thought Nick loved me, but now I'm wondering if I didn't make a mistake. Maybe Nick isn't the one for me after all. Maybe he'll be happier going off with Ross, and where does that leave me?"

"Just because he cheated doesn't mean he doesn't love you."

"I guess that's true, but if I can't trust him, how can I truly love him? You don't have to answer this, but have you and Ralph ever...slipped?"

"No," Jordan said. "I've been attracted to other guys, and I'm sure Ralph has too, but I've never cheated on him. I'm sure he's never cheated on me, either. We did break up for a time due to a misunderstanding. Both of us were with someone else then, but that's not cheating. To be honest, I'm not sure what I would do if I was in your position."

"I never dreamed Nick would cheat on me. It hurts so much!" Tears welled up in my eyes. I couldn't help it.

Jordan scooted closer and held my hand.

"If there is anything I can do, if you need someone to talk to, someone to hold Ross down while you beat him, or whatever, I'm here. Okay?"

"Where were you earlier when I needed someone to hold Ross down? He's strong," I said.

"I just don't know about that boy," Jordan said. "You know, Ross is twenty-two, but he acts like he's twelve most of the time. I'm really worried he's going to get himself into serious trouble someday. I'm surprised there aren't little Rosses running around."

"Maybe there are. He does seem rather out of control, especially where other guys' boyfriends are concerned. I imagine he's the same with girls."

"Most of the time he's okay. He's a sweet guy, and I love him to bits. He's this wacky screwball who just happens to have an amazing musical talent, but sometimes he displays such poor judgment. To be blunt, he thinks with his dick far too often."

"Like last night."

"Yeah. I really don't think Ross would have kissed Nick if he had stopped to think of the consequences. That's the trouble with him. He never thinks. He just acts. Everything has to be instant gratification with him. I really wonder sometimes if his fame and all the money have messed him up. I feel as though I'm his dad sometimes. Thank God, he doesn't control his own finances or he would have blown it all on something stupid by now."

"He doesn't control his own finances? Who does?"

"Ralph, actually. He handles everything financial for Ross. He pays his bills, makes investments for him and gives him an allowance. Ralph has even taken a few classes so he can take care of Ross's finances properly."

"Ross agreed to that?"

"Yes, he knows he'd blow everything he makes if someone else wasn't watching over him. Of course, the allowance he agreed upon is rather sizable. Few people make as much. Ralph has most of his money safely invested, so despite himself, Ross will always be provided for."

"He does sound like a child."

"He is in some ways. In other ways, he's brilliant."

"I don't know if Ross told you this, but I told him I don't want to see him again after the video is finished."

"I can't say I blame you Sean."

"I don't want to put you in the middle of things either, Jordan. I know you and Ross are close. I know you're also close with Nick. I have no intention of letting my problems with Ross and Nick affect the friendship you and I have developed. Even if Nick goes off with Ross, I want us to remain friends."

"Of course we'll remain friends Sean. I really don't think you have to worry about Ross and Nick developing any kind of relationship. Ross is too flighty. To be honest, I think he's incapable of a sustained relationship. I've never known him to stick with anyone for more than a few days. Well, Ross and Cedi do have something going, but it's casual.

I probably shouldn't be telling you that, but I'm sure you'll keep it to yourself."

"Ross and Cedi? Damn, Ross has Cedi, who is right here with him, and he still went for Nick? He *is* a slut."

"Well, I'm not going to argue with you, because I can't say I disagree. I think you are underestimating Nick, though. I know you're hurting right now, and I think it's causing you to see things as being a lot worse than they are. I'm not saying things aren't bad, but I am saying that things might not be over between you and Nick."

"You know, Jordan, I wanted to spend my whole life with Nick, but now, even if what you say is true, I really don't know if I want that anymore."

Jordan leaned over and hugged me. I felt as if my life was over.

Skye

I dove into the water. The stars were shining above, and the pool was illuminated from below. I'd had a busy day, and swimming at night was a great way to relax. I'd just finished an intense workout, and the warm water eased my tired muscles.

We currently had no guests, but *Phantom's* road crew and the film crew for their latest video pushed the population of Graymoor higher than it had ever been before—in this century, anyway. Most of both crews were busy throughout the day and night, but those who weren't dropped in to use the pool or gymnasium now and then.

I wasn't accustomed to being around rock stars, but Jordan, Kieran, Ross and Cedi all seemed really cool. They were all rather good-looking too. It was too bad Jordan was taken. He was exceptionally good-looking and had a tight, firm body I wouldn't have minded getting my hands on. Kieran was a hottie, but he was married. That left Cedi and Ross.

Cedi was the youngest of the group at eighteen and seemed even younger. He stood at only about 5'9" and probably weighed no more than 125 pounds. He had black hair and the most amazing eyes—greenish blue, with a sort of violet thrown in. Cedi had to be the most energetic guy I'd ever met in my life. He reminded me of a hummingbird, always zipping around and never sitting still for more than a moment. Cedi's sexual orientation was a mystery to me, but he was a sexy little guy. That taut little body of his and his tight ass made me want to jump on him.

Ross was freaking hot. He wasn't as good-looking as Jordan, but then who was? Ross was extremely attractive, with his long dark hair and mischievous eyes. He was a real wild boy, and I found that appealing. He looked as if he had a hot bod hidden under his clothes, as well.

As if summoned by my thoughts, Ross entered the Natatorium as I lounged in the pool. He grinned at me as he pulled off his shirt. I checked him out as he walked toward me. Yeah, he had a nice bod. He wasn't built like me, but he had some hard muscles, and his torso had a sexy V-shape. A thin trail of dark hair led from his navel into his swimsuit. I began to breathe a little harder.

"Hey, I'm Skye," I said. "We met briefly before."

"Oh, yeah, I remember," Ross said, his gaze lingering on my chest.

I grinned at him knowingly. I liked where we were headed.

Ross and I had the Natatorium to ourselves. We swam in the warm water under the stars while we talked, laughed and flirted. Ross's long hair clung to the sides of his face until he climbed out of the pool and tied it back in a ponytail with what looked like a rubber band. My eyes were glued to his backside as he lifted himself out of the water. His shoulders were broad and tapered down to a narrow waist. What drew most of my attention was the way his swimsuit clung to his butt cheeks. Ross had one fine ass.

When Ross turned around, another of his attributes was revealed. If I wasn't mistaken, Ross was partly aroused. If I *was* mistaken—wow! Ross caught me checking him out, which was my plan. He grinned at me and dove back into the water.

We swam around each other for a few moments, then stopped and treaded water as we gazed into each other's eyes. I could read the desire in Ross's eyes. He wanted me, and he wanted me bad. I closed the distance between us, leaned in and was just about to kiss him when Ross pressed his hand against my chest.

"You don't have a boyfriend, do you? Or a girlfriend?" Ross asked.

"No, I don't have a boyfriend, and I have no interest in girls."

"Good," Ross said. He removed his hand from my chest, pressed his lips to mine and kissed me.

We paddled our way to the shallow end of the pool as we made out, never parting our lips once. When we were in shallow water, I took Ross into my arms, pulled him tightly against me and kissed him harder than ever. We stood in the pool and made out while our hands roamed.

"Someone could come in," I said. "Let's go hop in the hot tub."

I climbed out of the pool and extended my hand to Ross. I pulled him up and we made our way into the gymnasium with water streaming off our bodies. I closed the gymnasium door and locked it behind me.

We slipped into the hot tub. The water was almost too hot to bear at first, but I knew from experience I would grow accustomed to it quickly. Ross and I drew together and began making out once more. Ross kissed my neck and worked around until he was sitting behind me. Once there, he gripped my shoulders and began to massage them.

"You have such a beautiful body," he whispered in my ear.

I moaned my appreciation for the expertise of his fingers.

"You're so tense," Ross said as he continued his massage.

"That feels good."

"I know ways to make you feel a lot better."

"I'm sure you do," I said.

Ross worked on my shoulders more, kneading my hard muscles and then floated around in front of me again. I guided him around so that his back was to me and began to massage his shoulders.

"Talk about tense," I said. "You're so tight."

"Yeah, a lot has been going on. I really fucked up last night and again today."

"We all make mistakes," I said.

"I'm the master of mistakes."

He didn't say more, so I assumed he didn't want to talk about it. I kneaded his tight shoulder muscles with my fingers, using their strength to work out the tension.

"Oh," purred Ross, "if you keep that up you're going to put me to sleep."

"Why don't we continue this in my room?" I suggested. "If you fall asleep, you won't drown there."

"Mmm, I don't want to fall asleep Skye. I want you."

"Don't worry. If you nod off, we'll just pick up where we left off when you awaken."

Ross and I climbed out of the hot tub, dried ourselves off and headed for my room on the third floor. I couldn't wait to get there. I was aroused to a nearly painful extent, and Ross was the hottest guy who had crossed my path since I'd left California.

We wasted no time in tearing each other's clothes off once we reached my room. We had been practically nude in the Natatorium, but Ross looked even better naked. I couldn't wait to get my hands on him, and I didn't.

Ross had a beautifully sculpted torso, perfectly proportioned. His wide, smooth chest had just the right swell of muscle and tapered down into a slim, well-defined abdomen. Ross also had some sizable equipment to offer, and I wasted no time in checking it out.

Okay, I know some of you who are reading this want me to go into every stiff, throbbing detail, while others no doubt think I've given too much information already. I'm not one to care what others think, but I also don't want my life to read like cheap porn. So, I'll just say we did pretty much everything two guys can do together. We went at it like wild animals with no inhibitions. I was right about Ross. He was wild and intense. He was my kind of guy. We were all over and in each other for over two hours before we were finally too exhausted to keep it up. We took a quick shower together, and then we crashed onto the bed and fell instantly asleep.

When I awakened in the morning, Ross was gone. I found a note on the pillow saying that he'd gone downstairs for the video shoot and didn't want to waken me. He thanked me for "an awesome night," but my favorite part of the note was the sentence that read, "I hope we can get together again soon. Tonight?"

"Definitely," I said out loud as I climbed out of bed and began to dress.

I stopped by the ballroom and watched *Phantom* shoot part of their video. I was amazed at the amount of equipment and people it took to film a short music video. I gazed at Ross as he sang and played the drums. He smiled when he saw me and licked his lips. I felt an immediate stirring in my groin. I'd had a lot of guys, but never one like Ross. He was even more intense than Jarret, although in a different way.

I almost couldn't believe I'd had sex with a rock star. I didn't sleep with Ross because of his fame. I slept with him because of his sizzling hotness. I knew I'd never be able to watch one of *Phantom's* videos or listen to one of their songs the same way ever again.

Ross and I skipped the pool and hot tub that night and went straight to my room. I didn't think anything could top the night before, but I was wrong! If I gave you the details, well...you just couldn't handle it.

After we'd finished our second round, Ross and I lay naked on the bed, panting and sweating. Ross rested his head on my chest and sighed as he tried to catch his breath.

"I really needed this, Skye."

"Me too," I said, smiling.

"You've really helped me to get my mind off things."

"Want to talk about it?"

"I did something really terrible, and I don't know how to fix it."

"What did you do?"

"You've probably noticed Nick hasn't been around and that Sean is down in the dumps."

"Yes."

"It's my fault."

"How?"

"Sean caught Nick and me together."

"Are you kidding me? You had sex with Nick?"

"No. We weren't having sex. We were just making out, but that is bad enough."

"Oh, shit, Ross."

"Yeah. I truly didn't mean for it to happen, and I know Nick didn't either, but it did. Nick tried to explain it to Sean, but he wouldn't listen. I tried to explain it too, but Sean and I ended up getting in a fist fight."

"Whoa. Sean?"

"Yeah, he got so pissed off while we were talking that he attacked me."

"Damn, I didn't think he was that aggressive."

"If I wasn't stronger than he was, he would have kicked my ass. He did a fairly good job of it anyway."

"So how are things between you and Sean now?"

"Not good. He said that when the video is finished he never wants to see me again."

"Damn. Maybe he'll cool off."

"Maybe, but I don't think so."

"I hope he does. I want you to come back."

"And why is that?" I couldn't see it, but I knew Ross had a mischievous grin on his lips.

"You know why."

I rested my hand on Ross's chest. I could feel his heart beating.

"Jordan is so pissed at me, and I'm not exactly flavor of the month with Kieran, either. Even Cedi is rather ticked off at me for what I did. I fucked up bad."

"So, have you and Nick gotten together since then?"

"No. I haven't seen him since that night. I think he's talked to Jordan, but he's avoiding me like a plague."

"Sean and Nick go way back. This has to be hard on them both."

"Yeah. I feel so guilty. They've broken up because of me. Jordan accused me of thinking with my dick. I think he's right."

"That's not always bad," I said.

"No, not always, but it was this time. I wasn't thinking about anything when I was kissing Nick except how bad I wanted him. If Sean hadn't caught us, I don't know what would have happened. I'd like to think I would have come to my senses, but I know myself better than that. The only thing that kept Nick and me from getting it on was Sean."

"I don't know what to tell you," I said. "I'm not the relationship type of guy, so I don't know how to go about getting back together after a fight."

"You mean you're not going to marry me?" Ross asked with pretend hurt.

"No, but I will fuck you whenever you want, big boy."

"I want it as much as I can get it," Ross said. "I'm going to miss you when we leave."

"And I'm going to miss you."

I instructed Ross to lie on his stomach, and I massaged his shoulders and back until he fell asleep. When I could hear his soft, regular breath, I lay down beside him and pulled a sheet up over both of us. I was already growing accustomed to feeling Ross's warm body next to me as I slept.

***

"A ghost tour?" I asked as I stood in the parlor with Sean and Marshall.

"Of course!" Marshall said. "Much of the draw of Graymoor Mansion is its history."

"Its notorious history," corrected Sean.

"Yes, people are fascinated by the ax murders. The only reason Kenneth Graymoor isn't as famous as Lizzie Borden is that the story was hushed up when it happened. Everyone who lived in Verona at the time knew the details, but few others ever found out. Even today, it's a Verona secret."

"It's not a secret," I said.

"Well, perhaps I should have said it's a little-known historical event. Everyone in and around Verona knows about it, but go fifty miles away, and no one has heard of the Graymoor ax murders. All that is about to change."

"What do you mean?" I asked.

"Marshall thinks we should play up the murders for publicity," Sean said.

"I can just imagine what Avery would say about that," I said.

"Yeah, Avery thought no one would stay here because Graymoor is haunted, but he was wrong," Sean said, "as usual."

"I've already ensured that the Graymoor murders will become famous," Marshall said.

"And how's that?" I asked.

"You've heard of Thad T. Thomas, right?"

"The novelist?"

"That's right," Marshall said.

"See, I told you Skye reads books that don't have pictures," Sean said.

I crossed my arms and scowled at Sean, but he only grinned.

"Doesn't he write vampire books?" I asked.

"Yes, but he thinks there is potential for turning the Graymoor murders into a novel, especially with everything else we found out."

I remembered the grisly discovery made beneath Graymoor at the end of my high-school years. The Graymoor ax murders were merely the end of a life-long killing spree by Kenneth Graymoor—a spree that took dozens of lives, all of them boys and young men, with the exception of Mr. Graymoor's wife and daughter. If that wasn't bizarre enough, Mr. Graymoor himself had been a victim, possessed by a malevolent spirit that forced him to kill against his will.

"Yeah, you're right about that," I said.

"If Mr. Thomas writes a novel based on the Graymoor ax murders, they'll become famous overnight and so will Graymoor Mansion," Marshall said.

"And what has that got to do with this ghost tour you're talking about?" I asked.

"Everyone who stays here is going to want to see where the bodies were discovered and where Mr. Graymoor was lynched by a mob. They'll also be interested in the crypt."

"So it will just be like some kind of historical-home tour?"

A disembodied giggle filled the air, causing the hair on the back of my neck to stand on end. I jumped as I felt something brush against my ass.

"Oh, no, it will be much more than that. Observe."

Marshall raised his arm, and I gasped as a silver candlestick flew from a marble-top table some twenty feet away right into his hand.

"How did you do that?" Sean said, his eyes wide.

Marshall grinned at us.

"That's nothing, guys."

Marshall looked around the room, and candles and lamps began to light, one after another. Sean and I turned in place, watching with open mouths. Marshall stared at the pump organ, and it began to play.

"Marshall, I don't like this!" Sean said, edging closer to me.

My heart pounded in my chest, but I stood my ground.

"I'm sorry," Marshall said. "Too much?" He made a slashing motion across his throat. The organ ceased to play, and the candles and lamps were extinguished one by one.

"Are you...okay?" Sean asked, peering at Marshall with fear and concern.

"It's okay, Sean. I'm not possessed."

I understood why Sean looked so pale. A few years earlier, he'd had some nasty experiences with possession that had nearly cost him his life.

"How did you do that?" I asked, repeating Sean's earlier question. "Did you learn that in that school of yours?"

"I'd like to take the credit, but I didn't do it," Marshall said. "I merely arranged for it."

"So it's all rigged," I said.

"No, nothing was rigged. You can check for yourself."

"Then how—" began Sean.

"With a little help from a friend."

A cold breeze blew through us, making Marshall's hair fly around as if he was in a windstorm.

"Okay, a lot of help," Marshall said to the air.

"Friend, Marshall? *You* have a friend?"

"You're a funny man, Skye," Marshall said.

"I'm almost afraid to ask, but what friend?" Sean asked.

"His name is Etienne."

"Etienne?" I asked.

"Etienne Blackford. Does the last name ring a bell?" Marshall asked.

"Blackford?" Sean asked. "So he's connected with the manor?"

I was lost, but only for a moment. I remembered the discovery made in Graymoor Mansion when I was in high school. At the heart of the mansion was a much older structure, Blackford Manor. The manor had been moved stone by stone from England before Graymoor was built around and over it.

"It was his home. When the manor was moved, Etienne came with it. He wasn't the only one."

"How do you know this?"

"He told me. He's thirteen. He died in 1348 of the Black Death. It might interest you to know, Skye, that he's quite cute."

"I don't do thirteen-year-olds, especially dead ones."

"Well, if you go by his birthday, he's *much* older, Skye."

"Yeah, about six hundred years older," I said. "No, thank you."

I felt a breeze whirl around me and heard a boyish giggle. I could feel my face pale, but I fought not to let my fear show.

"So, you see dead people?" I said. "I knew that was a freaky school you attended, but..."

"Get with the program, Skye. I could see dead people before I left Verona. Now, it's much easier for me, and I can communicate with them far more easily as well."

"So you've been hanging out with dead boys?" I asked.

"Well, they're more fun than you, Skye."

"Fuck you, Marshall."

Marshall just laughed. "It's always sex with you, isn't it, Skye?"

"So you didn't light the candles or make the organ play?" Sean asked.

"No, Etienne did that. He also tossed the candlestick into my hand. Unfortunately, telekinesis isn't one of my talents."

"Telekinesis?" I asked.

"It's the ability to move things with the power of one's mind," Sean said.

"Oh, then we know Marshall didn't do it."

"I wouldn't talk, Skye. Your mind wouldn't have enough power to lift a speck of dust."

119

"I've got my body for that," I said, flexing my bicep. Sean and Marshall just rolled their eyes.

"This is really cool!" Sean said. "Do you know what this means? We can prove Graymoor is haunted!"

"Exactly," Marshall said. "Skeptics can search for wires and any other sign of rigging all they want, but there's none to find, because it's all real. As long as Etienne and the Graymoor boys don't mind helping out, we can guarantee some astonishing sights for every tour."

"And here I thought your time in England was a complete waste. I guess you *can* make some money with it," I said.

"My studies weren't about making money, but this will help pay the bills."

"This will be great!" Sean said.

Sean and Marshall began discussing the details, and I quickly grew bored. I turned to leave, but a chair slid across the floor and blocked my path.

"Marshall, will you call your ghost off?"

"Etienne, leave Skye alone," Marshall said. "It's bad enough you spy on him in the shower."

My mouth dropped open, and I nearly gave myself whiplash jerking my head around to look at Marshall. He laughed. I didn't know if he was serious or not, but the idea of a ghost checking me out while I showered was kind of creepy. I wondered what other private moments were observed by the thirteen-year-old ghost—correction, six-hundred-thirteen-year-old ghost. I thought of all Ross and I had done in my room. That created a whole new line of thought. I quickly suppressed thoughts of the dead voyeur.

"Later, guys," I said, heading back toward the Natatorium.

"Bye Skye," called out the voice of a boy. I halted for moment, then walked on. I *knew* living in Graymoor would be a unique experience.

***

In the late afternoon, the new gardener dropped into the Natatorium to tend the ivy, palms, roses and various plants that made the pool area seem like a tropical paradise. I'd caught sight of him in the distance earlier as he worked outside tending the rose garden, but this was the first time I got a good look at him.

"Hey, I'm Skye," I said, extending my hand.

"I'm Kane. So you're in charge of this place?"

"Yeah, anything you need, just ask. Staff can come in any time they want to use the facilities."

"Great. I haven't had a chance yet. What with working full time here and restoring my Chevy, I haven't had a moment to spare."

"Your Chevy?"

"Yeah, a '57 convertible. She was a wreck when I started, literally, but I've been working on her since I was in high school. I'm finally seeing light at the end of the tunnel, so I've been putting in a lot more time on her."

"Sweet."

"You like vintage cars?"

"Oh, yeah," I said, "especially the '57 Chevy."

"You'll have to come by and see her sometime."

"I'd like that."

As we talked, I checked out Kane. He was a couple of inches shorter than I was, probably about six feet, not especially good-looking, but definitely not homely. He had a nice build, if the biceps pressing against his sleeves and his forearms were any indication. Kane had dark red hair and mischievous green eyes. I'd never cared much for redheads, as they tended to be pale and pasty, but Kane's hair was so dark it bordered on brown, and he had a nice tan. I especially liked his eyes. They hinted at a wild side.

Kane was gay. He didn't tell me, but there was no need. His mischievous green eyes gave him away as they roved

121

over my body, and so did his shy grin. Kane wanted me; there was no doubt about that. Little did he know he was going to get his wish.

"Maybe I could come by and check out your car some evening this week," I suggested.

"Tonight would be great," Kane said.

I suppressed a grin.

"Tonight it is, then."

Kane gave me his address and phone number just as Sean entered the Natatorium. Kane moved off to tend to the ivy trailing up the columns of the portico. I enjoyed the scenery as I walked away, and I'm not talking about the plants. Kane had a nice ass.

"I see you didn't waste any time with Kane," Sean said, grinning.

"There's no time like the present."

Sean laughed. "Hey, do you have those order forms you were working on?"

"Sure thing. They're on my desk." We walked toward my small office.

"Great. I've just about got the new system up and running that will allow us to do all this via computer. Everyone will be able to send me their forms on the intranet. That way I won't have to reenter the information, I can just transfer it to the master list."

"Trying to cut down on paperwork, huh?"

"Yeah, it's my least favorite part of the job. I'm setting up the system so everyone can see orders, track orders and view current inventory. That way, if you're running out of chlorine or whatever, you can check to see if it's been ordered and when the shipment will be arriving."

"Oliver would say you have the efficiency of a Vulcan."

"Maybe, but I still don't have the cool ears. So how's your day going?"

"Great, especially now," I said, throwing a meaningful glance at Kane.

"Just don't get too rough with him. You might hurt him."

"Hey, I never break my toys. He'll be able to work tomorrow. I promise."

"Any other cute guys wander into your web recently?"

"Well, there was a extremely cute boy in here a few days ago checking me out like mad, but nothing happened."

"Why not? It's not like you to pass up a cute guy."

"He was fifteen."

"Oh."

"I have a strict no-one-under-eighteen rule."

"You have rules?"

"Yep. No one under eighteen, no married guys, and no unsafe sex—that's the big three."

"I bet you do get your share of under-aged admirers. If I would have spotted a guy like you when I was fifteen, I would probably have creamed my shorts."

I laughed.

"Hey, I've got to run."

"Sure you do. I know you, Sean. You just pretend to be busy."

"Don't tell anyone. Bye Skye."

I eyed Kane as he watered, weeded and clipped his way around the Natatorium. His jeans were just a little tight and the sight of him bending over made me breathe a little harder. Yeah, I definitely intended to get to know Kane better...and soon.

Ralph

Jordan beamed as he looked at from the invitation that had just been delivered by Mike.

"Is it from your grandparents?" I asked.

"Better. It's from my other grandmother."

Jordan's other grandmother was Mark's mother. While Taylor Potter was Jordan's biological father, he also thought of Mark Bailey as his father. Had Taylor and Mark lived, there is little doubt they would have raised Jordan together as their son. Of course, Jordan's mom might have objected, but I'm sure that's what Taylor and Mark would have wanted.

"That's so wonderful, Babe!" I said, giving my partner an affectionate hug.

Jordan had met Taylor's parents only a few years before. After much resistance and a rough start, they had developed a relationship. It had been much harder with Mark's mom. There was a lot of old pain there, and she had initially refused to see Jordan at all. She finally did meet with Jordan, but being with him was difficult for her. An invitation from Mark's mom was indeed cause for celebration.

"She wants us to come to supper tomorrow night. You're invited too, as are Grandmother and Grandfather Potter."

"That's great!"

"Yeah, I haven't had a chance to visit them yet this trip. We've been so busy with the video."

"Isn't *Phantom* scheduled to shoot some night scenes in the Solarium tomorrow evening?" I asked.

"Yes, but that will have to change. This is too important."

"I'm sure Kieran, Cedi and Ross will find something to do, or in Ross's case, someone to do."

"He's been hanging out with Skye a lot," Jordan said.

125

"Please, that's a no-brainer. The moment I laid eyes on Skye I knew Ross would be drooling over him."

"I think you might have done a bit of drooling yourself," Jordan teased.

"Not me. Gorgeous guys have no effect on me. I have you. How could I possibly want anyone else?"

"Aw," Jordan said and grinned.

***

The next evening, Jordan and I drove to the Bailey home. Jordan's grandmother lived alone. Her husband, Mark's dad, had killed himself shortly after Mark's own suicide. Mark's dad blamed himself for his son's death, and while he wasn't solely responsible, much of the blame lay at his feet. It was too bad he hadn't come to his senses before the tragedy that cost Jordan both his dads. If Mark's dad would have been more understanding... but I guess there was no reason to ponder the 'what ifs.'

The Potters had already arrived by the time we pulled up in front of the Bailey residence. Grandmother Bailey ushered us inside. She gave Jordan an affectionate hug.

Most of the conversation wasn't particularly interesting, just the everyday sort of talk that one can experience, well— every day. Jordan's grandparents wanted to be updated on everything going on in his life. There was quite a lot to tell, of course, so Jordan did most of the talking. What was said wasn't nearly as significant as the fact that Jordan was sitting there chatting with the very family members who had once rejected his father. Jordan had forgiven them a long time ago, because he knew it was what his dad would have wanted. I'm sure Jordan's grandparents had a much more difficult time forgiving themselves, but they were trying to put the past behind them and make up for it where they could. Jordan's forgiving attitude said much about him. He could have hated his grandparents for what they'd done.

Instead, he had tried to understand and had forgiven them. As a result, they were together now.

I also appreciated how they accepted me. It showed that they really had learned from the past. They definitely weren't repeating their mistakes.

"So when do I get some great-grandchildren?" asked Taylor's mom.

Jordan grinned, "Um...well, Ralph and I have given some thought to our options, but our life is so hectic. We just don't know if it's the right time."

"It's something you shouldn't miss out on, either of you," Taylor's mom said. "Now is a good time. You're twenty-two, Jordan. If you have children now, you won't be too old to enjoy them later."

"True, although Ralph and I could adopt older kids later."

"That's also true, but..."

"Oh, stop pestering the boy, Shirley," Jordan's grandfather said.

"It's my duty to pester him."

Jordan grinned. "Well, I promise we'll give it some more thought."

Jordan's grandparents had truly come around. They treated Jordan and me as if we were a traditional couple. Knowing what I did of their past, the accepting attitude of Jordan's grandparents gave me hope that others could change as well. The world seemed so ugly at times, with so many groups spreading nasty lies about gays, that it was refreshing to see acceptance.

We had a nice supper that Mrs. Bailey had prepared— spaghetti and meatballs with applesauce and garlic bread. I'd been a little concerned that I'd feel ill at ease. I had met Jordan's grandparents before, and there had been short visits over the years, but I felt more at home around them now than ever before. They made me feel a part of the family.

When we drove back to Graymoor, Jordan was smiling. I reached across the seat, grasped his hand and held it.

"You know, every time we visit we're going to be badgered about providing great-grandchildren," Jordan said.

"Yeah."

"And I would like to see my grandparents more than I have in the past."

"Are you thinking again about us having kids?"

"Maybe it's time for us to think about it more seriously. It won't be easy, and it's going to take time. I'm thinking about something else too. Maybe it is time I slowed down a little. I don't want to look back someday and realize I've rushed through my life without enjoying it."

"I wouldn't mind spending more leisure time with you."

"The problem is how to slow down."

"That is a tricky one," I said. "You definitely can't give up your music."

"No, I'll never give up music, but maybe it's time to cut back on the tours. We don't have to tour *every* year. There are also enough *Phantom* CDs out there for a while, and we don't want people getting sick of us after all."

"They haven't so far."

"True, but it wouldn't hurt to cut back some. I know Kieran could use more time with Natalie. They may also want to get started on a family."

"And what about Ross and Cedi?"

"Cedi will be fine; you know how he is. I'm sure Ross will find plenty to fill his time."

"Maybe we should just put Ross on a leash."

"No, he'd like that too much," Jordan said and laughed.

"You're really thinking about this, aren't you?" I asked.

"Yeah. Why don't we go to our room, get in the tub and discuss it?"

"If we get in the tub together, I don't think we'll be able to keep our minds on the topic."

"True, let's make love first, then get in the tub and discuss it."

"I like this plan. Drive faster!"

Over an hour later, we climbed into the tub. We had just finished making slow, unhurried love. Sometimes we went at it like wild boys, but we prolonged the pleasure this time, showing our love for each other with our bodies. Our physical needs satisfied, we could now turn our minds to other matters. I'm glad we opted to make love first, because there was no way I could have kept my mind off sex while sitting naked with Jordan in the tub. He was just too sexy!

"So do you think it's time for us to get serious about starting a family?" I asked Jordan as the flame from a candle flickered by the edge of the tub.

"I'm happy with my life, but then I see parents with their kids, and it makes me feel like I'm missing out on something. Part of me really wants to have a son. Sometimes I imagine what he might be like. I think about all the things I could teach him, all the things I could show him. I almost feel like I'm cheating him out of life by not having a kid. I know that's not rational, but the feeling is still there."

"You sound like you're getting very serious about the idea."

"Well, Grandmother was right about one thing at least; this would be a good time for us to start a family. I'm twenty-two, nearly twenty-three, and you just turned twenty-four. If we have a kid now, he will be ten when we're thirty-two and thirty-four. When he's eighteen, we'll be forty and forty-two. That's not too old, but if we wait too many years, we could be in our fifties by the time he graduates from high school. If we are going to have a kid, we should do it soon."

"Unless we adopt."

"True, we could wait for ten years and then adopt a ten-year-old. I'm sure I could love an adopted child as much as I could a biological child, but let's face it, we are a gay couple, and with all the prejudice out there, adopting could be an uphill battle. It's a battle I'm not afraid to fight, but there is no guarantee of success, and to be perfectly honest, I would rather father my own child."

"I know we've discussed this before," I said, "but I've got to admit I'm a little scared of becoming a parent."

"Oh, I am too, especially since babies don't come with manuals. There will be problems we don't know how to handle..."

"And diapers," I added.

"And sleepless nights," Jordan said.

"And countless hours worrying when he's sick."

"And, well, a lot of things," Jordan said, "but we've never let difficulties stop us before."

Jordan paused and looked at me.

"What do you think, Ralph? If we have a kid, it will mean big changes. Do you want to change our life like that or would you rather we just keep things as they are?"

"I'm happy with the way things are, but I feel like you do. Sometimes, I yearn to have a son. It's a natural instinct, I guess. Sometimes I think about teaching him how to play catch or fish or swim. I don't want to miss out on all of that."

"Maybe we're closer to making a decision than we thought," Jordan said.

"It's not as if we haven't discussed this before."

"Several times," Jordan said. He grinned.

"There's something we haven't discussed. How would we do it? I mean, this isn't something we can do alone."

"No, we sure can't," Jordan said, "although I'm willing to try."

I playfully splashed him with water.

"Actually, we do have an option open to us."

"We do?" I asked.

"Yes. I didn't want to say anything unless we began to seriously consider having our own kid, but I know someone who might be willing to be the mother of our child."

"Jordan, there are probably millions of women who would be willing to have your child."

"I said *our* child, and I'm being serious."

"You've really discussed this with someone?"

"Yes, although it was more of a 'what if' discussion than anything else. Well, it was more than that..."

"Who?"

"You know Sam, in our road crew?"

"The old guy who helps with the lighting? Does he have a daughter or something?"

"Noooo, not that Sam. The other Sam: Samantha. She helps Chad with sound."

"Oh! That Sam! The two of you have discussed this? How did that come up?"

"Well, as you know, Samantha is gay, and we got to talking about having kids someday. We talked about some of the difficulties involved. To make a long story short, we ended up discussing the possibility that perhaps we could be the answer to each other's problem. It was mainly theoretical, you understand, because you and I had only been thinking about having a kid, and Samantha was only beginning to entertain the idea herself. I was thinking, though, that since we're getting serious about this, maybe we should discuss it with her and see what she thinks. She may reject the idea completely now that it's becoming a real possibility, but it's somewhere to start at least."

"Whew, this is getting serious," I said.

"Scared?"

"Yes, but excited. It's just that it seems so sudden. I know it's not. I know we've been thinking about it off and on for months. Now that we're talking about actually doing it... I guess it's just hard to get used the idea. I mean, us as parents? I've never really thought of myself as a dad. We could really do this, couldn't we?"

"Yes, but Samantha may not be willing. We may be facing a long, hard search."

"We'd best get started then," I said.

"Really? You want to do this? You want to start a family?"

"Yes, Jordan, I do. I think we would make great parents. We have a lot to offer. My mom will be so excited too! She never thought she would have a grandkid!"

"Well, let's not get ahead of ourselves. We definitely don't want to tell your parents or my grandparents until way down the road. Too much could go wrong."

"Yeah, I know. I'm just excited."

"I'll tell you what: let's both sleep on this and mull it over and then see how we feel about it. If we haven't changed our minds by tomorrow, we can take the next step."

"That sounds like a good plan," I said.

We lingered in the tub a while longer, smiling at each other. The thought of actually becoming a dad was overwhelming. I didn't feel ready, but if I waited until I felt ready, I knew I'd never have a kid. Maybe we would decide it wasn't such a good idea after all. Maybe it was something we wouldn't be able to accomplish, but just thinking about it filled my head with possibilities and questions.

***

The bright light of day did not change our thoughts on bringing a child into the world. We had an entire day of work before us, but after filming was finished for the day, Jordan invited Sam to join us for supper, saying only he had something important to discuss with her. Sean was kind enough to arrange for a table to be set in a small parlor so we could dine without being disturbed. Martha prepared roast Cornish hens with side dishes that were so delicious I nearly forgot what we were about to propose to Samantha.

"So," Sam said, when we'd finished supper, "what's your ulterior motive?"

Jordan grinned.

"You know me too well. Ralph and I want to discuss the possibility of something with you. You see, we're thinking of starting a family, and...well, we can't do that alone."

"I wondered when you two would get serious about having a child," she said.

"You're not surprised at all?"

"Jordan, if you could have seen the look in your eyes when we talked about children, you would have known, as surely as I did, that it was only a matter of time. Besides, I've seen you around kids. You love kids."

Jordan grinned.

"Ralph and I have decided we want to start a family."

"I take it you'd like me to be involved? I've heard of being hit on by the boss, but..." Sam laughed.

"Don't worry, there will be no repercussions if you turn us down. We're just beginning to explore our options, and since I've talked with you about this, I thought sounding you out was the best place to start. I'm sorry to just spring this on you, but I didn't really know a way to ease into the discussion."

"As I said, I knew it was only a matter of time. This is not a surprise."

"So...what do you think? Is the idea of being the mother of our child something you're willing to discuss, or is it out of the question?"

"I can't make any promises. This is a big decision after all, but I'm willing to discuss it. The devil is in the details. For instance, if we do have a child together, will I be allowed to be a part of her life, or will I be expected to disappear? I couldn't bear the thought of not being involved with my own child."

"We would never ask such a thing of you," I said. "This child wouldn't be just Jordan's and mine, but yours too. We would want you to be a part of his or her life. A child should have a mother."

"That's right," Jordan said. "Ralph and I have been discussing slowing down a bit. If we're going to have a child, we need to provide a real home for it, not a life spent in hotel rooms and a tour bus. I'm not going to give up music or touring, but I don't want our child growing up on the road. I know what it's like to grow up without roots. I want my child to have better than that."

"So, how would we work out my role in this?"

"Just tell us what you want," Jordan said. "Ralph and I have discussed this. We know having a child will cause a major life change. If the three of us have a child together, it's like getting married. The three of us will be permanently connected. How big a part you play is largely up to you. Obviously, Ralph and I want the child to live with us. We want to raise him, but that doesn't mean you can't raise him as well. We're asking no less than for you to become a part of our family. As family, you'll be welcome to spend as much—or as little time—with us as you desire. Wherever we are, there will always be a place for you, and you'll always be a part of our child's life, whether you're living with us or somewhere else."

Samantha smiled.

"Well, *if* we do this, I would want to see our child often," Samantha said. "I'll want her to know who her mother is and that I love her. I'll want to spend time with her. You'll be raising her, because I'm not ready to raise a child yet. I'm not quite ready to settle down, and I'd like to go to school. I can't do all that if I'm raising a child. If I was on my own, I wouldn't think of having a child at this point, but since the two of you will be raising her, it's a different situation entirely."

"I know you have your own life to live, and someday you'll find someone special to share it with," Jordan said. "We won't ask you to have any responsibility for the child. The level of your involvement will be entirely up to you. You can visit as often as you like, stay with us for as long as you like, and of course spend time with our child. I'll say it again, by *our* I mean the three of us, not just Ralph and me."

"I think the two of you will make great parents," Sam said. "Believe me, I wouldn't be discussing this with you if I didn't."

"We appreciate that you are talking about this with us," I said. "Jordan and I do want to have a kid, and as we said in the beginning, it's something we can't do alone."

"If your answer is yes," Jordan said, "we will fully take care of all the expenses involved—doctor appointments, medicines, hospital expenses, maternity clothes, and whatever you might need. I'll make sure your boss also gives you a six-month, paid maternity leave." Jordan grinned.

"That's good. I do get paid well, but I'm saving for college."

"That's something else Ralph and I thought about. I hesitate to mention this, because I don't want it to sound like a bribe, but if you do decide to become the mother for our child, Ralph and I would like to pay for your college education. We realize we're asking a huge favor of you, although favor doesn't seem quite the right word for it. This will involve a considerable amount of time and discomfort for you. I can't even begin to imagine labor pains, and I don't think I want to. Ralph and I feel that we should do something for you in return. We knew you had college plans. We know how expensive that can be, so we would like to send you to school, wherever you can get accepted. We'll pay for everything—tuition, books, housing, meals, miscellaneous expenses, everything."

"That's very generous of you," Sam said.

"Well, if you decide you're willing to do this for us, it's the least we can do. We're asking for you to devote part of your life to doing something for us. We're asking you to change your life. I will tell you that we were planning to give you a big bonus to help with school expenses when you someday left *Phantom*, so if you decide not to have a baby with us, we'll still help you out. I don't want to make it seem like we're trying to buy a baby from you."

"I know you would never do something like that, Jordan. Besides, if we do this, it will be our baby. You and Ralph will raise her, but I'll be a part of her life too."

"Yes, that's the way it should be. We don't want to find a mother who will just hand over her baby and disappear. We want our son to know his mother and be close to her whether she lives close by or far away."

"I notice you always say *he*," Sam said.

"Hey, I can't help but want a son. I'll love a daughter just as much."

"Me too," I added.

"I notice you refer to the baby as *she*," Jordan teased.

"Well, what mother doesn't want a daughter? I would love a son just as much though. I'll admit I'll be hoping for a girl, but I'll love any child of mine, no matter what."

Jordan actually got tears in his eyes and hugged Sam, who was also looking a little teary.

"I almost hate to bring this up at this time," I said, "but there are medical-history and legal implications involved. We would need to have papers drawn up specifying custody rights, financial responsibilities, et cetera."

"Yes, but that we can worry about later," Sam said. "First, comes the decision. I don't want to get your hopes up, because I have a lot of thinking to do. This is such a big decision. There is something I'm wondering about..."

"What's that?" asked Jordan.

"Well, in the future, if I meet someone special and would like to have a child with her, would the two of you be willing to be the father? I guess it would only take one of you, but what I'm asking is would you be willing to be on the other end of such an arrangement?"

Jordan and I looked at each other.

"I need to give this some thought before providing a certain answer," I said. "If I fathered your child, I would want to be involved with his or her life, but yeah, I think I would be willing."

"Me too," Jordan said. "I think you'll make a wonderful mother. That's one reason we're approaching you. You're the kind of mother we want for our child."

"Oh my, there is so much to think about," Sam said.

"Take all the time you need," Jordan said. "This isn't something any of us should rush into. Ralph and I have discussed having a child several times. We have decided it's what we want to do, but that's us, not you. We won't press you on this, and if your answer is *no*, we'll understand."

"Okay," Sam said. "Let me think this over, and I'll let you know what I decide. I may need to come back to you with more questions, but mainly I just need to think."

"As Jordan said, take all the time you need," I said.

Jordan and I sat alone in the small parlor after Samantha left.

"I'm still nervous," Jordan said. "I was almost shaking when I asked Sam to be the mother of our child."

"You appeared calm and confident."

"I felt anything but calm. If Sam and I hadn't discussed this before, I would never have had the nerve. Do you think she'll agree?"

"I think she's leaning toward it, but it's a huge decision, so who knows?"

"I guess we'll just wait for her answer and then decide on our next move."

"That's all we can do, Babe."

"I hope she says yes. I really want to have a baby with you Ralph."

I stood and took Jordan's hands in mine. "You're going to make a great father," I said.

"So are you," Jordan said and hugged me tight.

Sean

There was a knock at my office door.

"Come," I said.

"Hi Sean."

"Ethan," I said, surprised by his presence. "How are you? Please have a seat. What brings you to Graymoor?"

"To be honest, I've come to stick my nose in where it doesn't belong."

"So this involves Nick," I said, none too pleased.

"Yes."

"Did he ask you to come?"

"No. In fact, he would likely be angry if he knew I was here, but it's difficult for a father to stand by while his son is in pain."

"I'm not sure how wise it is for us to discuss Nick. To be honest, I'm pretty angry with him right now. Infuriated would come closer to the truth."

"I'm not here to discuss the situation between you and Nick. That's not my business. He did tell me what happened, and he is miserable about it. I can certainly understand your anger too. I am here to ask you to talk to him."

"I don't know if I want to do that. He hurt me very badly and now.... I just don't know about him."

"It's usually best to talk things out. If you aren't ready to do so now, maybe you can a little down the road. I hope it will be soon, though, because I've never seen Nick this upset before."

"Has anyone ever cheated on you? Someone you loved and who you thought loved you?"

"No. There has never been anyone in my life except Nathan. I had some crushes on guys in high school when I admitted to myself I was gay, but I never dated anyone other than Nathan. I did almost slip once."

"You did?" I was shocked. I couldn't imagine Ethan even thinking about cheating on Nathan.

"It was a long time ago, not that that makes any difference. It was shortly after Nathan and I got together. The most gorgeous boy came to live on the farm with us, and I was tempted."

"You mean Coach Brewer?"

"Yes, although he was still in high school then. We came very close to kissing each other—to cheating on the ones we loved—but at the last second, something stopped us."

"What?"

"I realized that as attracted as I was to Brendan, I loved Nathan. I knew that if he ever found out I'd cheated on him, it would break his heart. Later, I realized that my conscience would have tormented me forever even if he never found out. Almost cheating on him made me feel guilty enough that I told him what happened. He forgave me and even told me that the fact I was tempted and didn't cheat on him proved to him how much I loved him."

Tears began to flow from my eyes. "Why couldn't Nick have thought of me like that before he kissed Ross?"

"I can't understand Nick without being Nick. I only know that I came very, very close to cheating on Nathan with Brendan. My lust very nearly overpowered my good sense. Things could have easily ended up differently."

"I guess Nick doesn't love me like you love Nathan."

"I wouldn't say that, Sean. Ross is, well—a very attractive young man. His beauty is enough to turn anyone's head. There is also his fame. I'm not trying to defend what Nick did. He was clearly in the wrong. I know he loves you. I think his hormones staged a coup and overpowered his good sense. I think he's so star struck with Ross he can't think straight around him. Again, I'm not saying he didn't do wrong, but I know he would never intentionally hurt you. Yes, he's guilty of cheating on you and of being very, very stupid, but he would not hurt you on purpose."

Yeah, Nick was star struck with Ross. I remembered the three-way with Ross and how badly Nick had wanted it. He still cheated on me though; nothing could alter that.

"Sean, whether or not you forgive Nick, whether or not you continue to date him, Nathan and I want you to know we love you and that you're welcome in our home any time."

"Thanks, Ethan."

"Well, I've taken enough of your time, and I've been enough of an interfering busybody for today. Thanks for listening."

"You aren't a busybody. You're just trying to help someone you love."

"I'm trying to help *two* someones I love," Ethan said. He smiled at me and departed.

I sat at my desk after Ethan had departed, feeling the pain Nick had inflicted upon me. We'd gone through so much together. How could he forget, even for a moment? We had something that many searched for their entire lives— without finding it. How could he cheapen that by making out with another guy? I'd been hurt many times in the past. I'd been called every name in the book. I'd been tormented and taunted. Hell, Kyle and his crew had even tried to kill me. None of that hurt nearly as much as what Nick had done to me. I guess it takes a loved one to really, truly cause pain.

A disembodied laugh caused me to jump. It wasn't the mischievous giggle of Etienne, but the cold cruel laugh of...

"Devon," I said.

A cold wind whipped through the room. The laugh repeated. Was Devon somehow at the bottom of all this, or was he just taking delight in my pain? I guess it didn't matter. Nick had still betrayed me. My heart was still broken.

***

141

Nick fearfully approached me the next day as I was speaking with Jordan, Cedi and Kieran in the Solarium. Ross was also present, but I addressed him only as a part of *Phantom*. The guys were shooting some scenes for their video near the small waterfall and were setting things up for a night shoot as well. We were discussing the difficulty of making room for a small crane to get some overhead shots. That's when Nick appeared.

"Um, Sean, can we talk?" Nick asked when my conversation with *Phantom* had wound down.

"I don't have anything to say to you," I said, shooting Ross a glare. Ross at least had the decency to look contrite.

"Please Sean, just talk to me!"

"Okay," I said, "but I seriously doubt you have anything to say that I want to hear."

I led Nick into a small sitting room not far from the Solarium.

"So talk," I said.

"I know you're mad at me. I know I hurt you. I can't tell you how sorry I am, Sean, because there are no words to describe it. I never meant to hurt you. I never meant to kiss Ross at all. It just...happened."

"And did you just happen to fuck him too?"

"No, Sean! I told you nothing else happened between us. I swear!"

"How can I believe you Nick? How can I believe you now or ever again? You violated my trust. The one person in all the world whom I trusted the most has proven untrustworthy. How do I forgive that? How do I forget that? Damn it Nick, we had something special, and you had to go and fuck it up! You can't describe how sorry you are? Well, I can't describe how angry I am! God damn it, Nick, do you have any idea how seeing you with Ross made me feel? Do you? Why didn't you just rip my heart out and stomp on it?"

Tears flowed down Nick's cheeks, and a little part of me wanted to comfort him. Another part of me wanted to hurt him as he'd hurt me. Most of me just wanted him to go away so I could try to put him behind me.

"Please take me back Sean. I promise nothing like that will *ever* happen again! I love you! I don't want to lose you!"

"If you were happy with me, you would never have kissed Ross. Yeah, I know he's a rock star, and I know you're obsessed with *Phantom*, but you still wouldn't have made out with him if you were happy with me. You know what your dad told me? He told me that he was tempted once. He came so close to cheating on Nathan, but he didn't, because he stopped and thought about how much it would hurt the one he loved. Why didn't you stop yourself, Nick?"

"I...I...I didn't think. I..."

"Yeah, you didn't think of me. You only thought of your idol. You wanted him, Nick, and now you can have him. Go ahead; leave with Ross when he goes. It's obviously what you want."

"No! That's not what I want! I want to stay here with you! I want you, not Ross!"

"Well, it's a little late to make that choice, isn't it?"

"Please Sean."

"Listen, maybe you're telling me the truth when you say nothing more went on than what I saw with my own eyes. Maybe you really didn't mean for it to happen. Maybe you never cheated on me in college. You did cheat on me with Ross though, even after I agreed to that three-way with him a few years ago. I thought that would quench your lust for him, but I guess I was wrong. Maybe you even still love me. I don't know. I do know that neither of us has ever dated anyone else. We're both twenty-three years old, and we've never dated another guy. I think we need to, especially you. If I took you back, what happened with Ross would just happen again—if not with him then with some other guy you just couldn't resist."

"No, Sean. That will never happen again! I swear!"

"I'd like to believe you, but I don't. I don't want to be your boyfriend anymore, Nick."

Nick looked as if I'd struck him. He began to sob. Tears flowed from my own eyes. I felt as if I'd just ripped my own heart out.

"Please Sean."

"Goodbye Nick."

I walked past him and left the room without looking back. I passed Jordan and Kieran in the hallway, but I didn't speak or even slow down. I could still hear Nick's sobs as I walked quickly down the hall. I took no joy in hurting him, but I couldn't date him, not anymore.

I walked upstairs to my room and cried. Breaking up with Nick was the hardest thing I ever had to do. I didn't do it to punish him. I didn't do it because I wanted to. I did it because I didn't think things would ever be right between us again if I took him back. I would always wonder if I was enough for him. I'd always wonder if he yearned for experiences with other men. By breaking up with Nick, I gave him the opportunity to have those experiences without cheating on me.

Did I also want the freedom to date other guys? I honestly didn't know. Nick was all I'd ever wanted. I could have practically walked on air when we started dating. Then, as the years passed, my happiness with Nick had only increased. Yes, I had been attracted to other guys. There were times in college when I spotted a young hunk I wanted so badly I could hardly stand it, but I knew Nick was the one for me. Whenever I had lusted after another guy, it was just that—lust. Nick was the one I loved.

Nick needed to experience a relationship with someone else before he could ever be the boyfriend I needed him to be. It would have been easier on us both if I had taken him back, but something told me the easy path was not the right one this time. Nick's infidelity was a sign. It was a wake-up call that we weren't the perfect couple I thought we were. Okay... I never thought we were perfect, but close enough.

***

I was just coming down the stairs when the front door opened. I looked up and was surprised to see Brendan and Casper enter.

"Hi Sean."

"Hey, what brings you guys to the haunted house?"

"We came to visit an acquaintance of mine. He's with *Phantom's* road crew. Perhaps you can help us find him. Chad?"

"Oh yeah, Chad. I'll almost forgotten you know him. *Phantom* is filming in the Solarium tonight. He's sure to be there."

"That would explain all the lights. We could see them from the street," Casper said.

"Follow me," I said. "Few people can find their way alone."

"I'll bet," Brendan said. "So how are you doing, Sean?"

"Not so well," I said as we walked out of the parlor and down a long hallway. "Nick and I broke up."

"I'm sorry to hear that."

"I'm sorry to say it, but it had to be."

"I wish I had some sage advice for you, but I don't. There has never been another guy in my life besides Casper."

"You are both very lucky."

"True," Casper said, "but I'm sure you don't want to hear about us right now. There is nothing more obnoxious than a happy couple when your own relationship has just ended."

"I'm happy for you," I said. "I just hope I can find such a relationship for myself." I nearly said 'again,' but stopped myself.

"Here we are," I said after a while.

Bright lights illuminated the area near the waterfall where *Phantom* was performing. Loud music filled the usually quiet Solarium.

Someone yelled "cut," and the music abruptly halted.

"That fern was obscuring Cedi's face. We need to reset."

"Won't that improve the video?" Ross asked.

"Blow me, Ross!" yelled Cedi, laughing.

"I told you *after* we're done shooting."

I would have found the exchange amusing had I not been so pissed off at Ross.

"There he is," Brendan said, pointing.

Brendan broke away from us and walked toward Chad, who was fiddling with an immense soundboard.

"Dude!"

"Hello, Chad."

They hugged. I looked at Casper. He was smiling.

I was well-acquainted with the story of Brendan and Chad's escape from the despicable Cloverdale Center. Even though I knew it was true, it was hard to believe that places like the Cloverdale Center exist. I stood with Casper, and we watched Brendan and Chad chat with each other until Chad turned his eyes upon us. Casper joined Brendan and Chad then. I remained only a few moments longer before I turned and left the Solarium.

I walked back to the parlor where I found Marshall seated on a couch talking to himself.

"You've finally cracked. Huh, Marshall?"

"Not at all. I was just having a chat with Etienne."

"He's here?"

"He's sitting right there," Marshall said, pointing to a spot on the couch.

I peered closely, but could see nothing, not that I expected to see anything. Marshall was the one who saw dead people, not me. Well, I had seen my share of ghosts, but this was different.

"I think you were talking to yourself, and you're just trying to cover up," I teased.

146

"You shouldn't have said that. Now Etienne is walking around behind you."

I felt someone pinch my butt. I whipped around, but only heard a boyish giggle sweep past me.

"Okay, I believe you! Hmm, this isn't the first time I've had my butt pinched by someone I couldn't see. Could Etienne perhaps be what we used to refer to as the "Butt Grabber Ghost?"

Marshall looked to the side and then back at me.

"Guilty as charged."

"I don't know if I'm ever going to get used to your ability to speak with the dead," I said.

"Etienne prefers to refer to himself as 'breathing challenged.'"

"I'm sorry, I didn't know there were politically correct terms for spirits."

"There's a lot you don't know, Sean."

"No doubt."

"Any sign of our mutual enemy?" I asked. I'd told Marshall about my short, but unpleasant encounter with Devon.

"Not a whisper. I can say with certainty that he's not hanging around. Perhaps he's adapted a hit-and-run approach. Of course, my range is limited, and this is a huge house."

An uncomfortable thought occurred to me.

"You're sure about Etienne, right? About who he is, I mean? You don't think it could be..."

"No. You can relax. If Devon tries his old trick of masquerading as someone else, I'll be able to see right through him."

"That's going to piss him off. It's the only trick he knows."

"I wish. In any case, I haven't seen any sign of him while I've been here. You're the only one he's plagued lately."

147

"If you ever find a way to exorcize him for good, be sure to let me know."

"Will do," Marshall said.

"I'm going to take a walk. I have some thinking to do. See you later, Marshall—and Etienne."

"Later, Sean."

"Later," said a boyish voice, followed by a giggle. I paused only a moment before I continued.

Skye

Just before eight, I walked over to Kane's place to see his '57 Chevy convertible. Okay, I was more interested in Kane than his car, but the '57 Chevy was *THE* car in my book.

Kane greeted me at the door, wearing sleek, black soccer shorts and a Hollister t-shirt torn in all the right places. I'd worn ripped jeans and a tight Abercrombie & Fitch polo shirt that showed off my torso. Kane couldn't tear his eyes off my chest for a few moments.

"She's in the garage," he said leading me away from the house to a detached garage a few feet away. We entered through a side door, and Kane flipped on the light.

"Nice," I said.

"Thanks. What you see is the result of hundreds of hours of work."

"She's beautiful. You said you aren't finished with her? What remains to be done? She's perfect."

I meant it. The red and white convertible gleamed under the fluorescent lights. It looked showroom new. The top was down, and the white-leather interior was immaculate.

"For one thing, the taillights don't work, and neither do the windshield wipers. There are a lot of little things that need adjusting—the type of thing most people will never notice, but I want this car to be perfect."

"She looks perfect now," I said. "I think I'm getting a hard-on."

Kane laughed and swallowed. There was a sense of anticipation in the air that had nothing to do with the Chevy.

"I always wondered what it was like in the '50s," Kane said. "Driving to some secluded spot in a car like this and making out in the back seat. I guess it's a little fantasy of mine."

I stepped closer to Kane. "And I bet you dreamed about being in that back seat with the quarterback instead of a cheerleader, didn't you, Kane?" I said just above a whisper.

Kane's eyes nervously darted about, and he began to breathe harder.

"I was the quarterback in high school," I whispered and then pressed my lips to Kane's.

Kane responded, kissing me back with desire. He flipped off the overhead lights, leaving the Chevy lit only by the moonlight coming in through the window. Kane opened the door of the convertible, and we climbed into the back seat, pawing at each other all the while. I bit at Kane's neck and pulled his shirt over his head. Our clothes came off as we made out until we were both completely naked. Kane dove for my crotch, and I moaned.

Kane and I went at it for a good hour in the back seat of his '57 Chevy. Sex in the back seat of a car, even a big vintage automobile, isn't the most comfortable experience, but Kane and I were so focused on each other's body we hardly noticed the confined space and the occasional knob in the back (no pun intended). A convertible is the best of all cars for sex, because there's no end of head room (um, no pun intended again). I spent a fair amount of time sitting on the top of the seat with Kane kneeling in front of me.

When we were both spent, Kane and I lay panting and sweaty in the back seat. I was feeling energized but mellow, as I always did after good sex. There was nothing like sex to release tension, and Kane had proven himself to be quite talented. I was eager to go even further with him the next time. I had stimulating thoughts of Kane spread out on the hood of his Chevy.

I strolled toward home with a smile on my face. Maybe things weren't going to be so slow in my old hometown after all. I'd forgotten there were hot guys everywhere.

As I walked under the moonlight, I got a premonition to take a detour through the park. My instincts never led me wrong, so I altered course. I remembered the days when Taylor had appeared again and again, sending me off to

150

battle gay bashers. I no longer needed such direction. I'd developed a sixth sense for sniffing out trouble. I missed those days with Taylor though. I think I would have traded in my instinct for more time with him.

The air was beginning to cool but still carried a hint of the humidity of the day. I could hear frogs croaking and insects chirping out their various songs despite the fact that I was in the middle of Verona.

"Hey, faggot!"

I turned. Five high-school-age guys were crossing the darkened park, strutting toward me. I'd expected to find some boy in trouble, but I guessed the high-school boys would do for this evening's adventure. It had been a long time since anyone had called me a faggot to my face. One of the boys swayed a little. Alcohol was likely the source of his courage—or rather stupidity. I stood and waited for the gang to swagger to me. They were high-school boys all right. Two of them wore V.H.S. letter jackets.

"You're the faggot who used to be quarterback of the football team, right?" asked the largest of the five. He showed no sign of intoxication.

"My name is Skye. Call me a faggot again and you'll be picking your teeth out of the grass."

"Ohh, the old guy still thinks he's tough!"

Old guy? I was twenty-three, not eighty-three.

"I'm tough enough to kick your ass."

"Well, even if that's true, which I doubt, there's five of us and one of you."

"And your point would be..."

"Don't get smart queer," said the punk who had done all the talking so far.

I grabbed him, swiftly whipped him around and twisted his arm behind his back before he even knew I was coming for him.

"I don't like being called queer either," I whispered loudly into his ear so all his buddies could hear. I twisted his

151

arm just enough to make him cry out in pain. "If you want to refer to my sexual orientation, the term is gay, not fag, not faggot, or queer, or homo, or cocksucker, or any of the other names dipshits like you like to use. Got it?"

"Yes!"

"Now that we've got that settled, what's your name?"

"Bart."

I released Bart's arm and shoved him away. His buddies had not dared to make a move toward me while I was holding their leader captive. Perhaps they thought I'd break his arm. They were braver once I'd released him. Bart's own bluster made a quick comeback too.

"You really think you're hot shit, don't you gay boy?" Bart asked.

"Let's just say I'm good at handling losers like you."

"You definitely need to be taken down a notch."

"I can wait here if you like."

"For what?" Bart asked, confused.

"You said you were going to take me down. I thought you were going to get some more of your buddies. I'll be honest with you: five just isn't going to be enough."

"I'm gonna beat that cockiness out of you."

"You can try," I said with a sigh, "but I can guarantee I'll enjoy this far more than you. It's been a while since I've had the opportunity to kick anyone's ass."

"You are un-fucking-believable."

"I do think it's only fair to warn you that if you guys jump me, some of you may need to visit the hospital when we're finished. Since this is your first attempt at kicking my ass, I'll try to take it easy on you, but sometimes I find it hard to control myself once I get going."

"This is gonna be a pleasure," Bart said, punching his fist into his palm.

I could tell I'd been away from Verona too long. A whole new layer of scum had risen in my absence.

"The pleasure will be all mine," I said.

"Get him!" Bart yelled, and all five boys hurtled themselves toward me.

My most eager assailant, a blond boy who didn't look half bad, received a sharp jab in the abs for his efforts and dropped to the ground clutching his stomach. The next to come into range aimed a hard punch at my jaw, but I jerked to the side and landed a quick uppercut to his abdomen too. The next two came in together. I nailed one with a right cross. The other took at swing at me, missed and shot past me. I lashed out with my right heel and caught him in the back of the knee, sending him tumbling to the ground. Bart was the last to launch himself at me. Perhaps he wasn't quite as brave as he let on, or perhaps he was observing my defense, looking for a weakness. He charged me like a bull, wrapped his arms around my torso and knocked me to the ground. I'll say one thing for Bart. He was the first of the five to land a punch, a powerful jab to the face that I didn't particularly enjoy.

It became hard to keep track of my assailants after that. One of them nailed me in the lats, causing me to hiss in pain. Before I'd recovered, Bart slugged me in the jaw hard enough to rattle my teeth. I grabbed the blond boy and one of his buddies and rammed their heads together, sending them both to the ground dazed, if not unconscious. I went after the one who had punched me in the lats next, returning the favor and adding a few quick punches to the gut just for the hell of it. He was a tough bastard and came right back at me. Unfortunately for him, one of his buddies launched himself at me from the opposite direction. I tossed myself on the ground and let them collide. They butted heads even harder than the two boys I'd knocked together. Bart used the opportunity to stomp on the middle of my back with his heel, a move that royally pissed me off. I twisted to the side, hooked his ankle with my leg and pulled him down. Even as he fell, I rolled onto my back and flipped up into a standing position. Bart pulled himself to his feet, and I let him have it, pummeling his face, chest and abs with a flurry of blows that sent him staggering backwards.

I would have thought he would have learned his lesson by then. His buddies were strewn about on the grass, two of them more or less unconscious, and Bart himself was having trouble standing. He *still* hadn't had enough. Bart growled in anger and charged me, attempting to knock me to the ground once more. I sidestepped him and delivered a quick jab to his abs. He twisted around and snarled at me.

"I'm going to kick your ass, faggot!"

I slugged him in the mouth before he knew what had happened. That was the end of the fight. Bart spit blood and teeth from his mouth as he moaned in pain. I stepped back, careful not to trip on any of the high-school boys writhing on the ground.

"I told you you'd be picking your teeth off the grass if you called me faggot again. I always keep my word. Bart, it's been a pleasure. Boys, thank you for an interesting night. We'll have to do this again sometime. Bring your friends."

I stepped over the bodies and went on my way, enjoying the warmth of the summer night and the beautiful stars above. I felt exhilarated and alive, thanks to Kane and my new high-school buddies. There was nothing like a good fight to get the heart pumping. My only regret is that the struggle didn't last a little longer. I'd have to remember next time not to be so rough on my attackers. It was just so hard not to get caught up in the thrill of a fight.

A few minutes later, I was standing before Graymoor, gazing up at the lights in the windows. The place was more alive than it ever had been in my lifetime. I never thought I'd end up living in the big old mansion. Life was odd. It took weird twists and turns, and one never knew where one would end up. I certainly never thought I'd end up back in Verona. I'd set my sights on a big city with lots of hot young men to occupy my nights. I couldn't say that I was sorry things hadn't worked out as I'd planned. It felt good to be back.

I walked inside and found Ross sprawled out on one of the couches in the main parlor.

"You look exhausted," I said.

"It's been a long day. You look like crap."

"Huh? Oh, I got into a little fight. It was nothing—just five high-school boys who thought they were tough."

"Five? You call that a little fight?"

I grinned.

"You should put something on that eye before it swells any more."

"Nah, it will be fine in a few minutes. I heal quickly."

"Skye, that eye will be swelled shut by tomorrow morning."

"I don't think so, Ross. So, would you perhaps be loitering around down here waiting for me?"

"Uh-huh," Ross said, grinning.

"Oh? And just want do you want from me, Ross?"

"I think you know."

I grinned.

"Come on, let's go to my room."

"Are you sure you're up to it?" Ross asked.

"Oh, I'm always up to it, as you'll soon find out."

I pulled Ross off the couch, kissed him deeply and then pulled him toward the stairway. Soon, we were in my room, ripping each other's clothes off. Yeah, I know what you're thinking: two guys in one night is too much sex, but that's where you're wrong. There's no such thing as too much sex.

***

I awoke the next morning alone in my bed. Ross had disappeared once again before I'd awakened, rushing off to join the other band members as they continued to film their latest video. I was going to miss Ross when he was gone. He was one beautiful boy and was quite unrestrained in bed—at least when I didn't have him tied up. Ross had no inhibitions. He was ready to try anything, and talk about

155

energetic! He was like the Energizer Bunny; he just kept going and going.

I was glad to learn Ross practiced safe sex. His wildness didn't extend into foolishness. I'd been amazed at how many college boys threw caution to the wind. I'd turned down a fair number of extremely hot boys who wanted to go bareback. Perhaps it did feel better without a condom, but was a little extra pleasure worth a possible death sentence? Even if the HIV virus didn't exist, there were plenty of other sexually transmitted diseases I wanted to avoid. I was a wild man in bed, but I didn't take foolish risks. I'd even had myself vaccinated for hepatitis.

The only thing I'd contracted in my college years was a bad case of crabs. It's not a pretty topic and believe me, it's something to avoid. The crabs gave me the worst case of jock itch ever. I never thought I'd get rid of those little bastards. I ended up have to shave off my pubes, which I was not happy about at all. None of the remedies for crabs seemed to work until I smeared a thick coating of mayonnaise all over my crotch and left it on all night while I slept on my back. I guess it smothered the little fuckers or something, because after I showered the next morning they were gone. I never could figure out who'd given me crabs. I would have kicked his ass for sure if I'd found out, but enough about that.

After breakfast, I arrived at the Natatorium to find it filled with cameras, lights and cables. *Phantom* was filming a short scene there, so they were spending the entire day by the pool. I didn't get much work done, but then we didn't have any regular guests, so there wasn't as much to do. It was fascinating to watch the shoot, although there was a lot of down time while the crew set up for a shot. If it took that much work to film a short scene for a video, I wondered how producers ever finished a feature-length film.

I had a chance to hang out with Jordan, Kieran, Cedi, and Ross between takes. Ross and I kept grinning at each other—sometimes leering at each other. I'm sure Jordan knew we'd been sleeping with each other, but neither of us cared. Ross and I slipped off to the weight room for a little tongue action a few times. One thing we had in common is that neither of us could ever get enough.

I also saw some looks pass between Ross and Cedi. Those two definitely had something going. No doubt about it. Cedi was at the very least bi. I thought about seducing him, but I just didn't know if I could fit him into my busy schedule. Ross was keeping me busy nearly every night. Who would've thought I'd have too many boys in Verona?

Ross was hyper, running all over the Natatorium while he waited for the crew to set up for the next shot. I half expected him to start swinging from vines like Tarzan. I momentarily pictured Ross in a loincloth, and my shorts grew tighter. Cedi was just as hyper, if not more so. That boy could not sit still for a second. He and Ross were quite a pair. I found myself wondering how they went at it when they had sex. Now, that would have been interesting to watch, not that I usually got off on watching other guys. I much preferred to be a part of the action.

Ralph, Jordan's partner, was around much of the day. He was a nice guy, although just ordinary looking. Part of me wondered what Jordan saw in him. After all, Jordan was sizzling hot and could surely have any guy he wanted. Jordan and Ralph had been together for years, so I guess they were happy. I never could understand relationship-oriented guys. How could they stand to stick with just one guy for year after year? I'd go insane!

Sean popped in for a while, but didn't stay long. He was royally pissed off at Ross, and who could blame him? I'm not sure what Sean would've thought if he knew Ross and I were getting it on. He'd probably consider it my business. I didn't like what Ross and Nick had done, but I knew for a fact that Ross was remorseful.

Sean had a pained expression on his face, even though he tried to act cheerful. I never thought that day would come when Sean and Nick would no longer be a couple. Personally, I thought both Sean and Nick needed a few experiences with other guys, although I was sorry to see them break up. Sean walked around looking as if he'd lost his best friend. Nick wasn't around at all. I felt sorry for Sean. I couldn't imagine the pain he was experiencing. That was another reason not to get too involved with someone: get too close and you'll get hurt. I never let myself get too close to any of the guys I was with. I had a regular thing going with more than one in college, but it was never a boyfriend thing. We were just friends with benefits. That's as far as Skye went. I wasn't about to be tied down by anyone, except in the bedroom.

Sean looked so miserable at supper that evening that I followed him out into the hall when he left the table.

"How are you doing, Sean?"

"I've been better."

"I gathered. Come on, you're coming with me."

"Where?"

"The Natatorium. We're going to work out a little and then go swimming."

"I don't know, Skye."

"Did I say you have a choice? You need to get your mind off Nick, and a little workout will make you feel good. You could use a good dose of endorphins."

"Yeah okay, I guess. That sounds better than moping in my room or filling out work orders."

I led Sean to the Natatorium, regaling him with the tale of the fight the night before.

"You don't look like you've been in a fight."

"I heal a lot faster now. Just about any black eye, cut, or bruise lasts less than eight hours."

"How is that possible?"

"I don't know, but that's the way it is. I don't question it. That's your problem Sean. You think too much."

"Sometimes I wish I could stop thinking."

"Well, this evening we're going to be physical," I said as we passed the pool and headed into the gymnasium. "Don't worry. I'll go easy on you, but it is time you started working out again."

"Yeah, I know...I've just been busy."

"No excuses. From now on, you'll work out at least three days a week, or else! We'll start with the bench press. You do remember how to do a bench press, right?"

"Yeah, smart ass. Now step aside."

I watched as Sean knocked out fifteen reps. He was still kind of pudgy, but he had better muscle tone than he had had in high school. Despite his pudginess, he was kind of hot. I didn't usually go for his type, but there was something sexy about Sean.

I stripped off my shirt when my turn came. I liked to work out as unrestricted by clothing as possible. No, I never worked out in the nude. There was unrestricted, and then there was dangerous.

I ran Sean through an easy workout, and then we changed into swimsuits and went for a dip in the pool. Sean began to cheer up during our workout, and he actually laughed as we goofed off in the water. The combination of the endorphins released by the workout and getting his mind off Nick was doing the trick. We must have remained in the pool for a good hour before we climbed out and dried off.

"Thanks, Skye," Sean said.

"Any time."

Sean was about to depart, but part of me didn't want him to go. I'd known Sean for years, but I was looking at him in a whole new way.

"Hey, Sean, you want to come to my room and just...talk for a while."

Sean paused, but then nodded.

"Yeah, sure."

We dried off, changed back into our regular clothing in the locker room, and then walked through the twisting hallways and up the stairs to my room. Sean crossed to the window and looked out at the view. At night, the lights in the Natatorium and Solarium gave both glassed-in structures an enchanted glow. Some of the plants inside were even visible through the sides and roof.

"Beautiful, isn't it?" I asked.

"Yeah."

"I never thought I'd someday be living in Graymoor Mansion. I never understood how you could stand living in this creepy old place when we were in high school."

"I barely could at first. I remember how hard it was to get you to come here. You were scared of the ghosts."

"Me? Scared of a ghost. I don't think so!"

"I hope the ghosts of Graymoor haven't been giving you any trouble since you moved in."

"Something does like to jerk the covers off the bed at night."

"Maybe it just wants to see you naked."

"Well, if that's what it wants, it has plenty of opportunities."

"I'm sure."

"I've had my butt pinched a few times, and I keep hearing giggling, but other than that the spirits have left me alone."

"Giggling, huh? Does it sound like a boy?"

"Yeah."

"That's probably Etienne. Marshall has told me a few things about him."

"We've met, sort of. I guess I should start calling him by name if he's going to play with my ass. Marshall said Etienne likes to watch me in the shower."

I expected Sean to laugh, but he stared out the window and sighed.

"I really miss him, you know?"

"Yeah," I said. "I know."

I intended to keep Sean from talking about Nick, but maybe that's what he needed just then. I walked up behind Sean and put my arms on his shoulders. He surprised me by turning, hugging me tightly, and sobbing onto my shoulder. I wasn't the best at offering comfort, so I just held him and let him cry. I could hear the pain in his sobs, and my heart went out to him.

After a while, his sobs quieted and he released me. He stood back a pace and wiped his eyes.

"I'm sorry."

"Don't be. I don't mind. I know breaking up with Nick has been hard on you."

"Maybe you've had the right idea all along Skye. Just love 'em and leave 'em."

"Well, that's the right thing for me, but I don't think it is for you. I think you're the type who needs a boyfriend."

"Well, it's sure not going to be Nick."

"Are you really so certain? I don't think you would be so broken up over him if you didn't love him."

"I'm certain, for now at least. Maybe later, but...I don't know. I don't even want to think about him right now."

I put my hands on Sean's shoulders and gripped them.

"Man, you're tense."

"Yeah, well, I have this sadistic personal trainer who works me too hard."

"That was too hard? That's the program I designed for grade-school kids."

"Oh you did not!" Sean said, grinning slightly despite himself.

"Okay I didn't, but the workout didn't make you tense."

I began to rub Sean's shoulders.

"That feels good."

"Lie down on the bed and I'll give you a backrub," I said.

Sean lay down on his stomach. I climbed on top of him and straddled his butt. I began kneading the muscles of his neck, working slowly down to his shoulders. His muscles were as tight as a bowstring. I took my time, easing out the tension. I could feel Sean begin to relax. I rubbed his back and then firmly began to press on one side of his spine and then the other. His upper back popped, and Sean released a contented "ahhhh."

"Take off your shirt," I instructed.

While Sean did so, I put on some quiet, soothing music. I returned to my position on top of Sean, kneaded the muscles of his back and then ran my fingernails all over, lightly scratching his back.

"That feels soooo good, Skye."

I kept up the scratching and then massaged his neck, shoulders and back yet more. The tension was quickly leaving Sean's body. Sean had too many pressures in his life. Getting the bed & breakfast up and running couldn't be an easy task, and then on top of that was the whole situation with Nick. I was glad I was able to help Sean in a small way.

"Turn over," I said.

Sean did so and I massaged his shoulders from the front.

"Are you feeling better?"

"Yeah," Sean said, nodding.

Sean was no hunk, but he was kind of sexy in his way. Rubbing Sean's back had aroused me a little, but rubbing his chest turned me on even more. I really had not meant for us to end up on my bed together, but one thing had led to another, and there we were. I was sitting on Sean's crotch and I could tell I wasn't the only one getting excited.

I kept massaging Sean's shoulders and chest while he sighed with contentment. His eyes were closed part of the time, but at other times he gazed into my own. I wondered what he was thinking. I found myself leaning toward him, bringing my lips closer and closer to his. When I was mere inches away, I pulled back.

"I shouldn't be doing this," I said.

"Giving me a massage? I love it."

"No. In case you didn't notice, Sean, I was just about to kiss you."

"I noticed. I didn't tell you to stop you, did I?"

"No."

"Well?"

"It just doesn't seem right."

"What? You're analyzing the situation? I thought you were a man of action. I thought you just pounced. Or am I not hot enough for you?"

"It's not that, Sean. You're very attractive, but you just broke up with Nick. You're vulnerable. I don't want to be a vulture, swooping in and taking advantage when you might not be thinking clearly. We've been friends a long time..."

Sean reached up and traced my jaw-line with his finger tip.

"You're a good friend Skye, but I'm a big boy, and I know what I'm doing. If I had any reservations, I would have pushed you away when you leaned down to kiss me."

"I shouldn't..." I said, and I began to climb off Sean. Before I knew what happened, Sean grasped the back of my neck, pulled me down on top of him, and kissed me hard on the mouth. I resisted, but he hung on with both arms and forced his tongue between my lips. I gave into my desires and kissed him back passionately.

Sean was far more aggressive than I would ever have guessed. I had no time to think about whether or not what we were doing was right. Sean rolled over on top of me and began to tear at my shirt. He actually ripped it getting it off me and once he did, his hands and tongue were all over my torso. He had me moaning in seconds. I thought my boxers and shorts were going to split from the strain.

Off came socks, shorts and boxers. Sean and I writhed naked on the bed, pawing at each other like wild animals. Sean leaned down and engulfed me, causing me to moan so loudly I wondered if we could be heard downstairs. Sean went at it with everything he had. Even Ross hadn't been that wild!

We were all over each other in a frenzy of lust. Sean only paused for a moment when we'd been going at it nearly an hour to ask where I kept my condoms and lube. He jerked the drawer open, brought out the small leather case where I kept my supplies, and then returned to the bed. Sean shoved me onto my back, placed the condom on me, climbed on top, and then began to ride.

To say I was shocked is a vast understatement, but Sean rode me like a bucking bronco. Even when he rolled over onto his back and pulled me down on top of him, he was so forceful that I felt like I was the bottom. I pulled Sean's legs over my shoulders and slid into him. Sean constantly urged me to go harder and faster. I think he was trying to kill me.

We kept going at it as sweat streamed from our bodies. Finally, we both groaned with passion, and I fell upon Sean, gasping for breath.

We just lay there for a while, and then I rolled onto my back. I hadn't had sex that intense since my days with Jarret.

"Now I feel better," Sean said, still panting.

"Wow," I said. I looked over at him and grinned.

"Do you still have any doubts that I wanted it?" Sean asked.

"None whatsoever." I was still shocked and amazed.

Sean smiled. "Don't worry that you took advantage of me Skye, because you didn't. And don't worry, I know you're not a relationship kind of guy. This is what it is. Nothing more."

I nodded.

"I never dreamed you could be so aggressive."

"Just call it pent-up emotion and lust. Can I stay with you tonight Skye? I just want to sleep tonight in your arms."

"You're more than welcome to sleep with me," I said. I leaned over and kissed him lightly on the lips.

Sean and I both showered, separately. We were too exhausted and sated to think about more sex. We slipped into bed, and Sean snuggled up next to me and lay his head on my chest. I wrapped my arms around him, and in moments he was asleep. I'd had my doubts when we'd started, but I knew in my heart that what we'd done was right. Sean had needed it, and as for me, it was an experience I wouldn't have missed for the world.

Ralph

Our time in Verona was nearly at an end. Filming a video is a long and difficult process, but we had been at it a few days and were almost finished. Jordan and I were eager to hear Sam's answer, but we didn't press her. We both knew it was a monumental decision. After all, we were talking about bringing a child into the world together. What could be bigger than that?

Jordan and I spent most of our time together when he wasn't working. We revisited all the places connected with his father, including Ofarim's, Café Moffatt, Taylor's old high school and of course, the soccer fields. I think Jordan felt a special connection to his dad when he went to the places his dad had known. We drove by his mom's old house too. Jordan had lived many places, but he would always think of Verona as home.

We stopped at the graves of Taylor and Mark briefly to leave roses and carnations, but we did not linger because we both knew without a doubt that the graves contained only their bodies, not their spirits.

We visited with Taylor's grandparents and also with Ethan and Nathan. Nick was very distressed over what had happened with Sean, and it pained me to see him suffer so. Jordan was still angry with Ross over the incident, but he believed, as I did, that it wasn't something planned. It was just another case of Ross thinking with his dick instead of his brain. This time it had cost Sean and Nick their relationship. I wondered if Ross would ever learn.

On the last day of filming, Samantha asked if we could have dinner together again. Jordan and I knew she'd reached a decision, and I must admit I was powerfully tempted to ask for her answer. I knew she would reveal it in her own good time, and that the waiting was nearly over. We could easily have had a far longer wait. Sam could have required weeks or even months to reach a decision, instead of days. I was glad she had quickly made up her mind, because the suspense was killing me. If she turned Jordan and me down, it didn't mean we couldn't have kids, but we would have to search hard for a mother for our child. It was a process that I didn't even know how to begin, but if begin it we must, it would be best to do so as quickly as possible.

We arranged for supper in the same small parlor as before. Jordan and I anxiously awaited Sam's arrival. She took a seat and smiled at us both.

"The answer is yes," Sam said, ending our agonizing wait instantly.

"You're sure?" Jordan asked.

"I'm sure."

Jordan stood up and hugged Sam, as did I. I felt myself getting a little teary. Jordan and I were going to have a child.

"This is wonderful news," Jordan said. "I can't tell you how happy I am."

"I'm very excited myself. I thought I would have to wait for years to have a baby, but I can have one right now instead."

"Well, I do think it takes a few months," I said.

"Ralph!" Sam said, laughing.

"This calls for a celebration!" Jordan said.

"And how are we going to celebrate?" I asked.

"Hmm, I don't think we can improve on this meal," Jordan said, looking down at the eggplant parmesan, bread sticks, Caesar salad and bruschetta.

"Perhaps with a special dessert!"

"Like cherry cheesecake," Sam said, pointing to the table.

"I guess fate has planned ahead for us," Jordan said smiling. He gave Sam another hug.

We chatted excitedly as we ate, making plans, discussing what we could buy the baby and basically laying out his or her entire future, including college and a profession. Yes, we were getting ahead of ourselves, but we couldn't help it. I would have laughed at Jordan and Samantha for their boundless enthusiasm, but I was right in there with them. It was all I could do to keep myself from running out and buying a stroller and a teddy bear.

After dessert, our talk turned a bit more serious, but was still joyful.

"I'll have the lawyers draw up the necessary paperwork," Jordan said. "I want you to select your own lawyer to advise you. We'll pay all your legal costs, secretly so the lawyer won't feel obligated to protect us."

"That isn't necessary," Samantha said.

"No. I want you to be absolutely certain of what you're getting into and all the details. Having your own lawyer will prevent any conflict of interest. I want you to be as comfortable with this as possible. Once all that is completed, we can proceed."

"That brings up another question," Sam asked. "How do we proceed? I know we should do some genetic and STD tests, but I mean, do we do this by artificial insemination or the old-fashioned way?"

"I think whichever you are the most comfortable with," Jordan said to Sam, looking at me for confirmation. Jordan and I had, of course, discussed this amongst ourselves before.

"I agree."

"But what do you think?" Sam asked. "Even if you leave the decision up to me, I still want your input."

"Well," I said. "I'm going to be a little uncomfortable doing it the old-fashioned way. We are talking about a very intimate act after all. I'm also going to be uncomfortable if we use artificial insemination. The idea of leaving a...sample in a test tube is a bit embarrassing."

Jordan laughed. "I have to agree with Ralph. I think I'm going to be a little embarrassed and ill at ease whichever method you choose."

"In that case, I'd like to do it the old-fashioned way. I just don't like the idea of my child being conceived with a turkey baster. Artificial insemination also increases risk of multiples. I don't think we want to end up with quintuplets.

We're about to become a part of each other's lives. I don't think we should fear a little intimacy."

"So, the old-fashioned way it is," Jordan said. "While we're on uncomfortable topics, we need to discuss something else. Ralph and I want this to be our baby, 'our' meaning the three of us. It will only take one of us to father a child, of course, but we want to share this. It doesn't really matter which of us is the father; we'll both love this child the same. Ralph and I have decided that we don't even want to know which of us is the biological father, so if you don't mind, we both want to be a part of the conception."

"I don't mind," Sam said. "I think it's a wise idea. Leaving it to chance stands as proof that you'll both love our child no matter which of you is the biological father. It will also double our chances of success. No offense, but I am hoping we won't have to try too many times before we succeed."

"None taken," I said. "We're all friends here, but I would also rather limit the physical side of this as much as possible. It's going to be...awkward to say the least."

"It's going to be a first for both Ralph and me," Jordan said. "We may need a little guidance."

"Are you turning red, Jordan?" Samantha teased. He was indeed, but I didn't say anything because I could feel my own face going a bit hot.

"I'm not very experienced with men," Sam said, "although I have been with a couple— well, with boys really, not men. When I was a teenager, I had a couple of boyfriends. That was before I realized I liked girls. I think I can remember how to do it."

Sam smiled. Her humor helped set me at ease.

"So I guess when the time comes, one of us will be with you and then the other," I said.

The others nodded.

"I'll be honest with you Sam," Jordan said. "I'm going to be very nervous about this. We're friends, but...procreating is going to take our friendship to a whole new level. I may have trouble looking you in the eyes the next day."

"We'll all do just fine," Sam said, reaching across the table and grasping our hands. "We're doing something wonderful. This baby is going to have three parents who love her very much. There's no need for embarrassment, but if you tell anyone what I look like naked, you'll be in big trouble."

I grinned. We were all excited over the big event: the birth of our baby that is, not its conception. The conception scared the crap out of us. We talked more about our plans for becoming parents, but mostly about our baby who was yet to be conceived. I reached out and grasped Jordan's hand as we talked. I didn't know if I'd ever been as happy as I was at that moment.

***

Later that same evening, Jordan was scheduled to give a talk at the Potter-Bailey Gay Youth Center. I went along with him. The gay-youth meeting was already in progress when we arrived. It was seven-thirty, and Jordan wasn't scheduled to talk until eight p.m. It gave us a chance to look around by ourselves for a while. It had been quite some time since we'd visited.

The center was quite impressive. We stopped first at the large display case in the reception area. There, memorabilia of Taylor and Mark were on display.

"I bet Dad never thought his soccer uniform would be on display in a gay-youth center bearing his and Mark's names," Jordan said.

"Well, you made it happen."

"I helped."

"Bullshit. Plenty of others pitched in, but without you, this place wouldn't exist."

"Just think," Jordan said, "with the endowment, this center is funded forever. Even with all the expenses, there is far more money in the account than when we started."

"You planned well."

"The financial experts I hired planned well," Jordan said. "No one will ever be able to shut this place down."

We continued our tour. On the first floor, there were offices for counselors, a room with phones for the twenty-four-hour crisis line, a large reception area, meeting rooms, a lounge, a library, a kitchen and a large living room with a big screen TV, DVD and more. In the basement was a game room and the second floor had rooms where troubled youth could stay for a while.

"I wish we would've had a place like this in southern Indiana when I was growing up," I said.

"I think I'm more proud of this place than I am of any of my other accomplishments," Jordan said. "I love my music, Phantom World is beyond cool, and we've been able to raise tons of money for charities, but this place is something special."

"You're special," I said, kissing Jordan on the cheek.

"And you're sappy," Jordan said, giggling and returning my kiss.

"It's nearly time for you to go be a celebrity," I said, looking at my watch.

We wandered to the meeting room and quietly entered the back. Casper was speaking to a group of some four-dozen kids. About three-quarters of them were boys, and they ranged in age from about twelve to twenty. Nick was also present, which wasn't much of a surprise.

"I see our guest has arrived," Casper said. "I'd like you all to welcome Jordan Potter."

Jordan walked forward while I took a seat among the kids. The seating was arranged in a horseshoe to encourage discussion. While the kids were quieting down, I took a moment to look at Casper. I knew he was fast approaching forty, but he sure didn't look it. He could have passed for my age with ease. I hoped I looked that good when I was his age.

"Speeches are really boring," Jordan said to the group, "so I would just like to answer questions. Who has one?"

"What's it like being a rock star?" asked a dark-haired boy of about thirteen.

Jordan laughed. "Let's keep most of the questions centered on gay topics, but to answer your question I feel very lucky to do what I do. I love music, both composing and performing it. The success of *Phantom* has allowed me to do a lot of other things that I would not have otherwise been able to do. You need to keep in mind that my life isn't the way you probably picture it. My life is a lot more like yours than you think. Being a performer isn't all about doing concerts and appearing on TV. Most of it is a lot of work, although even the work can be fun."

"Was it scary for you to come out?" asked one of the girls.

"Yes. I think it's scary for anyone to come out. The unknown is always frightening. I didn't know how my friends would take it, and I didn't know how my fans would react, either. It was quite a risk, because at the time, most of *Phantom's* fans were girls. There were those who tried to discourage me because of that. They were afraid I'd derail *Phantom's* success.

"It took far less courage for me to come out than it would for most of you. I was already on my own, and I didn't have to worry about losing my home. I also didn't have to worry about how my parents would react. I knew my mom was more or less okay with it, and...I never got the chance to know my dad.

"It's especially hard to come out when you're young. There are certain groups out there that work very hard to make gays look like monsters. They claim that being gay is a sin. Let me tell you right now, it's not. These groups try to make gays look immoral, dirty and vulgar. One thing you must never do is allow anyone to tell you that you are this or that, just because you're gay. Gays are just like anyone else.

We're not angels. We're not devils. We're people, just people. Some of us aren't so nice, while others are wonderful. Don't ever let what others think or say influence how you feel about yourself. You know whether or not you're a good person."

"Is it true your boyfriend was a fan before he met you?" asked one of the older guys.

"Why don't you ask him? He's sitting right back there," Jordan said, pointing to me.

Suddenly, all eyes were on me. It was not what I'd expected.

"It's true," I said. "I had a major obsession for *Phantom* and Jordan in particular. Getting to meet Jordan was like...well, just picture getting to meet someone you idolize. As we spent time together and got to know each other, I grew to understand that Jordan was a real guy...with faults and problems just like all of us. I very quickly ceased to think of him as a rock star. To me, he's just Jordan."

Jordan smiled.

There were many more questions, quite a few of them having to do with *Phantom* rather than with gay topics, but I guess that was okay. Jordan was trying to instill a sense of pride in those kids, seeking to undo the negative images often hurled at them by fanatical religious groups. Jordan's message was one of love and acceptance. I was very proud of him.

After the meeting, we went to visit Ethan and Nathan once more. With the video shoot wrapped up, we finally had some time on our hands. Nothing particularly exciting or interesting happened as we sat at the old kitchen table in the Selby farmhouse, but not everything needs to be exciting to be enjoyable. It was good just to spend time with friends. Jordan's visit helped Nick cheer up too. I knew Nick had a long and difficult road ahead of him. I didn't even want to think about how I'd feel if Jordan and I broke up.

That night, Jordan and I lay side by side, talking about the child we would have with Samantha and how our life would change when the baby became a part of it. We were both excited. We knew we were setting out on a grand adventure.

Sean

My cell phone awakened me as I lay slumbering in Skye's bed. I glanced at the clock. It was not yet six a.m.

"Yeah?" I asked.

"Sean, I'm sorry to call you this early," said Matilda, our head housekeeper, "but could you please come to the Dining Room? We have a problem."

"Okay, I'll be right down."

I hopped out of bed, trying not to disturb Skye. I was unsuccessful.

"Is something wrong?"

"Nothing major. I hope. Something in the Dining Room."

I quickly dressed, running my fingers through my hair in an attempt to make myself presentable.

"Skye?"

"Yeah?"

"Thanks for last night."

"No. Thank you."

I blushed. I left Skye's room, walked downstairs and into the Dining Room.

"Whoa!" I said as I entered.

Matilda, along with my mom and dad, were standing there gazing at the pyramid of tables and chairs standing on the huge dining table. Pieces of expensive crystal and other glassware were precariously balanced on the stack of furniture. I whipped out my phone and called Marshall.

"Marshall, get down to the Dining Room. There's something you've got to see."

Marshall arrived no more than two minutes later.

"Cool," he said.

Matilda gave him a withering look. She did not share his opinion.

177

"We need this room put back in order if breakfast is to be served on time," Matilda said.

"I'm sure we can whip it into shape before Martha is ready for us," I said, looking at the precarious stack.

Skye came into the Dining Room just then.

"Rearranging the furniture, Sean?"

"I'm so glad you're here."

"Uh-oh, I don't like the sound of that."

"We need to get this down, preferably without breaking anything."

"How are you going to reach the stuff on top?" Skye asked.

"By standing on your shoulders."

"Let's do it."

Skye kneeled down, and I climbed onto his broad shoulders. When I was seated, Skye stood and then helped me stand up. It wasn't an easy process, but I had fairly good balance. Skye held my legs tightly to help steady me as I reached out and began handing delicate crystal down to Marshall.

"Do you think your little friend did this?" I asked.

"Hmm, it doesn't seem his style. He's mischievous, but this is going a bit too far. This looks like the work of someone a bit more malicious. If it was Etienne, he'd be here giggling. The perpetrator is not in the room."

"Well, if you discover which of your ghostly friends did it, tell them to knock it off."

"Why, Sean?" Skye asked beneath me. "This is kind of fun."

It took several minutes, but finally we had everything down and back in place. It was an interesting way to start the day.

I sat across from Skye during breakfast, smiling at him occasionally. Marshall noticed the looks passing between us, but I was willing to bet he would never guess we'd slept together. I was definitely still upset about Nick, but I was much less tense. It also made me feel a bit more secure to know that someone cared about me. What happened with Skye wasn't the beginning of a romantic relationship, but it wasn't just sex either.

Breakfast was delicious, as always. Martha served buttermilk pancakes with blueberries, blackberries, and strawberries piled on top. There was also bacon, scrambled eggs flavored with orange, and heavenly hash browns. There was also the usual selection of juices, coffees, and teas. It was a good thing I had trained myself to eat moderately or the gourmet buffet that awaited me every morning would have packed the pounds around my middle. I wanted to lose weight, not gain it.

Ross behaved as if he wanted to speak to me just after breakfast, but I ducked him. *Phantom* was departing in less than an hour, and soon Ross would be gone from my life forever. I had no desire to bid him goodbye. Unfortunately, I didn't escape from Ross so easily. He tracked me down and cornered me as I was interviewing candidates for staff in my office.

"We need to talk," Ross said.

I frowned.

"Just a minute," I said to my potential employee.

I followed Ross out into the hall, taking a moment to close my office door. We walked several feet down the hallway so we wouldn't be overheard.

"The last time we talked didn't end so well."

"I just wanted to say I'm sorry. I didn't mean for what happened between Nick and me to happen, but it did and it's my fault. Jordan says I think with my cock, and he's right. I can't tell you how bad I feel that you and Nick have broken up over this. I wish I could do something to set things right, but I can't undo what happened. You may not believe me, but we really didn't mean for it to happen. I think Nick was also thinking with his dick. If he'd been thinking with his head or his heart, he would have never cheated on a boyfriend as wonderful as you."

"He cheated on me Ross; that's the bottom line. If you had ever loved someone as much as I loved Nick, you would understand how much it hurts to be betrayed. I don't know if I'll ever be able to trust him again."

"How about forgiving him then?" Ross asked.

"In time, probably, but forgetting is another matter."

"Try to forgive him and forget, Sean. I know you hate me, but I also know you love Nick. What happened was my fault. If it makes you feel any better, I initiated it. If I hadn't been so thoughtless, you and Nick would still be together. I'll regret what I did for the rest of my life."

I didn't know what to say to Ross, so I said nothing.

"I won't bother you any more Sean. Thank you for letting me stay here. Thank you for letting us use the mansion. And again, I'm truly sorry. I hope that someday maybe you'll be able to forgive me."

With that Ross turned and departed. I was no longer angry enough to want to beat him into a pulp, but I was still angry. Ross was right about one thing; if it hadn't been for him, Nick and I would still be together. Nick was just as guilty though. If he had been faithful to me, we would still be a couple. Maybe this was one of those painful things that has to happen for some reason, but I could see no reason in it. I returned to my office.

I tried not to think of Nick as I interviewed potential employees. I failed. Thoughts of Nick kept slipping in. When I'd finished the last interview, Nick flooded my mind. To force him out, I thought about the night I'd spent with Skye. I had no regrets concerning what had happened between us, but it still seemed strange having sex with Skye after knowing him for so many years. In high school, I never dreamed I would ever get the chance to be with him. Of course, it was out of the question most of the time I'd known Skye, because I was with Nick. I could certainly understand why guys flocked to Skye. In a word, he was magnificent. Not only did he have the most incredible body I'd ever seen in my entire life, but his sexual prowess was without parallel.

What had happened between Skye and me was more than just sex. Our time together was about more than satisfying our mutual lust. After breaking up with Nick, I needed companionship and intimacy. Sleeping beside Skye after we'd finished was even more important than the sex. I needed to be close to someone. I needed to be held. Skye had been there for me.

If I knew less about Skye, I could have fallen for him. He was gorgeous, of that there was no doubt, but he'd shown me his caring, loving side, and that attracted me as much as his incredible body. Still, I knew Skye wasn't the relationship type of guy. He was too restless, too eager to make conquests. I respected him no less for that, but I knew that even if he desired a relationship with me, he'd never be happy with it. No. Skye was not boyfriend material, but that was okay because I was in no way, shape, or form searching for someone who could hurt me as Nick had. No one was going to be given that opportunity ever again.

"Sean, we need to talk."

I looked up, relieved to see Marshall and not Ross sticking his head through the open door of my office.

"I hope this conversation is more pleasant than the last one that started with that sentence."

"I can't guarantee that. Who were you talking with earlier?"

"Ross."

"Oh."

Marshall peered at me closely.

"Don't worry. We didn't get into a fistfight this time."

"Well, that much is good."

"So what's this about?"

"The workmen are having a little trouble proceeding with some of the restoration."

"How so?"

"I think you should come and see."

"Has our ghost created a pyramid of tools or something?"

"No," Marshall said. "This is more serious."

This was not turning out to be a good day. Marshall led me through the twisted hallways of the fourth floor, far away from my office. Some minutes later, we arrived at our destination.

"This is the problem."

"Holy crap!"

The workers had hit a brick wall, literally.

"This wasn't here before," I said, indicating the wall, which blocked the hallway.

"Uh-huh, hence the problem."

"Are the construction guys playing some kind of practical joke?"

"No, it's no joke."

"How can you be sure?"

Marshall crossed his arms and gave me a condescending glare.

"Okay, okay. Let me rephrase that: how did you find out it's not a practical joke?"

"That's better. I had a chat with some of the resident ghosts of Graymoor."

"Edward? William?"

"Yes, and Etienne."

"So, what did Etienne and the Graymoor boys have to say?"

"That it would be dangerous to open up this part of the house to guests."

"Why?"

"They didn't say...exactly, only that death, destruction, and disaster could result."

"Hmm, what do you think?"

"I think we should listen. Edward and William have been nothing but helpful all along. Etienne is mischievous, but good at heart. I sensed only concern when I spoke with our friends from the other side."

"So, we're definitely not dealing with Devon again? He's not posing as other ghosts?"

"Oh, no, I can sense Devon if he's near. If I'm talking to a spirit, I can be certain it's not him."

"It's too bad you didn't have that ability a few years ago. You could have saved us a good deal of trouble."

"Don't I know it? So, what do you think?"

"I suppose we don't really need to go into this part of Graymoor. There are plenty of other directions to take and plenty of other bedrooms. I'll talk to Dad, but I think we can avoid whatever is down this hallway. I am curious, though. I've explored here some, but I haven't been in all the rooms yet. I wonder what's behind this wall that is so dangerous."

"Maybe I can dig up some more details."

"I'd appreciate that."

***

After supper, I walked to the Natatorium for a swim. I needed to relax after my day. At least, Ross was gone now. Every time I'd crossed his path, it was a reminder of what had happened. I would miss Jordan, Ralph, Kieran and Cedi, but as far as Ross was concerned, it was good riddance. I hoped I never saw him again.

I thought about Cedi for a moment. I'd seen very little of him during his stay. Of course, I'd spent precious little time with any of the *Phantom* crowd, but Cedi never seemed to be around. I'd likely get my chance to know him better. He was a permanent member of *Phantom* now. Our paths were sure to cross again.

Other than the departure of Ross, it had not been a good day. As I walked toward the Natatorium, I turned my thoughts away from the unpleasantness of recent hours and onto the crystal waters of the pool. I still couldn't believe I had an Olympic-sized pool inside my own home. I could remember when Graymoor didn't even have electricity! Times had changed. I couldn't wait to get into the warm, relaxing water.

Skye was swimming when I arrived, cutting through the water with powerful strokes. His body was so perfect he seemed like he'd stepped from the pages of an Abercrombie & Fitch catalog. Even that description doesn't do him justice. The A&F models could only dream they might one day be as hot as Skye. He was so handsome, so beautifully built that he almost didn't seem real. He was masculinity perfected.

Skye had quite an ego, but it was a miracle that he wasn't as conceited as hell. He was conceited to a point, but not as much as he pretended to be. Skye sometimes hinted to us mere mortals how god-like he was, but it was always done with a touch of humor. Skye didn't take himself too seriously, at least not any more. There was a time when his conceit was quite real, but he'd mellowed and grown wiser with age. There was no doubt he thought he was hot, but how could he have any other opinion of himself?

I pulled off my shirt and dove into the water. Skye finished his laps and swam to me. We treaded water, floated, and swam around while we talked of nothing in particular. My eyes were drawn again and again to Skye's chest and handsome face. He'd held me in his powerful arms and kissed me with his perfect lips. The mere sight of him filled me with sexual desire.

I drew close to Skye, gazed into his eyes, leaned in and kissed him. There was a moment's hesitation on Skye's part, but then he pulled me to him and kissed me forcefully.

A few minutes later, we were in Skye's room, our wet swimsuits on floor, Skye and I wrestling naked on his bed. My entire body felt as if it was on fire with lust. I didn't feel like myself, or perhaps I should say, I felt as if I'd been stripped down to my most basic, primitive level. I was completely controlled by hormones and instinct.

Skye and I didn't make love. We had sex, and it's just what I needed. When we finished, more than an hour later, we lay on our backs, panting and sweating.

"Damn," Skye said, "it is true what they say about the quiet ones."

I laughed. "I feel so relaxed now."

"Sex does that for you."

I lay there enjoying the afterglow of sex while I stared at the ceiling. Skye was magnificent. The control he had over his own body was amazing. He was just—wow.

"I didn't mean to sleep with you again," I said after a while.

"Oh? Was I that bad the first time?" Skye grinned. He knew he was a god in bed.

"Are you kidding? I would describe how incredible you are, but your ego is already quite big enough."

"Everything about me is big, Sean, but you know that." Skye laughed.

"Oh I know, but I still didn't mean to end up in your bed again."

"Why not?"

"Sex changes things. We've been friends for so long, and our friendship has come to mean a lot to me. Sex with you is incredible, but our friendship means even more to me. You know?"

"Yeah."

"We also work together and live in the same house. Things could get...complicated."

"I know what you mean."

"I don't know how I can resist you though. You're so attractive, so fucking sexy that you drive me out of my mind with lust. Any time I see you without a shirt I just... or with one on for that matter. I feel like I've opened a door I can't shut."

"Maybe we should never have had sex at all," Skye said.

"No. I needed what happened between us the first time. Well, I needed this too, but the first time I needed to be with someone. You know? It was about a lot more than just sex."

"And this time?"

"This time was about sex—sex and pure animal lust."

"I could promise never to have sex with you again, but I won't make that promise, because I'm not sure it's one I could keep. If you started kissing me again like you did in the pool, I doubt I could maintain my resolve. Sex is my weakness, you might say."

"You have a weakness?"

Skye laughed.

"Maybe you need to see other guys, Sean. Maybe you need to take your own advice and play the field."

"I don't think so, Skye. I definitely don't want a boyfriend."

"It doesn't have to be anything serious, but maybe you should find a guy to casually date, or just to sleep with. Hell, find a few guys; experiment. You'll forget all about me."

"Not likely. Besides, I don't want to play the field."

"Are you sure? Listen, don't take this the wrong way, but you slept with me rather fast after you dumped Nick. Maybe there's a reason for that."

"Yeah, lack of sex."

"I think there's more to it than that. Maybe you told Nick he needed to play the field because subconsciously you feel that need yourself. Maybe you want to see what else is out there. While you were dating, you wouldn't let yourself think about it, because to do so would have been like being unfaithful. You're not that kind of guy. In the back of your mind, though, you wondered. Maybe it's even more hidden than that—maybe subconscious. Nick's infidelity gave you an out. I'm stepping way over the line here. I hope I don't piss you off, but the Sean I know would have been more forgiving. I think there's a reason you broke up with Nick. Part of it is what you told him, but I think you're ignoring the

186

fact that Nick isn't the only one who needs wider experience."

"I just don't know Skye."

"Nick was your first boyfriend, right?"

"Yeah."

"And you're Nick's first?"

"His first real boyfriend. I think he sort of dated someone before he came here, but it wasn't serious."

"So you both have no real experience, except with each other. You guys dated since high school. I'm sure you both passed up plenty of opportunities to be with other guys in college. Before what happened with Ross, both Nick and you probably thought you'd grow old together, right?"

"Yeah."

"Both of you must be curious about other guys. You were curious, weren't you? At the very least, you were curious about me."

"But you're different, Skye! You're the hottest guy I've ever seen in my life. Who wouldn't be curious about you?"

"You're in danger of enlarging my ego, Sean," Skye said, laughing. "If you're truthful with yourself, I think you'll find that you weren't just curious about me. You're curious about who else might be out there. There are all kinds of guys, Sean—all kinds of different body types, sizes, shapes, nationalities, and personalities. There are guys who are dominant, submissive, tender, rough, caring, brutal, sensual, and more. There are many you would never want to meet, but there are just as many that you'd find sexy and fascinating."

"But I'm not like you, Skye, I'm not..."

"Were you going to say a slut?"

"No, I know you're selective, but you do sleep with lots of guys. I'm a one-man kind of guy."

"I'm not saying you should become a whore, Sean. I just think that this might be a good time for you to see what else is out there. When you were dating Nick, I bet you sometimes wondered if getting so serious with the first boy you met was wise. I know this is none of my business, but I don't like to see you in pain. Or Nick, either, for that matter. You're both suffering right now, and I think this is something you both need to resolve. You were smart enough to see it when you looked at Nick, but not quite wise enough to see that you need the same thing. I think you're so loyal, so faithful that even now you feel like you would be cheating on Nick if you dated other guys. I'm willing to bet you felt guilty after sleeping with me the first time, and you're probably feeling a little guilty right now. I'm right about that, aren't I?"

"Yeah."

"It's a big world, Sean, filled with hot guys. You're young, and you're sexy. Now is the time to explore. You can settle down when you're an old man, although in your case I have a feeling you'll be settling down long before that."

"You think?"

"Yes, and you want to know what else I think?"

"You're going to tell me whether I want to know or not, right?"

"You know me so well."

"Then I want to know!"

"I think that things aren't as over between Nick and you as you think. Even I can see you guys were made to be together. You're hurting right now, probably worse than ever before. You're also scared to death because you're afraid it really is over. You guys love each other too much to let things end. You guys will get back together. I'd bet my balls on it."

I would have made a joke about Skye betting one of his most prized possessions, but he was so serious it wasn't the time for levity. I wasn't in the mood to kid around either. Some of what Skye was saying made sense. Hell, maybe all of it did. I would have to think long and hard on it to be sure.

"Aren't you supposed to just be a dumb jock? When did you get so smart?" I asked.

"When you're as gorgeous as I am, you have to hide your intelligence. People just couldn't take it if they found out I have beauty and brains."

I laughed. I couldn't help it. Now that Skye had made his point, he was back to his old self. I rolled over and kissed him lightly on the lips.

"Now get out of my bed," Skye said. "I've had you twice; I'm tired of you!"

Yeah, he was back to his old self.

"Thanks Skye."

Skye

I'd come to rather enjoy one of the perks of working in a bed & breakfast: namely, breakfast. Each morning Martha prepared an incredible feast. The spread she laid out on the Dining Room table and the large buffet might be peach pancakes with whipped cream one morning, coconut crepes the next, and banana-walnut waffles the following morning. In addition to the main dish, there was a varying combination of bacon, sausages, muffins, Danish, ham, biscuits, bagels, toast, juices, coffees, teas and just about any breakfast item one could imagine. There was always something wonderful awaiting me in the Dining Room, and it made getting up in the morning much easier.

My defined abs would have been in danger of disappearing, but I practiced moderation and led such an active lifestyle that I burned whatever calories I consumed. I weighed myself weekly just to make sure my weight remained consistent, but over the years I'd become adept at controlling my eating habits. Moderation was the key.

Breakfast was especially delightful due to the presence of Martha. I found her company as enjoyable as any of her delicious goodies. Martha was feisty, energetic and witty. Sean had described her as everyone's grandmother. If that was true, she was the sort of grandmother who rode a Harley. She always had delightful stories to tell of her years in Paris as well as her travels throughout the U.S. She had worked in several B&Bs, moving from one to the next when she pleased. I hoped she would stay with us for a good long time.

Matilda was an interesting character too, but I liked Basil even better. Basil tended to be somewhat quiet, but when he did speak he was fascinating. He knew everything there was to know about plants. He had a sort of wizardly air about him, and I couldn't get the image of Gandalf the Grey from *The Lord of the Rings* out of my mind when he was near.

After a heavenly and slightly spicy Italian omelet, filled with mozzarella, red peppers and Italian sausage, served along with the story of Martha's years of working in a B&B in Hollywood—she'd actually known Elizabeth Taylor—I headed for the Natatorium to begin my work for the day.

With *Phantom* gone, it was back to business as usual. Guests were in and out of the Natatorium all day. The pool was extremely popular, and there was someone in the water more often than not. One of my duties was to act as a lifeguard. There was a notice posted that no lifeguard was on duty, but what that really meant is that there was no lifeguard sitting at the edge of the pool. Anytime there was a lone swimmer or unattended children, I remained in the Natatorium and busied myself with tasks there while keeping an eye on the situation.

I had feared I would lose my California tan when I returned to Verona, but the warm soothing sunlight shining down through the glass roof of the Natatorium ended that worry. I often worked dressed in only a swimsuit or shorts and sandals, so my torso received plenty of sun. I smiled to myself when some of the guests checked me out.

It was mostly middle-aged women who ogled my body, but there were some guys of about the same age who looked at me with interest. Some of those who checked me out were married. I guess it didn't hurt to just look, but I'd always thought being married meant committing to your partner—until death do us part and all that. I'd had more than a few married men and women hit on me during my years in college. I was not the relationship kind of guy, but if I did commit to someone, I would never be unfaithful. I had never slept with a married man; at least that I know of. Very few of them would interest me in any case, but I wasn't about to help someone cheat on their partner. In California, a married student had tried his best to get into my pants. He was my age and extremely good looking. Had he been single I would've been all over him, but he had been married for three years. He even had a one-year-old daughter, and he was hitting on me! I thought about the big fuss some people made over the idea of gay marriage. Such indignation seemed so hypocritical when so many of those who were married took their marriage vows no more seriously than the due date on a library book.

"Hey Skye."

I placed the stack of towels on the rack under the portico by the pool and turned.

"Oliver! I haven't seen you in a while. We haven't had a chance to talk yet. How is Clay? I barely had a chance to see him at the graduation party."

"Incredibly sexy."

"I know that. I mean how is he doing?"

"Great! We're both great!"

"Wow, Oliver, I can't get over how good you look. Where is that pudgy little boy who used to work with me at Wahlberg's Farm Store?"

"Oh, I'm still a little pudgy. I just have better arms now, so it's not as noticeable."

"You've been working out. I can tell."

"I'm just trying to keep my sexy boyfriend."

"Liar. Clay doesn't care what you look like. He loves you for you."

"True," Oliver said, grinning. "I like to be as sexy as I can be for him though, and working out just makes me feel good."

"Hmm, now where did you learn something like that?" I said.

"So, how have you been Skye? Had any hot guys recently?"

"I couldn't be better, and as for the guys, what do you think?"

Oliver laughed.

"Hey, we need to get together for supper or something sometime," I said. "We have a lot of catching up to do. Clay can come too, of course. I'm sure you two are still inseparable."

"That sounds great. I'm staying at Mom's. You can reach me there anytime."

"I'm easy to reach—just call my room," I said.

"I know you're easy Skye. Everyone knows it."

"Hey, you may not be the little kid I remember from our days at Wahlberg's, but I can still kick your butt."

Oliver laughed.

"So you're staying in the haunted mansion, huh? I almost couldn't believe it when I heard you were working here and living in."

"Ah, you get used to the messages written in blood on the walls after a few nights."

Oliver's mouth dropped open.

"I'm kidding, Oliver. I've seen a few freaky things, but nothing *that* freaky."

"How are Sean and Nick getting on now that they're both back in Verona?"

"You haven't heard?"

"What?"

"They broke up."

"No! When?"

"Just a few days ago."

"What happened?"

"Sean caught Nick making out with Ross."

"Ross?"

"You know, Ross, the drummer in *Phantom*?"

"No way!"

"Yeah. *Phantom* was here filming a video. I don't know how it came about, but Sean found Nick and Ross going at it. He was furious and hurt. He broke up with Nick and got into a fist fight with Ross."

"That's...rough. I thought Sean and Nick would stick together."

"I have a feeling they'll get back together sooner or later. Sean just needs some time to cool off."

"How is Sean?"

"He was depressed and angry at first, but he's doing a lot better now."

"And Nick?"

"I haven't seen much of Nick, but he was all torn up over it. Of course, it was his own fault, but I don't like to see him suffer. I hope he's beginning to get over it too."

"Neither of them is going to be able to get over breaking up, Skye."

"I don't mean that they'll forget about it and each other. It's going to hurt them both for a long time. I just mean that the initial pain and shock of it are done."

"I don't think I could handle breaking up with Clay. I seriously don't know what I'd do."

"You would survive Oliver. It would be painful, but you'd survive."

"Well, I don't want to find out."

"Hopefully, you'll never need to experience it."

"I guess I need to do a better job of keeping up with things. I didn't know about any of this," Oliver said. "So is Jarret around?"

"No, he's long gone. I have no idea where that boy is now. We've lost touch."

"You two had quite a thing going before you left for college."

"Yeah. We got together a few times when I was back in Verona too, but you know how it is."

"I always thought you two would start dating."

"You're a funny guy, Oliver!"

"No, really!"

"You should know better than most that I'm not a relationship kind of guy."

"You should give it a try, Skye. You don't know what you're missing."

"I know. I'm missing the pain of breaking up with someone. I'm missing all the worries that come with dating."

"Those worries are worth it, Skye. I have no doubt you get plenty of sex, but you're missing out on the best parts of being with someone."

"I'll live."

"You never change, do you Skye?"

"Oh, I change. I get hotter and hotter."

Oliver shook his head and rolled his eyes.

"Where is Clay staying? His parents moved, right?"

"Yeah, they moved last year. He's staying with me."

"Your parents are cool with that?"

"Yeah. They love Clay. They consider him their son-in-law."

"That's really cool, Oliver."

"Yeah, it is," he said, smiling.

Oliver and I chatted a while longer, and then he went in search of Sean. I'd seen Oliver a handful of times during my college years, but I always expected to see the pudgy Harry Potter lookalike who had worked with me at Wahlberg's Farm Store. Oliver was so naïve then and had so many problems. I was glad that I'd been able to be a big brother to him.

Ralph

Jordan and I drove down to our cabin in southern Indiana after wrapping things up in Verona. It felt good to have my boyfriend all to myself again, although I guess I didn't truly have him to myself, as Mike was once again accompanying us. At least he was in a second vehicle trailing us and not in the SUV with Jordan and me.

I'd enjoyed our stay in the Graymoor Mansion, but I couldn't wait to get away from it all. We drove up the grassy drive that led to the cabin, parked, and then Mike helped us carry in boxes of supplies.

We hadn't visited the cabin for quite a while, but it was just as we left it. We stacked the boxes of groceries and other supplies on the floor and began to pull the sheets off furniture. It was a process that did not take long. The cabin was small, no more than twenty by twenty feet, so floor space was limited. There was a half loft above where Jordan and I sometimes slept, but we usually slept in the antique double bed that occupied the northwest corner of the cabin.

Mike departed to set up his campsite within sight of the cabin. He was a seasoned camper, and I had no doubt he would be just as comfortable in his tent as Jordan and I would be in our cabin. He was far enough away to give us privacy, but close enough to be on the scene in seconds if there was trouble. I anticipated no danger, but I always felt more secure with Mike around. He was the perfect bodyguard, always on the alert but unobtrusive. I'd hardly noticed him at all while we were staying at Graymoor. Mike was a good friend as well, so we enjoyed his company. The best part was that he generally kept to himself.

We had owned the cabin for a few years now. It was furnished with antiques we'd found on our travels—a step-back cupboard, our antique bed, a kitchen cupboard, an empire dresser, a turn-of-the-century oak kitchen table and chairs. There was stoneware sitting on the ledge that ran the length of the south wall and more on the edge of the half loft. There was a spinning wheel, a large old mirror, and lots of old framed prints, including one by R. Atkinson Fox of cattle grazing in a misty forest. There was even a painting of the cabin done by Estelyn Eversoll, who lived in the nearby town of Petersburg. The old kitchen cupboard was filled with Blue Willow china that we actually used. It looked beautiful behind the glass doors.

Our little property, which we'd named Phantom Farm, was comfy, quiet, and cozy. It wasn't a true farm of course; it was much too small for one thing. We'd planted lilacs, roses, peonies, and a snowball bush and even had a small garden plot, but there were no fields of waving corn. We had no farm animals, but there were plenty of deer, squirrels, turkeys, rabbits, and a few raccoons. There was no barn, but we did have a small, rustic-looking building that housed the bathroom facilities. They were separate from the cabin and gave the farm a summer-camp feel. Phantom Farm lacked much that defined a farm, and yet it seemed like one. The old log cabin with wild raspberries growing up its side, the wildflowers, and the old stepping-stone path made our little property feel like a pioneer farm.

I knew plenty about farms. I'd grown up on one less than five miles away from our cabin. It was I who suggested the name of Phantom Farm for our property. It might not be a farm in fact, but it was in my heart. We spent most of our time in far more luxurious surroundings, but I was the most content while we resided at Phantom Farm.

It did not take long for Jordan and me to settle in. We put our few groceries away in the step-back cupboard and the dorm-sized refrigerator that also acted as a nightstand by the bed. Not everything was antique in our cabin. Jordan and I were willing to do without many modern amenities, but a refrigerator was a definite necessity.

Jordan and I stepped out onto the porch and sat, looking out into the woods. Birds called in the near and far distance, and insects made their presence known. It was quite hot in the sun, but the porch, surrounded as it was almost entirely by trees, was cool. The cabin also stayed cool for most of the summer days. The surrounding trees and the thick logs insulated the interior to such a degree that I'm sure our few visitors thought we had central air. Only in the late afternoon did the cabin become too warm; then we opened the windows and let the heat flow away. We kept the windows open all night and then shut them in the mornings to hold in the cool, night air. Such was the life on Phantom Farm. It was quite a contrast to our usual hectic pace.

"Are you nervous?" Jordan asked as we sat and admired the tranquil view. I knew exactly what he was referring to: fathering our child.

"Yeah," I said. "I just don't know if I can...perform. I've never had sex with a woman, and I know Sam, so that makes it even more difficult. Well, people usually know each other when they have sex, but...I don't know. It's just going to seem so weird."

"I understand. I've been thinking much the same thing. It's going to be awkward and embarrassing, but we're all friends."

"What if it comes down to it and I just can't? I don't mean I'm thinking about backing out, but what if I physically can't do it?"

"I'm a little concerned about that myself. Sam is beautiful, but she's a *girl*."

"If she wasn't, there wouldn't be much point in the whole thing," I said, grinning.

"True, but I'm a little concerned that my body won't cooperate."

"Exactly," I said. "They say almost no one is exclusively heterosexual or homosexual. I am a little attracted to females, but very little."

"Same here. I've felt an attraction to a few, but a very few, and the attraction wasn't strong."

"It will all work out," I said. "Even if one of us isn't up to the task, the other can take care of it. One of us has to get lucky."

"I just hope we're successful on our first try. I don't want to have to do it again and again."

"I'm sure Sam feels the same way. At least we know from that over-the-counter ovulation test when she's fertile."

"I almost can't believe she's doing this for us. I know she also wants a child, but just think of what it will be like for her. Our biggest worry is the conception, but that's only the beginning for her. We're going to be experiencing this with her to a degree, but she's the one who will actually be going through it. We'll just be there worrying about her health and how the baby is doing. I can't even imagine going through pregnancy."

"Or labor."

"Oh man! Men are supposed to be tough, but damn, can you even imagine?"

"I try not to."

"We're going to have a child Ralph," Jordan said, taking my hand. "We're going to have our very own son."

"The baby could turn out to be a daughter," I pointed out.

"I'm hoping for a son, but I know I'll fall in love with that baby no matter if it's a girl or a boy."

"I think we're getting ahead of ourselves—counting our chickens before they hatch."

"Or in this case, our baby before it's born. I'm going to be so nervous the whole nine months!"

I squeezed Jordan's hand, leaned over and kissed him.

***

Jordan and I visited my mom and dad the next day. It felt good to be back home on the farm. My years there seemed so far in the past now, but it wasn't that long ago that I was living on the old farm and listening to *Phantom* while I yearned for someone to love me. Little did I know back then how my dreams were soon to come true.

We sat on the screened-in front porch with my parents looking out at a view that was quite different from that seen from our cabin's porch. Here, there was a yard with large maple trees and a fence. Beyond that, there were fields of corn trailing off into the distance until they reached a wood. A gentle breeze, bringing with it the scent of honeysuckle and clover, blew across the fields.

I kept in touch with my parents, but I didn't get to see them nearly as much as I would have liked. Life with Jordan was a whirlwind of concerts, photo shoots, appearances, and recording sessions. There never seemed enough time for everything. I couldn't wait until Jordan began to slow down. I was greedy for more time with him.

We didn't speak of our family plans with my parents. Such a discussion would have been premature. Too much could go wrong, and it would have been cruel to give my parents hopes of a grandchild when it might never happen. Mom and Dad had resigned themselves to having no grandchildren when they found out I was gay. I must admit I yearned to tell them our plans. I could just imagine the look of joy on my mother's face.

Chris and Denise joined us for lunch. They were my best friends from high school. They had been there for me through the rough and lonely years and had accepted me just as I was—sexual orientation and all. Chris had always delighted in teasing me about my *Phantom* obsession. He loved to make fun of my favorite band, but he had changed his tune when he came face to face with *Phantom*. I still remembered the look of terror on his face when Jordan confronted him and brought up some of the unkind things Chris had said about *Phantom*, and particularly about Jordan himself. Jordan was just jerking his chain though, and let him off the hook after he'd made him squirm a bit. I laughed my ass off. I was even closer to Denise. She and I had spent long hours looking at pictures of Jordan, Kieran and Ross in teen magazines, never dreaming that someday Jordan and I would be a couple. I'd shared my dreams with Denise, and she was as happy as I when they came true.

Jordan and I had a very pleasant day at Mom and Dad's. Nothing particularly interesting happened, but I enjoyed myself. The acceptance of my family and friends made me feel good inside. There were many in the world who worked very hard to spread hatred and discord, but my family had triumphed over them.

***

The days passed, and Jordan and I came closer and closer to the big event. The legal papers were drawn up, examined, and signed by Jordan, Samantha, and myself. Sam was coming to join us on Phantom Farm, and we nervously awaited her arrival. It was really going to happen. The three of us were going to conceive a child.

Jordan and I picked her up at the Evansville Airport and drove her back to our cabin. There was a sense of nervous anticipation in the air, but our conversation flowed easily, all things considered. Sam had been with *Phantom* for a long time, joining the road crew not long after those terrible days when religious fanatics tried to assassinate Jordan and very nearly succeeded in killing Ross instead. We lived in close quarters while on tour, so everyone got to know everyone else. We were like a little family on the road, and as many members of the road crew as could manage returned tour after tour. Some even worked with the band almost year 'round.

"Oh, I love your cabin!" Sam said as soon as she walked in. "It looks like a picture in *Country Living*. Did you decorate it yourselves?"

"Of course," Jordan said smiling. "You know homos are natural-born decorators."

"Oh stop!" Sam said.

"We browse antique shops and malls wherever we go," I said. "There is stuff in here from all over. We try to find just the right pieces."

The three of us settled in on the porch, talking and laughing, and I grew more and more at ease. We spoke of shared experiences, crazy stunts Ross had pulled, Cedi's wild

British ways, and plans for another tour. Our conversation eventually made its way around to the reason we were together: making a baby.

"We haven't discussed exactly when we're going to do this," Sam said, "but sooner is better. In other words, the time is now. Also, I know we'll all be more at ease once we're finished."

"I can't tell you how nervous I am," Jordan said.

"I'm rather nervous myself," Sam said. "That's why I think we should start immediately—as soon as it's dark."

The light was already failing, and I felt a sense of panic. My old fears surged to the surface, but I tried to quell them. My performance anxiety was somewhat eased by the fact that Jordan and I had not had sex for a week. We had intentionally deprived ourselves to increase our chances of success. Not only would we be more likely to be able to perform, but the odds of impregnating Sam would be improved. Jordan and I had made out several times, and naturally we slept side by side. That had increased our need for sex to a fever pitch. I felt like my body was on fire with lust. The deprivation would be well worth it if it meant success. My intense need for release also lessened my fears that I wouldn't be able to get it up with Sam. I'd hardly been able to keep it down!

Jordan and I would both be having intercourse with Sam, but we thought it would be more comfortable for all if we did it separately. Sam agreed. I don't know if I could have done it if Jordan was in the room, and I sure didn't want to see my boyfriend having sex with someone else. I knew what we were doing was a necessary act, but I still didn't like to think of Jordan with anyone but me.

When it grew dark, Jordan and Sam retired to the cabin, and I went for a drive in the SUV. I couldn't just sit on the porch while Jordan and Sam were inside trying to make a baby, and I couldn't walk around in the woods in the dark. Driving helped me take my mind off of what was happening back in the cabin.

We decided I should stay away for an hour, then Jordan and I would exchange places. The situation had a somewhat perverse feel to it, as if Jordan and I were tag-teaming a groupie. I reminded myself that there was nothing wrong with what we were doing. In fact, making a baby was something special. We weren't engaged in some kind of three-way sex act. We were trying to bring a new life into the world.

I drove around the back roads and to some of the little towns in the county—places that were familiar. I couldn't keep from thinking about what was going on back in the cabin. I was worried about my time with Sam too. I kept reminding myself that Jordan, Sam and I could well have a child in less than a year. I wondered how I would react to having a son or daughter. I wanted a child and knew I would love it, but that still didn't tell me what it would feel like the first time I held him or her in my arms.

The hour crawled by, but at last neared its end. I headed back to the cabin, but made sure I didn't arrive early. I wanted to make sure that Jordan was finished before I got anywhere near the cabin.

Jordan and Sam were sitting on the porch talking when I arrived. Neither looked as if they had been trying to make a baby only a few minutes before. Jordan smiled at me, no doubt to put me at ease. He looked far more relaxed than he had in days. I'm sure he was glad to get his part over with. His week-long chastity had also ended, and that had to be a considerable relief.

"Are you ready?" Sam asked.

"Yeah," I said, not certain if it was true or not. I didn't think I could ever be ready for what was about to happen.

I tossed Jordan the keys and followed Sam into the cabin. Jordan headed for the SUV. I wondered what was going through his mind. I was soon much too occupied with my own thoughts and feelings to wonder what Jordan was experiencing.

The cabin was lit by romantic candlelight. The covers on the bed were turned down waiting on us. I gazed at Sam and shyly smiled. We didn't speak but began to slowly undress. My hands trembled. I flushed with embarrassment as I pulled off my shirt and even more so as I began to unzip my shorts. Sam had never seen me naked. Few others had. I wasn't ashamed of my body, but still, getting naked in front of Sam was disquieting. The fact that she was also getting naked helped. I tried not to look at her, but I also tried not to be obvious about not looking at her. I didn't want to make her uncomfortable.

Sam took me by the hand and led me to the bed. Her smile put me at ease. I could almost forget that both of us were completely naked and were about to engage in the most intimate of acts.

"It will be okay, Ralph," Sam said.

"Should I...kiss you?" I asked as Sam lay on her back.

"If it will help you, go right ahead."

I didn't kiss her, but lay on top of her instead. I rubbed up against her and massaged her shoulders. I kept it up for a few minutes. The week of deprivation did the trick. I didn't feel attracted to Sam, but I was fully erect.

Sam helped to guide me in. I was grateful. I wasn't completely ignorant of female anatomy, but it set me at ease to know I was going about it the right way. Sam removed her hand and I slid inside her. It was a curious but not unpleasant sensation. I began to slowly thrust. Sam didn't react much, but I kept on going. It was actually a lot easier than I'd thought. I hadn't anticipated the intercourse itself to be difficult—if I could maintain an erection that is— but I had been very worried about embarrassment and nervousness. Instead, I focused on the physical sensation and even more upon the fact that the act we were engaged in could result in a child. My body could actually play a part in creating another life.

My breath came faster, and my heart raced. I began to sweat. I thrust more violently and then groaned with release. A week of self-denial was at its end. I buried myself deep inside Sam as I released my sperm. I lay upon her panting and then rolled over onto my side to catch my breath. Sam leaned over and gently kissed me on the lips. Oddly, or perhaps not, I didn't feel embarrassed or even self-conscious. Sam and I had just had intercourse. We were lying naked side by side. I had feared this moment, and yet I felt completely at ease and closer to Sam than I'd ever felt before.

I arose and dressed. Sam remained lying down for a while to increase our chances of success. I went outside and watched the fireflies in silence until Jordan returned. Sam came outside then too, and we all sat close together—Jordan, Sam and me, shoulder to shoulder. The feeling of love and intimacy I'd felt as I'd lain beside Sam continued, only now the three of us shared it. What we had done had created a bond between us that I knew would never break. Hopefully, we were going to become parents.

Sean

I hesitated as I sat down in front of the computer. Was Skye right? Should I take my own advice and see what else, or rather *who* else, was out there? Nick was my first boyfriend, and my experience with guys beyond Nick was practically nil. I had fooled around once with my high-school classmate Ken, but that hardly counted. Marty, my best friend in high school, had kissed me during a dance, but that was his way of coming out to our classmates. Making love with Nick had always been exciting and fulfilling, but I didn't know what it was like with other guys. I had gay friends, but when it came down to romance or sex, my experience was limited.

I truly did not want to date. I wasn't ready for another serious relationship. The sting of Nick's betrayal was still with me, and I didn't want to risk getting hurt again. I wasn't so sure about how I felt about hooking up for sex. Skye did it plenty, but he was Skye. I feared hooking up would make me feel slutty. Then again, I didn't think of Skye as a slut. Still, I wasn't sure I could hook up with someone just for sex. I wanted something more to be there. Perhaps I could find something in between—something more than just sex but less than a relationship. Perhaps a friend with benefits. Maybe I didn't even need to look for that online. Maybe I needed to look at my friends in a new way. The problem with that was that most of them were paired up. Even if they weren't, I couldn't picture myself getting intimate with Oliver or Clay or the others. Skye and I had done it twice, but I had the feeling we wouldn't do it again. I yearned to return to him, but it was probably best that we just remained friends. Sex complicates things. That was reason enough not to consider any of my other friends. Besides, I just couldn't feel that way about them. There was already another relationship there that precluded it. My other friends weren't like Skye. He was in a class by himself.

I signed on to Gay.com. I was ridiculously nervous as I entered the chat room. It had been a long time, but I had once gone into the Indiana room to chat. Not many guys actually chatted in the room though. They just sat there and said nothing. It was the same this time around. Very few guys talked. There was no one in the room who really interested me. A few guys I didn't find of interest harassed me. Well, harassed is too strong of a word. Let's just say I was hit on, and when I said "no," some guys seemed to have trouble understanding the word.

I'm going to skip to the next night, because that's when someone of interest finally began to chat with me. I liked several things about him: he was near my age—only a couple of years older; he wasn't just trying to get into my pants, he was kind of good looking, he was nice, sexy, and funny, and he lived not far away. I soon learned his real name was Doug. We began talking, and I confessed that I didn't really know what I was seeking because of my recent breakup. Doug was mainly looking for friends, but if that led into more he was all for it.

We chatted about an hour that first night until Doug had to go. We exchanged e-mail addresses and added each other to our Yahoo Messenger buddy list before he departed. I didn't often haunt Gay.com, but I kept my Yahoo Messenger on a lot when I was online. Marshall and several other friends were on there now and then, and it was nice to chat with them. Some of my friends from college were on there too, so if I didn't mind being interrupted I kept my messenger on.

Doug and I chatted the next few nights, mainly on Yahoo Messenger. After getting to know each other on the Internet, we agreed to meet at The Park's Edge.

I recognized Doug from his photo as he walked toward the table. He was about six feet tall, had short brown hair, brown eyes and was reasonably good-looking. He wasn't the kind of guy I'd call hot, but he did have a nice smile and definitely wasn't hard on the eyes. The fact that he wasn't a major hottie like Skye set me at ease. I was more or less comfortable with my own looks, but I knew I was no Abercrombie & Fitch poster boy. Nick had always been much better looking than I was. There was always a fear lurking in the back of my mind that Nick would decide he wanted someone hotter. My fears were justified, because in the end he had gone for Ross, who was definitely much hotter than I.

Doug was dressed in jeans and a nice orange t-shirt that read "Thames Rowing Team" on the front. I was also wearing jeans and a muscle-cut Abercrombie & Fitch shirt I'd borrowed from Skye. I liked the muscle-cut shirt. The sleeves were a little shorter than normal and made my biceps look bigger.

We shook hands and Doug sat down.

"I kind of feel like I already know you," I said.

"You do. It's nice to finally meet you in person."

"I'm just a little bit nervous," I said.

"Yeah, I'm told I can be pretty intimidating," Doug said smiling. "I'll try not to frighten you too much."

"How was work today?"

"It was a thrill a minute. Watermelon was on sale, so I got quite a workout."

Doug worked in produce at the Kroger in Plymouth.

"I spent much of my day hiring staff and trying to figure out a new scheduling program."

'Sounds like fun."

"It wasn't bad. I don't like being stuck in my office, but I'm really not in there all that much. I'm out and about most of the time."

Doug and I enjoyed ourselves. We talked and laughed and ate. Doug ordered a grilled tuna hoagie and I had the Mediterranean Penne Pasta.

It felt odd to be sitting across the table from someone besides Nick. I went out with friends plenty of times, but sitting there with Doug was different. I knew we weren't going somewhere after supper to get it on, but there was a possibility of a physical relationship somewhere down the road—perhaps not very far down the road. There was even the remote possibility that Doug and I would date, but I didn't even want to think about that yet. I just wanted a friend, perhaps with benefits.

I *really* liked Doug. I hadn't counted on that. Okay, maybe I'd better explain. I obviously wouldn't have met him in person if I thought I wouldn't like him, but I hadn't counted on feeling something for him. I don't mean it was love at first sight or anything like that, but I realized as we sat there that I *could* fall for him. Perhaps I was even beginning to do so. I felt guilty and surprised as well. I'd never felt drawn to anyone like that other than Nick and hadn't even realized I could. I couldn't shake the feeling that I was cheating on Nick somehow, although Doug and I were doing no more than talking, and Nick and I were no longer a couple.

After supper, Doug and I crossed the street and took a walk in the park. We strolled along under the stars, and Doug charmed me with his quick wit and quirky sense of humor. We got into a discussion about space travel and how long it would take to get to some of those stars. We debated whether or not Einstein was right: that nothing could travel faster than light. We both hoped he was wrong and that space travel like that in *Star Trek* would someday be possible.

We parted without so much as a kiss. Doug did hold my hand in both of his when we shook hands at the end of the evening. He gazed into my eyes for a moment, grinned, and told me he was glad we'd met. My heart felt lighter than it had in days. I knew I'd just made a friend.

I was also a bit troubled by the encounter, so I sought out Skye as soon as I returned to Graymoor. He was not in the Natatorium or gym, so I walked to his room and knocked on the door.

Skye peered at me cautiously when he opened the door. He was dressed only in sleep pants. His tan chiseled chest was bare, momentarily drawing my eyes to his muscular pecs. I feared he would get the wrong idea about my nighttime visit, so I quickly locked my eyes on his own.

"I'm just here to talk," I said.

Skye grinned and stepped back so I could enter. He closed the door as I took a seat in one of the Victorian armchairs.

"So what's up hot stuff?" Skye asked, dropping into the other chair.

His bare chest was distracting, and I almost wished he would put on a shirt—almost I say, because Skye's chest was a sight I never wanted to miss. I remembered running my hands along his abs, licking his pecs and... I forced myself back to the topic at hand.

"I went on a date tonight, sort of, not a date really, but I went out with a guy."

"So you've bowed to my immense wisdom, at last."

"Well, we won't go there, but I had supper with Doug tonight, and then we went for a walk in the park."

I told Skye about my evening and hoped he wouldn't get bored because no sex was involved.

"So, you had fun?"

"Yeah!"

"But?"

"I feel a little guilty and a little scared. I know I'm completely free to do whatever I want with other guys, but I still feel attached to Nick. That creates guilt. I know it doesn't make sense, but I feel like I'm cheating on him."

"I suppose that's only natural. Old habits die hard, and you guys were together for a long time. Just remember, you're not cheating on him. Hell, what you did tonight wouldn't be cheating if the two of you were still together."

"Yeah I know, but it still feels that way."

"Maybe that feeling will pass in time."

"Yeah, maybe."

"So why did you feel scared?"

"Because I *really* like Doug. I don't mean I'm in love or even lust with him, but I didn't expect to feel anything."

"You are human Sean. I know you've been lonely. You've been developing a friendship with Doug on-line, so why wouldn't you feel something for him?"

"You're probably right, but it's still scary. I don't want another boyfriend. I just want to spend time with some different guys, just hang out and maybe...have sex."

"Now you're talking!"

"You're so bad Skye."

"And don't you ever forget it."

"I don't want to just sleep around, but I do want to see what it's like with others. Making love with Nick was incredible. Sex with you was...unbelievable, and it was so different from when I was with Nick. I wonder what it would be like with others, but..." I trailed off. I didn't even know what I wanted to say.

"Maybe a little part of you is afraid you'll find someone you prefer over Nick. Maybe you're afraid sex will be better with someone else than it was with him."

"I...I don't know. Nick and I aren't a couple anymore, so what would it matter if I did like it better with someone else? In some ways, it was way hotter with you."

"Just some ways?"

I grinned and shook my head. "The situation was different with you. I was in love with Nick. You're a friend. I love you as a friend, but not like I love Nick."

"I know," Skye said, "I'm just jerking you around."

"I don't even know what I'm trying to say. I just feel kind of guilty because I had a good time. I guess maybe I'm scared of what will happen if Doug and I continue to see other each other. Things might go in a direction I don't want."

"Or maybe you're afraid you'll change your mind and decide you do want another boyfriend. If that happens, you risk getting hurt again, and you're not ready for that. Right?"

"Yeah maybe. I don't know. I just feel so confused."

"And you wonder why I won't settle down? You think I just try to nail as many guys as I can, but maybe I'm really avoiding all the emotional entanglements guys like you experience."

"Nah, you're just always horny, Skye."

Skye laughed. "Maybe you're right. Listen Sean, I think you're being too hard on yourself. There's no reason to feel guilty about going out with Doug. There's no reason to feel guilty about having slept with me. You're a free agent and you can do what you want. As for the fear, you can't let it control you. There is always going to be something to fear in life, but you can't let it stop you. There is no use in worrying about what could happen. Just go with the flow; do what makes you happy right now. Life is for living Sean, not for pondering and not for worrying about. You and I both know you need to get out there and explore what it's like with other guys, both sexually and non-sexually. You just had a great time with a great guy, so be happy and go out with him again. Go out with a few other guys too! Live life for a while Sean."

"I wasn't living life before?"

"You were, but the situation has changed. Now is the time for exploration. Take advantage of it, because knowing you, it won't last long."

"You think?"

"I know you Sean. You have a lot of love to give, and very soon you will be falling for some cute guy."

"That scares me. I don't want to fall for anyone."

"Ignore the fear Sean. It's meaningless. When you do fall for someone again, you'll want to. I know things are rough for you now, and you're a little gun-shy so to speak, but things won't be like this forever. So get your ass out there, go out with Doug, nail a few hotties and see where life takes you."

"Hmm, why am I not surprised that your advice includes having sex?"

"Hey, sex is one of the great joys of life. Most people are too prudish or too scared to embrace it. They foolishly deny themselves one of the greatest pleasures that exists."

"I'm sure you'll never be that foolish."

"You can bet your balls on that Sean."

"Hey, bet your own, I might need mine!"

Skye laughed.

"It's getting late. I should go. Thanks Skye."

We stood and hugged. Skye's body felt incredible in my arms. I took his advice and didn't fear how that made me feel. I just enjoyed it.

I returned to my room, climbed into bed and fell fast asleep.

Skye—July 2004

I walked into the Dining Room for breakfast ready to start another day at the Graymoor Mansion B&B. I was filling my plate with crepes, strawberries, blueberries, and raspberries when a strikingly handsome man entered the room. He was my height, 6'2", with broad shoulders, a slim waist, dark-brown hair, and brown eyes. I usually went for guys my age or younger, but there was something about this man. My description of him truly does not do him justice. He was probably thirty, but he was decidedly sexy. Oh, I should add he was wearing small, round glasses. I didn't usually go for the studious type, but the glasses gave him a quiet strength and steamy passion hidden behind an intellectual façade. His gaze was penetrating when his eyes met mine. His gaze was dangerous, almost menacing. I felt my heart beat faster as I gazed at him.

"Skye, this is Thad Thomas," Sean said by way of introduction. "Thad, this is Skye Mackenzie. He's our personal trainer and in charge of the Natatorium and Gymnasium."

I shook Thad's hand. I had heard of Thad's vampire novels, although I had never read one. Despite what others thought, I did read, but I didn't have much time for it.

"I'm sure I'll be seeing you later," Thad said. "I always need a short workout after I've been pecking at a keyboard all day."

I stole a quick look at Thad's body while we made idle chitchat. Hidden as it was behind a long-sleeve, button-down shirt and khaki slacks, I couldn't make much out, but something told me I'd like what I'd see if he was naked. There was a stirring in my boxers as I turned from Thad and carried my plate and orange juice to the table.

I took a seat between Marshall and a guest I'd met the day before, a middle-aged librarian who had driven in from Missouri just to stay at Graymoor. She was fascinated by the grisly history of the house and hoped to see a re-enactment of the Graymoor murders. Marshall was scheduled to give her a ghost tour, so I had little doubt she would get her fill of ghosts.

I listened in as Marshall talked with Thad. Marshall had read all of Thad's books—no surprise there. Vampires were right up Marshall's alley. I had never heard Marshall speak of vampires as if they were real, but I guess his interest in the supernatural delved into the fictional world as well. I smiled when I remembered all the monster magazines he toted around during our high-school years. What a freak.

I wondered if I shouldn't give one of Thad's books a try. I didn't share Marshall's interest in the supernatural, but Mr. Thad Thomas intrigued me, and I thought perhaps reading one of his books might give me some insight into what made him tick.

I didn't have time to linger at the breakfast table. I had a busy day ahead. There was all the usual pool and weight-equipment maintenance, and I was still developing programs and materials for use in the gymnasium. Add to that the guests who came to use the facilities, and I stayed quite busy. I was well aware that my job appeared nearly effortless from the outside, but like most jobs, it wasn't quite so simple when one took a closer look. I had little spare time during working hours, so most of my workouts now took place after my day was done. I didn't mind at all. I would rather have spent my time in the gym than anywhere else, except maybe in bed with a hot guy. My thoughts momentarily flowed to Kane. I needed to give him a call soon.

I had plenty of time to think about Thad while I worked. Most of my tasks don't require a lot of concentration. There was something about that guy that intrigued me. Rarely did an older guy excite me. I had a thing for Coach Brewer in high school, and Nick's dads were both extremely hot, but I don't think I'd run across an older man who did anything for me since I was eighteen. Thad was different. I tried to puzzle out why. I'd wanted Coach Brewer and Ethan, because both were not only achingly handsome but also incredibly well built. Nathan was smaller than the other two, but he had an exceptional body as well. Thad looked like he had a nice build hidden under his clothes, but he definitely didn't have a build like Coach Brewer or Ethan. Perhaps he was well-defined, but there was no way to tell, so that couldn't be what had made my heart race when I'd met him. Was it his fame? I didn't think so. The fact that Ross was a famous rock star added another level of arousal to our encounters, but fame itself wasn't an aphrodisiac for me. I could think of tons of very famous guys I wouldn't touch with a ten-foot pole.

Sean or Marshall had mentioned that Thad would be sticking around for a while, several days at least, so I'd probably have plenty of time to figure out what made me hot for Thad Thomas. Even if I couldn't get to the bottom of the little mystery it was no loss. Hot guys are like buses; if you miss one, another will be along in a few minutes—well, at least if you're me.

***

Each day was so full it passed quickly. I did everything from maintaining the weight equipment and pool to teaching beginners how to lift weights and swim. I was running my own miniature YMCA. I almost couldn't believe I was getting paid!

I remembered working at Wahlberg's Farm Store in high school. Time passed so slowly in that old store. There were few customers and not much to do. If it hadn't been for Oliver I would've died of boredom. It wasn't a bad job to be sure, but it paled by comparison to my current career. I used to dream of working in an Abercrombie & Fitch. What an idiot I was. Had I known what life could be like, I would have been dreaming of my current job instead. I guess I'd grown wiser over the years.

Guests were in and out all morning. The pool and hot tub were the most popular features of the Natatorium and Gymnasium, but quite a few guests were interested in working out. Any time a boy came in I knew he would head for the weight equipment. There was just something about barbells and curl machines that drew boys, like honey draws flies. My nephew Colin, who was now thirteen, had his own weight equipment at home. His mom feared he might hurt himself because he was so young, but Colin knew what he could and could not do. Of course, Colin had been under the influence of his Uncle Skye since he was a toddler. He'd told me more than once he wanted to look just like me when he grew up. He probably had been the only first grader at Verona Elementary School who did perfect pushups and ab crunches. Colin was now in the eighth grade and had already progressed to working out with free weights. He was just beginning to put on serious muscle now that puberty had set in. He was already the best-built thirteen-year-old around. Little girls were probably already drooling over his well-defined abs.

When guys got older, their interest in working out dropped off. Even most guys my age had already given it up. Most every guy wanted to be buff, but few were willing to put in the effort. The vast majority of those with dreams of a hot body fell by the wayside one by one. Laziness, beer, hectic schedules, work, girlfriends, boyfriends, and so much more killed the dream of a buff bod. The guys who married and had kids had almost no chance at all of staying in shape. A few managed it, but most didn't even seem to care after they got hitched. That's one reason I didn't care for married guys; they almost always carried a gut. Of course, the main reason I didn't sleep with married guys was because they were married. I wasn't the relationship kind of guy, but I did respect commitment. It's too bad more people didn't. See, I'm not so bad after all, am I?

Anyway, whenever a guy under twenty came in, I knew he'd hit the weight machines. I spent a great deal of time showing boys how to work out. The Hiltons were even considering offering a YMCA-like membership, but that would come later. Some days there were so many kids I felt like I was running Camp Skye, but that was okay. I was good with kids. Perhaps that had something to do with the summers I'd spent working as a camp counselor.

Some girls were interested in working out too, and I was just as eager to help them. Most of the girls were more into aerobics than muscle-building, but in my book, any interest in keeping in shape is a good thing—period.

The only problem the munchkin crowd caused me was when one of them developed a crush on me or a simple case of lust. With the girls, it was usually limited to staring when they thought I wasn't looking and giggling. Most of the boys who had a crush on me were the same, minus the giggling (usually), but some were more aggressive. I didn't mind when a boy asked me to flex my bicep so he could feel it, but some wanted to feel more than my arm. A couple had asked to feel my chest, but that's where I drew the line. Sure, letting a twelve-year-old boy feel my pecs didn't constitute sexual activity, but it was too close for comfort. During my college years I'd become an expert in turning down advances without being rude or hurting feelings, and I sometimes had to put that into practice in the gym. Of course, it wasn't just the under-aged that made unwanted advances.

It wasn't too difficult to fend off my under-aged admirers. Most of them just hung around a lot watching me, following my movements with yearning glances. Sometimes I had to fight not to laugh. Kids aren't the best at hiding their feelings, and a few of them practically drooled over me. I knew they thought they were being quite secretive, but they were terribly obvious.

Thankfully, most had no such interest in me and were only there to swim or work out. I found their innocence refreshing. I enjoyed guiding kids along a path that had benefited me so much during my own life. I knew I'd never have kids of my own, and that was fine by me. The times I spent with my nephew and the kids who visited the Natatorium were quite enough.

Just after one of my junior weightlifters departed, I heard a slightly familiar voice behind me.

"Hey Skye."

I turned.

"Oh, hi...Craig, right?"

"Yeah."

Craig smiled. Craig was the high-school boy I'd rescued from three bullies in the park in the not-so-distant past. He was an attractive boy with shaggy black hair, blue eyes and a shy smile. He was nearly my height, but very slim.

"Um, I was wondering something Skye. Next year, I'm taking my senior art classes, and then I'll be applying to art schools. I'm putting together a portfolio to show to schools, and I was wondering if you'd pose for me."

"Pose for you?"

"Yeah, I'm working on a multimedia approach—modeling the same subject in different media. Do you have a minute? I can show you what I mean."

"Sure."

I followed Craig to one of the ornate marble-and-cast-iron tables that surrounded the pool. He set an oversized album on the table and opened it.

"This is a study I did of a daisy," Craig said, slowly turning the pages.

First, there was a photograph of a daisy. It was of such high quality it looked like it should be framed and hung on a wall. Then, the very same daisy was rendered in a pencil drawing, watercolor and paint. There were photos of the same daisy featured in a collage and a sculpture.

"You did all this?"

"Yes," Craig said, smiling. "What I want to show the art schools is that I'm not limited to one media. I can sculpt as well as I can draw and paint as well as I can photograph."

"Well, hello Leonardo da Vinci. You're a Renaissance man Craig. I especially like that mosaic."

"I'm hardly a Leonardo, but thanks. The actual mosaic looks better than the photo, but it won't fit in a portfolio."

"So you were saying you wanted me to model?"

"Yeah. I've been carefully choosing subjects for studies, working my way up to a live model, and I think I'm ready. I would love to work on you, so to speak," Craig said, reddening just a bit. "You're exceptionally handsome and extremely...strong. I think you'd make the perfect model."

"I'm flattered."

"I know you're probably busy, but I could do a lot of the work from photos. It would still take a few hours here and there, but it wouldn't all have to be at once. I know it's a lot to ask, but I know I'm not going to find another guy who would be as perfect for it as you. There is one thing you might not like and it's not a must, but if you're willing, I would like you to pose in the nude."

"Hmm, I've never been asked to model before, not for an actual artist. I was asked to model for an Internet site, but that was porn."

"Really?"

"Yeah, and I have no desire to do porn."

"What I have in mind isn't porn. It's something like...that," Craig said, pointing to a statue of a beautiful nude by the side of the pool.

"Okay. I'll do it," I said.

"Really?"

"Sure. It might be an interesting experience."

"Thanks, I really appreciate this. I didn't think you would say yes, but I had to try. This is going to be great! With you as my model, I know I'll get into art school!"

"I think it's your talent that will get you into a good art school."

"Yeah well, true, but you're going to make it possible for me to truly show off my talent. Leonardo searched all the time for beautiful youths. His work wouldn't have been half as impressive if his subjects were mundane."

"You're going to make me conceited, although my friends believe my ego can't get any bigger."

Craig laughed.

"So you won't mind posing in the nude?"

"No. I'm not at all shy about my body."

"If I looked like you, I wouldn't be either."

"You shouldn't be shy Craig. What I see looks very nice."

Craig blushed.

"Wow, I'm so excited! Oh, before I forget, who do I see about getting permission to take some photos inside Graymoor? I'd also like to do some drawings. This place is awesome."

"Sean will be the one to ask—or his parents. They own the place. I'm sure they'll have no objection. Hold on a second, and I'll see if I can track Sean down."

I stepped into my office and picked up the phone. I tried Sean's office first, but there was no answer. Next, I dialed his cell phone. Sean was in the kitchen working out a supply order with Martha.

I returned to Craig and gave him directions to the kitchen.

"If you get lost, just wander around until you find someone and they'll point you in the right direction."

"Thanks."

Craig and I exchanged phone numbers and e-mail addresses so we could arrange my first modeling session. I wondered what Sean would say if he knew I'd obtained yet another cute guy's phone number. Craig went in search of the kitchen and I returned to my work.

***

Thad entered the gym in the early evening hours. He was wearing long basketball shorts and a gray t-shirt that read, "Culver Military Academy." My heart beat a little faster as I gazed at him even though his attire wasn't much more revealing than what he'd been wearing that morning. It was his dark eyes that got to me—so stern, knowing and sexy. I felt as if he could pierce right through me with them.

"Is there anything I can do for you?" I asked.

"No. I keep it simple. I like to work out a little to offset sitting still so much of the day. Of course, I haven't been sitting much today. Marshall has been showing me around Graymoor."

"Incredible, isn't it?"

"To say the least. I had no idea a private home this large even existed. It's amazing. The history of the house makes it truly fascinating."

"Marshall is definitely the one to tell you all about that," I said. "He knows more about Graymoor than anyone else."

"My hand nearly cramped from taking notes."

"Well, I'll let you get to your workout. Just let me know if you need anything."

I stuck close to Thad while he worked out. The sight of his muscles flexing made me want to run my hands all over his body. I wanted to do plenty more too, but I tried not to think about that too much or the front of my shorts would give away my interest.

I watched Thad for signs of interest in me. He looked me over, but I didn't catch any glimmer of lust. I'd grown rather adept at detecting lust directed toward me, but I wasn't picking up much of anything from Thad. I stripped off my shirt and began my own workout. I'd seduced more than a few guys in gyms that way. Thad took only slightly more notice of my body once I was shirtless. He wasn't going for the bait as I'd hoped.

Thad didn't linger when he'd finished his workout. I was frustrated and in need of release. I'd hoped to seduce him, but no dice, so I was left with a throbbing groin and no one to help me with it. Ross was gone. It probably wasn't wise to get together with Sean again. My thoughts immediately went to Kane. Yeah, it was time to give the sexy new gardener a call even though my thoughts kept going back to Thad. I couldn't quite get him out of my mind.

Ralph

"Sam is pregnant," Jordan said as he put down the phone. We were in the penthouse of the Graymoor Mansion in Phantom World, not to be confused with the original Graymoor Mansion in Verona. We'd been expecting a call from Sam all day, and were nervously awaiting the news. We'd both jumped when the phone rang and Jordan had rushed to answer it. I could hardly bear the anticipation as he'd spoken to Sam, and I couldn't tell the outcome until he spoke the words.

Jordan smiled from ear to ear.

"We're going to be parents," I said, grabbing Jordan and hugging him.

"This is the most incredible feeling in the world. I never thought anything could match standing on stage performing, but this...this surpasses it."

"Are you going to tell your mom?" I asked.

Jordan and I had already discussed whom and when to tell about our unborn child. We'd decided to hold off until late in the pregnancy to tell most of those around us. Jordan and I feared the press would hound us as soon as word got out. Leaks were inevitable, but I definitely wanted to tell my parents as soon as possible. Jordan was more indecisive when it came to his mother. They didn't have a bad relationship, but it was somewhat distant. Stephanie had never quite gotten over the whole situation with Jordan's father. She was truly in love with Taylor, and discovering that he loved Mark and not her was a blow that no doubt still brought her pain. Taylor's suicide had lessened her anger, but she'd never quite forgiven him. Jordan was the spitting image of his dad, so things became more and more difficult as Jordan grew to resemble the boy who Stephanie felt had betrayed her. I knew Jordan wanted to share this moment with his mom, but she came with a lot of baggage.

"Are you going to tell your mom?" I asked again when met with silence.

"Yeah," Jordan said. "I am."

Once the decision was made Jordan moved quickly, just as he did with so many things. He was on the phone minutes later.

I pulled a Diet Sunkist from the refrigerator and walked to the large picture window that looked out over Phantom World. The park was filled with guests having a blast. I almost couldn't believe my life sometimes. I was "married" to a rock star who owned his own theme park, among other things. Jordan and I traveled the world, toured museums, and explored the best the world had to offer. My life was like a waking dream, and yet all that wasn't important. Jordan was my world. When it came right down to it, the fame and money meant nothing. It was Jordan I loved. That's the way it had always been.

"She'll be here the day after tomorrow," Jordan announced when he joined me at the window several minutes later.

"She's coming here? What did you tell her?"

"That I had some very big news and that I wanted to see my mom."

Jordan stepped up beside me, and I put my arm over his shoulders. I leaned over and kissed his cheek.

"I don't think I can get any happier than this," I said.

Jordan beamed. He'd never looked more beautiful.

"When do you want to tell your parents?" he asked.

"Can we tell them this evening?"

"Of course we can."

"Let me make a phone call. I'll invite us to supper!"

Jordan laughed.

I left him alone while I called my parents to make sure they weren't busy that evening. Mom said she would be delighted to have us over for supper. She detected the excitement in my voice and asked about it, but I passed it off as merely the result of a great day.

We killed some of our leisure time by visiting with Avery, who was working in the park. We said nothing about our big news. While we considered Avery a friend, he was one of those who would be told about our child shortly before his or her birth.

"Have you heard from Sean?" I asked Avery as we sat around in the penthouse sipping drinks.

"Yeah, he's still busted up over Nick, but I think he's doing better."

"He was barely holding it together when we were in Verona," Jordan said. "I was hoping he and Nick would be back together by now, but I guess it's going to take longer than a few weeks."

"I don't think they'll be getting back together at all. Sean was really hurt. I think he'd be too afraid to get back with Nick even if he wanted to do so. The last time I talked with him he was still steamed."

"Ross truly needs his ass kicked sometimes," Jordan said.

"Ross was just being Ross," Avery said.

"I don't think he's capable of thinking ahead," Jordan said.

"Isn't that the truth?" I said.

"Sean has gone out with a guy from Plymouth a couple of times," Avery said.

"Really?" asked Jordan.

"Yeah. Skye talked him into seeing someone new. Sean is cautious, but he also seems excited."

"That's great," Jordan said. "I really hope he'll get back with Nick, but if not, it will be great if he can find someone else. I hate to think of Sean being alone."

"I think this new guy, Doug, is giving a much needed boost to Sean's self-esteem. It was a real blow to Sean's self-image when Nick cheated on him. I think this new guy makes him feel attractive."

"Sean should feel attractive. He has a lot going for him."

"True, but I don't think he can see it sometimes. We're all like that, I guess."

"Except Skye," I said.

Avery laughed. "I see you spent some time with Mr. Buff Boy."

"Yeah. He's gorgeous," I said.

"And he knows it," Avery said, grinning.

"How could he not?" Jordan said.

"I try not to hang around Skye too much when girls are around," Avery said. "I don't want to look pathetic by comparison."

"Hey, you're a very attractive guy," Jordan said.

"Not compared to Skye. Thank God he's gay."

"Have you seen Toby?" Jordan asked. "We should spend some time with him while we're around."

"He'd love that," Avery said.

Our conversation flowed into other areas. We must have spent two hours talking with Avery. We enjoyed catching up with each other.

***

Mom and Dad's farm was not far distant from Phantom World, much less than an hour's drive. Mike saw us safely out of Phantom World and reluctantly allowed us to travel to my parents' farm without his protection.

Mom and Dad hugged us both upon our arrival. Jordan was treated like a son-in-law or second son. For all practical purposes, Jordan and I were a married couple. Indiana law discriminated against us and would not allow us an official marriage, but as far as my family and we were concerned, the legality of it was meaningless. God acknowledged marriages, and that was good enough for us. We had given some thought to a commitment ceremony, but Jordan and I were so committed to each other such a ceremony seemed redundant.

Jordan had long ago insisted that legal documents be drawn up giving us each visitation rights if the other was hospitalized, and so on. We had used legal means to obtain virtually everything that the prejudiced tried to deny us. I didn't like to think about it, but when one of us died, the other would inherit nearly everything, just as if we were married. While Jordan had a far greater fortune in his name than I, vast sums of money were held solely in my name just in case. That was another of Jordan's ideas. I just hoped that I'd be the first to go.

Mom had promised not to go to any trouble, but she began frying catfish and French fries as soon as she had welcomed us home. There was a chocolate cake cooling on the counter waiting to be frosted.

Jordan and I gave no hint of our big announcement as we sat and talked with Mom and Dad. Jordan told Mom about our latest antiquing expedition while Mom moved about the kitchen. Mom liked antiques, but she was amazed that things she and Dad had used when they were first married were now collectible. Jordan and I usually went for older stuff than that. Our latest acquisition was a beautiful brown stoneware pitcher that was probably 150 years old.

I set the table and got drinks ready for everyone to save Mom a bit of work. She would run herself ragged preparing a meal if allowed to do so. In just a few minutes everything was set, and a platter of steaming catfish and French fries sat in the center of the table. We all helped ourselves and were soon too busy eating to talk much.

After supper, Mom frosted the cake while I made hot tea. Soon, the four of us sat around the kitchen table eating dessert and talking yet more. Jordan was telling my parents about Phantom World and how it was beginning to pay for itself. The park had made a considerable profit already. It would take some time, but Jordan, Ross and Kieran would get back all the money they had put into it in only a few years time. The three had pooled their funds to buy the park and make improvements, so not a cent had to be borrowed. That saved them a fortune in itself.

When there was a lull in the conversation, Jordan looked over to me, raised his eyebrows and smiled. The time had come.

"Mom, Dad, Jordan and I have some news that I think you'll be happy to hear."

"You're going to visit more often?" asked Mom, half teasing.

"Very likely, but that's not the news. What we have to tell you is much bigger."

"Now I'm curious," Dad said.

"You're going to be grandparents. Jordan and I are going to have a baby."

"A baby?" my mom asked, shocked, but delighted.

"Yes."

"But how?" Dad asked, looking back and forth between Jordan and me.

"I'm pregnant," Jordan said. "We didn't think it could happen, but..."

Mom laughed.

"A good friend of ours is having the baby for us," I said. "Well, it will be hers too as well. I don't think you've met Samantha, but I'm sure you'll want to now. She's awesome and the nicest person you can imagine."

"I...I don't know what to say," Mom said. "I'd given up on the idea of grandchildren. This is...*wonderful*!"

"I thought you'd be happy. How about you Dad?"

"I do hope it's going to be a boy. I'd like a grandson."

"Well, we did our best," Jordan said.

"So this Samantha...she's pregnant?"

"Yes," I said. "We didn't want to say anything until we knew for sure, but we just found out today."

"This is a delicate question, but which of you is the father?" Mom asked.

"We don't know, and we intend to keep it that way. It doesn't matter which one of us is the biological father. This child is going to be ours," Jordan said.

"I'm so happy for you both," Mom said, taking our hands across the table. Tears began to run down her face. She got up and kissed both Jordan and me on the cheek.

"We're very excited," Jordan said. "The idea of being a dad is overwhelming. I don't think either of us feels ready, but if we waited until we felt ready we'd never have a family."

"A lot of planning went into this decision," I said. "Jordan and I never mentioned the possibility of kids to you because we didn't know if it would happen. We didn't know if we'd adopt or try to have our own. We didn't want to get your hopes up. We were going to wait until things were further along, but we just couldn't wait to tell you."

"Have you told your mother?" Mom asked Jordan.

"Not yet, but she's flying in and will be here in a couple of days. We're going to tell her then."

"I bet she'll be so happy!"

"I hope so," Jordan said with a touch of sadness.

"Oh, I want to go shopping," Mom said. "We'll need a lot of things for when you come to visit with the baby."

"I don't think we need to go out right now Lois," Dad said. "We have a little time." Dad grinned.

"Just wait until your grandmother finds out. She'll be a great-grandmother!"

"You know, I hadn't thought of this before, but we should tell your grandparents and "Uncle" Tristan, Jordan."

"Yeah, that's right," Jordan said, smacking his head. "You know, I hadn't thought of that. I've just been so excited since we found out!"

"This is wonderful news!" Mom said.

"You and Dad are the first to know. We're not telling any of our friends yet, so this is to be a family secret."

"I promise. I'll only tell your grandparents."

"Good, let's keep it at that for now. Don't tell anyone else, not even other family members. If too many people know, word will get out, and then we'll have the press to deal with." It was true: being married to a rock star did create a few problems. When the press found out Jordan was going to be a father, it would be all over the news and unfortunately the tabloids as well.

"I'm glad I'm taking some time off," Jordan said. "We're going to have to make another trip to Verona to give my grandparents the news."

"Hey, I'm up for it."

"So what about Samantha?" Mom asked. "How will she fit in once the baby is born?"

"Sam is going to attend college and hasn't quite decided what she wants to do with her life. We'll have joint custody, but the baby will be living with us permanently. We're going to make sure there is always a place for Sam in the baby's life. Sam will probably be living with us part of the time."

"We don't want our son growing up without his mother," Jordan said.

"You two seem to have thought this all out. Son, huh? What makes you so sure the baby won't be a girl?" Mom asked.

"Well," Jordan said, smiling, "I have to admit I'm hoping for a boy."

"I think you two will make great parents," Mom said.

We talked long into the night with Mom and Dad—all about the baby, of course. Even though Phantom World wasn't far, Jordan and I decided to spend the night in our cabin instead. We made the short drive there after bidding my parents goodbye.

"I still can't believe all this is real," Jordan said as he lay by my side, the candlelight illuminating his handsome features.

"It's real; you're going to be a daddy."

"So are you."

"This does feel weird," I said. "I feel like I'm still sixteen, and now I'm going to be a father. It's just...*wow!*"

"Wow is right."

"I love you, Jordan."

"I love you too, Ralph."

Jordan and I wrapped our arms around each other, lay back and fell asleep.

***

Jordan tapped his fingers against the glass of the penthouse window as he looked out over Phantom World. He'd been pacing the floor for half an hour and only stopped to peer out at the theme park from time to time.

"You're turning into Ross," I said.

"Gee, thanks."

I stepped up behind Jordan and rubbed his shoulders. Jordan moved his head from side to side as my fingers worked the tension out of his body. He turned to me after a few moments and gave me a light kiss.

"She'll be here soon," he said.

Jordan had sent a car to pick up his mom at the airport in Evansville. If her flight was on time, she could walk through the door any minute. I was nervous about meeting Jordan's mother. In all the time Jordan and I had been together, I'd never met her. It was hard to believe, but true. Jordan saw her rarely, although he and his mom kept in touch with infrequent phone calls. Their relationship was a rather distant one.

The door opened and Mike stepped in, carrying bags in both arms. An attractive woman who didn't look much like Jordan followed him. Jordan had obviously obtained most of his features from his dad.

Mother and son hugged each other briefly. Mike took the bags to one of the guest rooms.

"Did you have a good trip?" Jordan asked.

233

"Oh yes, but I'm not fond of flying. I hope this news of yours is worth the trip."

I stood there awkwardly, feeling naked and nervous. I took a deep breath. Jordan and his mom turned to me.

"Mom, this is Ralph. Ralph, this is my mom, Stephanie."

I nervously shook her hand.

"It's very nice to meet you..."

"You can call me Stephanie."

Jordan's mom was neither rude nor unkind, but I sensed that she did not approve of her son's lifestyle or me. I didn't know how long she would be staying with us, but I feared each hour would be an eternity.

Mike slipped out with only a nod to Jordan, and the three of us were completely alone. Jordan led his mom to a large couch and sat beside her. I took a seat in a nearby chair.

"So do I get to hear this news of yours, or are you going to make me wait?"

"I think when you hear what I have to say you'll understand why I didn't want to tell you over the phone."

"You're not sick, are you? You don't have..."

Jordan's mom obviously couldn't bring herself to say the word AIDS, but there was suddenly such fear and concern in her features that I knew she loved Jordan.

"No, Mom, I'm in perfect health. The news is good news."

"Well what is it?"

"You're going to be a grandmother."

"I...don't understand."

"It's a simple concept Mom. Ralph and I are having a child, with the help of one of our female friends."

"But you're...um..."

"Just because I'm gay doesn't mean I can't reproduce, Mom. Samantha—she's the mother—is pregnant."

"I...I don't know what to say."

"I hoped you would be happy," Jordan said with an edge of disappointment in his voice.

"I'm going to be a grandmother," Stephanie said to herself, "a grandmother!"

The barest hint of a smile appeared on her face, and soon it grew.

"Oh, Jordan."

Jordan's mom hugged him again, but this time with far more affection. Jordan smiled, and tears actually ran down his cheeks.

"If you don't mind, I think I'll go out and enjoy the park for a while," I said.

Jordan grinned at me. "I'll see you later Babe."

I made my exit so Jordan and his mom could be alone. I walked out the back of the Graymoor Mansion and then down the hill into the park. Unlike Jordan, I could walk around the park without being recognized. An occasional *Phantom* fan did stop me now and then, but those who did were friendly and calm. I didn't inspire the same screaming and fainting fits as my boyfriend sometimes did. I didn't mind in the least.

I got some cotton candy and strolled around the park to give Jordan and his mom time to talk. Something had changed between them when our news sank in. Something softened in Stephanie. Maybe this baby would bring mother and son closer. Jordan had everything he could wish for except for parents. Jordan's dad had died before he was born, never even knowing he was destined to be a father. Jordan didn't talk about his mom much, but I knew she'd grown distant as he grew up. He'd talked of a happy childhood, but then things began to change. Jordan's mom had never been neglectful, but she had slowly pulled away as he grew older. Then Jordan became famous, and his busy lifestyle meant he saw very little of his mom. That only served to widen the gulf between them. I hoped that was about to change. I loved Jordan and wanted him to be happy.

I spotted Toby working the Ferris Wheel, so I walked over and chatted with him a bit. He seemed in good spirits. I think I would have enjoyed his job. Working in an amusement park seemed like fun. Of course, it probably wasn't as enjoyable as it appeared from the outside, but I was sure it beat working in K-Mart.

Shortly after moving on from the Ferris Wheel, a couple of college-age girls latched onto me. I had nothing to do, so I patiently answered their questions about Jordan and *Phantom*. I went on the Scrambler with the girls, followed by the Ghost Pirates raft ride and the Phantom World Railroad. I actually had quite a good time, and the girls seemed excited to be hanging out with Jordan's partner. I'd long ago grown accustomed to my vicarious fame. It came along with being married to a rock star.

Before I knew it, three hours had passed. Jordan probably wondered where I was, although he would have called my cell phone if he was worried.

"Hey, I have to get going," I told the girls. "I've been having so much fun I've lost track of the time."

"It's been a blast Ralph," said Daphne. "If we gave you our addresses, do you think you could get Jordan to send us an autograph?"

"Hold on," I said. I pulled out my phone and called Jordan. "Hey Babe, can you get away for just a few minutes? There's someone I'd like you to meet. Yeah. Bring a couple of photos."

We spoke for a few moments while the girls watched me with rapt interest.

"That was Jordan you were talking to, right?" asked Daphne, as if she just couldn't believe it.

"Yeah, I'd be in trouble if I called anyone else Babe. I'll take you to meet him, but don't spread it around that Jordan is here, okay?"

"We promise," Cheryl said.

"Okay, follow me. He's going to meet us in the conference room."

I led the girls toward the back of the park. After a few minutes, we passed a sign that read "Employees Only" and entered a long, low building. We walked down the hallway and entered the conference room. Jordan was already waiting on us. I wasn't surprised. His route was much shorter. I had no doubt he used the service tunnels to avoid being spotted. The tunnels were one of the little-known secrets of Phantom World.

"Oh my gosh!" Cheryl said. "It's really you!"

"Hi," Jordan said, extending his hand.

Both girls shook his hand and began talking excitedly, but still managed to stay fairly calm. There was no screaming. Daphne and Cheryl were *Phantom* fans, but not obsessed fans. I'd gotten to know them well enough in the short time I was with them to know it was safe to bring them to meet Jordan.

"How about a picture?" I asked, since Daphne was carrying a camera with her.

I took photos while the girls posed with Jordan, both separately and together.

"Could we get pictures with you too Ralph?"

Jordan took his turn behind the camera and then signed the photos he'd brought for the girls.

Daphne and Cheryl told Jordan how much they loved his music, and he spent a few minutes talking with them.

"We should go," Daphne said after a bit. "I'm sure we've taken up too much of your time already."

"I do have to get back," Jordan said. "It's been very nice talking to you."

"I'll walk you out," I said.

I led the girls outside while Jordan waited on me. We said our goodbyes, and then I returned to my boyfriend.

"So, that's what you've been doing for the last three hours: hanging out with girls, huh?"

"Yeah, we had a blast! Did you have a good talk with your mom?" I asked as he headed down the hall and downstairs to the service tunnels.

"Yeah we did. Thanks for giving me some time alone with her."

"No problem. I know when to get lost."

"We talked through a lot of things. I think things are going to be better between us, but we still have a long way to go. There's no way to work through all of our issues in a few hours, but I have a good feeling about this. I think we'll also be seeing a lot more of Mom when the baby comes. She's very excited."

Soon we were back inside the penthouse. It was our little private world hidden away within Phantom World. Few even knew of its existence.

Stephanie came out of her room when we returned, and we all had a seat. The disapproving edge was gone from Stephanie's gaze, just like that.

"Are you nervous about the baby Ralph?" she asked.

"Yeah. This is something completely new to me. Babies really should come with instructions."

Stephanie laughed. "I'm only a phone call away if you need help or advice, and sometimes I'll be closer than that."

"I know I speak for Jordan when I say you're always welcome to be with us, wherever we are. I hope we'll be seeing a lot more of you. Now that I've met you, I'd like to get to know you better."

"I think that can be arranged," Stephanie said, "although I know you two lead busy lives. I won't make a nuisance of myself."

"We're going to be less busy," Jordan said. "We're going to cut back so we'll have more free time when the baby comes."

"That's what you think," said Stephanie, laughing. "I remember a baby who didn't want to sleep at nights. You used to keep me up at all hours, Jordan. It's payback time."

"Yeah, Mom has told us some stories," I said. "She said babies are more trouble than you can possibly believe, but they're worth it."

"They certainly are," said Stephanie, gazing at Jordan. "Your father would have been so proud."

Jordan looked at his mom in surprise. I think it was the first time Stephanie had mentioned Taylor in years.

"You look so much like him," Stephanie said. "Of course you're older now than he ever was, but I remember when you were sixteen. You could have been your father's twin. He was so beautiful."

Jordan took his mom's hand. "I know things didn't end well Mom, but Dad loved you. I know he did."

"It's taken me a lot of years, but I'm beginning to realize that. I shouldn't have let my problems with your father come between us. For that I'm truly sorry."

"It's okay Mom. I know things were rough."

"Um, should I leave again?" I asked.

"No, you stay right there Ralph. You're part of the family. Jordan and I have already talked most of this over while you were gone. We're just rehashing a few things. Sometimes, saying 'I'm sorry' once just isn't enough."

Stephanie stayed with us for a few days. Jordan seemed happier than he had ever been. As Jordan had said, they still had a long way to go, but I think they settled a lot of their differences before Stephanie returned home. The healing had definitely begun.

Sean

I led Tobias toward my room. I felt a stirring of guilt for picking up a guy off the Internet, but most of the stirring I felt was in my pants. Still, I wondered if I was doing the right thing. I'd advised Nick to broaden his horizons, and Skye had told me I needed to follow my own advice. I knew he was right, but...it just seemed so...slutty to hook up with a guy I didn't even know.

Another glance at Tobias chased most of my inhibitions away. Tobias was nineteen, about 5'7" and 145. He was from Costa Rica and had curly black hair and sexy brown eyes. He was dark and handsome, and the things we'd talked about online turned me on like mad. I'd met Tobias in Ofarim's just to be safe, and he'd shown up looking better than his photo. He was just as nice and as sexy as he'd been online. It hadn't taken me long to ask him back to my place. I wondered what I'd say if Mom or Dad spotted us. Sometimes I still felt as if I was sixteen.

We made it safely up the stairs to the third floor without seeing a living soul. Skye spotted us before we made it to my room and gave me a knowing grin. I just know I turned crimson. I'd been caught in the act and was sure I'd hear about it later.

Soon, Tobias and I were safely behind my locked door. Tobias turned to me, smiled, pulled me to him, and kissed me on the lips.

Tobias and I made out while our hands roamed. The thrill of anticipation was intense. Here was a guy I'd never been with before. My fingers were beginning to unravel the mystery of Tobias's body, but I had only the vaguest idea of what remained hidden under his clothing. Just as his body was a mystery, so was how he would react to my caresses and to words spoken in passion. This new experience was both frightening and thrilling.

I pulled off Tobias's shirt to reveal his sleek, tanned torso. His skin was so much darker than Nick's, even darker than Skye's. I ran my hands over his smooth skin, feeling the sleek muscles underneath. Tobias pulled my own shirt away and admired my chest and abdomen with his fingers and then his tongue. Tobias made me feel sexy and desirable.

We kicked off our shoes and socks. Our jeans fell to the floor. Soon, my boxers and Tobias' bikini briefs had joined the pile. We sank onto my bed, exploring each other with fingers, lips, and tongues. Our moans began to fill the room, and I lost myself in intense male-to-male sex. I didn't know Tobias. I felt a freedom to explore as I never had with Nick or even Skye. I had no inhibitions. If Tobias found my sexual desires odd or my performance poor, it was okay because I wouldn't have to face him the next day. I never had to see him again unless I wished it or I bumped into him in the grocery store.

My heart raced as we writhed on the bed, our hands and lips seemingly everywhere at once. There was something so basic about sex, so instinctual, that it took place almost without thought. It was pure sensual pleasure. How odd it was that so many denied themselves that pleasure out of a sense of shame. How could something so natural be sinful?

Tobias and I kept at it until both of us had cried out with release. When we finished we even took a shower together. We dressed once more, putting on the clothing that had been so thrilling to take off, and I led Tobias downstairs to the front door. There I bid him goodbye with a kiss and then returned to my room.

I lay back on my bed somewhat aroused by the mere memory of what we'd done. I compared Tobias to Nick and Skye in my mind, not in an effort to decide who was the best but merely noting the differences in personality and technique. Each of them was unique, and I found myself wondering if Skye found every guy he was with different from the one before. My experience was quite limited, but it definitely wasn't the same with Tobias as it had been with Skye or Nick. I guess I should have expected that. They were individuals after all.

Now that my passion had cooled, the sense of guilt returned. I pushed it aside. It was groundless. I'd done nothing wrong. I did feel slightly cheap for hooking up with someone off the Internet, but how else was I to explore? All the possible meeting places that came to mind, such as the library, the grocery, or the park were no good. It might take forever to meet someone there. I wasn't getting any younger. I was already twenty-three.

Still, "hooking up" didn't seem like me. Sure, I'd hooked up with Ken before I met Nick, but somehow this seemed different. I felt like a stranger to myself. I didn't know if I liked the feeling or not.

I wondered if there wasn't a better and safer way to meet guys. Surely some of the gay guys I knew could point me in the direction of someone I'd never met. Maybe we could create a Yahoo Group or have monthly dinners or socials or something. It was tough meeting someone in a small town. I was truly lucky to have met Nick all those years ago.

Thinking of my ex saddened me, so I pushed him from my mind. Instead, I thought of Doug as I lay there. Doug and I had gone out a couple more times but we had yet to have sex. That was okay because sex wasn't the sum total of what I needed to experience with other men. I just needed to be with other guys, at least if I was to follow my own advice.

I missed Nick. I'd been avoiding him, but perhaps it was time to make peace with him. I couldn't stay angry with him forever. I couldn't forget what he'd done but I could forgive him. Our relationship as a couple was over, but that didn't mean we couldn't still be friends.

The bed & breakfast was operating smoothly. We had expanded from eight to twelve rooms. Housing the *Phantom* film crew had turned out to be a blessing in disguise. Every restored room was put to use while *Phantom* was residing in Graymoor, and their stay had given the entire staff and me some much-needed practice. Since they were non-paying guests they weren't demanding and were more forgiving of mistakes. The presence of so many guests also gave us an idea of the size of staff we would need later when all those rooms would hopefully be occupied on a regular basis.

I'd been slowly increasing our staff as needed. The key areas were housekeeping, the kitchen and gardening. With so many carpenters, plumbers and electricians at work restoring Graymoor, we had no need for a regular maintenance staff. If there was a problem, Dad just temporarily put whoever was needed on the task. By keeping the staff adequate but small we were actually turning a small profit. Of course that didn't include the restoration costs. There was no way we'd ever make *that* much money. Our operating profit was extremely small, but I was amazed there was any profit at all. It was a good sign indeed.

When I felt we were ready I'd open up more rooms, and then hopefully our profits would increase. Some staff areas such as gardening required the same number of staff no matter how many guests were in Graymoor. The number of plants and the size of the grounds didn't change based on the number of guests. Skye could probably handle the Natatorium and gym by himself, no matter how many rooms we opened. At most he'd require one assistant. Housekeeping and kitchen staff would need to be increased as we opened more rooms, but at least theoretically the extra expense would be outweighed by the increased income. The problem with the theory is that every available room would not necessarily be occupied. So far, every room was filled every night, but I knew that would change as we opened more rooms. Once we were operating at full capacity, I'd have to calculate how many staff we needed based on how many rooms we could realistically expect to be occupied on a regular basis.

I enjoyed meeting our guests. I checked many of them in personally. Most of our guests so far had come from northern Indiana, southern Michigan, northeastern Illinois and northwestern Ohio. We did get a few from much farther away, which was probably thanks to our website. There were also some locals—those who had lived all their lives in the shadow of Graymoor Mansion and were at last ready to brave the interior. Since guests had been coming and going on a regular basis with no fatalities and no missing persons, I think the locals were becoming a little more comfortable with Verona's most notorious haunted house.

As I predicted, Skye tracked me down the day after I'd slept with Tobias. It was just after lunch. I was coming downstairs after showing a couple to their room, and Skye was entering the front parlor from the kitchen. He grinned when he spotted me.

"Okay, I want all the details. Start talking," he said.

"What makes you think there are any details to share?"

"I'd say the fact that your dick was about ready to rip through your jeans as you were walking to your room is a pretty good indication."

I could feel myself go slightly red. Skye had noticed *that*?

"Okay, we had sex."

"I said details Sean."

"Uh-unh. You just want to see me turn completely red."

"Well, I hope you had a good time."

"Definitely," I said with a yearning lilt to my voice.

"I'm glad you're taking my advice. You're so lacking in experience you're practically a virgin."

"Hey, Nick and I dated for years. Believe me, I'm not a virgin."

"Yeah, but it was all with one guy. Now you're beginning to explore and you like it, don't you?"

"Yeah," I admitted. "I just don't want to take it too far. Last night was awesome, but left me feeling slightly slutty."

"You're going to have to sleep with way more guys before you can consider yourself a slut Sean, and I never advised you to go that far. You don't have to sleep with everyone, just a select few."

"It still feels weird."

"I'm sure it does choirboy, but when you settle down with someone again, and I know you will, these experiences will allow you to be certain he's the one you want. You'll have experienced other guys, and your curiosity will be satisfied. You've heard the saying: curiosity killed the cat? Well, it can kill relationships too."

"Do you think that's what killed my relationship with Nick?"

"That relationship may be on the critical list, but it's not dead yet Sean."

I shrugged my shoulders.

"So what was that guy's name? He was hot."

"Tobias."

"Nice. You have good taste Sean. I wouldn't mind borrowing Tobias myself."

"Feel free. I met him online."

"Are you going to get with him again?"

"I don't know, maybe, probably. That depends largely on whether he's interested in being with me again."

"How could he not be hot stuff? Hey, I need to get going or I'll be late. The guy who runs this place can be a real dick, you know?"

"I've heard that," I said, smiling. "Later Skye."

"Later."

***

Doug and I sat at a table near the fountain in The Park's Edge. This was our fourth date. I suppose date was the right term for it, although we weren't actually dating. Doug was well aware of my recent breakup and my confused state of mind so I was comfortable with him. I knew he had no expectations beyond having a good time.

As we shared an artichoke-dip appetizer, I found myself thinking about kissing Doug. We had kissed already, but we hadn't made out. No tongues were involved. I wondered what it would be like to *really* kiss Doug. I daydreamed about what might come after.

My face darkened as Nick walked by our table. It wasn't the sight of my ex-boyfriend that upset me, but the fact that he wasn't alone. I had never met, but still recognized his companion, a blond hottie I'd seen on gay.com. Worse still, I'd hit on hung-jock-4-u or whatever his screen name was and had been rejected. I wasn't hot enough for him, but Nick obviously made the cut.

"What's wrong?" Doug asked.

"My ex just walked by."

Doug turned his head to follow Nick and what's-his-name.

"Which one?"

"The one with dark-blond hair."

"He's a nice-looking guy."

"Yeah, too good-looking for me. Look at the guy he's with. He should be on the cover of a magazine."

"His companion isn't that good looking Sean, and I could take your comment as an insult."

"What do you mean?"

"If I was insecure, I could think you feel safe going out with me because I'm not good-looking."

"No! I didn't mean it that way at all Doug. You are good-looking. I'm sorry if..."

"I said I *could* take your comment as an insult, not that I did," Doug said, grinning.

"You're toying with me."

"It's my sadistic side. I just wanted to see you squirm."

Nick looked up and spotted me gazing at him. I quickly looked away.

"You don't look very happy," Doug said.

"Sorry, it's just that I haven't seen Nick since we broke up. Bad memories."

I wasn't telling Doug the whole truth. To be honest, I was angry and jealous. Nick was out with another guy. How could he do that? I reminded myself that we were no longer a couple and that I had suggested he see other guys. Seeing him actually do it was unpleasant, however, and deepened my suspicions that I hadn't been hot enough for Nick.

"We can go somewhere else if you're uncomfortable," Doug said.

"No, that's okay, but that's very considerate of you to suggest it. I'm sorry you have to deal with my baggage."

"We all carry around some of that. If only we could each lose our baggage as easily as an airline does."

"Isn't that the truth?"

I did my best not to look at Nick while Doug and I had supper, although I was curious as to whether or not Nick was watching us. I wondered what Nick was thinking. Was he jealous, angry, sorry he'd ever cheated on me, or did he just not care? I was fairly successful at keeping my attention focused on Doug and our meal. We were sharing barbequed ribs and coconut tempura shrimp, and they were beyond delicious.

We opted to skip dessert because both of us were too full. Having an appetizer at The Park's Edge was usually a mistake. The portions were huge, and even an appetizer could be a meal in itself.

"Let's go for a walk," I said when we'd finished. "We can walk to Graymoor and I'll show you around."

"What about my car?"

"I can drive you over later. It's such a nice night I want to walk under the stars a bit."

We walked in silence, just enjoying each other's company. Despite my best efforts, my thoughts kept drifting back to Nick. Had he known hung-jock-whatever for long or had they just met? Had they had sex together, and if so, had they gone all the way? Were they dating? Had Nick already replaced me with a new boyfriend?

I had plenty of questions, but no answers, and I wasn't going to get anywhere by pondering Nick's relationship with the buff blond. Thinking about it would only upset me. Nick's life should not concern me at all, so I did my best to shove him out of my mind.

"Whoa, that is big," Doug said when we reached Graymoor. Only a dark outline of the mansion was visible, but it was enough to give an idea of the vast size of my home.

"I told you."

"You know, when you said you'd lived here for years but hadn't been in all the rooms yet, I thought you were kidding."

"Oh no, Graymoor is not only vast, it has some bizarre architectural elements. It's very easy to get lost in many parts of the house. The hallways are labyrinthine in places, and I swear they change. Some of the rooms seem to disappear at times too. There are rooms I entered once years ago and have yet to find again, even though I've searched for hours. Some believe the house itself is alive, and as fantastic as that seems, I must admit it wouldn't surprise me greatly to find out it's true. Now, I bet I've freaked you out."

"No, I'm not that easy to freak out."

Doug and I walked across the lawn and entered through the massive front door of Graymoor Mansion.

"This is the parlor," I said, "and also our lobby."

"It looks like a hotel lobby."

"I've always thought so, although it was built as a private residence and was never used as a hotel before this summer."

"Your family owns all this?" Doug asked. "It must have cost millions. The furniture alone is worth a fortune."

"Graymoor Mansion is Verona's most notorious haunted house. If fact, my friend Marshall believes it to be one of the most haunted spots in the country, if not *the* most haunted. The house had such a bad reputation that my parents were able to buy it for practically nothing several years ago. Of course, it was a dilapidated wreck then. The restoration has costs millions, and it isn't finished, but a silent investor is footing the bill. My family doesn't have that kind of money—not even close."

"Your investor must be mega-rich."

"I'm sure you've heard of Jordan, the lead singer of *Phantom*?"

"Of course."

"He's the one paying for the restoration of Graymoor."

"I didn't think even he had that much money."

"Apparently, in addition to being a awesome musician Jordan is also rather talented with financial investments. He's been able to take the profits from his share of *Phantom* and multiply them many times over."

"Have you met him?"

"Of course. Actually, I've known him for years."

"Oh wait, I read something about *Phantom* filming a video here."

"Yeah, quite recently. The B&B will get tons of free publicity out of it. Let me show you around."

I took Doug through the Dining Room, a sitting room, the main study just off the parlor, the Solarium, and finally the Natatorium. A special treat awaited Doug there, because Skye was swimming. He climbed out of the pool as we entered, water cascading down his smooth muscular body. His swimsuit clung to his skin, revealing quite a lot. I noticed Doug check Skye out.

"Doug, I'd like you to meet my friend Skye. He's in charge of the Natatorium and the gymnasium. Skye, this is Doug."

"Sean has told me quite a bit about you," Skye said.

"He's mentioned you as well."

"What are you guys up to?" Skye asked.

"We had supper at The Park's Edge, and now I'm giving Doug a little tour of Graymoor."

"You'll have to come back in the daylight. The Natatorium looks completely different during the day, although it's beautiful at night."

"It's extraordinary," Doug said.

From the way Doug was looking at Skye, I had the feeling he would have said the same about him. When we departed a few minutes later, I learned I was correct.

"Oh my God," Doug said as soon as we were out of earshot, "I have never met a guy that gorgeous in my entire life. I'm not one for casual hookups, but if your friend snapped his fingers I'd come running."

"Skye has that effect on most people."

"The women must go wild over him."

"They do, but Skye prefers men."

"You mean he's gay? No way!"

"Why does that come as such a shock?"

"I don't know. I guess it just seems too good to be true."

"He's not perfect, that's for sure, but Skye is awesome, and I'm not just talking about his appearance. He has been standing up for gay boys since he was in high school. Anyone who harasses gays around here has to answer to Skye, and he has no reservations about kicking ass. Verona is much safer for gays because of him."

"He looks like he could deliver a serious ass-kicking."

"I've seen him do things you wouldn't believe. Some of the things he has done are like something out of a movie."

"Like what?"

"I've seen him jump through a picture window, without getting cut. I've seen him take out five opponents and walk away with little more than a scratch. I've seen him move so fast he's just a blur. You have to see him fight to believe it."

"He sounds like a superhero."

"I think that description is closer to the truth that you might imagine."

I hadn't realized it, but while we were talking I'd been steadily leading Doug to my room. I was almost shocked to look up and see my own door.

"This is my room," I said.

We went inside.

"Wow, this is nice. Are the guest rooms like this?"

"Yeah."

"This isn't a B&B, it's a luxury hotel."

"Jordan spared no expense in restoring the place, that's for sure."

"I want to live here!"

"I don't think we're that close to getting married yet," I teased. Doug grinned.

"You know what I mean."

"Yes, and thank you."

Doug sat on the edge of my bed.

"I've had a really nice time tonight Sean."

"Yeah, me too, and...it doesn't have to end just yet."

Did I just say that? I thought to myself. It sounded like an overused pickup line.

Doug smiled.

"This is the fourth time we've gone out," Doug said. "I don't really know where we stand though. I like you a lot Sean. You've become a good friend in a short time. I know you're not looking for a relationship. I'm not sure that I am either. What I mainly want is a friend, and if something more than that develops, then okay."

"So what are you saying? Am I being rejected after such a pathetic pickup line?"

Doug laughed. "That *was* a bit pathetic, but that has nothing to do with what I'm saying. As to whether or not I'm rejecting you, that depends on what you're after."

Doug gazed at me, putting me on the spot.

"Well, I'm not exactly sure. You may or may not believe this but I didn't bring you to my room with an ulterior motive. I do find you rather attractive, and I'd be lying if I said I wasn't interested in getting more intimate. I'm not quite sure how much intimacy I'm ready for yet. I like you a lot, and I like what we have together, so I don't want to mess it up, but...I would like a little more time."

"Well," Doug said, "would you be satisfied, at least for now, if we just made out and went no further than that?"

"Yeah," I said, grinning shyly and perhaps stupidly. "That would be good."

"Then come here Sean," Doug said, patting the bed beside him.

I walked to him and sat down. I turned to face him, and we leaned toward each other. Our lips met, but this time instead of a simple kiss, our lips parted and we became passionate. After a few moments our tongues began to explore.

We climbed onto the bed and held each other close while we kissed. We took no more than our shoes off and our hands didn't wander beyond our backs and chests, but our make-out session was intense. Part of the time we held each other so close, I could feel Doug's body against mine. Part of the time we kept some distance between us, but continued to let our tongues entwine. It was sexy, steamy and arousing. It made me want to go further, but I contented myself with making out with Doug. We kissed for over an hour before our lips parted for the last time.

Instead of driving Doug to his car I walked him back, and then he dropped me off at Graymoor. I sighed with contentment as I went back inside.

Skye

Craig and I climbed the main stairway of Graymoor to reach the study where he'd chosen to work. Sean had graciously granted him permission not only to sketch anywhere in Graymoor, but also to use the study for our sessions. It worked out perfectly for me. I didn't even have to leave the mansion to meet Craig.

"Sean even gave me a key," Craig said as we entered and he locked the door behind him. "This will ensure no one walks in on us."

An easel stood at the ready, as did a small artist's table covered with wood cases that I supposed held Craig's art supplies. Two large lights on stands were already sitting in the room as well. Craig set down the camera bag and tripod he'd carried in from his car.

"I'm going to have you pose here," Craig said, indicating a space in front of a large hunter-green velvet curtain. "The curtain will be the perfect backdrop. I want to start with photos since I'll be doing some of my work from them. I really appreciate that you're posing for me, so I want to take up as little of your time as possible."

"It's no problem," I said. "I can give you two hours this evening. I'll have to leave just before eight."

"Great. I might even have time to start sketching you."

While Craig set up his camera and positioned his lights I stripped naked, neatly folding my shirt, boxers and shorts. I wasn't usually a neatness freak, but I was meeting Kane just after my session with Craig, and I didn't want my clothes wrinkled.

Craig surreptitiously watched me as I stripped. When I pulled off my boxers, he gawked. He turned red when he realized I'd caught him staring.

"I'm sorry, I've just never... You're huge."

"It's okay," I said, grinning. "I never mind when a guy checks me out."

Craig turned crimson.

"Am I *that* obvious?"

"Well, let's just say your interest in me is not a secret."

"I'm so embarrassed."

"Don't be. What is there to be embarrassed about?"

Craig busied himself with his preparations. He had some impressive camera and lighting equipment for a high-school boy. In just a few minutes he was ready for me.

"Okay, if you'll stand right here. Now, I want you to turn like this."

Craig had some trouble demonstrating what he wanted, but seemed fearful of contact.

"You can touch me Craig. Just position me how you want me."

Craig swallowed, gripped my shoulders and guided me into position. Next he moved my arm, running his hand over my biceps in the process. His face reddened again, and I noted the front of his khaki shorts were under considerable strain. I pretended not to notice. The poor guy was embarrassed and flustered enough. It was funny when I thought about it. I was the one standing there naked, and Craig was embarrassed.

Craig grew more at ease as he began to shoot photo after photo. He constantly adjusted my stance, the lighting, or the camera. He shot me from every conceivable angle, even from the top of a small stepladder. As our two hours progressed, I grew more adept at following his instructions until I could deliver what he wanted with ease. I felt as if I was modeling for an Abercrombie & Fitch catalog. I'd given modeling some consideration, but I didn't really know if that's what I wanted to do with my life. Besides, models had only a few short years until they were considered too old. I was twenty-two so the clock was already ticking. What would have been my prime modeling years were quickly drawing to an end. I knew I'd made the right choice. I was happier working at Graymoor than I would have been as a model. Besides, if I had become a model, Sean, Marshall and my other friends would have never let me hear the end of it.

"So, tell me about yourself Craig. I guess you still live at home?"

"Yeah, with my mom and dad. I can't wait to move out, not that it's that bad, but my dad is a control freak."

"Does he know you're gay?"

"Oh, hell no! He gets bent out of shape when information comes through the mail for art schools. He thinks art is effeminate. I've had to buy all my own art supplies, although Mom has secretly helped me out. Dad is determined that I join the family business."

"What's that?"

"Wholesale hardware, the most boring business in the world. Would you want to spend your life selling toilets and bolts to hardware stores?"

"I can't say that would excite me."

"There is no way I'm spending my life doing that just because my dad and granddad did it. No way!"

"Does your father know how you feel?"

"No. He knows I'm interested in art, but when I've tried to talk to him about it, he cuts me off and says that I'll come to my senses when I'm older. It's very frustrating."

"Parents can be difficult. I haven't seen my dad in years."

"Where is he?"

"I have no idea. He took off when I was a teenager."

"How about your mom?"

"She lives in town. We get along okay now, but things were rough for quite a while there."

"My mom is okay, but she lets Dad make all the decisions. I wish she had a little more backbone. Of course I'm one to talk; I'm not that good with confrontation."

We talked a good deal more, mostly about art. It wasn't exactly my area, but Craig did most of the talking, telling me about his plans for the future and what he hoped to accomplish with his life. I was impressed. I didn't have that kind of focus when I was his age.

"I've got to take off in ten minutes," I announced finally.

"Okay, just let me get a few last shots. I'll work on the sketches next time. I should be able to do a lot of work right from these photos, although a live model is always better."

The shutter clicked a few more times.

"Okay, that's it Skye. Thank you so much. You were great."

"No problem," I said, walking over to the chair where my clothing sat.

I pulled up my boxers and then my shorts. Even though I'd been standing before him naked for nearly two hours and he now had dozens of nude photographs of me, Craig still couldn't help but check me out. Had Craig not been a little too young, I might have made a move on him. He was cute, he obviously wanted me, and he just as obviously would never have the balls to approach me. He was a bit young, but not illegal, in Indiana at least, but I didn't think I'd be quite comfortable having sex with someone even just a little under eighteen. I wanted to help Craig, but I feared that adding sex into our forming relationship might unbalance it. Besides, I had Kane. I didn't need a high-school boy.

"Just give me a call when you want to schedule another session, or catch me in the Natatorium."

"I will, and thanks again Skye."

"You're welcome. See you later."

"Bye."

I headed straight for my room. I'd barely entered and taken off my sneakers when there was a knock on the door.

"Right on time," I said to myself.

I opened the door, grabbed Kane, and pulled him inside. I shoved him down on the bed, climbed on top of him, and we began to make out. We weren't finished with each other until nearly midnight.

***

Thad showed up to work out daily. I rarely saw him any other time, except occasionally at breakfast, but I could always count on his presence in the gym. Thad intrigued me. He was downright hot. He never took his shirt off but his clothing couldn't quite hide his hard body. I tried to catch him swimming in the pool, but unless he swam late at night, I never saw him in the water. I wondered if his chest was smooth or hairy. My own was smooth, with only the barest hint of hair below my navel. I generally preferred smooth guys, but sometimes a hairy chest could be hot. It all depended on the guy: some looked hot with hair on their chest, and some didn't.

I didn't usually go for guys with glasses either, but Thad's made him look sexy as hell. I wanted Thad more with each passing day.

I had Kane and others to satisfy my needs. I'd even tracked down Tobias, the hottie Sean had slept with, and I hooked up with him. I was always ready to experience a new guy, and there was just something about Thad that made me want him—badly. I had little doubt that once I got him going he'd be wild.

I flirted with most cute guys, but I began to be a little more obvious with Thad. I also timed my workouts to coincide with his. I stripped off my shirt and made sure he got a good look at what I had to offer. I can't even begin to tell you how many guys I'd seduced by taking off my shirt. If they were the least bit interested, it was soon obvious. Thad didn't show the slightest interest. He looked at me, but there was no lust-filled glaze to his eyes and no telltale bulge in his shorts.

I stood close to him while he talked, but he didn't lean in. I'd learned over the years that guys who wanted me would lean toward me if I got close enough. It was like they were drawn to my lips. Thad showed no such interest. In fact, more than once he took a step back. I was not encouraged. Finally, I resorted to a more direct approach.

"Hey, would you like to go out and get something to eat?" I asked as we finished a workout.

"Thanks for offering, but no."

Ouch. Rejection. What made it worse is that Sean chose just that moment to enter. He heard every word.

"Okay, well...have a good night."

"Goodnight, um..."

"Skye."

Thad nodded and left. Sean waited until Thad was out of earshot to speak.

"Did I just see Skye Mackenzie get rejected?"

I stood there a bit dazed. Thad couldn't even remember my name!

"Are you okay Skye?"

"Uh, yeah," I said, looking at Sean, trying to hide my embarrassment.

"Maybe he's not gay Skye."

"Ross told me he is, or that's he's at least bi."

Sean blew out a breath in disgust. "Ross would know. He's a slut."

"Ross said Thad had a thing going with Cedi at one time."

"Really?"

"Yeah."

"I wonder how that happened?"

"They both live in the same town. I have no idea how they got together."

My attention was drawn to the exit. I stared at it hard, as if I could make Thad come back by force of will.

"Why isn't he interested in me?"

I didn't really mean to say it out loud.

"Skye, have you never been rejected before?"

"Well, once, sort of, but that was in high school, and I didn't outright ask; I just hinted, and Coach told me not to go there. Well, twice, kind of...if I count Scott."

"Coach Brewer? You hit on Coach Brewer?"

"Well, kind of. I guess I did. I didn't exactly hit on him, but close. I think he shot me down because of the teacher/student thing, and he was also already taken. Thad...he's single as far as I know."

"Maybe he's not into younger guys."

"I'm not that much younger. I'm twenty-three and he's thirty-one. That's just a difference of eight years. It's not as if he's old enough to be my dad or something. If I was fifteen and he was my age, then I could understand the age difference being a problem, but not now. Besides, Cedi is younger than I am."

"I don't know what to tell you Skye. Personally, I didn't think even a straight guy would turn you down."

I laughed, although I wasn't feeling particularly cheerful at the moment. "You realize if you tell anyone about this I'll have to kill you."

"Of course," Sean said, as if I was actually serious. "Cheer up Skye, worse things can happen. You've probably been rejected less than anyone else in the world. If we count Coach Brewer and Scott, that's only three guys in twenty-three years. Most guys get rejected that much in a week."

"You don't."

"That's because I'm too chicken to ask guys out."

"Hey, how are things going with Doug?"

"Great. We have a blast. We even made out."

"Awesome," I said, but without much enthusiasm.

"Skye, why don't you call up one of your boy toys and get naked with him? You'll forget all about Thad."

"I like that prescription, doctor, but I don't think it will cure me."

"It will at least get your mind off things."

"I guess it's worth a try," I said, smiling.

261

"That's more like the Skye I know."

I bid Sean goodbye and walked to my room. I was tempted to lose myself in hot sweaty sex, but I didn't know if that's what I really wanted. I couldn't get Thad, or his rejection of me, out of my mind, and I didn't know why being turned down bothered me so much. I could have any guy I wanted...except Thad. Was that what was bothering me? Was I upset because he ruined my perfect record? Well, my record was perfect if I didn't count Coach Brewer and Scott. I didn't think it was fair to count them. After all, I just barely hinted with Coach. I didn't actually come onto him. If he'd slept with me, it would probably have been a felony. He had good reason to push my advance to the side. No, I didn't have to count Brendan, but surely I wasn't so shallow that I couldn't take rejection.

I thought about Thad far too much that night and the next day too. I didn't spend *all* my time thinking about him, but he kept slipping into my thoughts. I was confused. I'd never been preoccupied with a guy before. Dozens of different guys had been in my thoughts, but none of them had lingered—until now.

Thad came in for another workout the next afternoon about four. I spoke to him and flirted a little, but my efforts fell dead. Finally, I couldn't stand it anymore. I walked over to him and waited until he finished a set of curls.

"Why don't you want to go out with me?"

"I don't have casual sex."

"Who said anything about sex? I asked you out to dinner."

"Your reputation precedes you. I have no intention of becoming another notch in your headboard."

"What?"

"I've only been in Verona for a few days, but I've heard a lot about you. You stick up for those weaker than you, and that's commendable. You also seduce every guy you find attractive, so again, I have no wish to add another notch to your headboard."

"What's wrong with sex?"

"Nothing is wrong with it, but I don't go out with someone if their sole interest in me is getting in my pants."

My face blanched. For some reason, I felt as if Thad had struck me.

"You've never been rejected before, have you Skye? I bet it's just killing you."

My face darkened. Thad was enjoying this too much.

"That's not what's bothering me."

Thad raised an eyebrow. "So I'm right; you haven't been rejected before."

"I like you," I said. "I don't know what it is, but there's just something about you."

"Find someone else. I'm not interested."

"Go out with me."

"No."

"Just for supper, no sex."

"I've heard that line before, from both men and women."

"When I say something I mean it. No sex, just supper. We'll eat and talk. We'll come back here. You'll go to your room. I'll go to mine. I won't bring up sex once."

"I don't think you're capable of that Skye."

"Try me."

Thad smiled slightly. "Okay," he said, "I'll meet you in the lobby at seven. We'll just see if you can handle it. I don't think you can."

"You drive me crazy, you know that?"

"Quit pretending you don't like it. Now leave me alone so I can finish my workout."

I nodded and walked away. What was it about this guy? He acted so superior, so smug in a quiet, understated sort of way. He was the kind of guy I usually told to fuck off, and yet I pursued him.

So he didn't think I was capable of having supper with him without trying to seduce him? I'd show him. I had self-discipline beyond his imagination. I wouldn't have the body I did without self-discipline. I was a self-made man, and I'd done it through self-denial and self-control. What was so hot about him, anyway? Guys way hotter had fallen to their knees before me. Our date would be a piece of cake.

I dressed casually for supper: a pastel-yellow polo shirt, khaki shorts and leather sandals. Just before seven, I headed downstairs. I met Thad on the stairway. He was wearing a shirt similar to my own, but his was navy blue. He was wearing khaki Docker slacks and Sketchers athletic shoes. How did he manage to look studious, mysterious, and sexy all at the same time?

"Where would you like to go?" I asked. "There's The Park's Edge; if you like Italian, there's Mama's Pizza, and there's The Iron Kettle, which is kind of an old-fashioned country restaurant, sort of a non-franchised Cracker Barrel."

"Pizza sounds good."

"Okay, next question. Would you rather walk or drive? It's only a few blocks."

"It's a nice evening for a walk. I've been cooped up inside all day."

"Were you hanging out with Marshall again?"

"No. Marshall has been very informative about the house, but I spent the day writing."

"Do you often write away from home like this?"

"Not usually, but Graymoor is special. There is nothing like actually experiencing a place to get a feel for it. The mansion itself is giving me a lot of ideas. It's an inspiration."

"So have you met any of the ghosts yet?" I asked.

"I didn't think you were the type to believe in ghosts," Thad said.

"There's a lot you don't know about me. I'm not just a dumb jock."

"I never said you were."

"There was a time I didn't believe in ghosts, but there is nothing like seeing to make one believe, and I've seen some seriously weird shit in Graymoor."

"Such as?"

"Chairs moving by themselves, paintings that seem alive, lamps and candles that light themselves, an organ that sometimes plays when no one is sitting there, and that's not the freakiest stuff."

"I've experienced some of that myself. That's one of the things that's special about Graymoor. There seem to be few truly haunted houses. Many are said to be haunted, but go there and you'll see nothing. I must admit I was skeptical of Graymoor's reputation, but I've learned in the short time I've been here that it's accurate. So tell me about some of the 'freakiest' stuff you've seen."

"I think you're just using me to get material for your book," I said, grinning.

"Definitely."

"Have you seen the reenactment of the Graymoor murders yet?"

"Yes, Marshall arranged that for me. He knew just when and where to be to observe the phenomena."

"Sean was the first to see it. He thought Mr. Graymoor was actually chasing him. He just about crapped his pants."

"I can imagine," Thad said, laughing.

By that time we had reached Mama's Pizza. We entered and were ushered to a quiet booth. I hadn't been in Mama's for a while, as I usually ate at Ofarim's or The Park's Edge, but I liked its dark atmosphere. Everything was still done up in reds, as it had been when the restaurant opened at the end of my high-school years—red carpet, red-and-white-checked table cloths, red candles and even red globes on the hanging lamps over the tables. Something else hadn't changed over the years either.

"Noah, you still work here?" I asked when I spotted him. Noah had started working at Mama's when it first opened.

"Only in the summers and winter breaks now. I'm at IU in Bloomington the rest of the year."

"It's great to see you again."

"You too Skye."

"I'm working at the B&B now. Stop by and see me sometime. I'm sure Sean would love to see you too. Oh, this is Thad," I said, remembering that Thad didn't know everyone in Verona. "Thad, this is Noah Cummings, one of my friends from my high-school days."

"It's nice to meet you," Thad said.

"You too. Do you guys know what you'd like to drink?"

"Diet Coke or Pepsi," Thad said.

"Same here."

"Okay, two Diet Cokes. I'll have them out in a minute."

"So what kind of pizza do you like?" I asked as Noah walked away. I made it a point not to check out Noah's ass.

"I'm not picky."

"Have you ever had a Hawaiian pizza?"

"I can't say that I have."

"It's incredible. I discovered it years ago. Well, actually I discovered Hawaiian omelets and that led me to Hawaiian pizza, but it has pepperoni, onions, pineapple and lots of gooey cheese."

"I live for danger," Thad said. "Let's go for it."

His eyes flashed when he said he lived for danger, and he did indeed look perilous. How did he manage that? How could he look so much like a college professor and yet also like a hit man? Thad should have been an actor. He could articulate so much with his facial expressions, and I knew he wasn't even trying. I wanted to lunge across the table and shove my tongue into his mouth, but I calmed myself.

When Noah returned, we ordered a large Hawaiian pizza—deep dish of course.

"So you were telling me about what you've seen in Graymoor," Thad said.

"My most frightening encounters involve Devon," I said.

"Ah, Marshall has mentioned him."

"I'm not surprised. His spirit has plagued Graymoor for almost as long as I can remember. He's extremely malevolent and despises gays. He seems to grow more powerful as time passes. If it weren't for Taylor and Mark, I truly believe he would destroy us all."

"Taylor and Mark?"

"Marshall hasn't mentioned them?"

"No."

"I'm not sure you're ready to hear about Taylor and Mark. You might say they are the most unbelievable part of Graymoor's story."

"Then I definitely want to hear about them."

"O-o-kay," I said, drawing out the word, "they're angels."

Thad's left eyebrow went up, reminding me of Spock on one of the old Star Trek's that Oliver got me to watch.

"Angels? Fascinating."

I nearly laughed at Thad's choice of words. One of the things I remembered most about Star Trek was the way Spock said "fascinating."

"So you don't think I'm out of my mind?"

"We're talking about ghosts and otherworldly phenomena, why should I think you're crazy for mentioning angels? Besides, I have the feeling you're the type who doesn't much care what others think."

Thad was right about the last part, although for some reason I very much cared what he thought about me.

"I think a lot of people have their own experiences with ghosts, so it's easier to believe. Angels are beyond what most people can handle," I said.

"I'm not most people. I could probably tell you a few things that would shock you."

"Oh could you? Let's see, I've dealt with ghosts, evil spirits and angels; just what would shock me?"

"What if I told you vampires exist?"

"Are you telling me you are one?" I asked with a smile.

"No. I'm not. I realize I am a bit pale, but I do get out in the sun."

"Vampires huh? That is a bit far-fetched."

"Why is that?"

"I don't know, it's just...it seems like something out of a fantasy."

"Ghosts and angels don't?"

"I get your point. So you're telling me you know for a fact that vampires exist?"

"Yes. You don't think I make up everything in my novels, do you? That would be far too much work. I do research for all my books, not unlike what I'm doing at Graymoor now."

"Ah, and here I thought you had a brilliant literary mind," I said, teasing Thad. "Now I find out you're just taking dictation like some kind of glorified secretary."

Thad laughed out loud.

"I'm a little more creative than that. The research is merely to establish a factual basis for my fiction. As for what you think of my writing, I seriously doubt you've read any of my books."

"Oh do you? Why?"

"You don't seem the type."

"As I said, I'm not just a dumb jock. In fact, I have read *The Pain of Eternity* quite recently."

"Watch your step. There could be a quiz."

"Bring it on," I said.

"Perhaps later. My point, which I've strayed from, is that I have no difficulty believing in angels. I've never come into contact with one myself, but then I've never seen the

Great Pyramid for myself either, but I'm quite sure it's there."

"You've seen photos of the pyramid though."

"Yes, and I've seen drawings of angels. The point is I don't have to see to believe if I trust the source."

"Do you trust me?"

"Yes. So tell me about the angels."

I told Thad about the origins of the angels first: how they had once been gay boys not unlike myself, but had been driven to their own destruction by prejudice and hatred. I described my own encounters with them, which few would believe. Among other things, I'd been brought back from the edge of death by their intervention. Thad didn't bat an eye at my tale, which made me believe he was telling the truth when he said he'd met an actual vampire. Only someone who had experienced the extraordinary could believe my tale.

Our pizza arrived before I'd finished the story, and we spent more time eating than talking for a while. Thad loved the Hawaiian pizza. I continued to relate my adventures with Mark and Taylor to him between bites. Thad laughed when I told him I'd put the moves on Taylor, not realizing he was anything more than a sixteen-year-old boy. That incident had been years before, but I was still a bit embarrassed about it. I'm not sure why I told Thad.

We talked more about the supernatural. Marshall would have loved it. The entire conversation would have been right up his alley. I wasn't sorry I hadn't invited him though. I wanted Thad all to myself.

After supper we walked back to Graymoor in the moonlight. I felt a strong desire to hold Thad's hand, but I kept my arms at my sides. I felt an even more powerful desire to ask Thad to my room, where we'd make mad, passionate love, but I restrained myself. I had to prove that I was about more than just sex.

"I had a great time," Thad said when we were once more standing in Graymoor.

"I did too."

"You didn't mention sex once."

"I told you I could do it."

"Perhaps there is hope for you yet. Have a good night Skye."

Thad turned and headed for the stairway.

"Thad?" I called after him.

"Yes?"

"Would you like to go out again? I didn't get to hear anything about you tonight. Want to see if I can stretch my record to two dates without mentioning sex?"

"Dates? I don't think 'date' is quite the appropriate term. We aren't dating Skye. We just went out together. That's all."

"Okay, it wasn't a date, but will you go out and eat with me again?"

"Yeah, I'll go. Next time I'll bore you with my books."

"If the others are like the one I read, they could never be boring."

Did I just say that?

Thad laughed. "Have a good night Skye. I'll see you tomorrow."

"Good night Thad."

Thad walked up the stairs, and I sighed. What had I gotten myself into?

Ralph

Jordan pulled our rented Jeep to a stop in front of Graymoor Mansion. We had flown from Evansville to South Bend and then driven to Verona instead of driving the entire way this time. I was glad to be back in Verona, even though it hadn't been terribly long since we'd left. We had come to give Jordan's grandparents the news of our child-to-be.

Sean greeted us warmly, but there was no sign or mention of Nick. Leave it to Ross to foul things up. The boy could be a menace. Ross was twenty-two, but he seemed more like fifteen most of the time (my apologies to fifteen-year-olds, I know most of you are far more mature than Ross). Jordan and I feared Ross would never grow up. He was a real live Peter Pan.

That very evening, we were getting together with Jordan's three surviving grandparents on his fathers' side: Taylor's mom and dad and Mark's mother. Jordan had offered to take everyone out to eat, but his grandmothers preferred to cook for us instead. They insisted we didn't get enough home-cooked meals, which I supposed was true enough. In any case, it was better because we needed privacy to give them our news. Jordan's grandparents had no idea what it was, but he had told them that we had an important announcement to make.

We drove over to the Potter house about six. Jordan was attacked with hugs and kisses by both grandmothers as soon as he walked in the door. I was next on their hit list. I was pleased to be treated like family. Jordan's grandfather was more reserved, but hugged us both after shaking our hands. He even kissed Jordan on the cheek.

We kept in touch with Jordan's grandparents and had seen them recently, but there was still much to share with them. Jordan did most of the talking, but we told them what we'd been up to, and in turn they told us about their lives. We did our talking in the kitchen, since preparations for supper were well under way.

Supper halted most of our conversation. Jordan's grandmothers had roasted a turkey breast and had prepared stuffing, a broccoli casserole, mashed potatoes, sweet potatoes, corn and freshly baked rolls to go with it.

As we ate, I wondered if Jordan thought it odd to be sitting in the very kitchen where his dad had once eaten his meals. From the look of the table, it was likely the very same one used when Taylor was alive. A picture of Taylor was displayed in the living room, and it was a reminder that the resemblance between Jordan and his dad was uncanny. Taylor had died at sixteen, and Jordan was turning twenty-three on July 31st.

Jordan and I offered to help clean up when supper was finished, but his grandmother told us she would see to it later and ushered us all into the living room.

"So," she said, "what is this announcement that brought you all the way back to Verona?"

Jordan and I looked at each other and grinned.

"Ralph and I are going to be parents," he said. "You're going to be great-grandparents."

The news took a bit to sink in. When it did, there were some confused looks on the faces of Jordan's grandparents, so he explained. The confusion soon turned to happiness.

"Jordan, Ralph, that's wonderful," Grandmother Potter said.

All three great-grandparents-to-be were quite excited, and there was much discussion about the sex of the baby, possible names and so forth. It was much the same conversation we'd had with my parents and with Jordan's mom.

Taylor's mom insisted we spend the night. We had a room at the Graymoor Bed & Breakfast, but she was so enthusiastic about us staying that we agreed. We were set up in Taylor's old room. Jordan's other grandmother was also staying the night. Everyone was so excited about the baby I don't think they wanted our time together to end.

"It looks as if nothing has changed in this room since the 1980s," I said when Jordan and I were alone in his father's old room.

"It hasn't. My grandparents have kept everything exactly as Dad left it. The only exception is the few things they gave me, like his soccer uniform."

"It's kind of strange, isn't it? I don't mean bad-strange, but just odd to think this room has sat here just like this for all these years."

"Yeah," Jordan said, sitting on the edge of the bed. "When I first visited, Grandmother showed me this room and let me stay in here by myself for as long as I wanted. It felt very peculiar to open a drawer and realize my dad was the last one to open it. I mean, look around, there are bookmarks in some of the books, unfinished homework and so many signs of my dad's life. It feels as though he could come back through that door any minute."

"You know he's okay," I said, sitting beside Jordan and wrapping my arm around his shoulder.

"I know. I'm not sad. I like being in here. It's just that the whole room is a moment frozen in time. Time has gone on, but here it stands still."

"I wonder what your dad would have thought if he knew his son and his boyfriend would someday be sleeping in his very own bed."

"He would have been freaked out. You're forgetting: he didn't know about me when he died. Mom didn't even know then."

"Yeah."

Jordan stood and walked around the room, examining various objects left behind by his father. I followed him, but didn't feel right about touching anything myself. The room felt like a museum.

That night we lay in Taylor's bed side by side. I couldn't help but grin as we lay there. I was so excited about our child that I wished he or she was already here. I didn't know how I was going to stand waiting all those months. I drifted off to sleep, dreaming of cribs and baby shoes.

Jordan and I had a breakfast of pancakes, scrambled eggs and bacon with the grandparents the next morning. After breakfast, we were all quite lazy and sat around the kitchen table drinking hot tea and coffee. Everyone was still buzzing over our new baby, and he wouldn't even be born for months yet!

Jordan's grandparents told us stories about their sons, and Jordan eagerly listened. Jordan had his dad's old diary and Mark's too, but there was still plenty more to be learned about them both. I was so glad Jordan had made peace with his grandparents all those years ago. He had forgiven them, just as he knew his dads would have wished. Thanks to that forgiveness, Taylor and Mark's parents were a part of our lives. It was such a shame that Mark's dad had taken his own life, but I understood. He couldn't handle knowing he was largely responsible for the death of his son. I could understand Mark's father more now than I could in the past because I was soon to become a father myself. One thing was for sure: I would not repeat his mistakes. I was going to be there for my child no matter what.

Jordan and I didn't head back to Graymoor until well past eleven. It was getting close to lunch time, but we'd eaten such a large breakfast neither of us was hungry yet. We each took a shower and changed clothes. We hadn't planned on spending the night at Jordan's grandparents' so we were still wearing the same clothes we had the day before.

"So what's on the agenda for today?" I asked.

"We really should get out to see Ethan and Nathan while we're in town. Nick would be rather hurt if he found out we were in Verona and didn't visit him, especially since we're staying here with Sean."

"You know, Sean and Nick were together so long that the two of them breaking up is like a divorce."

"I thought they would stay together forever," Jordan said. "Leave it to Ross to foul things up. I love him, but he can be such an idiot."

"Idiotic is the best way to describe what he did."

"Yeah, Ross doesn't have a mean bone in his body. If he would just think before he acts, he could avoid so much trouble—for himself and others."

"Maybe he'll learn his lesson. This whole thing with Sean and Nick tore him up."

"Yeah, but you know Ross. He's so flighty. He's probably already forgotten all about it. I seriously think he's impervious to information and experience. He never learns."

"Well, enough about Ross for now. We'll be spending plenty of time with him when we get back to work."

"Don't remind me," Jordan said, but he was grinning. He truly did love Ross, as did I. Ross was so energetic and upbeat it was impossible not to like him.

We drove the short distance to the Selby farm. Ethan, Nathan and Nick had just finished lunch. Nick ran to us as soon as Nathan opened the back door and hugged first Jordan and then me.

"What are you guys doing here?" Nick asked. "I didn't think you would be back in Verona so soon."

Jordan and I hadn't discussed telling anyone but our immediate families about the baby, but Jordan silently asked my opinion on the matter with a glance, and I nodded.

"Well, we had some big news to give my grandparents."

"What?" Nick asked.

"Ralph and I are going to be parents."

"Congratulations," Ethan and Nathan said.

"Parents? You're adopting?"

"No, the baby will be ours," I said. "Well, it will biologically be either Jordan's or mine, but which of us is the biological father doesn't matter. This will be *our* baby."

"How did you manage that?" Nick asked.

"I thought we had this talk with you when you were in high school," Nathan said, teasing Nick.

"I don't mean *that*. I mean, how did you arrange it? Who's the mother?"

Jordan and I explained our arrangement with Sam.

"It works out well for all of us," I said after we'd explained. "Someday, when Samantha wants to have a baby, Jordan and I have agreed to do our part."

"Wow," Nick said. "I can't believe you're going to have a kid. He'll be so lucky."

I smiled.

"So what have you got going, Nick?" I asked.

"I'm helping my dads out with the farm, of course. They even pay me."

"We figured we had to pay him now that he has that horticultural degree from Purdue," Ethan said.

"Why don't we get paid?" Nathan asked.

"We don't have degrees," Ethan said.

Nick rolled his eyes.

"I'm also working part-time at the gardening center in town. I was going to work for the B&B, but well...you know."

"Yeah," Jordan said.

"Have you met any nice guys yet?" I asked.

"No boyfriend material, if that's what you mean," Nick said. I could tell the topic saddened him, so I dropped it.

"It sounds like you're busy. Jordan and I are men of leisure for the moment."

"That comes to an end soon," Jordan said. "We have to go over the edits for our video soon, and then it's back to the studio."

"A new CD?"

"Eventually. We're recording three new songs right away, but it will be a while before we've come up with enough new material for an album."

"Once the baby comes Jordan is cutting back, so things will move even more slowly."

"You're still going to perform though, right?" Nick asked with a worried edge to his voice.

"I'll perform as long as someone is willing to listen. *Phantom* isn't breaking up, we're just slowing down; at least I am. Kieran is married now, so he needs more time at home. As for Ross and Cedi, well—who knows with them? They're single, but I'm sure they have plenty to keep them busy."

"So where are you off to next once you leave Verona?"

"Phantom Ranch, at least that's what we call it," Jordan said.

"I read something about that," Nick said.

"Yeah, you'll have to see it sometime. We finally have our own recording studio. Studio time is so expensive that it made sense to build our own. Besides, we can use it whenever we want, and we also let a few other promising groups use it."

"So what's the ranch like?

"Well, it's not really a ranch, but since it's located just outside Tulsa, it seemed a good name. It's an old farm, and we had the old barn redone. That's where the studio is located. There's a sound booth and recording equipment where cattle and horses once stayed. From the outside, it still looks like an old fashioned barn except for the addition of a few large windows."

"I would love to see that!"

"Well, you're welcome to visit any time we're there. There's an old farm house we had renovated on the property. It looks like a ranch house, long and low; that's what inspired us to call the place Phantom Ranch. There are plenty of rooms. Either the previous owners had a big family, or their farm hands lived in the house too. There are what, nine bedrooms, Ralph?"

"Ten."

"So, we have plenty of room. There are sleeping areas in the old loft too, where we can handle a lot of guests if necessary."

"Why did you buy a place in Oklahoma?" Ethan asked.

"We wanted to get away from L.A. where we had been doing all of our recording. We wanted to avoid big cities, period. Oklahoma is centrally located, so it makes a good base of operations. We could really work from anywhere. We thought about putting a recording studio in Phantom World, but we needed more privacy. The ranch is just minutes from Tulsa, but it feels as though it's in the middle of nowhere. It's the best of both worlds."

"It sounds like a great place," Nathan said.

"Yeah, we were keeping our eye out for a place. Kieran found it when he was in Tulsa visiting Natalie, then his fiancée. Natalie's mom is a real-estate agent, and when Kieran mentioned we were looking for somewhere to put a recording studio, she told him about the property. He went out and had a look. He e-mailed his description and photos to the rest of us, and we decided to buy it. It works out great for Kieran, because Natalie will be close to her family whenever we're at the ranch. Kieran and Natalie spend quite a bit of time there even when the rest of us are elsewhere."

We talked more about Phantom Ranch, the Selby farm, and the small events of our lives in general. I was glad we had met Ethan, Nathan, and Nick all those years ago.

After a long visit with the Selbys we returned to Graymoor Mansion for a rest. We lingered there for the few remaining days of our vacation and then headed for Tulsa and Phantom Ranch.

Sean

"Good night Noah," I said and gave him a kiss on the lips that was quite tame compared to the tongue wrestling that had gone on in my bedroom...

"Good night Sean."

I closed the front door and turned to see Skye standing there.

"Sorry," Skye said, "I didn't mean to eavesdrop. I was just going to my room. It looks like you had fun tonight. Hey, are you okay?"

I wasn't smiling. In fact, I felt a little like crying.

"I don't know," I said.

"What's wrong?"

"Can we talk about it in your room?"

"Sure," Skye said. "Come on up."

I followed Skye to his room. He ushered me inside, and then we sat on the edge of his bed while I tried to rein in and figure out my emotions.

"So, what's wrong Sean? It looks to me as if you just finished an enjoyable night with Noah, so why do you look like you're about to lose it?"

"I don't know," I said. "I guess I feel guilty. I've known Noah for a long time. He's only a year younger than I am, but I felt protective of him when we were in high school, and now I've just had sex with him. I feel...I dunno...like I'm a child molester."

"Sean, Noah is twenty-two, not twelve. I'm sure he's quite mature enough to make his own decisions. I'm sure nothing happened he didn't want."

"I know, but...I feel so stupid for feeling like this. It doesn't make any sense. Every time I sleep with someone I feel as though I've done something wrong. These one-night stands just aren't me."

"Well, you know, Sean, what you've got with Noah doesn't have to be a one-night stand."

"How do you do it, Skye? How do you manage to pick guys up, have sex with them, and then not feel guilty about it?"

"Perhaps because to me, sex itself is something special. When I choose to be with a guy like I was with you, I'm sharing an intimate experience with him. To me, that's a very special relationship."

"Even if you never see him again?"

"Yes. I don't sleep with a guy unless I'm attracted to him. I don't have sex for money, or to influence someone, or just to get off. When I have sex with someone, it's because I want to share an intimate relationship with him."

I had never thought of sex in such a way. I'd felt something when I was with Skye, but I thought that was because we were already close. Skye had been there for me when I needed him, and that made it special, but perhaps it was special for another reason as well. We had shared something intimate. I understood Skye just a little better now. To Skye, a one-night stand wasn't just a one-night stand; it was an intense meaningful relationship. It was as if Skye had the ability to distill an entire relationship down into its concentrated essence.

I had felt something when I'd slept with Skye, but I didn't feel that intimate connection with Tobias or Noah. With them, it was just sex for the sake of satisfying my lust. Skye could look at sex with any partner he chose as a special intimate act, but it wasn't that way for me.

"I don't feel like that. To me, it's just sex. With Nick, it was different... it was so much more."

"Do you think you're still feeling guilty because of Nick?"

"I don't know. I don't think that's it. I've been seeing Doug and..."

I trailed off. I didn't know what to say.

"And what? Have you guys had sex yet?"

"No, the most we've done is make out with our clothes on. We have gone out several times though, and we have a lot of fun."

"This is just a theory, but maybe you're hooking up for the wrong reason, and maybe it has nothing to do with Nick. You said you have fun with Doug, and the most you've done with him so far is make out. The two of you are taking things slowly. It sounds as if you're trying to develop a real relationship with each other."

"That's not what I want!"

"I know that, but maybe you feel as though it's happening anyway. Maybe that scares you, so you're having sex with other guys to sabotage any possibility that things might get serious with Doug."

"I don't know. I'm so confused. Maybe I just feel guilty because I believe you shouldn't have sex with someone unless you really love them. I don't love Tobias. I don't love Noah. But I had sex with them anyway. I love you, but as a close friend, not as a boyfriend and not romantically. Skye, this whole 'seeing what's out there' thing isn't working out so well for me."

"Maybe you're not cut out for life in the fast lane."

"Yeah, while you're speeding down the highway of sex in a Viper, I'm chugging along in an AMC Pacer."

Skye laughed out loud.

"I wish I could tell you what to do Sean. I wish I could say something wise to put everything in perspective. The only bit of wisdom I have to give you is to follow your heart, and I realize that's pretty damned vague."

"Vague, but far better than nothing," I said. "Thanks for listening to me anyway Skye."

"Any time Sean."

We stood and Skye hugged me. He seemed like an older brother, even though he was actually a little younger than I was. I was glad we were keeping our relationship platonic now. What I needed from Skye had nothing to do with his

281

body. We bid each other goodnight and I retired to my room to sleep alone.

***

Doug and I had supper at Ofarim's, where we talked and laughed like old friends. Just before seven p.m. we walked down the street to the Paramount to take in a movie. Doug looked handsome in the flickering light of the screen, and I found myself remembering our make-out session on my bed. My heart raced and I yearned to take him home with me again, but my heart was also troubled. I had so much fun when I was with Doug. We hadn't known each other long, but I had dreamy thoughts of him throughout the day—the kind of thoughts I once had about Nick.

After the movie we stepped out into the warm summer night. The lights from the marquee lit up the sidewalk and street like day. Doug was smiling, but I felt sadness envelop me as we walked across the street to the park. This wasn't right, none of it—Doug, Tobias, Noah, and maybe even Skye. I felt as if my life was a movie, but I was playing the wrong role.

"Sean, what's wrong?" asked Doug.

I didn't realize it until just that moment, but tears were streaming down my cheeks. My heart ached.

"I don't think we should see each other anymore," I said.

"What? Why?"

I could tell I'd taken Doug unawares. I didn't know I was going to utter those words myself until they came out of my mouth. I turned to Doug and gazed into his eyes.

"I'm falling for you Doug. I haven't let myself see it, because I didn't want to see it, but it's true."

"What's wrong with that Sean? I know you aren't looking to get into another relationship, and I'm not either, but I really like you. You're a special guy. We have a blast together, and we have so much in common. Maybe..."

282

"No," I said. "I can't. I'm still in love with Nick."

That's when I lost it. I started bawling right there in the park. Doug pulled me to him and held me close, and I cried even harder.

"I miss him so much," I said. "I was so angry with him when he cheated on me. I tried to make myself believe we were finished. I wanted to hate him, but I could never hate Nick. I love him so much! Oh God, what am I going to do without him?"

I'd bottled up the pain inside me. I'd forced it down with anger refusing to feel it, but emotional pain can't be contained like that. The more it's bottled up, the more it grows. It all came bursting out as I cried into Doug's chest.

When I quieted, Doug led me to a park bench and sat by my side holding my hands. When I looked at him, his eyes had tears in them too.

"I think I'm out of luck," Doug said. "As much as I hate to say this, I think it's time you go back to Nick. Damn! I'm going to miss you."

I wiped the tears out of my eyes with the back of my hands.

"I'm so sorry if I've hurt you," I said. "I truly didn't mean to fall for you. I never meant for us to be more than friends. You're so good and so kind that I couldn't help myself. Even now you're being so kind to me when you should be angry."

"You can't help feeling what you feel, Sean. What kind of friend would I be if I was angered by that?"

"I want you," I said. "I'm falling for you, but I know in my heart it can't be. I love Nick, and I always will."

"I never intended to care for you either Sean, not like that. I'll be honest. I don't love you. I care for you, and I think what we've got could grow—or rather could've grown— into something more. I wish we could let things take their course and see what happens, but...I'm not the one for you. I wish I was, because you're a special guy. You can't change your feelings though, and you shouldn't. If you tried you would only hurt us both."

"I'm sorry."

"Don't be sorry Sean. I'm just glad you realized you're still in love with Nick now. If it had happened later, I might have fallen for you by then too. As it is, I'll miss you. I'll miss our time together, but my heart won't be broken—not quite."

"You're going to make someone a wonderful boyfriend," I said.

"I hope so," Doug said, smiling for a moment. "You know Sean, just because our relationship can't go anywhere romantically doesn't mean it has to end. I know you won't be able to see me for a while, and I know things can never be the same, but later, maybe after you and Nick are back together...maybe then we can be friends."

"I'd like that, but...I can't make any promises."

"I know that," Doug said.

"You're being so kind. It makes me feel even worse about all this."

"I've had a wonderful experience with you Sean, and you're not a bad kisser either. I wouldn't have missed out on our time together if I'd known in advance how it would end. So don't feel bad, but do say 'hi' to me when you see me. Then, when you can, *if* you can, maybe we can go out again. You can even bring your boyfriend along."

"Thank you Doug."

We stood and hugged.

"I'm going to get going," Doug said. "I think you need some time to think."

"I surely do."

"Say hi to Nick for me."

I managed a small laugh.

"Good night Doug."

I watched Doug walk across the park, then across the street to his car. He got in and drove away. Soon, even his taillights had disappeared. I felt miserable, but I knew in my heart I'd done the right thing.

I walked home alone feeling a profound sense of loss. Doug was one in a million, the kind of guy many dreamed of meeting. If we had continued to go out, I might have grown to love him as much as I loved Nick. Maybe not. I don't think I could ever love anyone as I loved Nick. Through everything, even when I tried to hate him because he'd hurt me, I still loved him.

I suddenly felt very guilty. I'd said such nasty things to Nick. I hadn't listened to his explanations. Well, I had listened—I'd heard the words, but I hadn't paid any attention. I was so hurt by what he'd done with Ross that I wanted to hurt Nick right back. I'd turned my back on him when he asked for forgiveness. What had he been going through all this time we were apart? Would he even want me now?

I walked through the warm summer night toward Graymoor. I thought of Doug, Tobias, Noah, and Skye. Each was unique in his own way, even special. I could understand a little of what Skye had said about the meaning he attached to intimacy. His was not my way, but I did feel now as if I'd shared something more with Tobias and Noah than mere sex. My nights with Skye were the most meaningful. Skye had been there for me when I needed him. He understood that I needed to be held and feel loved. It hadn't been just sex between us. Doug and I had never had sex, but my relationship with him had also been special. In another life, he could have been my boyfriend. All four paled in comparison to Nick. What I had with him was...beyond description.

Had, that was the key word. Could I get back what I'd thrown away? What would I do if I couldn't?

***

285

"Sean, you've got to see this!" Marshall said, rushing into my office.

"What is it this time?"

"Something you're not going to believe!"

"It must really be something, then. There is very little I won't believe these days."

"Come on!"

"Okay, calm down."

"Grab your flashlight."

I wasn't really in the mood for one of Marshall's little adventures, but at least it would get my mind off Nick for a while. I'd spent most of my day thinking about how I should approach him. I had even picked up the phone a few times to call him, but I needed to see him in person. I was so nervous about facing him I had butterflies in my stomach. After all this time, he was as likely as not to throw my apology back in my face. I guess it would serve me right if he did.

Marshall led me to the very hallway he had found blocked with a new brick wall several days before, or was it weeks? I was losing track of time.

"It's gone," I said when we reached the spot where the wall had been located. "Did one of the work crews remove it?"

"No. That's not what I brought you to see. I've discovered why the spirits warned us to keep guests out of this part of Graymoor."

"Marshall, are you sure we should even be going into this part of the house? Didn't Etienne and the Graymoor boys say death, destruction and disaster could be the result?"

"That's why I've proceeded slowly and cautiously. Follow me."

We switched on our flashlights. I reluctantly followed Marshall through twisting hallways until I was hopelessly lost. I had no idea how he managed to navigate back to whatever it was he'd discovered. After several minutes, we came to a large, heavily carved doorway. We shined our flashlights upon it to illuminate the carvings.

"It's incredible," I said.

"Yes, but it's not what we came to see either. You can check it out later."

Marshall opened the heavy door and I reluctantly allowed him to pull me into a dark circular room. There were no windows, and the only light came from our flashlights and the dim illumination coming from the hall. I turned around in a complete circle. Nothing but doors met my eyes. There must have been two dozen of them, as the room was quite large. I shined my flashlight to the ceiling. A large dome hung overhead, covered with painted panels depicting...I don't know what. There just wasn't enough light to see properly.

"Okay, this is bizarre," I said.

"You haven't seen anything yet."

Marshall walked to one of the doors and opened it. Sunlight suddenly streamed into the room. I had expected to view a darkened upstairs hallway, but instead I was looking into a peaceful, grass-covered valley. My eyes grew wide, and I took a step back. My heart pounded in my chest. I looked at Marshall in shock.

"I told you it was something you wouldn't believe."

I looked back through the doorway. I could not believe what I was seeing.

"I'm dreaming," I said.

"No. I assure you that you're wide awake."

"But...this is impossible!" I said.

"Hmm, just like the spirits floating around Graymoor are impossible? Or impossible, like the existence of angels? Or perhaps you mean impossible, like being able to communicate with the dead? Or impossible like..."

"Okay, I get your point. I still think this is a dream and I'm going to wake up soon. If it is, I guess it doesn't matter. If not, well..."

Marshall shut the door and opened another. At first I glimpsed nothing but dark, but then I began to make out stars in the sky and a large moon partly visible through trees. I rubbed the bridge of my nose.

"This is some dream."

"I think you'll find this doorway interesting," Marshall said.

He opened another door.

"It's Main Street!" I said.

I could see cars driving down the street and pedestrians walking along the sidewalks. There was Café Moffatt just down the street. I looked over at Marshall, astonished.

"I told you Graymoor had secrets upon secrets."

"This is way too much," I said. "I can't handle this."

I backed away from the doorway as Marshall closed it.

"Sean, are you okay?"

I shook my head. "Let's go back now."

"Okay." I could tell from his tone of voice that Marshall was disappointed.

We walked through the winding, twisting hallways. I was in a dream-like daze and still mostly convinced that I was indeed dreaming. I'd seen plenty of weird shit over the years, but this was in a class all by itself.

"That can't be real," I said.

"Nothing unreal can exist," Marshall said.

"I mean...it's some kind of illusion, right? There was some force making us see it."

"No," Marshall said. "I could detect such a force at a great distance. We weren't under the influence of a supernatural force, malicious or otherwise."

"Have you...gone through any of the doorways?" I asked.

"I've done no more than stick my hand through. I didn't think it wise to enter by myself. That's why I brought you."

I exhaled loudly. "I'm going to have to think about this Marshall. This is just too weird. That room can't be what it seems. It's not possible!"

"As Captain Picard once said, 'It's only impossible until it's not.'"

"I'm going to wake up here in a bit," I said. "That's what I'm going to do. I'm going to wake up and find this is all a dream."

"Did you wake up when the ghost of Mr. Graymoor was chasing you with an ax? Did you wake up when Devon possessed me and I tried to kill you? Did you wake up when an angel appeared to you? Did you..."

"Okay, okay, I get your point, but...damn! This is...fantasy!"

"It's not fantasy, Sean. It's just something new. Think of how fire must have seemed to primitive humans when they saw it for the first time. Think of how a flashlight would have astonished George Washington. Think of how people during WWII would have reacted to seeing a microwave oven for the first time. None of these things is fantasy. They're not magic. They would have appeared to be so at one time. Any technology that is sufficiently more advanced that those observing it will seem like magic. Of course, I'm not ruling out the possibility that magic is involved here, but I'm saying that room back there is what it seems. We've just come across something we've never seen before."

"Most likely something no one has ever seen before."

"Just try to keep an open mind."

"I'll tell you what Marshall. If this isn't a dream, then I'll think about it. Right now, I'm pretty sure I'm asleep and none of this is real. If it's not real, then there is no reason to worry about it."

"Okay Sean," Marshall said, laughing a little. "I'll talk to you about this tomorrow when you're sure you didn't dream it."

"I sure hope it's a dream," I said. "I have enough to deal with without...whatever that was back there."

We were soon back at the main stairway and Marshall and I parted ways. I returned to my office, my mind spinning. I reassured myself that soon I'd wake up and have a good laugh over my messed-up dream.

Skye

I hesitated as I stood before the door to Sean's room. I wasn't sure I wanted to share my feelings, even with Sean. Opening up emotionally wasn't the easiest thing for me, but I needed to talk to someone, and Sean and I had grown close. I took a deep breath and knocked. Sean opened the door.

"Hey Skye."

"Do you have a few minutes?"

"Of course. To be honest, I welcome the distraction from my own thoughts."

"Nick?"

"Yeah. Nick and...other things. I'm still working up the courage to approach him. I'm terrified he'll turn me away."

"Nick loves you."

"I hope so, but you're not here to talk about me, and if I think about Nick any more my head will explode. So what's up?"

Sean and I took seats in large comfortable armchairs near his bed.

"I *really* like Thad. I've had my eye on him since he arrived. We went out on a date...well, not a date, but we went out and..."

"You had sex with Thad T. Thomas?" Sean asked.

"No."

"No? But I thought you said..."

"It wasn't like that. At first, he wouldn't go out with me. He thought I was only trying to get into his pants."

"You don't want in his pants?"

"I do, but...there's something about him—something mysterious. I *feel* something for him—something that's not just lust."

"Whoa," Sean said. He just sat there for a few moments, stunned into silence. "Whoa. Are you telling me you're falling in love with him?"

"No. I'm not in love with him. I just *feel* something for him. I've never felt like this before. I don't know what to do about it." I sighed.

"Ohhh, I've heard sighs like that before. If I'm not mistaken, I'm detecting just a hint of infatuation here. You're falling for this guy."

"I think that's putting it a bit strongly."

"I haven't spent much time with Thad," Sean said. "He's with Marshall most of time or writing in his room. What's he like?"

"He's smart and sexy, and when I look at him...mmm. I want him so bad I can't stand it, but there's something more. We went out for pizza, and we just ate and talked, and it was incredible! I've even...I've even daydreamed about walking in the moonlight with him."

"Are you sure you aren't ill, Skye?"

"No. I'm not sure. I feel...weird. I don't like it, and yet... I don't know. I just want to forget about him, but I keep thinking about him."

"Like it or not, I believe you're beginning to fall for him, Skye."

"I don't know. I don't want to fall for anyone. I never thought this could happen to me. I know it happens, but I didn't think it would happen to me—you know?"

"Skye, we're talking about love, not cancer."

"I don't love him; I just...I don't know. It's so complicated. When I spot a guy I want, I just go for it, you know? I take him to my room, and we get it on. This isn't anything like that. I tried all the usual tricks to get Thad's attention, and...nothing."

"He went out with you. He must have some interest in you."

"I'm not sure why he went out with me. With other guys it's so simple: they want my body. Thad isn't like that. I don't know what he wants. He doesn't seem interested in me at all—not like that. I wonder if he's just toying with me.

292

I know he thinks I'm a player, but I did manage to go through our entire date without bringing up sex once. The scary thing is I liked it. He scares me, Sean."

"You? Afraid? Skye, I've seen you take on five guys at once. I've seen you hurl yourself through a window without a moment's hesitation. You're the closest thing we have to Batman around here, and you're afraid of a writer?"

"Weird isn't it? I just don't know how to deal with Thad. He won't sleep with me, so I don't even know why I don't just walk away."

"Maybe Cupid has shot you in the ass."

"Don't make me smack you."

"Sorry, I didn't mean to compare you with the rest of us mere mortals, but would it be so bad? Would it really be so horrible if you were falling for him?"

I just shook my head and stared at the floor.

"It's not easy sometimes, but the rewards of a relationship can be incredible. I don't have to tell you what I've been going through. I'm scared to death right now because I'm afraid Nick won't take me back after I've made such an ass of myself. I don't know what I'll do if he doesn't want me anymore, but even if he doesn't, all the pain and suffering is a small price to pay for all the joy I had when things were good between us. Knowing that things may be over and that I may never know the same happiness with Nick again is hard, but even if I go down in flames, I wouldn't change things. I wouldn't give up what I had with Nick, even to spare myself what I'm feeling now and what may be to come. It's taken me a long time to realize that, but it's true."

"So what do you think I should do?"

"Just see where events take you. Go out with Thad, and just be yourself."

"If I do that I'll try to seduce him, and then it's all over."

"Okay. Other than that, be yourself. Spend time with Thad the way you would with Marshall, or Nick, or me. Well, excepting the times we slept together. You know what I mean."

"I really should tell him to go fuck himself. I should just forget about him. There's just something about him though."

"So just have fun with him—with your clothes on."

"I guess. Okay, let's quit talking about me. I'm getting tired of it. Let me give you a little advice: go talk to Nick. Say whatever it is you have to say to him. Waiting isn't going to make things easier and will likely make them harder. I know you're scared, but putting things off only serves to torment you. It's time to face your fear and talk to Nick."

"What if he rejects me?" Sean asked with a pained expression.

"Then at least you'll know things are truly over, and you can begin to move on."

"I don't want to move on."

"I know that Sean, but putting off your confrontation with Nick will only torment you."

"Maybe not knowing is better than knowing. If I talk to him and he tells me to go away..."

"Sean, you can't let fear stop you. I know you're miserable. You're going to go on being miserable until you talk to Nick. Maybe you will go down in flames, but maybe you won't. You've got to at least try Sean, because if you don't, then all is truly lost. Your only chance to be back with Nick, to recapture that joy you lost, is to tell him how you feel."

Sean nodded. We both sat there in silence for a while. There didn't seem to be anything left to say.

"I guess I should get back to my room. If you need to talk, my door is always open."

"Thanks Skye."

"Thank you."

We stood and hugged, and then I made my way back to my own room. Talking things over with Sean had helped, but I was still uneasy. Could I really be falling for Thad? I'd never considered an actual romantic relationship with a guy. Well, that wasn't quite true. When I had first realized I was gay I had thought about dating guys, just as Sean and Nick were dating each other. My thoughts had quickly turned to sex, and I had all but forgotten those thoughts of romance. Was it time for me to settle down with one guy instead of hooking up with every hunk who crossed my path? Damn, I sounded like Sean.

My thoughts were premature in any case. I'd gone out with Thad once. Surely he'd lose interest in me soon, or I'd lose interest in him. I'd never been with a guy who wasn't just after my body (except for Sean), and what else did I have to offer? True, there was more to me than my muscles, but I didn't even know how to talk about feelings and stuff. Life was far too complicated.

A few short hours later, I sat across from Thad in The Park's Edge feeling a nervous anticipation I had not previously experienced. I simply did not know how to date. Even if Thad wouldn't call it a date, a date it was. I'd never spent an evening with a guy that didn't end up in sex. I'd been with plenty of guys, but they were all hookups. I rarely even ate out with a guy before we got it on. We met, went to his place or mine, had sex, and then went our separate ways. Sometimes we met again. Sometimes we didn't. It was all very simple and clear cut. There were no complications. This was another matter entirely. I felt like I was lost in the wilderness without map or compass.

"So tell me about Thad T. Thomas," I said as we waited for our orders to arrive.

"I thought you wanted to discuss my books."

"I'm more interested in the author."

"Hmm, well, I've lived all over the world, although I spent most of my years in Chicago, L.A. and New Orleans. I lived in London for a while, Edinburgh, Stockholm, Rome and Paris. I was brought up in southern Indiana, mostly by my grandparents, and I've recently returned there to settle down."

"What about your parents?"

"That's a long story and one you don't get to hear. Grandfather Kurt and Grandfather Angel are the ones who really raised me."

"You took turns living with each of them?"

"Oh no, Kurt and Angel are a couple. They've been together for decades."

"Really?"

"Yes. They met in high school. You wouldn't believe some of the stories they've told me about their early years. By the time I came into the picture, things had settled down. Angel and Kurt were great parents, although I didn't make it easy for them at first."

Our food arrived. Thad had ordered a fried chicken hoagie and fries. I had a blackened yellowfin tuna salad. It was delicious.

Thad remembered his childhood fondly, and he told me quite a bit about those years as we ate. He was less forthcoming about other aspects of his life—secretive really. When I sensed I'd stepped into an area he didn't wish to discuss, I headed in another direction.

"It must have been fascinating to live in all those places. I've lived in Verona for my entire life, except for my college years in California."

"Fascinating yes, but none of them ever really felt like home. That's why I returned to Blackford. I bought an old farmhouse from my grandfathers that I recently finished having restored. It sits back in the woods away from everything. It's very quiet there."

"You sound like you miss it."

"I do, but I don't mind experiencing other places. Having my own home in Blackford gives me a sense of roots. I know that no matter how long I stay away, I can always go back home."

"Well, I hope you stay in Verona for a while."

"And why is that Skye?" Thad asked, with a devilish look in his eye.

"I want the chance to get to know you."

"Not just sleep with me?"

"No. If you'll notice, I haven't mentioned the three-letter word that begins with s."

"I keep waiting for it to pop up."

"You still think I'm just after your body?"

"Let's just say, others—both men and women—have told me they only want to be my friend. That usually means they don't proposition me until after dessert."

"I didn't ask you last time."

"We didn't have dessert."

"We will this evening, and then you'll see. I won't try to seduce you."

"So you have no interest in my body?"

"I didn't say that. I'm curious, intrigued even, but I'm also interested in you. I want to get to know you. Maybe we can be friends. Maybe we can be more than friends."

"I don't know about that Skye. I'm not really looking for a relationship, and I'm not going to be around long enough for one."

"To be honest, I don't even know what I want. I'm not asking you to commit to anything, just to remain open to the possibilities."

"Fair enough. I must admit that what I'm seeing doesn't fit with your reputation. I thought that once I turned down your advances, you would lose interest and go on to your next target."

"My reputation is deserved, but you're not like any other guy I've met. There's something about you that...well, I can't even put it into words."

"Well then, what about you Skye? Tell me about your past."

I told Thad some of the events of my life as we ate, although I realized as we talked that most of my life revolved around sports and other physical activities. I didn't mention my sexual conquests. Thad knew enough about them already.

"I hear you have a reputation as the champion of gay boys around here," Thad said.

"Someone has to look out for them. If I don't stick up for them, who will?"

"That can be a rather hazardous endeavor."

"I'm not afraid of danger."

"What are you afraid of Skye?"

I paused before answering. "You."

"And what is so intimidating about me?"

"I like you. I feel something for you. For the first time in my life, I want something more from a guy besides his body. I feel drawn to you, and I'm not exactly sure why. You're an unknown. I don't know how you feel about me, and I really don't know how to proceed."

"Are you sure you don't just see me as a challenge because I turned you down?"

"Oh you're a challenge alright, but in another way. I'm not accustomed to rejection, but I'm tough. I can take it. No, there is something else here that I've never experienced before—something that's drawing me toward you. I must admit I'm lost and bewildered."

"Let's see if we can dispel some of the mystery," Thad said. "Hmm, how do I feel about you? At first, I thought you were a conceited frat boy who thought of nothing more than his next one-night stand. I've discovered you are more than a pretty face. You're intelligent, and you care deeply about those around you. I've talked to Marshall about you, and I must say I'm impressed. From what he tells me, you continually put yourself in danger to help others. I admire that. My opinion of you has improved dramatically since we met."

I still had no idea what I was feeling. I wasn't even sure what to say. My head was beginning to hurt. I didn't want to think about it anymore.

"Let's talk about *The Pain of Eternity*..."

Thad and I spent the remainder of our meal discussing the only book of his that I had read so far. It was fascinating to be able to discuss the novel with the author himself. Thad was very willing to discuss his book, the plot, the characters, and the hidden meanings. He was even impressed that I'd caught on to some of the subtle nuances of his work. He was open about his work in a way he was not about himself.

We parted once more at the foot of the stairs in Graymoor. I resisted the urge to jump on him. It wasn't easy.

Ralph

Jordan drove the jeep through the gateway and under the rustic sign made of branches that read "Phantom Ranch." If I didn't know better, I would've thought we were out in the middle of nowhere in some remote section of Oklahoma. Less than thirty minutes before, the tall buildings of downtown Tulsa were visible. Jordan pulled up beside Kieran's old Jeep and a yellow Corvette convertible that belonged to Ross.

Jordan and I had spent very little time at the ranch so far, just a weekend now and then usually on our way somewhere else. I'd barely had time to explore the place. I loved the old ranch house. It was long and low and rustic looking with a porch running its entire length. Hanging pots holding geraniums were spaced at intervals along the porch, and several different types of cacti were set along the edge, giving the ranch house almost a southwestern feel, despite the fact we were in the Midwest. Chairs and settees made of bent branches were interspersed with white wicker along the length of the porch. Natalie had handled the decorating, and the result was like something out of *Country Living*.

Jordan and I pulled our backpacks and bags from the back of the Jeep and walked toward the ranch house. Kieran and Natalie greeted us as we reached the front door. There were hugs all around.

"How was your trip?" Kieran asked.

"Perfect," Jordan said.

We stepped into the large living room.

"Jordan!"

Ross bolted across the room and jumped into Jordan's arms. Jordan had to drop his bags to catch him. Ross planted a quick kiss on Jordan's lips. I didn't mind. It wasn't overtly sexual. Ross was just being Ross.

"Hello Ross," Jordan said in a long-suffering tone, but I knew he was glad to see him.

"You missed me didn't you?" Ross said.

"Like a hemorrhoid."

Ross scowled. He jumped on me next.

"Ralphie!" he said, giving me a hug.

"Hey Ross. Run out of Prozac again?"

"I choose to ignore you!"

"You say that a lot," Jordan said.

"Where's your boy toy?" I asked.

"He's out, but he'll be back! No one can stand being parted from me for long!"

"Yeah, right," I said.

Jordan and I retired to our room to unpack. Our bedroom was rather large, with a queen-sized bed, a private bathroom and a nice little sitting area. Natalie had decorated it and had chosen a rustic-ranch theme. There was a saddle sitting across a beam above the large windows, a red-and-black Navajo rug hanging on one wall, and various farm implements decorating the other walls. Interspersed with these were photos of Jordan, Ross, Kieran, Cedi and myself in groups and singly. The foot and headboard of the bed were made of branches, much like the chairs on the porch, and it was covered with a Native American blanket in tan, red, white, and black. There was Native American pottery displayed in a primitive cupboard along one wall and a few baskets hanging overhead. Somehow it all worked together. Natalie could easily have been a professional decorator.

"I think we should wait until everyone is here before we make our announcement," I said.

"I'm dying to tell the guys," Jordan said.

"You just want them to know what a stud you are."

"You could be the father you know."

"I know," I said. "We have to wait until Sam arrives anyway."

"True. Chad should be here by then too."

We put our things away in the antique dresser and wardrobe and then headed for the kitchen for something to drink. The kitchen was a thing of beauty. It had all the modern conveniences, yet looked like an old-fashioned kitchen. The stove even looked like an old, wood-burning range, although it was electric. The floor was tile, with a southwest design that matched the rest of the décor.

Natalie pulled out a pitcher of iced tea from the refrigerator, which was disguised as an old ice box, and filled glasses for us.

"You did such a remarkable job on this place Natalie."

"She's incredible, isn't she?" Kieran said.

"I think he just married me so he wouldn't have to hire a decorator," Natalie said.

"Nonsense. I married you to get a discount on the real-estate commission. How else could I get your mom to cut her usual fee?"

Kieran kissed Natalie. Ross chose just that moment to enter.

"Get a room, you two!" Ross yelled.

"Look who's talking," I said. "You and Cedi spend more time making out than breathing."

"Yeah, like you and Jordan aren't just waiting to go at it."

"We have self control," Jordan said.

"We're having a cookout later," Kieran said. "It's all arranged. I'm grilling steaks, and Natalie is preparing her famous California Chicken Sunburst Salad. You will love it."

"I'm sure," I said.

The kitchen was a comfortable place to relax as well as cook. There was a very large carved table from an old Southwest Spanish Mission that could easily seat twelve. In addition, there were more branch-chairs like those on the front porch. These had comfortable padded cushions in various patterns dominated by red.

We all sat around the kitchen for a while, drinking our drinks and catching up on recent events.

"So, where is Cedi?" I asked.

"Natalie sent him into town for groceries," Kieran said.

303

"You trusted Cedi with a grocery list?" Jordan asked. "That's almost as bad as sending Ross shopping."

"I take offense at that remark!" Ross said loudly.

"You came back with ice cream and potato chips instead of hamburger and buns the last time we sent you out," Jordan said.

"I've got your buns right here!" Ross said, beginning to unfasten his shorts.

"No one wants to see that," Kieran said.

Ross scowled at him, but sat down.

Jordan and I took a nap after we'd visited in the kitchen. Our flight had been a short one, but we were still a bit sleepy. I awakened before Jordan and quietly walked to the multi-paned windows that took up the west wall of our bedroom. Just outside was a flower bed of cacti, some of them quite large. Beyond the flower bed was a small area of mown grass that quickly transformed into a meadow a few paces from the house. Off to the right, I could see the large patio with rustic wooden chairs gathered around a central fire pit. An outdoor cooking area was located in a small covered pavilion that reminded me of a shelter house in a park. It, like most everything else, was rustic, with large shaved wooden posts like those on the front porch and a red-tile roof. Sheltered from the elements was a large gas grill, an outdoor sink and a long table for food preparation. The pavilion was surrounded by more cacti and flowers, as was the entire patio.

"This place is remarkable isn't it?" Jordan said as he walked to my side. I was so taken with the view I hadn't even noticed him getting out of bed.

"It sure is different from Indiana," I said.

Jordan and I stood admiring the view for a few minutes, then we headed into the living room.

"Jordan! Ralph! HIIIIIII!" shouted Cedi as he leaped from a love seat and hugged us both. "How are you guys? I am so excited about recording!"

"You're always excited Cedi," I said.

"Hey, I've got something for you to hear," Cedi said. "Grab a guitar and meet me on the porch."

Intrigued, we did as we were told. Jordan picked one of the acoustic guitars hanging on the wall, and we walked outside. It was warm, but not unpleasant. Cedi joined us a couple of minutes later carrying his violin and sheet music.

"Here, listen to this," he said.

Cedi began to play a sweet almost melancholy tune on his violin. Somehow, it brought to mind fields of flowers and babbling brooks.

"That's excellent Cedi," Jordan said.

"Thanks! I wrote it in my head while I was in the checkout line at the grocery. I jotted it down when I got home. Here, now play along with me." Cedi handed Jordan a few pages of sheet music.

The two began to play. I was amazed at how the instruments each followed their own tune but together wove a complex musical dance. I'd never heard anything like it.

"What do you think?" asked Cedi.

"It's incredible," Jordan said. "You just wrote this?"

"Yeah, it just came to me. I was working out the keyboard sections in my head when you guys came in. It's nowhere near a complete song, but I thought we could do something with it."

"We'll definitely try," Jordan said.

Natalie came out onto the porch. "Kieran wants to know if he should start grilling."

"It sounds good to me," I said.

"Yeah! I'm starving!" Cedi said.

"I'll tell him to grill away," Natalie said.

Jordan and Cedi played around with Cedi's new creation for a few minutes. I just sat back, watched, and listened. Cedi was a welcome addition to *Phantom*. The guys had asked him to fill in for Kieran during the last tour because Kieran's arm was out of commission. He had worked out so well they'd asked him to join the band permanently. Cedi was a bit too intense at times, but I enjoyed his extreme enthusiasm and zany sense of humor. He resembled Ross in many ways, but despite being younger, he was far more mature. He also didn't share Ross's tendency to fuck everything that moved, and that was a very good thing indeed. I had seen Cedi making out with both guys and girls, but he was far more discreet than Ross, as well as far more selective. There was no reason to worry about Cedi the way I did about Ross. Cedi and Ross also had a thing going. I wasn't quite sure what it was, but I'd seen them make out a number of times and was quite sure they'd slept together. They probably wouldn't make a bad couple if they could both settle down.

We moved from the porch to the back patio. The smell of grilling steaks filled the air. The sizzle made my mouth water, and I wasn't even that big a fan of steaks. Ross was nowhere to be seen, but that was a good thing. A little Ross goes a long way.

"You guys wanna play Frisbee?" Cedi asked, jumping with excitement. If anything, Cedi was more hyper than Ross, although before meeting Cedi, none of us would have thought that possible.

"Sure," Jordan said. "You in Natalie?"

"No, I'm going to see to my salad."

Cedi zipped inside for his Frisbee and returned in a flash. Jordan and I followed him to the stretch of grass between the patio and the meadow. Cedi whipped the Frisbee toward me. I caught it—surprisingly—and sent it sailing toward Jordan, who gracefully plucked it out of the air and sent it hurtling toward Cedi.

Cedi jumped up, twisted in the air and sent the Frisbee rocketing back toward Jordan who was caught off guard. The Frisbee smacked him in the chest. Cedi danced around, wiggled his butt and did cartwheels. Jordan and I couldn't help but laugh at him.

It took us no time at all to get sweaty, and the three of us pulled off our shirts.

"Yeah! Take it off, baby!" Ross yelled as he came outside. He stripped off his shirt also, and joined us.

With the addition of Ross, our game became truly crazy. Ross or Cedi alone was a wild and intense experience, but put them together and...well, there just isn't a word to describe it. We ran around the yard like little kids, trying to outdo each other with difficult throws and catches. Cedi could actually jump in the air, do a flip and come down with the Frisbee. Ross tried it. He managed the flip just fine, but the Frisbee hit him in the ass.

"Nice catch, Ross! There's using your brains!" Cedi yelled.

"Oh, you're dead squirt!"

Jordan and I lost it. The sight of Ross dashing around trying to catch Cedi was just too funny. Ross was fast, but Cedi was nothing but a blur. Cedi giggled and laughed as if he was twelve. No wonder he and Ross got along so well. Ross finally gave up. His chest was heaving, and sweat dripped off him. The rest of us were rather sweaty as well.

"The steaks will be done in just a few minutes children," announced Kieran.

"Yes Daddy!" yelled both Ross and Cedi. Yeah, they were too much alike. I didn't even want to think of them in bed together.

"Let's grab a shower," I suggested to Jordan.

"I'm in!" Ross yelled.

"Group shower!" Cedi shouted.

"Uh, no," Jordan said. "You guys have your own bathrooms."

Jordan and I showered together, although mostly to save time. We did make out just a bit while washing off, but there wasn't time for more.

The steaks were incredible. Kieran knew how to season them just right. Natalie's California Chicken Sunburst Salad was awesome. When I spotted small slices of orange and pineapple among the mixed lettuce leaves and strips of chicken breast, I had my doubts, but it was delicious.

We spent the reminder of our evening sitting around and talking. When it was dark, the guys took down guitars from the walls, played, and sang. Natalie and I sat back and listened. The guys played until it grew late; then we all headed for bed. Jordan and I were tired, but we had enough energy for a little love-making. By the time we fell asleep, we were truly relaxed.

Sean

Before I realized where I was going, I was there. My feet walked up the winding gravel driveway to Nick's home. The scuff of my shoes on the concrete sidewalk soon replaced the crunch of gravel. Light from inside the house cast skewed rectangles of brightness on the grass. As I knocked on the glass of the back door, my heart pounded in my chest as if I'd run all the way from Graymoor at top speed.

Nathan opened the door.

"Well hello Sean. Come in."

"Is Nick here?" I asked in a trembling voice.

"Yeah. He's upstairs in his room. Go on up."

Nathan watched me as I crossed the kitchen, entered the living room and climbed the stairs. Soon, I was out of his sight, stepping down the hallway toward Nick's open door. I trembled with fear as I never had before. I almost couldn't force myself to move forward, but I couldn't stand the torment any more. I hadn't intended to walk to Nick's house when I'd begun my stroll, but some part of my mind forced my feet toward the old farm.

I swallowed hard and stepped into the light falling from Nick's bedroom into the hallway. Nick was unaware of my presence. He sat writing at his desk. I took a shuddering breath and took a step into his room. Nick turned at the sound of my feet upon the carpet and stood. A look of surprise crossed his handsome features. I opened my mouth to speak, but no words would come out. I swallowed and then finally made my voice work.

"I'm sorry," I said. My voice broke even before I could get 'sorry' out, and I began to cry.

Then something wonderful happened. Nick raced across the distance that separated us, took me in his arms, and held me tight.

"I'm so sorry," I said, sobbing into his shoulder.

"It's okay baby. It's okay," Nick said as he rubbed my back. "Come here and sit with me on the bed."

I let Nick lead me to the edge of the bed. We sat close and turned to look at each other.

"I've been so horrible to you. I didn't mean the things I said. I'm sorry I didn't believe you when you told me that what happened with Ross wasn't planned. I knew it in my heart, but seeing you kiss him hurt me so much. I know you've always been faithful to me. I've been an absolute beast."

Nick laughed a little.

"Only you could turn this around so that you're the guilty party, you silly ass," Nick said.

"But I was so horrible..."

"I'm the one who did wrong," Nick said. "I should never have kissed Ross. I should never have let my *Phantom* obsession control me. I'm the one who should be sorry Sean, and I am. What I did was wrong and it was stupid. I was weak. I gave in to a momentary temptation I should have resisted. I should have been stronger."

"I was afraid you were going to leave me for him. I've always been afraid you'll find someone better."

"Oh Sean, haven't you realized by now it's you I love? Haven't our years together taught you that? Why else would I remain with you when we were so far apart all through college?"

"I'm beginning to realize it now."

"Well it's about time!"

I grinned.

"Please forgive me," I said. "Please take me back."

"I forgive you, although there is nothing to forgive. As for taking you back... you're the one who broke up with me, remember? Will you forgive me? Will you take *me* back?"

"Yes and yes," I said, grabbing Nick and hugging him tight. "I love you so much Nick!"

"And I love you."

Nick stood, walked across his bedroom and then closed and locked the door.

"I've heard that makeup sex is intense," Nick said.

"Well, I guess we'll—" that's as far as I got. Nick jerked me up off the bed, pressed his lips to mine and kissed me passionately.

I feel a little embarrassed to admit this, but I cried while we were making out. I was just so happy to be with Nick again I couldn't help myself. My tears soon stopped though, and we sank onto the bed, making out and ripping each other's clothes off. Our need for each other was at a fever pitch. It had been so very long since we'd been together.

I'm sure Ethan and Nathan could hear us going at it as they sat downstairs, but I didn't care. I was consumed by lust and love for my boyfriend. Nick and I were all over each other, and I had never been so turned on in my entire life. Neither Tobias, nor Noah, nor even Skye could begin to compare to Nick.

We made love for hours until finally we were spent. We lay on our backs panting and grinning at each other.

"I needed that," Nick said.

"So did I."

Nick turned off the light and we cuddled up with each other. We lay there side by side until we slowly drifted off to sleep.

I woke up the next morning with a grin on my face. I turned my head and there lay Nick beside me. Everything felt as right now as it had felt wrong when we were apart. The pain I'd suffered during our separation was my own doing. I should have been more forgiving, but I understood why that wasn't possible for me when I found Nick and Ross together. Time had to pass to dull the pain. Those close to me had the greatest power to hurt me, and I loved Nick the most of all. When I discovered his infidelity, it was more than I could take. The world as I'd known it was destroyed, at least it seemed so then. In my pain, I'd struck out like a wounded animal. I'd wanted to hurt Nick as he'd hurt me.

I'd made the situation worse in my own mind by assuming greater infidelity on Nick's part than was really there. Yes he had kissed Ross, but he had been faithful to me at all other times. I knew in my heart it was so, but in my anguish I couldn't see it. I wasn't capable of forgiving Nick until I'd followed the path set out before me. It was a necessary journey that made me realize Nick truly did love me and that I was foolish to think I wasn't good enough for him.

Nick stirred, opened his eyes, and smiled. I leaned over and kissed him. That led to another intense lovemaking session, although a far shorter one. It was early, but I had a busy morning ahead. I wished I could just spend it with Nick, but we were back together. We had our whole lives ahead of us!

Nick drove me to Graymoor and dropped me off. I rushed inside and met Skye as he was coming down the stairs.

"That's some grin," Skye said when he spotted me. "That smile can only mean one thing: you got laid last night, and the sex was intense."

"Yes, but that's not the best part."

"Come on Sean, what could possibly be better than intense sex? Wait, I've got it, you're meeting him tonight to do it again?"

"I'm definitely getting with him again tonight, but that's not it either. Nick and I are back together."

Skye smiled. "So that explains it. Even the Raposo triplets weren't able to put a grin like that on my face."

"Triplets?"

"Yeah, but that story will have to wait. I'm so happy for you Sean!" Skye grabbed me and hugged me. "I guess you finally worked up the courage to talk to Nick."

"Yeah. I finally came to my senses last night."

"You should have listened to me. I told you not to put off talking to Nick. No one ever listens to me. They think that a guy with such stunning beauty couldn't possibly be smart too."

"Uh-huh," I said, rolling my eyes. "Maybe I'll listen to you next time."

"Sure you will. I'm truly glad you two are back together. Everything seemed so wrong when you were apart."

"Yeah, it was a rough time for me. Thank you for being there for me Skye."

"Hey, what are friends for? Besides I knew it was my only chance to get you into bed."

"Yeah, like I'm so hot."

"You *are* hot Sean. You just don't realize it." Skye leaned in and whispered conspiratorially even though we were quite alone: "And I happen to know you're very talented in bed."

I smiled.

"Okay, I'll admit I possess some hotness if you'll admit there was more on your mind than sex when we slept together. You were there for me when I needed you. You were very sweet."

"Nope, sorry, I can't admit that. I just wanted your ass."

"Yeah, sure you did."

"Well, I need to get going. I'm late already."

"Thanks, Skye—for everything."

I leaned in, kissed Skye on the cheek and then raced upstairs. Once there, I took a quick shower, changed, and went back downstairs to the kitchen for breakfast. The staff often ate in the kitchen. We were welcome in the Dining Room, but we sometimes liked to sit and talk away from the guests. Skye was already seated, as were Basil, Kane, Matilda, Mom and Dad. Martha was far too busy seeing to the guests to join us.

I helped myself to blueberry pancakes and bacon and then joined the others at the table.

"Hey Basil, Nick will be able to start work soon."

"Good. I can definitely use the help."

Mom and Dad quickly looked at me. I grinned. My parents smiled back. They knew everything was okay.

"What's this?" Skye asked, pretending ignorance. "Nick? Could this be Nick Selby perhaps?"

"Yes," I said.

"Mr. Hilton," Skye said, turning to my dad, "I'm afraid your son is practicing nepotism, hiring his boyfriend."

"Nick happens to have a degree in horticulture from Purdue, and Basil himself recommended him as his first choice from the current applicants, thank-you-very-much," I said.

Skye laughed. I thought of mentioning that if we hired all of Skye's boy toys, we could easily staff the mansion—even if it was running at full capacity, but I didn't think it proper in front of the older crowd.

After breakfast, I went upstairs to double-check some of the as-yet-unused guest rooms. I was thinking of opening up a few more. I'd already discussed the possibility with Matilda, and she thought we could open up four more rooms without hiring additional staff. Any more than that would require more housekeeping staff. I was eager to open up as many rooms as possible, but I was intentionally taking things slowly. The quality of the service we provided was far more important than profit. If the guests were happy, they would come back and recommend us to their friends.

I had comfortably settled into my new role in Graymoor. Now that things were rolling, I could handle the paperwork more efficiently and spend less and less time in my office. I was out and about most of the day seeing to the needs of the guests and troubleshooting. Whenever an unexpected difficulty came up, I was the one to call. I carried my cell phone with me at all times.

When I was satisfied that the additional rooms were indeed ready for guests, I made a mental note to begin taking reservations for them. We had been steadily booked so far, and I knew I could probably have the additional four rooms filled by the very next night. Many people were curious about Graymoor, and with such a limited number of rooms available, it wasn't difficult to sell out. I only hoped we could continue to sell out as we expanded.

I grinned every time I thought of Nick. All was forgiven, and we were back together again at last. Nothing mattered more to me than that.

***

"You had sex with Skye? Details, I want details!" Nick said.

Nick and I had no secrets, so we were telling each other about the guys we'd been with during our separation.

"I don't think we need to get into details."

"Oh yes we do! Was it incredible? How big is he?"

"Yeah, it was incredible, but it's even more incredible with you."

"You don't have to say that, but thanks!" Nick said, giving me a peck on the lips.

"I mean it Nick. Sex is better with you than with anyone else."

"You didn't answer my second question."

"Okay, okay. It's not like I measured, but I'd say damn close to ten inches."

"Are you shitting me?"

"No."

"Damn, some guys get everything."

"I love what you've got Nick. Skye was incredible, but not as incredible as you. No one can even come close."

"Aw. I feel the same way about you Sean, now more than ever."

We talked more, and I discovered that Nick did have sex with hung-jock-4-u or whatever his name was. His real name was Bill. How boring was that?

"I didn't want to be with other guys," Nick said. "I only wanted to be with you, but I took your advice, and you know what? You were right. I think I did need to see what it was like with other guys. The past weeks have been difficult and painful. I'd never want to go through them again, but I learned something important: you are without a doubt the one for me."

I don't think I'd ever been as happy as I was at that very moment.

We kept talking, getting everything out in the open. It didn't bother me to hear about the handful of guys Nick had been with during our time apart. He was only following my advice, and in the end—he'd chosen me.

Nick and I were meeting Marshall in a few minutes to explore the room of doorways. I couldn't put him off any longer. Marshall was chomping at the bit to take a closer look. I would just have soon forgotten the room even existed, but Marshall could think of little else. He had been pestering me to go back with him. I was surprised he hadn't set out to explore it himself. Nick and I were sitting on my bed making out when Marshall knocked on the door and stuck his head into the room.

"Don't you guys ever stop? Come on. It's time."

"I'm not so sure about this Marshall," I said as Nick and I stood and smoothed out our clothing.

"Come on Sean. I've been waiting forever! You've got to be curious about what's behind those doors. No one has ever discovered anything like this before!"

"And therein lies the danger. We don't know what we're getting into."

"You promised."

"Okay, okay. Lead the way."

Nick and I followed Marshall up to the fourth floor and through the twisting hallways of Graymoor. I had told Nick about the room and how I had at first believed it was part of a dream. Most people would've thought I was a nut case if I'd told them about a room with doorways to distant places, but Nick accepted my story without a doubt.

When I was a kid, I thought I understood things, but my concept of reality had been shaken up so many times I didn't know what to expect next. There was a time when I thought ghosts only existed in stories, but I learned they were as real as my friends and family. Then, I was faced with angels—real angels—and my concept of reality had to shift again. Every time I assimilated new information, something new and startling was thrown at me. I truly didn't know what to make of the circular room with all those doorways leading to other places. What was in that room shouldn't have been possible, but there it was and I was forced to shift my concept of reality yet again. I just wondered how far I could shift it without going insane.

I secretly hoped that the room of doorways would be one of those that could not be found when we tried to return. Marshall led us right to it all too soon and far too easily. I wondered if he'd returned there himself, gazing through the doorways but not daring to enter on his own.

"Weird," Nick said, looking around.

"If you got turned around in here you might never find your way back out," I said. The very thought made a chill run up my spine.

"I've thought ahead," Marshall said. He marked an X on the inside of the door we'd come through. "Besides, I don't think many of these doors open on darkened hallways."

"All these doorways really lead to...other places?" Nick asked, swallowing hard.

"Most of them, at least. One looked as if it opened onto just another hallway in Graymoor, but I'm not sure. The others definitely lead elsewhere. They seem to be stable. As far as I can tell they don't change with each opening. Take a look at this."

Marshall opened a door. Through the opening, we could see a dense forest. The undergrowth was swaying in a slight breeze. The forest could have been anywhere.

"It's kind of like *The Lion, The Witch and The Wardrobe*," Nick said. "Think any of these doors will get us into Narnia?"

"I think they only lead to real places, Nick," I said.

"Maybe Narnia is real. Maybe C.S. Lewis only wrote about it as fiction because he knew no one would believe it was a real place."

"You have been spending far too much time with Marshall," I said. Nick only grinned.

"So, are you guys ready?" Marshall asked.

"Yeah," Nick said. My boyfriend looked ready for any kind of adventure.

"I'm not, but this is as ready as I'll get, so let's do it," I said.

"Let's start with something familiar," Marshall said. He walked to a door and opened it, revealing downtown Verona. "This shouldn't be too scary for you guys."

We stepped closer, but I hesitated. "How do we know we can get back?"

"We don't. That's another reason we're trying this door first. If it's a one way door, we can just walk back to Graymoor the long way."

I supposed that was true enough, but I still felt a sense of nervous anticipation. One would not have thought downtown Verona could be intimidating, but I felt as if I was about to step onto the moon.

"Here goes," Marshall said. He stepped through the door. Nothing unusual at all happened. I halfway expected a flash of light or some whooshing noise. The event was rather anticlimactic, but it set me more at ease—somewhat.

I could clearly see Marshall standing only a few feet away. He was on the sidewalk on the west side of Main Street, looking around at the buildings.

"Let's do it," Nick said.

Nick and I stepped through the doorway together.

I felt no sensation of movement. Walking through the doorway felt like just that—walking through a doorway. The only thing odd about passing through the doorway was that it took us from the fourth floor of Graymoor Mansion to downtown Verona. It was nothing like the transporters on

Star Trek. We didn't go all sparkly or anything. I felt almost disappointed.

The first thing I did was look back to see if the doorway we'd come through was visible, and indeed it was. It made for the most peculiar sight. There was a doorway off to one side of the sidewalk, nearly in the street. There weren't many people around, but they took no notice of it at all.

"I don't think they can see it," Marshall said.

"Can they see us?" I asked.

Marshall turned to an elderly lady I didn't recognize who was just then walking past.

"Hello," Marshall said.

"Well, hello, young man," she said. "Beautiful day, isn't it?" She smiled and walked on down the street.

"Well, that answers that question," I said.

"Come on, let's have a look around," Marshall said.

"Let's see if we can get back first," I said.

"Okay, okay. You try it."

I walked back to the doorway and stepped through. I was in the darkened room of doorways once more. Marshall and Nick peered at me from the sidewalk. I rejoined them.

"Satisfied?" Marshall asked.

"Yes. I'm beginning to feel a good deal better about this."

We walked down the street. There was Café Moffatt, looking so familiar and yet strange, but I knew it was my own disorientation making it look skewed. Although I'd grown more at ease, I was not quite fully comfortable. You wouldn't be either if you'd just walked through what could only be described as a magical portal.

"Let's walk to the park," Nick suggested. "We might as well get some exercise while we're looking around."

We walked through the town toward the park. Something bothered me. Something didn't seem quite right. I chalked it up to nerves, however, as I could put my finger on nothing amiss.

It was a bright sunny day, a bit too warm, but enjoyable nonetheless. I felt ever so slightly nervous, but also excited. It's not every day one steps through a portal.

We entered the park. Verona was a small town, but a lot of effort went into making the park a pleasant place. People of all ages came to enjoy the park: kids to play on the playground equipment, teenagers to use the volleyball courts, families to picnic and older people to just sit and admire the flowers. Nick and I had strolled there plenty of times, just enjoying each other's company.

Everything seemed so normal it was easy to forget how we'd arrived.

"Hey look!" Nick said. "It's Taylor and Mark!"

Rarely did we cross paths with Verona's resident angels, but there they were, just a short distance away. We changed course and headed in their direction.

"Maybe now we'll get some answers," I said. "Taylor and Mark will know all about the room of doorways."

"Yeah," Marshall said. "But, will they tell us?"

"Hey Taylor!" Nick called out as we neared.

Taylor and Mark stopped talking and looked in our direction as we walked toward them.

"What are you guys doing here?" Marshall asked.

"Um... the same thing you are, I suppose," Taylor said. "We're spending some time in the sun. Nice isn't it?"

"It's been a long time since we've seen you guys," I said. "What have you been up to?"

"I'm afraid I don't remember you," Mark said, looking at us curiously. Taylor peered at us as if also trying to place us.

"Uh..." I said.

"You're Taylor Hilton right?" Marshall asked.

I stared at Marshall. He knew full well Taylor's last name was Potter. Nick and I exchanged a look.

"Um, no."

"This is incredible! You look so much like Sean's cousin. Doesn't he Sean?" Marshall said.

Marshall's voice trembled as he spoke. His face was chalky white.

What is going on? I thought.

Nick and I looked at each other again.

"Um, uh, yeah," I stammered.

"Our mistake," Marshall said. He turned to us. "I guess you were right Sean. You told us it couldn't be him."

Nick blinked stupidly, and I fear I did too.

"Well, we need to run or...we'll be late," Marshall said. "Sorry to intrude."

"That's okay," Taylor said, looking at the three of us as if we were a bit simple. "It was nice meeting you."

Marshall turned and walked quickly away. Nick and I followed on his heels, struggling to catch up.

"Marshall wait up. What's the hurry?" Nick asked.

"What was up with that?" I asked.

When Marshall turned, his features were etched with fear. He was visibly shaking, and tears were in his eyes.

"What's wrong?" I asked.

"We've got to get out of here!"

"What?"

"We've got to get out of here NOW! Don't talk to anyone. Don't look at anyone. Just follow me."

Marshall turned and bolted back toward Main Street. Nick and I tore out after him.

"Marshall! Marshall, wait! What's wrong?" I called.

Marshall turned to us once again. "We're not where we thought we were, or rather we're not *when* we thought we were."

"Huh?" Nick said. "This is Verona, Marshall."

"Yes!" he hissed, "but we're in the past!"

321

"That's why Mark and Taylor didn't recognize us!" Nick said. "They haven't met us yet. They aren't angels yet. They're just boys!"

"Yes," Marshall said. "We have to get out of here before it's too late! Hurry!"

"What do you mean?" I asked.

"This is so cool!" Nick said. "Come on, let's go back and talk to them. Wow, if Taylor and Mark are boys that also means my dads are boys now. We can meet them and see what they were like when they were teenagers."

"NOOOOOOOOOOOOOOO!" Marshall yelled so loudly I jumped.

"Why not?" Nick asked.

"Please!" Marshall said, actually beginning to cry. "Don't ask questions! Just trust me! We've got to get out of here now!"

Marshall turned and ran again. He was in a state of total panic. Nick and I raced after him silently. I'd never seen Marshall run so fast before. Soon we were huffing and puffing our way down Main Street. I could see the doorway up ahead. Marshall bolted through it. Nick and I soon joined him in the room of doorways. Marshall slammed the door shut and leaned back against it, panting. I could not for my life figure out what had frightened Marshall so badly.

Skye

"Let's go for a walk in the Solarium," I suggested after Thad and I returned from another evening out.

We walked through the twisted hallways of Graymoor. I'd lived in the old mansion long enough now that I at least knew my way to some of the key rooms. I still swore some of them moved at times, but perhaps my memory merely failed now and then.

So far, I had not made the least mention of sex. Thad and I had discussed his books, my life as the champion of gay boys' rights (his words, not mine), ghosts, archaeology, astronomy, astrology (which both of us thought was a load of crap), life, death, and myriad other topics.

Thad was stern. His demeanor was almost intimidating. That is not to say he intimidated me, but when he wanted, he could terrorize most anyone simply by gazing at them. I admired that kind of strength, and it drew me to Thad, but I was also attracted by his intellect, his charm, and the aura of mystery that surrounded him. I'd never come across a man as strong and self-assured as Thad. It was only natural that I felt drawn to him.

"This may be my favorite part of Graymoor," Thad said as we walked among the tropical plants softly lit by unseen lights.

"I often come here to walk," I said. "It's peaceful and beautiful, and a certain solitude permeates the air even when others are here."

We stopped and stared up at the stars shining bright through the glass overhead. When I returned my gaze to earth, Thad was looking at me. I drew nearer. My heart pounded in my chest. I leaned in, but Thad put his hand on my chest.

"Don't."

I drew back.

"That's not what I want with you Skye."

"Why not? You are single, right? You aren't dating anyone. You're not married. What's to stop us?"

"Not everything has to be about sex Skye."

"I know that, but..."

I didn't know how to continue.

"Don't you get tired of guys who are just after your body?"

"Not really," I said. "Sex is incredible. Why shouldn't I enjoy it?"

"I didn't say you have to be chaste."

"What are you saying?"

"What I've already said: not everything has to be about sex. Do you sleep with every guy you know?"

"No. I have friends I've never had sex with."

"Do you enjoy the time you spend with them?"

"Well, yeah."

"That's how I want it to be between us, Skye. Despite my initial first impression, I've discovered much to admire within you. You're not just the horny frat boy I thought you were. We could sleep together, but what would it mean? What would be the point beyond physical pleasure?"

"Physical pleasure is a pretty good reason," I said.

"There are lots of kinds of pleasure Skye. As I told you before, I don't want to be another notch in your headboard. I would like to be your friend."

I let out a long breath.

"You're very frustrating."

"I've been told that before," Thad said with a slight smile.

"You sure I can't change your mind?"

"I'm sure."

"Well, if you won't change your mind, then I guess we'll just have to talk."

"Are you sure you can endure it?"

I loved that little smile of Thad's. It was barely there, but it carried a lot of weight. Thad was a mystery I wanted to solve, but somehow I knew I'd never truly understand him. He was an enigma. We looked up and continued gazing at the stars.

***

I met Craig for another session late the next afternoon. This time a large sketch pad and easel were set up, rather than a camera and a lot of lights. I stripped and Craig positioned me in a pose somewhat reminiscent of the discus-thrower statue downstairs. Sean and others had mentioned how that statue looked a lot like me. The pose I held for Craig was original and not a mere copy of an old statue. I found it surprisingly easy to maintain.

Craig gazed at me from behind his easel, sketched, and then gazed some more.

"I'm amazed at how at ease you are about being naked," Craig said as he sketched.

"I don't think anything about it. I wouldn't want to run around naked all the time, but here it's fine. Growing up, I was naked in the locker room and showers after gym classes, football, wrestling, and other sports practices so much I guess I grew accustomed to it, although I can't remember it ever bothering me."

"I'd die of embarrassment, but then again I don't look like you."

"I'm sure you look very good naked."

Craig grinned shyly. "I don't think so."

Craig sketched for a while longer in silence. He was intent upon his work, but I detected distraction, and the distraction had nothing to do with my nude body.

"Is something wrong?" I asked.

"No... well, yes. Dad is trying to force me to go to a small conservative school here in the Midwest instead of an art school in a large city. He has always been against the idea of art school, but now he's becoming adamant. Maybe he's afraid I'll engage in an alternative lifestyle."

"He knows you're gay?"

"No, but he's not stupid. He probably suspects. Anyway, now Dad is saying he won't pay for an art school. It has to be a small conservative, preferably Christian, college. It's his way or no way."

"Damn, that's harsh."

"He can be harsh. It sucks. Art is all I care about. It's my life. There is no way I'm going to find a good art program at any of the schools on my dad's acceptable list."

"What are you going to do?"

"I don't know yet, but I'm damned well not wasting four years in some little holier-than-thou shit-hole where people think they can tell me what to think."

"Good for you."

"I'm so sick of being told I'm a pervert by self-righteous control freaks who can't stand it if anyone is the least bit different."

"It sounds like you've had a rough time of it."

"Yeah, when I was a kid my parents used to be so proud of my artistic talent—proud of me, period—but when I got a little older, Dad expected me to leave art behind. To him, it's something for children—and homos."

"That's just odd."

"Mom isn't as bad, but Dad is prejudiced to begin with. I've heard Dad use words like 'nigger,' 'faggot,' 'spic,' and 'gook' all my life."

"Spic? Gook?"

"Spic is a nasty way of saying Hispanic. It's what fag is to gay. Gook is a disparaging way to refer to someone of East Asian descent."

"You know, I've never heard those words before?"

"Well, you don't live with my dad. Things got a lot worse when my parents began attending this Southern

Baptist church. That's when they became convinced that anyone who is not a heterosexual, white Protestant is in league with the Devil."

"That's something that has always amazed me. It seems as though it's the religious who are always the most prejudiced and the most filled with hate. I know not all religious people are like that, but any time you hear about some group attacking gay rights—or any minority's rights, for that matter—it's a church. The hypocrisy of it astounds me."

"I'd likely be in the same fix now, even if my parents weren't attending that church, but it's definitely made matters worse."

"I'm very sorry to hear that Craig. Do you belong to the local gay-youth group?"

"Yeah. Dad would freak if he knew I went, but I go behind his back whenever I can manage it. It helps."

"Good. Just remember, you can count on me."

"Thanks Skye. Somehow I'm going to art school. I'm going to live my life as I see fit. I may have to get some crappy job and save up for years, but I'll manage somehow."

"There are Point Foundation Scholarships and National PFLAG scholarships. You might want to consider those. Perhaps you could work here. I'm sure the Hiltons will be hiring more people as the B&B expands. I can put in a good word for you with Sean. I bet he'll hire you. He's one of us, you know."

"Cool. I may take you up on that. Wow, you've saved my butt from bullies, you're posing nude for me, and you're willing to help me get a job. Should I sleep with you to pay you back?"

"Don't tempt me."

"That night you saved me and then walked me home...I thought about...well...I thought about expressing my appreciation physically." Craig turned a bright shade of red.

I tried to calm myself, but I was becoming aroused. There was no hiding it from Craig.

"You didn't owe me anything for giving those bullies what they deserved," I said.

"It would be more of a reward for me anyway. I'm sure you can have any guy you want."

I thought of Thad, but didn't mention him.

"Don't sell yourself short, Craig. You've got a lot to offer. If you were just a little older..."

"Thanks Skye."

"How's the sketch coming?" I asked to change the subject. If I didn't, I knew I'd soon be fully erect.

"I'm getting you roughed in. I'm afraid it won't look like much today. I'll work on it at home using the photos I took as reference."

"Your parents allow you to draw naked men at home?"

"No, but what they don't know won't hurt me. I spend a lot of time in my room, and they seem a little afraid to come in there. Perhaps they think I'm communing with the Devil."

"From the little you've told me it seems more as if *they* are."

Craig laughed.

"Have you ever read *The Last Battle* by C.S. Lewis?" I asked.

"No."

"It's the last book in his Narnia series. Near the end, Aslan is speaking with a young soldier who has followed a rival god, Tash, all his life. This soldier doesn't think Aslan will accept him because he has served Tash instead of Aslan. In the book, Aslan is basically Jesus or God, and Tash is the Devil. Aslan tells the soldier that he counted all the service he had done to Tash as service done to himself. The soldier didn't understand, so Aslan explained that he and Tash were opposites, so that no service that is good could be done to Tash, and no service that is vile could be done to Aslan, even if it was done in his name. The soldier had been serving Aslan the whole time, even though he thought he was serving Tash."

"So you're saying people who discriminate and preach hatred are serving the Devil, even though they say they are serving God?"

"Exactly. No evil service can be done in the name of God. Those performing evil may claim to be serving God, they may even believe it themselves, but in fact they are serving the Devil. It is to him they pay tribute when performing evil acts."

"My dad would go ballistic if he heard you say that."

"It's okay. I'm sure I could handle him."

"I have no doubt about that. I get what you're saying. I hardly turn on the news anymore because everything seems so twisted. It's as if truth has become unimportant. People seem to think that merely saying something makes it true. Like this whole uproar over gays getting married. There's this big fuss about the institution of marriage being under attack. It's so ridiculous I don't see how anyone can even say it with a straight face. I think they know it's bullshit, but they're using it as a smokescreen so they can discriminate. Groups like Focus on the Family act as if the whole country is going to disintegrate if gays are allowed to marry. Marriage will be strengthened when gays are legally allowed to marry, not weakened. And remember back when the Boy Scouts began openly discriminating against gays? I don't, but I read about it. Suddenly there was all this bullshit about protecting the Boy Scouts, as if they were under some big attack, when it was the Boy Scout leadership that was attacking its own members by forcing out gays. It makes me so mad I could spit nails."

"I'll tell you something that might put you at ease," I said.

"What?"

"Evil often wins battles, but in the end good always prevails. Even if gay marriage is outlawed throughout the land, even if the prejudiced find more ways to discriminate against us, in the end all their efforts will fail. It's inevitable. In the future, people will look back on this time and see all these fundamentalist-religious and family-values groups for what they are. They will be held up as examples of an evil that must never again be allowed to flourish."

"Do you really believe that?"

"Yes. I think a lot of these groups know it too. Why else would they be so desperate to legislate discrimination? They know their time is limited, so they're attempting to carve their prejudices in stone. They might as well be writing them on the air for all the good it will do them."

Craig actually laughed.

"You're so calm about everything Skye, while I get so worked up."

"Oh, I also get worked up, but I've experienced things that have opened my eyes to the bigger picture. I often feel as if I'm fighting a losing battle, but then I remember that victory is inevitable. You might even say that we've already won."

"Then what's the point of fighting?"

"Just because I know the destination doesn't mean I can skip the journey. Without the journey I can't reach the destination, and it's the journey that is important. It's what defines us."

"You're very philosophical."

I laughed so hard I completely lost my pose.

"You are the first person who has *ever* said that to me. I'm not philosophical. In fact, in my book thinking is often a waste of time. I prefer action. When you've had the experiences I've had, you can't help but pick up a few ideas."

Craig guided me back into the pose I'd been holding.

"What experiences are those?"

"I don't think you're ready to hear about them. Perhaps someday, but not today."

"You're being mysterious. It makes you even sexier."

Craig didn't know how much he was affecting me. It was only with a supreme effort that I was able to control my arousal. Craig was a very attractive young man.

Ralph

Samantha and Chad finally arrived at Phantom Ranch. Our inner circle was complete. Jordan, Samantha, and I wasted no time in delivering our news.

"We've gathered you all here to share something very special with you," Jordan said as we all sat around the living room. "I'm sure our announcement will come as quite a surprise, but I hope you'll be happy for us. Sam?"

The three of us had decided that Sam should reveal our wonderful secret. After all, she was having the baby. Kieran, Ross, Cedi, Natalie and Chad were all gazing at Sam expectantly, probably wondering what in the hell was going on.

"I don't quite know how to say this, so I'll just say it: Jordan, Ralph, and I are having a baby."

Sam's announcement was met with stunned silence.

"What do you mean?" Kieran asked.

"I can explain where babies come from if you don't understand," Ross said.

"Or we could demonstrate!" Cedi said.

"Shut up, you two," Kieran said.

Jordan stepped in to rescue Sam.

"Ralph and I want to have children, and since we can't do that alone, so we're having a child with Sam."

"There was an orgy and I wasn't invited?" Ross yelled.

"Shut up Ross," said almost everyone. Ross grinned.

"You're going to be dads? That's fantastic!" Cedi said. He ran to us and gave Jordan and me hugs. Sam was his next victim.

"This is wonderful!" Natalie said. "Congratulations!"

Congratulations came from every direction as our friends recovered from their shock. I knew they would be happy for us.

"Hey Sam, when you've finished with having Jordan's and Ralph's baby..." began Ross.

"Don't even think about it Ross. You should not be allowed to reproduce," Samantha said.

"Hey, I already have lots of kids!"

I sincerely hoped that wasn't true. Jordan and I turned and looked at each other.

"Can you even imagine?" Jordan said quietly.

"Hey!" Ross yelled.

Jordan rolled his eyes and smiled.

"When are you expecting?" Natalie asked Sam as they walked away toward the kitchen.

"A celebration is in order!" Cedi shouted.

"Yeah, it's not every day three homos have a kid!" added Ross.

"Ugh! I'll never get used to Ross and Cedi together," Kieran said. "They're like twins."

"Now that was a nasty thing to say about me!" Cedi said loudly.

"You should be lucky enough to be my twin!" Ross yelled. "I'm completely awesome! Everyone wants to be just like me!"

"Make that no one and you've got it right," Cedi said, giggling.

Ross pounced on him and began to wrestle Cedi down on the couch. Their wrestling quickly became a make-out session.

"It's your fault there're two of them. I believe it was your idea for Cedi to join the band," Kieran said.

"A lapse of judgment," Jordan said, but I knew he didn't mean it.

"Hey women!" Ross yelled, coming up for air. "Since you're already in the kitchen where you belong, fix us some food! We're gonna have a party!"

Jordan put his hands over his face and shook his head.

Natalie looked over the antique counter that was all that separated the living room from the kitchen.

"Fix it yourself hyper-boy!"

"I'll order pizzas!" Cedi said as he struggled to escape from Ross. Pizza was the magic word. Ross immediately released him.

"Whew," Kieran said, letting out the breath he'd been holding. "I thought that was going to get ugly. I was picturing Natalie and Sam beating Ross senseless."

"I'd pay to see that, but they know Ross is mentally incompetent," I said. "He isn't responsible for his own actions."

"Hey!" Ross yelled. "I heard that!"

"Yes," Jordan said, "but do you know what it means?"

"Shut up!"

Life was never dull with Ross around.

We feasted on thick gooey pizzas that evening. Cedi ordered far too many, but leftover pizza was easy to heat up in a microwave. It was wonderful to be surrounded by friends who were happy for us. I knew that some people would see what we were doing as some kind of unnatural aberration, but I'd long ago learned not to care what others thought. Jordan and I were going to be great parents. Maybe we didn't know what we were doing when it came to raising kids, but who did the first time around? I kind of wished I'd done some babysitting when I was younger, but it was too late for that now. We weren't experienced as parents, but Jordan and I would love our child no matter what and be there for him always. That was more than I could say for many of those who wouldn't approve of our parenthood.

The next day the guys returned to making music. Their main goal was to record the three songs they had completed for the next album. That task required long hours in the recording studio, far longer than anyone not familiar with the music business would probably believe. Natalie and I spent a lot of time alone together while the guys were recording. I didn't mind that at all. She and Kieran had been married for a few months, but during most of that time *Phantom* had been on tour without Kieran. I barely knew Natalie.

During one of the recording sessions in the barn studio, Natalie and I sat on the long front porch drinking iced tea.

"Kieran and I have discussed having a baby, but we're not sure if it's the right time," Natalie said.

"I don't think there is a right time. Kieran is like Jordan. He's always going to have a full life. You just have to make time for things that are important. When the baby comes, Jordan intends to slow down. He's involved in so many things. Luckily, he knows how to delegate or he wouldn't have time to sleep."

"I'll admit I didn't quite know what I was getting into when I married Kieran. I don't know if I could have handled it if he would have gone on tour right after we were married. Hopefully I'll be settled in before *Phantom* hits the road again."

"Touring is an interesting experience: sleeping in a different hotel room every night, or on the bus, waking up not knowing where you are... it all kind of blurs together after a while."

"I don't know if I like the sound of that."

"Oh, don't get me wrong; it can be a blast, but it's disorienting until you get used to it. There are also the bodyguards to deal with. They're great guys, but I had a lot of trouble getting used to having someone following Jordan and me around everywhere."

"I've already experienced some of that. I can't say I enjoy it. I'm glad we don't have to deal with it right now."

"I'm a little surprised the guys are getting away with not having bodyguards here. Perhaps Jordan convinced Mike and the others there are enough of us here for safety."

"How do you get used to the fans?" Natalie asked.

"It just takes time. I know it's overwhelming at first. Things have actually calmed down considerably. When I began dating Jordan, the guys couldn't go anywhere without causing complete havoc. It was crazy. We couldn't even get in and out of buildings without a police escort. If you think there are a lot of fans now you should have seen them back then."

"I don't know if I could handle that."

"Things still get crazy sometimes, but I think the fans have grown a little older along with the guys. There are still tons of teenage fans, but even more of them are in their twenties and thirties now and even older. There are probably almost as many fans now; they just don't get as wild."

"Do you ever get jealous?" Natalie asked. I could tell from the tone of her voice that she had some issues with jealousy.

"Well, I used to be bothered by the attention guys gave Jordan. I'm not talking about the vast majority of the fans, but those who were a little more aggressive and suggestive. A lot, and I mean *a lot* of guys come on to Jordan. Most of them are way hotter than I'll ever be. For a time I feared that Jordan would find someone he liked better, but I learned quickly that those guys didn't have a chance with him because he loved *me*. I'm sure a lot of women will throw themselves at Kieran even though they know he's married, but you've just got to trust in his love for you. Remember, Kieran could've had just about anyone he wanted, but he chose you."

Natalie smiled.

"Talking to you really helps Ralph."

"That's because I've been there before. It's not easy dating a rock star. A lot of people think it's a dream come true. It is with Jordan, because I'm so in love with him, but no one considers in advance all the problems that come with such a relationship. I work with the band, so I'm right there most of the time. I'm sure it's going to be hard on you when you aren't able to tour with Kieran, but you just have to make the most of it. There have been more times than I can count when Jordan and I couldn't be alone because he had to make an appearance or the fans demanded his time, but at the end of the day, I'm the one he loves. Knowing that makes it all okay."

"I suppose Kieran is worth all the trouble," Natalie said laughing. "So just how excited are you about this baby?"

"Incredibly! Despite the fact that the baby must remain a secret for as long as possible to remain out of the tabloids, Jordan and I have been running around telling everyone we can."

"I bet."

"I'm going to be so nervous when it comes time for the birth. I've been trying not to think about all the things that could go wrong."

"There's no use in worrying. Most pregnancies don't have any complications. I've never had a baby myself, but some of my friends have."

"I don't see how women do it. I don't think I could face the pain or even the discomfort before the birth."

"I think most women are aided by the thought of what's going on. When Kieran and I have a baby, knowing the end result will help me through the less-than-pleasant parts."

"I still can't believe this is happening. Jordan and I have talked about having a child for a few years and have been planning for a long time, but now that Sam is actually carrying our baby, well—it's overwhelming."

"Your child is going to be very lucky. He or she will have two wonderful dads."

"Thank you."

We sat and talked on the porch for a good, long time. I enjoyed the leisure time. Jordan and I had recently been on vacation, but even so, just sitting and doing nothing was a novelty.

Sean

Marshall stood with his back against the doorway, panting, trembling and crying. His eyes were squeezed shut as if trying to block out a sight he couldn't handle. Nick and I looked at each other. I could see my worry mirrored on Nick's features. We gazed back at Marshall.

"Marshall, are you okay?" Nick asked.

Marshall slowly opened his eyes. Tears streamed down his cheeks. He tried to talk, but he was trembling so violently he could hardly stand. Nick and I each took one of his arms and led him from the room.

I tried to puzzle out what had happened as we guided Marshall through the hallways and down to the first floor. The doorway we had entered didn't take us to present-day Verona, but to the Verona of years past—to a time before Mark and Taylor had died. It was very shortly before they died, because Taylor had resided in Verona for only a few months before he was driven to suicide. Stepping into the past was shocking, disturbing, and according to Einstein— impossible, but it didn't explain why Marshall had lost it. Marshall had no fear of ghosts and was more likely to run toward an unexplained supernatural phenomenon than away. If anything, I would have thought he would be fascinated to step into Verona's past. That was my own reaction. I wanted to go back and have a look around. I wanted to talk to Mark and Taylor and meet Nick's dads when they were teenagers. Marshall's reaction made no sense.

"Nick, can you run to the kitchen and get us some tea?" I asked Nick as we led Marshall into a quiet little sitting room. "Marshall spent years in England. Tea is their solution to everything over there."

"It's Dad's solution too. I'll be right back."

Marshall didn't react at all to quip about the British love of tea. I wasn't even sure he heard me. He just stared off into nothingness as I sat him down in a comfortable Victorian armchair.

I took a seat across from Marshall and wondered what I could do to help him. I was at a loss. I didn't even know what was wrong.

Marshall calmed down as we sat. At last his breathing began to return to normal, and his tears stopped. He was still trembling somewhat and looked as if he'd just witnessed the murder of his parents. Marshall wasn't acting like Marshall at all.

Nick came in with a tray bearing a teapot and three cups and saucers and set them down on a table. He poured Marshall a cup and handed it to him. Marshall looked at Nick and said, "Thank you." It was the first words he'd spoken.

"Marshall, what happened back there?" I asked quietly. "What's wrong?"

Marshall took a sip of tea to compose his thoughts before he answered.

"I guess you would call it sort of a panic attack. It's not that anything happened but that I feared what could happen."

"What could happen?" Nick asked, clearly as confused as I.

"We could have changed the future. If I would have had any hint we were stepping into the past, I wouldn't have dared."

"We could hardly change the future just by having a look around—not significantly—could we?" I asked.

Marshall turned his gaze upon me. "There is no way of knowing the consequences of any change, no matter how large or small."

Marshall shuddered, and a pained look crossed his face. Nick and I looked at each other again, quite concerned.

"I'm afraid I still don't understand your panic. True, we were somewhere we probably shouldn't have been, but we

338

could have just turned around and walked back instead of bolting for the doorway as if the hounds of hell were pursuing us."

"I overreacted," Marshall said, with tears welling in his eyes. "When I realized we were in the past, I lost it. I was afraid that..." His voice trailed off.

"You were afraid that what?" I asked. "What did you fear so badly?"

Marshall looked me in the eyes. "I was afraid it was going to happen again."

"Again? What do you mean?"

"I've been to the past before," Marshall said in a hoarse whisper. He shuddered again, and I thought he might cry.

"You've been there before?"

"Yes. Remember the book we found in the library while we were in high school? The one we destroyed?"

"Yes."

"It was a book of spells—spells that actually worked. I...tried one."

"You sent yourself into the past?"

"Yes."

Marshall had never explained why he was so frantic to destroy that book. He'd merely told Nick and me it was dangerous. He'd been so earnest we didn't doubt his word. I'd tried to ask him about it more than once, but he would never give me a straight answer.

"What did you do Marshall?"

"I nearly destroyed us all."

Nick and I listened as Marshall told us about traveling into the past. He had tried to make life better for everyone by preventing Taylor from killing himself, but his good intentions led to disaster. Marshall had altered reality, and the reality he'd created was a nightmare. Some of the things he told me about actually made me cry.

"I was so stupid," Marshall said. "If I'd had the abilities I have now, or if I'd even stopped to think, I would've known

I was being tricked. He tricked me into changing the past. I was such a fool."

"Who tricked you?"

"I'll give you one guess."

"Devon," Nick said.

Marshall nodded.

"I'd love to be rid of that pain in the ass," I said. "You just know he's up to something, even when he's not around. He's been so quiet recently that it scares me. I know something's coming. I keep waiting for the Gates of Hell to open up."

"Why would Devon want the past changed?" Nick asked. "How would that benefit him?"

"He wanted Mark and Taylor out of the way. He knew they'd have no power over him if they were alive instead of dead."

"But his past changed too," Nick said.

"It was a chance he was willing to take. He's thwarted here, for the time being at least. Perhaps he thought his chances to destroy us would be better if the past was changed."

"That's truly disturbing," Nick said.

"I didn't want to tell you. I didn't want to tell anyone," Marshall said. "I didn't want you to know what a fool I'd been."

"You meant well," I said.

"The road to hell is paved with good intentions. I nearly sent us all there."

"We actually lived different lives," Nick said. "I wonder what mine was like?"

Marshall remained silent.

"You know, don't you?" Nick asked.

"After the book was destroyed, Mark came to me. He told me some of what had happened in the altered reality—things I didn't see for myself. I don't know what happened to you Nick, except that you never came to Verona, because your dads weren't here to adopt you."

"Did something...bad happen to them," Nick asked.

Marshall nodded. "You don't want to know."

Nick looked at me, anguish in his eyes.

"Everything is okay now Nick," I said. "Everything was set back to way it was supposed to be. Right Marshall?"

"Yes. Mark said all was as it had been—except for me. He said I was changed. I alone among the living, remember what happened."

"I'm sorry," I said.

"I thought you'd be angry."

"That's all in the past," I said.

"Yes, and the past is something I will never again disturb," Marshall said.

I pitied Marshall. What horrible memories did he bear? He'd never been quite the same after we destroyed that book all those years ago. I can't explain it. He didn't act differently; it was just...something in his eyes. Now it all made sense.

"So you see why I panicked. We could have changed the past. We could have destroyed everything."

"That's one doorway we can never go through again," Nick said. "I wonder if we dare try any of the others."

"No," Marshall said. "I was thrilled to discover that room, but now...the risk is too great. We have to keep this among ourselves. No one else can ever know about that room. No one can be allowed to go there—ever."

I nodded. Marshall was right. Some things shouldn't be tampered with. I was just glad Marshall had grown wise enough to realize it. At least, that much good had come from his trip into the past.

Skye

"What do you mean you just saw me talking with Thad?" I asked.

"I saw you walking towards the library with him not two minutes ago," Nick said.

"Nick, that's impossible. I've been right here in the kitchen for the past half hour." The color drained from my face. "That wasn't me."

Nick and I stared at each other. I bolted from the kitchen and up the stairs. I could hear Nick's footsteps pounding behind me. I nearly knocked Sean down as I darted past him on the stairway but didn't stop to explain. I shot up the stairs. Panic consumed me. I knew in my heart something horrible was about to happen to Thad. I had to get there in time to stop it.

I thundered down the hallway as I raced for the library. The distance had never seemed so great before. I reached the end at last and jerked open the door just in time to see myself sink a dagger into Thad's chest. I launched myself at my double, but by the time I reached him, he was no longer there. I crashed into the wall nearly knocking myself unconscious. I struggled to my feet as evil laughter filled the air.

Nick and Sean bolted into the room as I crawled to Thad. I cradled him in my arms and gazed down at him, blood was spreading over his chest.

"Get an ambulance!" I screamed.

Sean whipped out his cell phone, but I paid him no more heed. I gazed down at Thad. His eyes were open, but his breath was ragged.

"It wasn't me," I said, tears streaming from my eyes. "It wasn't me."

"I know," Thad said, his voice wavering. "It seems I got to meet your nemesis after all."

Thad's body convulsed, and he grimaced in pain.

343

"An evil spirit posing as a man—that would've made a great scene for a book," Thad said.

"It will. You'll put it in your next book."

"I'm not so sure about that," Thad said.

"You will. Don't leave me."

"What is this power I have over younger men?" Thad said, smiling slightly. His voice was growing weaker. "I think you're still just trying to get into my pants."

I shook my head.

"You're my friend. I value my friends," I said.

We were silent for a while. I held Thad in my arms, willing the ambulance to get there. The minutes crawled by—each an eternity.

Thad drew a ragged breath, shuddered slightly, and then he was still. His eyes gazed sightlessly.

"Thad? Thad!"

Thad drew another breath, flooding me with relief. I looked up at Sean standing there. Tears pooled in his eyes. I felt so helpless. Thad was barely breathing.

I heard footsteps approaching and looked up to see Sean's dad leading in paramedics. I watched as they checked Thad's body for signs of life.

"I've got a pulse," said one of them.

I watched as the paramedics bound gauze to Thad's chest, slipped an oxygen mask over his face and carefully lifted him onto a gurney. One of them was quickly talking into a radio, but I was too dazed to hear what was said. I wanted to follow as they took Thad away, but I feared I might hinder them. I turned to Sean.

"Get Marshall," I said. "I want to know where Devon is NOW. I'm going to kill that fucker."

"Skye," Nick said hesitantly, "Devon's already dead."

"Then I'm going to do whatever it is I have to do to get rid of him *permanently*! Get Marshall!"

I had never been more determined in my life, but I also had no idea how I was going to rid Verona of its evil menace.

Before the police arrived, Sean, Nick and I created a story to tell them about Thad's assailant. Obviously, the truth would not do, so we kept it simple. Sean and Nick saw a young man running down the stairs from the fourth floor, went to investigate, and found Thad lying in the library. Only Thad and the three of us knew the true identity of Thad's attacker.

We left the library so the police could do their thing. I wondered whose prints they would find on the dagger. I guess it didn't matter. All that mattered was Thad. Sean called Marshall on his cell phone but couldn't reach him. It was just as well. Now that my initial fury had cooled, I could think of nothing but Thad. The cops told us he'd been taken to Memorial Hospital in South Bend for surgery. We were the closest thing Thad had to family in Verona, so Sean, Nick, and I drove up to await the outcome.

Thad was already in surgery when we arrived, but we were forced to sit there for over three hours with no word on his condition other than that he was alive when he was brought in, and he was listed in critical condition.

"I guess we should have warned Thad about Devon's old trick of appearing as someone else," Sean said.

"Who would have thought he'd go after Thad?" Nick said.

"Maybe he did it to hurt me. Thad and I have been spending a lot of time together," I said.

"Oh?" Nick asked.

"Not like that, not that I didn't try."

"Wait a minute," Nick said. "Did I hear you right? Did Skye Mackenzie get shot down?"

"If you tell anyone, I *will* kill you. I wish I could kill Devon. He's brought far too much pain into too many lives. It has to end."

"I wish they would come out and tell us something," Sean said. "I hate this waiting."

"Maybe no news is good news. It means they're still trying to save him," Nick said.

Sean's eyes met mine. He was as worried as I.

"You really like him don't you Skye?" Nick asked after we'd sat there in silence for a while.

"Yeah I do. I could almost..." I trailed off.

"Almost what?" Nick asked.

"I could almost date him."

"You mean as in relationship?" Nick asked. "As in *boyfriend*?"

"Hey, I said 'almost,' okay?"

"Wow, this is almost as big of a shock as you getting shot down."

"Remind me why I like you?" I asked.

I was glad Sean and Nick were with me. They helped me pass the time. I realized as I sat there that I cared for Thad more than I thought. I wasn't sure what I'd do if he died.

At last we got the word: Thad's surgery was over and he was in recovery. His condition was serious, but no longer critical. There was more waiting after that, but at least he'd jumped the first and most difficult hurtle. I was not at ease, but I felt a good deal more hopeful.

I lied to the pencil-pushing hospital employees and told them Thad was my uncle so they would let me in to see him when he'd awakened. He looked pale, but his eyes were alert and once more filled with life.

"I told you you weren't going to die," I said. "You're not getting away from me that easily."

"I hate being wrong," Thad said.

"How do you feel?" I asked.

Thad glared at me for a moment.

"Okay, stupid question. Is there anyone you would like me to call?"

"Yes, my grandparents and Cedi."

"Cedi?"

"Yeah."

I wrote down the numbers as Thad recited them

"Okay, I'll make these calls and then I'll be right back. I'm staying with you tonight."

"You don't have to do that."

"Yes I do. No one else would want to stay with your grumpy ass."

Thad began to laugh, but then grimaced.

"Sorry. I'll go make those phone calls now."

I updated Sean and Nick on Thad's condition and told them I was staying with him. They offered to stay with me, but I told them I'd be fine. I had my cell phone, so I could call if I needed anything. Sean and Nick left. I made the necessary phone calls, then returned to Thad's room. He was sleeping, so I sat down in a chair and just gazed at him. I eventually nodded off.

The sound of voices awakened me the next morning. I opened my eyes to see two older guys standing by Thad's bed talking to him. My neck popped like crazy when I sat up in the chair. I stood and arched my back so that it popped too. I stretched to work out the stiffness in my muscles. Hospital chairs aren't the most comfortable places to sleep.

"Hey Sleeping Beauty," Thad said.

"Shut up."

Thad was alert and his color was much better than it had been the day before. I began to relax for the first time since he'd been attacked. He really was going to recover.

"Skye, these are my grandfathers, Angel and Kurt. You spoke to them on the phone. They drove up from southern Indiana last night."

"I'm pleased to meet you," I said.

We nodded to each other. Thad's grandfathers were probably both in their mid-60s, but they looked good for their ages. Angel had white hair that he wore in a ponytail. That style of hair looked just plain nasty on most old guys, but it suited Angel perfectly. Something told me he'd probably worn it that way all his life. Kurt had far shorter hair, but was quite handsome as well.

"Thank you for taking care of our grandson," Kurt said. "He can't seem to stay out of trouble."

"He takes a good deal of looking after," Angel said.

"They still think I'm twelve," Thad said.

"Thank God he's not," Kurt said. "He was a terror at that age and his teenage years...what a nightmare."

I grinned. I could tell Angel and Kurt were teasing Thad. I was glad to know he had such a family.

"I think he does a pretty good job of taking care of himself," I said.

"He is starting to grow up a little," Angel said.

"I bet you have some interesting stories to tell about Thad."

"There will be no stories," Thad said firmly.

"Aw, I was looking forward to hearing about your embarrassing moments."

"Later," Angel said in a stage whisper.

Thad exhaled loudly. "Why didn't I just stay in Europe?" he asked no one in particular.

I knew Thad was only pretending to be annoyed. He loved those old guys. I could tell. I was growing rather fond of them myself.

Angel, Kurt, and I left the room when the doctor came in to examine Thad. We talked quietly in the waiting room, not about Thad's embarrassing teenage moments, but about the James-Egler farm where Angel and Kurt had resided most of their lives. We were all trying to get our minds off how close we had come to losing Thad.

When the doctor exited we went back in.

"So what's the news?" Angel asked.

"I've got to take it easy for the next six weeks, but other than that I'm fine. One of my ribs deflected the blade of the dagger so that only the outside edge of my heart was sliced. The doctor said it took a good deal of time to repair but that damage was minimal."

"When can we take you home?" Kurt asked.

I didn't like the sound of that. I was just getting to know Thad. I didn't want him to leave.

"The doctor said he would release me in a few days."

Angel grinned. Despite his years, he looked boyish when he did so.

"Could you two give me some time alone with Skye?" Thad asked.

"Of course," Angel said. "We'll go take a stroll."

I walked to Thad's bedside.

"You didn't have to stay all night with me," he said.

"Yeah I did. I was worried about you."

"Thanks. I appreciate it."

"Do you have to go home when you're released?" I asked. "You could come back to Graymoor, you know. I'll look after you."

"You have a life Skye, and you don't need to spend it babysitting me."

"I wouldn't mind."

"I've done all I can in Verona. It's time for me to go home."

"Are you sure I can't convince you to make Verona your home?"

"Are you proposing to me Skye?" asked Thad grinning. Before I could answer, he spoke again. "Our time together has been special Skye, but I think we both know it can't go on forever. My life is back in Blackford; yours is in Verona."

"This sucks. I was just getting to know you," I said.

"I'll be back sooner or later. Graymoor Mansion holds an irresistible lure for me. There are enough stories there for several novels. Besides, I'm absolutely impossible to get along with if you spend too much time with me. I like things

349

my way. You and I are both too headstrong to get along for long."

"You might be right about that."

"Yeah, I've heard some stories about the Alpha male."

I rolled my eyes. "I was such a freak in high school. I had quite a superiority complex. How did you find out about that anyway? Did Sean tell you?"

"I can't reveal my sources."

"It's just as well. Not knowing will save me the trouble of killing someone."

***

I visited Thad daily, but his grandfathers stayed with him. Finally, Thad was released from the hospital and returned to Graymoor to pack his things. I assisted him, while Sean's mom gave Angel and Kurt a tour of the house.

All too soon Thad was packed.

"I guess it's time to say goodbye," he said.

I grabbed Thad and hugged him, although not too tightly since he was injured.

"Here," Thad said, indicating a stack of books sitting near his bags. "These are for you. There will be a quiz the next time we meet."

"I'll be ready. I'm going to miss you."

"Just remember, if you miss me too much, you'll find me in there," he said, pointing to his books. "And Skye, I'm going to miss you too."

"I'm only a phone call or e-mail away," I said, "or a not-so-short drive."

I carried Thad's bags downstairs. He had no business lifting anything. He was determined to help carry his bags, but I wouldn't allow it. We found Angel and Kurt in the parlor with Sean's mom admiring the many antiques.

"I don't envy you the task ahead," I told Angel and Kurt. "He wanted to carry his own luggage downstairs. He's so stubborn."

"I only wanted to carry one bag," Thad said in his defense.

"The doctor said NO lifting," I admonished. I turned to Angel and Kurt. "If he gives you any trouble, you just let me know, and I'll come down and kick his butt."

Thad laughed. "Great, now you're treating me like a child too."

I carried Thad's bags to the car and returned to the front porch where Thad, Kurt, Angel, and Sean's mom were standing. Everyone said "goodbye," and then Kurt and Angel walked Thad to the car. All too soon, they were driving away. I just stood there watching until the car disappeared down the street. I felt an arm across my shoulder. It was Sean's mom.

"If I didn't know better, I'd say you liked him."

I looked at her and grinned.

I stayed out on the porch for a while after everyone went back inside. Now that Thad had departed I turned my mind to Devon. It was time to make that fucker pay.

Ralph

"Why did you buy that thing?" asked Jordan as I pulled a tabloid out the grocery bag.

"Our secret is out," I said, "and you're not going to like what the tabloids are saying about it."

"Do I ever like what the tabloids say?"

"They have outdone themselves this time."

"How could anyone have found out this quickly? Sam isn't even showing yet!"

"Beats me, but someone did."

I unfolded the tabloid so Jordan could read the front page headline.

Jordan's Coming Out a Sham

Phantom's Lead Singer Impregnates Roadie During Road Trip Orgy?

Six years ago, Phantom's lead singer gained international attention when he publicly announced he was gay. Since that time, Jordan has capitalized on his notoriety by making high-profile appearances at gay fundraisers and other events. Reliable resources have now reported, however, that Jordan is expecting the birth of *his* child in a matter of weeks. The mother of Jordan's illegitimate baby is rumored to be a member of Phantom's own road crew, which leads many to wonder just what goes on in the tour bus after Phantom's concerts.

"This is exactly the kind of immoral behavior that public personalities should not exhibit," stated Dr. Thomas Dotard, the founder and spokesperson for *Focus on Family Values* (FFV), when asked for his comment. "It's also proof that sexual orientation is a choice. Here we have a public figure who had proclaimed himself a homosexual, yet he has had intimate relations with women. Jordan Potter is exactly the kind of individual we do not need influencing our youth. Homosexuality is the scourge of modern civilization and far more damaging to our culture and family values than any terrorist attack. An individual such as Jordan has great influence over our youth, and look at the message he is sending through his deviant actions: it's acceptable to have indiscriminate sexual intercourse with members of either sex. This is exactly the type of immorality that the FFV works so fervently against."

Rumors suggest that Jordan fathered his illegitimate offspring during a private orgy after one of Phantom's concerts during their last tour. Jordan's long-time "boyfriend" is rumored to have been involved, but these rumors could not be confirmed.

"This is typical behavior for rock stars," says Dotard. "Rock music is all about sex. Just look at the lyrics, the groupies, and the wild orgies that would make a Roman emperor blush. This news comes as no shock to me at all. The only surprise is that it didn't happen years ago, but then again who says it didn't? No one has any idea of what goes on in Jordan's private world. He may have already fathered dozens of children for all we know."

This clear demonstration of heterosexuality has led some to wonder if Jordan's homosexuality is nothing but a sham designed to pull in gay fans. After Jordan publicly outed himself, Phantom's fan base grew tremendously.

"It's a shame that someone would stoop to taking advantage of an already confused group," said Dotard, "but when dealing with someone who cares about nothing more than record sales and the almighty dollar, nothing would surprise me."

Immoral behavior?   A scheme to take advantage of gays? Both? Only Jordan himself knows the answers to these questions.

Jordan's eyes were blazing when he put down the paper.

"This is ludicrous!" he shouted.

"Of course it is Jordan. It's a tabloid. This is the same paper that claimed a Sherman tank from WWI was found on the moon. It even contradicts itself! I thought you learned long ago not to get worked up over tabloids."

"This goes too far. This Dotard guy is trying to undermine all the work I've done. He's trying to create doubt, trying to make me look like some kind of pervert. What are all the gays who look up to me going to think when they read this?"

"That this is the same paper that claimed a Sherman tank from WWI was found on the moon," I repeated.

Jordan actually smiled for a moment.

"I'm sorry. I know I'm overreacting, but I just get so tired of being attacked. I'm so tired of all the bullshit lies spread against gays. I'm particularly tired of groups like this Focus on Family Values bunch who think they have the right to dictate how everyone else should act and think."

"The country does seem to be overrun with little groups that believe they should do the thinking for everyone."

"Maybe I'm also upset because this takes something wonderful and makes it look sordid. An orgy? What is Sam going to think about this?"

"Hmm, she might punch this Dotard guy in the nose, but other than that I doubt it will affect her."

"Is the press going to hound our child Ralph? Is he going to have any chance for a normal life, or will he be going off to preschool with a bodyguard?"

"He or she is going to have a wonderful life Jordan. We will make sure of that."

"You're disrupting my fury," Jordan said.

"Good. Now forget about the article, forget about all the idiots like Dotard. None of that can hurt us. The truth is the truth no matter how anyone tries to twist it. People are going to believe what they want to believe, and all we can do and should do is set an example by the way we live."

"I agree with most of that, but there's something more I can do. I wanted to keep the birth of our child a secret, but the cat's out of the bag. I want to tell our side of the story."

"I'd have to say that's a good idea."

"I wonder how the press found out?"

"Who knows?" I said. "I'm sure none of our friends or family talked, but you know how it is. Perhaps someone overheard; perhaps someone connected with Sam's doctor or hospital talked. We knew we couldn't keep this a secret forever."

"I wish we could have at least told our friends first."

"We told our families and our closest friends."

"That's true."

"So cheer up, Jordan. Nothing has changed. I wouldn't have shown you that tabloid at all, but I knew you would find out about it sooner or later, and sooner is probably better."

"Yes it is. Now we can do something about it."

***

"Next up, an exclusive interview with *Phantom's* lead singer, Jordan Potter, about the upcoming birth of his child."

356

"Jordan! It's coming on if you want to watch it!" I yelled.

Jordan joined me in front of the TV.

"I guess you still won't tell me what you said?"

"You can watch the interview in two minutes Ralph."

"O-o-k-a-a-y," I said.

After a bunch of commercials, the evening news program was back.

"Here in an exclusive interview recorded last night with Tulsa reporter Murphy Florence, Jordan Potter talks about the rumors swirling around the upcoming birth of his child."

The view switched to my partner, sitting across from Murphy, a local Tulsa TV reporter and friend of Natalie. Jordan had opted to give her the interview so he wouldn't have to travel to New York or L.A. and also because handling the exclusive story would give Murphy airtime on the national news. She hoped it would be her big break.

"Let's get right to it," Murphy said. "Are the rumors true? Have you fathered a child?"

"My partner Ralph and I are eagerly anticipating the birth of our child, so yes, there will be a baby in our future. A close friend of ours has agreed to act as a surrogate mother, although I hesitate to call her a surrogate because she will be very much involved in her child's life. Both Ralph and I believe it's very important that our child be close to its mother."

"What about the rumors that your baby was conceived during an after-concert orgy?"

"That's complete nonsense. Ralph and I have been discussing our options for a few years now. We've considered adoption, but the prejudiced attitude that currently prevails would have made adoption extremely difficult. We hoped to eventually find a surrogate mother for our child, and we are very lucky that a close friend of ours was willing to have a child with us. This baby will have three parents who love him, or her, very much."

"How did the rumors of conception during an orgy get started?"

"The first I heard of it was in a tabloid, and I imagine the rumor was started by the tabloid itself. Unlike more traditional news organizations, tabloids are not known for their adherence to the truth. Tabloids have claimed that Ross, Kieran, and myself are aliens, that various women have had Bigfoot's baby, and that Amelia Earhart has been discovered alive and well, living on Mars."

"And of course, none of these rumors is true?"

"Well, I've often suspected that Ross might be an alien, but other than that I'd have to say I don't have confidence in the reports."

"Ross is going to get you for that," I told Jordan.

"The reason I'm doing this interview is that once a rumor like this gets started, it tends to spread no matter how disreputable the source. Unfortunately, groups such as Focus on Family Values are only too ready to jump all over a story like this to advance their agenda. I do a lot of work with various gay groups to educate and increase understanding so that hopefully, prejudice and ignorance can be lessened. Some groups such as the FFV, don't want positive gay role models out there, so they do whatever they can to tear them down, even stooping so low as to ally themselves with a tabloid. The FFV's connection to a tabloid makes me wonder how truthful they are in their other endeavors."

"Ouch!" I said grinning. "Direct hit!"

"Just wait."

"You don't seem fond of such groups as Focus on Family Values."

"I'm not. I think they do a tremendous disservice to society. Supporting family values is a wonderful, worthwhile endeavor, but groups such as the FFV are a perversion of what they claim to be. Take a close look and you'll see that the FFV and similar groups have an agenda that has nothing to do with strengthening families. Anyone who falls outside of their narrow definition of family—mother, father, and their heterosexual children—is automatically excluded. Rather than strengthen families, their work does nothing but erode the strength of the family. Because of the message spread by such groups, many turn their backs on family members who are gay. These groups are narrow-minded and prejudiced, and their real goal is to legally ensure their right to discriminate. Gays are often depicted as a dangerous element in society, but groups such as the FFV are more fanatical than any Middle Eastern terrorist cell."

"How do you define a family, Jordan?"

"I think the term 'family' can have many definitions. It can mean parents and their biological children, parents and their adopted children, any couple and their children whether or not the parents are married, unmarried, gay, or straight and whether or not their children are biological or adopted. In many cultures 'family' refers to the extended family: aunts, uncles, cousins, grandparents and so forth. I believe it also includes friends who are so emotionally close they are 'adopted' into the family. There doesn't have to be a biological or legal connection. When all is said and done, a family is a group of people who care about each other. Unfortunately, some special-interest groups refuse to see it that way."

"What about the accusations that you've committed an immoral act since you have taken part in conceiving a child out of wedlock?"

"There is nothing immoral about intentionally bringing a child into this world. Our baby was not an accident. As for the baby being conceived out of wedlock, what choice did we have? We are denied our God-given right to marry, so how could anyone object to the fact that Ralph and I are not married?"

The interview continued for a short time, but the rest was anti-climactic.

"I'm surprised the networks were willing to run that interview," I said.

"I'm sure some didn't, but I told Murphy to inform all concerned parties that this was the only interview I would give on the topic, period. It was a take-it-or-leave-it proposition."

"You know you'll get flooded with interview requests and with questions."

"Yes, and they will all be politely turned down. When I say exclusive, I mean exclusive."

"I'm very proud of you, Jordan."

"Well, let's just hope it does some good. I've had my say. I've told our side of the story. Now, I'm just going to concentrate on you, Sam and our child. People can say and think whatever they want."

Sean

"He's not here," Marshall said as we sat in the tower room with Nick, Skye, Oliver, and Clay.

"Well, he sure as hell was the other day!" shouted Skye. "He almost killed Thad! I've had enough of his shit! I want him dead, destroyed—whatever it takes!"

"He can't be killed," Oliver said. "We can't destroy him. Taylor said that's not the way."

"Then how do we get rid of him?" Skye asked, more calmly.

"If we knew that we would've done it long ago," I said.

"Then let's figure it out and do it now. This has got to end. Oliver and I would be dead if Taylor hadn't intervened. Thad was nearly killed. Devon has stirred up trouble from day one. He's a menace, and who knows what he'll do next?"

Marshall's face blanched, and I knew he was thinking about how Devon had tricked him into altering the past. The consequences had been disastrous. The fact that everything had been set right did not alter the malevolence of our enemy. If Skye knew about it, he'd go ballistic.

"What did Mark say?" Oliver said, thinking. "Wasn't it something like: we can neither defeat nor destroy him. Our only hope is to change him. Devon is a tormented soul. He seeks vengeance for wrongs. Our task is to make him see he is following the wrong path. He must release his hatred and his pain. He must realize he is a part of the whole, not an outsider."

"Well *that* sounds easy," Skye said, rolling his eyes.

"It's the key," I said. "Mark told us what must be done. Helping Devon is the only way to rid ourselves of him."

"Help that thing?" Nick asked.

"Yes," Oliver said. "Look, I have as much reason as any of you to hate Devon. He tricked me. He made me look like a fool. He tried to kill me, but he is a tormented soul. He's doing what he's doing because something made him the way

361

he is. When Mark first told us we needed to help him, I didn't want to do it either, but I've thought a lot about what Mark said. Devon is not evil. He has lost his way; he's confused, shunned, lonely, and in pain. We may consider his actions evil, but he is not so."

"He sure seems evil to me," Nick said.

"You're going to argue with an angel?" Oliver asked.

"So how do we find out what made Devon the way he is?" Skye asked. "It's not as though we can just ask him: *Hey Devon, what turned you into a sadistic, fucked-up bastard?*"

"We could go back in time," I said.

"NO!" shouted Marshall so loud that everyone in the room, except Skye, jumped.

"We need to take him back in time," I said. "We need to make Devon see where he went wrong."

"NO!" Marshall said. "Absolutely not! After what I told you, you should know better Sean. It would be far better to just leave things as they are instead of meddling with the past."

Everyone in the room except for Nick, Marshall, and me looked profoundly confused.

"I think I've missed something here," Oliver said. "What are you guys going on about?"

"It's a very long and unpleasant story, and I'm not up to telling it now," Marshall said. "Just take my word for it: the past must absolutely be off limits."

"What if we could go into the past without changing it?" I asked. "What if we could merely observe it without altering it?"

"It doesn't work like that Sean," Marshall said. "You were there; we talked to Mark and Taylor. You *know*."

"Okay, you guys are going to have to do some explaining. I feel like you're talking in Swiss or something," Skye said.

"Swiss isn't a language Skye," Clay said.

"You know what I mean!"

I looked at Marshall, silently asking his permission. He nodded. We could trust our friends.

"Okay," I said. "Only Marshall, Nick, and I know about this so far, and this has to remain an absolute secret, but there is a room in this house with doorways that lead to...other places."

"Other places?" Skye asked.

"And at least one of them leads to another time," Marshall said. "We cannot go through that doorway again. It should be boarded up."

"Oh, God, what next?" Skye asked, rubbing the bridge of his nose. "Why-oh-why did I return to Spook Central? I swear all the weirdness in the world is centered in this house. I was in California with all those hot guys...."

"Calm yourself Skye," Oliver said.

"We do seem to have more than our share of bizarreness," I said.

"No kidding," Skye said.

"Okay," Nick said, "so if we can figure out a way to go back in time without changing it, and if we can figure out when and where to go back to, and if we can figure out a way to force Devon to go back with us...well, what then?"

"That is way too many ifs," Skye said, "and there are some huge if's there. Are you listening to what you're saying? I say we just find a way to kick Devon's ass."

"You would," Marshall said.

"We should have tried this a long time ago," Oliver said. "We should have started working on it right after Taylor and Mark told us about Devon. We should have listened."

"Yes, you should have Oliver."

We all turned at the sound of a new voice, a voice we recognized but did not often hear. Mark was sitting in one of the comfortable chairs under the large stained-glass window of daffodils, as if he'd been sitting there the entire time. Perhaps he had. Who knew with angels?

"Mark!" Oliver said.

"So," Mark said, rubbing his hands together. "Now that you're finally ready we can begin."

"Wait a minute," Skye said. "You mean we can actually do this—what we've been talking about? Why didn't we do this six years ago when you first told us we needed to show Devon he's following the wrong path?"

"Because you weren't prepared, you didn't truly understand, and you weren't determined enough to succeed. Everything happens in its own time."

"Why do I even bother talking to you?" Skye said, exasperated, but not angry. Mark merely laughed.

"Since you've come this far, I can give you a little help," Mark said. "Marshall, the doorway that you entered with Sean and Nick has been altered. You may now go through it without fear of altering the past."

"So if we go through the doorway, nothing we do can change anything?"

"That's correct. You will not be able to interact with anyone or anything from the past."

"What good is that?" Clay asked.

"You haven't been listening," I said. "It's perfect. We have to show Devon that things aren't as they seem to be. We don't have to change anything. We don't want to change anything. We just have to show him what he missed the first time around."

"How do we do that?" Oliver asked. "How do we take him where he needs to be and show him what he needs to see? He's a spirit. It's not as if we can force him."

"If he was human, I could force him," Skye said.

"Done," Mark said.

"What?" Skye asked.

"You said you needed him to be human, so he's human."

"Just like that?"

"Yes."

I was stunned. Taylor and Mark could so rarely intervene in human affairs that I wasn't expecting such

364

tremendous help. I considered asking Mark why he was able to help us now, but I knew he'd only tell me the time had come or something just as useless.

"Then our next task is to find Devon," Marshall said.

"Taylor should be making sure he's arriving at Graymoor just about now," Mark said. "I think you'll find Devon in the parlor."

"Leave this task to me then," Skye said, standing.

"Meet us on the fourth-floor landing," Sean said. "We'll take you to the doorway."

"Skye," Mark said, before Skye could leave the room. "Remember, your task is to convince Devon he's following the wrong path, not to punish him for what he's done. You're going to have to forgive him—for everything."

Skye looked angry for a moment, then perplexed, but then he nodded his head and left.

"There's one more problem," I said. "Just what is it we need to show Devon in his past?"

Skye

I fought to calm myself as I walked down the stairs. My nemesis awaited me. Devon had very nearly killed Oliver and me, and most recently, Thad. I didn't enjoy the sensation of hating any being, but I hated Devon. He was now mortal. For how long I didn't know, but at last I could deal with him—my way. I could beat him senseless for all that he'd done. I could wrap my fingers around his neck and squeeze the life out of him. Still, I knew that's not what I was about. As much as I yearned to make Devon pay for his crimes, my true goal was that shared by all of us: to eliminate the danger that was Devon, not by destroying him but by showing him the error of his ways.

I gazed into the parlor as I descended the last few steps. Devon had his back to me. He was facing Taylor, who barred his escape. Taylor looked fierce and beautiful, and Devon did not dare to make a move toward him. Devon turned at the sound of my footsteps and glared at me with pure hatred. He appeared as he must have when he died, a middle-aged man against whom the ravages of time had already begun to take their toll. Even though he was now a mere human, I could feel the malevolence flowing from him. We were supposed to bring understanding to this foul creature?

"So you've come to gloat, have you Skye?" spat Devon. "Or more likely you've come to kill me while you can. Now is your chance Skye, while I'm vulnerable to even your crude and pathetic prowess."

"I haven't come to harm you Devon."

"Oh? Not even after what I did to that old man you lusted over? The one who rejected you? I assure you his survival was quite accidental. Had I more accustomed to being in a solid form, I would have struck true and buried that dagger in his heart."

I seethed with anger.

"How is your little friend Oliver? Is he feeling healthy Skye?"

I refused to play Devon's game and quelled my anger.

"Don't waste my time Devon. My guess is you want me to kill you so you can go back to your spirit form. Surely even you realize that Taylor would merely force you back into human form again."

Devon growled at me and I grinned.

"Come on," I said. "We have an appointment to keep."

I moved forward and Devon shrank back. He feared me. He was playing on my turf now, and he knew I had the advantage. Devon was trapped. He could not step back far without bumping into Taylor, and I had no doubt he feared him far more than me. Devon darted to the side, but I tackled him around the midsection and took him down. He hit the floor and groaned in pain.

"We can do this the easy way or the hard way Devon," I said. "I do so hope you'll choose the hard way."

"I will remember your arrogance when I destroy you," Devon said. "I assure you your death will not be pleasant. I promise you also that you'll watch your little friend die before you meet your own fate."

"Charming, isn't he?" I said to Taylor.

I grabbed Devon by the hair and jerked him toward the stairs. He shrugged me off and began to climb on his own. I watched him for any sudden moves, but for the moment he was cooperating. We climbed all the way to the fourth floor where Mark, Marshall, Sean, Nick, Oliver, and Clay awaited us.

Devon snarled at Mark and the others, but did not speak. Sean gazed upon Devon with a mixture of fear, hatred, revulsion, and, oddly enough— pity. Marshall merely looked upon Devon with fascination.

"He is human. I sense nothing more from him."

"Hello Marshall. Read any good books lately?" Devon said with a smirk.

"None so revealing as the one you're about to read," Marshall said. I suppressed a grin.

Devon's eyes darted this way and that like a cornered beast. He looked most fearfully upon Mark. Devon knew there was no escape.

Marshall led us through twisting hallways until we came at last to our destination, a circular room that was nothing but closed doors. Mark opened one of them and through it I could see green grass and a distant goal. Boys in blue-and-white soccer uniforms were running about the field—vying with others dressed in green and gold for control of a ball. Devon looked fearfully at Mark, and I did not understand his trepidation.

"This is our first stop," Mark said, pointing through the doorway.

Marshall looked at the doorway with nearly as much dread as Devon. Mark smiled at him.

"Have no fear Marshall. The past we are about to enter is immutable."

Marshall swallowed, turned, and stepped through the doorway. I expected a flash of light or some such display, but there was none. I peered through the doorway to see Marshall standing upon the grass. The players darted around and *through* him as if he wasn't there. Sean followed. I took Devon by the upper arm and guided him forward. He offered token resistance, but no more. He knew there was no escape. I could have easily forced him if I had to, and Mark was more powerful still. I must admit I was not entirely comfortable in the presence of an angel, although this was not my first time. I felt very weak and small, almost like a child, in Mark's presence.

I was curious to see what miraculous events we were about to see unfold, but nothing more than a soccer game awaited us. I looked with interest upon Mark, Taylor and Devon running up and down the field. They all looked to be about sixteen, and I guessed that the game I was seeing occurred not many weeks before the deaths of Taylor and Mark. Devon's own demise would not come for many long years.

What I witnessed upon the green field was a scene of struggle, but only between the two opposing teams. Mark, Taylor and Devon were not enemies, but friends. There was no trace of hatred in Devon, no trace of bitterness or malice. We were viewing a time before he had turned. I saw Devon in a new light. Taylor had told us Devon was not always a malicious spirit, but I had to see it to truly comprehend. The hatred I felt for Devon began to ebb. The attractive blond boy I saw playing on the field bore no resemblance other than physical to the Devon who stood beside me.

I stole a glance at the present Devon as he watched himself and his friends in the past. What I saw was not hatred etched upon his features, but an epic sadness that almost made me want to cry. I began to pity the man who stood beside me. He had truly lost his way.

I glanced now and then at Mark and Taylor in their angel form as they watched their human selves play. Seeing them both in two places at once was bizarre. My mind didn't want to accept it.

I don't know how long we stood there—a half hour, perhaps. It seemed longer in some ways, maybe hours even, but it could not have been long, for we merely watched the game until its end.

Mark led us closer to Taylor, Devon, and his former self. I kept my gaze on the Devon of the past, and his features told a tale I had not suspected could even exist. Devon looked upon both Mark and Taylor with a sense of longing, of quiet desperation—even of love and desire.

"You were in love with them...both," Sean said quietly, gazing at Devon.

Devon jerked his head toward Sean and glared at him, but the expected angry outburst did not come. Instead, Devon remained silent and tears began to well in his eyes.

"There is more," Mark said.

Devon shook his head. "No. No more. Please." His tone was pleading, another first for Devon.

Mark smiled at Devon sadly, and I could tell that he loved him despite everything. Devon jerked his head, gazing into Mark's eyes as if he also noticed the love for the very first time.

"It's a difficult path my old friend, but you must follow it to the end. Come with us."

Mark and Taylor both extended a hand, and surprisingly, or perhaps not, Devon grasped them. In the next moment, we found ourselves gathered in what I guessed must have been Devon's own room. There were photos of soccer players upon the walls. Many of the photos were torn from the pages of magazines, but some were snapshots of Devon's very own teammates. Devon from the past held one of these in his hand. It was a picture of Mark in his soccer uniform. A ball balanced under one foot; his shirt dangling at his side. Devon picked up another photo—this one of Taylor. In it, Taylor stood, arms crossed, legs spread, smiling and staring directly into the camera. He was also clad in his soccer uniform. Devon from the past sighed.

I had not noticed before, but it was dark outside the windows. Devon got undressed and went to bed. He looked so very sad and lonely that my heart went out to him. Devon drew a shuddering breath, and tears rimmed his eyes. He did not cry, but I could sense his torment.

Devon laced his fingers together and closed his eyes. He remained silent, but I knew he was praying. Was he asking God for a soul mate? Was he praying that God would bring him together with one of the boys he loved? Even standing there in the past, we could not intrude upon Devon's prayer, but the Devon from our own time remembered. He knew what passed between himself and God all those years before. That Devon began to sob, even as his younger self finished his prayer and hugged his pillow to himself to ward off his feelings of guilt, isolation, and despair.

What followed were quick scenes of Devon gazing upon Taylor and Mark as they laughed together. So many times Devon had begun to join them, but had drawn back in fear. He was afraid of revealing his feelings. He was afraid his friends would discover his secret and turn their backs on him forever.

There were scenes with Devon's parents too. It took only a few of these for me to understand the fear that had permeated Devon's life. He'd been forced to hide his true nature completely. He didn't dare reveal he was anything less that 100% percent heterosexual. He also knew that his parents would not have loved him if they'd known the truth, for he wasn't the son they believed him to be. No doubt the fear of his parents discovering his secret spread within Devon until he didn't dare to reveal himself to anyone.

Next, our little group looked on as Devon carefully picked out a handsome journal in a stationery store. We watched Devon as he watched it being carefully wrapped. We followed him as he walked away carrying the gift tightly in his hands. I could feel his nervousness and his joy. I knew he'd made a decision to reveal his feelings at last, but was it to be to Taylor or Mark?

"I don't want to see any more," the Devon from our own time said.

I heard Devon begin to sob. I heard Sean gasp. He was staring at Devon. I turned to look at him, and I noticed it too. He looked younger, as if the years were beginning to peel away. The Devon standing beside us crying did not look the same as the one from the past, but he looked far more like him than he had before. I realized that the change wasn't so sudden as I at first thought. Hadn't Devon looked a bit younger even as we began our journey and he had watched his former self play soccer with his friends?

"Please," Devon said, turning to Mark and Taylor. "I don't want to see any more!"

Even Oliver and Clay began to look upon Devon with pity. They had as much reason as anyone to hate him.

"I'm sorry," Mark said. "I truly am, but we're almost there Devon. Just a few steps more."

Devon looked at each of us in turn with a pleading look in his eyes that nearly tore my heart out. Devon's gaze made both Sean and Oliver begin to cry. I felt such pity for Devon as I looked at him. Here was the creature who had tormented us all. Here was the very being who had tried to destroy my friends and me. He had stopped at nothing and struck out at us without conscience. The Devon who stood before me now already bore little resemblance to the twisted creature he had been. I had thought our mission folly from the beginning. I thought it impossible that such a being could change, but Devon was changing before my very eyes. I felt my hatred for him falling away, despite all that had occurred in the past.

Mark and Taylor next took us to a wooded area where we stood upon the path. I wasn't entirely sure, but I thought we were on the paths behind the high school. Just up the path, Mark, the Mark from the past that is, turned away from the path and walked among the trees. Devon from the past stealthily trailed him. Devon was holding the wrapped journal and gazing at Mark's retreating form expectantly. I felt sadness well up in my heart, as if I already knew what was about to happen. I felt a sense of impending tragedy.

We followed closely behind Devon until he stopped. The angel Mark led us on just past Devon so we could look back and see Devon's face.

"No! No!" said the Devon from our time. "I can't!"

"You must," Mark said in a quiet, but commanding tone. "It's almost over, Devon."

Taylor placed his hand on Devon's shoulder to comfort him. Devon did as he was told and watched the scene unfold with the rest of us. Rain began to fall from the darkened sky above, just a few drops at first, but soon in a steady downfall. It was an odd sensation, standing there in the rain and not getting the least bit wet.

I saw the Devon from the past take a few deep breaths to steady himself. A smile crept across his face and he began to step forward, but then cruel fate intervened. Devon's head jerked a bit to the side at the sound of a voice. Taylor's voice.

We followed Devon's gaze as he watched Taylor walk toward Mark. Both of them were getting soaked, but they didn't seem to care. Devon's face began to pale as the two drew closer together. Mark took Taylor in his arms and kissed him while the rain beat down upon them from above. Devon's face fell and he began to sob. His own tears mingled with the raindrops that fell on him from above. His gift fell from his fingers onto the damp soil of the forest as Devon's entire body was racked with sobs. Thunder rent the air, and Mark and Taylor scurried away. Devon from the past began to howl in pain.

The angel Mark touched Devon on the shoulder, and we all found ourselves watching Taylor and Mark yet again, but this time they were talking alone in a darkened room that I was quite sure was somewhere in Graymoor Mansion.

"How could so many have turned on us?" Taylor asked, crying. "So many that we counted as friends only a few days ago?"

"I'm so sorry Babe," Mark said, taking Taylor in his arms and holding him tight. Mark was sobbing too. "Not everyone has turned on us. Some have stood by us. I would have thought that..." Mark began to cry louder. His sobs drowned out his voice.

"What?" Taylor asked.

"Devon. I thought he would stick by us. I've always counted him as one of my closest friends. I loved him. I don't understand how he can turn his back on me now when I need him the most. I actually thought he loved me once upon a time. I guess I was wrong."

Mark broke down, and Taylor comforted him just as Mark had done for him only moments before.

"I didn't know."

I turned at the sound of the voice. It was our Devon from our time who spoke, although with difficulty as he fought against sobs of his own.

"I'm so...so sorry Mark. I didn't know how you felt about me. I did love you. I'd always loved you. I wanted us to be together. That night when I thought I saw you and Taylor kissing in the graveyard during the party, that made

374

me so angry, but I was drunk. I convinced myself it never happened. Then I saw you and Taylor together, just as we did moments before. That was the day I was going to reveal my feelings for you at last, but I was too late. I waited too long. You already had Taylor. It hurt so bad Mark. I didn't stop crying in the forest. I cried all the way home and the entire night. I thought I'd die. When I awakened in the morning, I started to hate you. I didn't understand how you could do that to me—how you could be with *him*. I hated you both then. I had to hate you, or I would have gone mad. I didn't know how you felt about me. I didn't know you cared. All I knew is that I could never have you. My dream died when I watched you take Taylor in your arms. I'm sorry Mark. I'm sorry for everything."

I could understand, at least to an extent, how love could turn to hate. Devon's pain was so intense, his disappointment so bitter, that he blamed Mark and Taylor for it. It wasn't logical, but I could understand it. Devon had said that he had to hate Mark. He'd hated him in an attempt to shut off the unbearable pain. I didn't get how Devon's hatred of Mark was transferred to all gays, but no doubt that happened over time. We clearly weren't seeing everything. I was glad. I felt guilty that we were trespassing into such private moments of Devon's life.

Devon broke down and cried. Mark took him in his arms and held him as he sobbed. Taylor joined Mark and Devon in their embrace. Devon held tightly onto them both, sobbing his heart out. None of us who stood there had dry eyes.

I felt the last of the hatred I held for Devon in my heart disappear. How could I hate someone who had suffered so through all the long years? Devon had been so wounded he'd turned to hate to dull the pain, only it was a trap that sucked him in deeper and deeper until he'd forgotten why he hated. After a while, hate was all he had left. Mark and Taylor had been right and I had been wrong. Devon wasn't evil; he was just a lost soul enduring unbearable pain. He was trapped in his own hell—until now.

When Devon stepped back from Mark and Taylor at last, they smiled at him. Devon grinned, and he looked truly beautiful. I noticed that the years had fallen away and he looked like the boy of sixteen he once was. It was as if the events of all the years since were swept away.

Sean drew close to Nick and Oliver to Clay. I found myself wishing Thad was there so I could hold him by my side too. It was a peculiar sensation.

In the blink of an eye, we were in the tower room. I wondered for an instant if this was some other scene from Devon's past, but no, this was the present. Sean, Nick, Oliver, Clay, Marshall and I were seated in comfy chairs.

"He's gone," Oliver said.

I looked around. Devon wasn't there anymore.

"Mark is gone too," Sean said.

Taylor remained with us, and all eyes naturally turned to him.

"Is it over Taylor? The battle with Devon, I mean?" Oliver asked.

"What you refer to as the battle is finished," Taylor said.

I had the feeling there was hidden meaning in Taylor's words, but I didn't even know what questions to ask to get at it. Taylor turned to me and smiled.

I felt emotionally drained and yet more at peace than I had been in a long time. I couldn't believe the battle with Devon was over. I would not miss the evil spirit who had plagued us, but he'd been a part of things for so long it just seemed odd that he wouldn't be around anymore. Even when I was away at college, he'd somehow been a part of my life. I'd felt a threatening presence looming. I felt as if I've kept my guard up for half my life because I was afraid Devon would find some new way to come at me or my friends.

Devon had done tremendous harm, but he was also a victim—a victim of life. I wondered what it must have been like for him all those years ago. There he was, on the verge of expressing his love for Mark, and then he saw him with Taylor. It must have been devastating. Then, he became trapped in a hell of his own creation. True, many of his problems were of his own doing, but Devon couldn't help but be himself.

"Where're Mark and Devon?" Oliver asked.

"They had some unfinished business."

"What will happen to Devon now?" Oliver asked.

"That depends largely on all of you."

From the confused looks on the faces of my friends, I knew they were as perplexed as I.

"What does that mean?" Sean asked.

"You're about to find out." Taylor looked almost mischievous as he smiled.

A blinding flash of white light filled the room. Taylor was gone. In his place stood...

"Devon!" Sean said.

The handsome, sixteen-year-old boy we'd observed playing soccer stood before us. He gazed at us fearfully. He reminded me of a very frightened cornered beast.

"What the..." began Clay, but then faltered.

Devon trembled as he gazed at us with his eyes filled with tears. No one quite knew what to do.

Oliver stood up slowly and approached him. Devon swallowed hard and looked at Oliver, with eyes wide with fear. He trembled. He would have backed away, but he was already up against the wall.

"It's okay," Oliver said. He paused. "You're still human, aren't you?"

Devon nodded. How different he was now. He bore no resemblance at all to what he'd once been. Or rather, he was once again as he had been before hate had blackened his heart. The malicious Devon was gone.

"It's okay," Oliver repeated. "No one's going to hurt you."

Oliver inched forward and slowly extended his hand. This was Oliver's task, without a doubt. He was the least intimidating of us. He also had been the closest to Devon once upon a time. Even though Devon had sought to destroy his chances with Clay, there had been something between them—perhaps something that had touched Devon's heart.

Oliver grasped Devon's shoulder. Devon flinched.

"Come on. Sit down."

Oliver took Devon by the arm and led him to a chair. Devon looked at us as if he expected us to jump him at any second. No one moved. We all just sat there and watched with rapt fascination.

Devon sat there and stared at us fearfully. His eyes were filled with tears, but I think they were tears of remorse rather than fear.

"I'm sorry," he said, his voice racked by a sob. "I'm so sorry. I don't care what you do to me. I deserve it. I'm sorry."

Devon sounded so pathetic that I could not find it in my heart to be angry with him. I would never have believed I would speak the words that were about to come from my lips, but there was nothing I wanted to say to him more.

"I forgive you," I said.

Devon's eyes locked with mine for several moments while the room remained perfectly silent.

"I forgive you too," Oliver said.

"And me," Sean said.

"And me," Nick said.

Soon, everyone had forgiven Devon. I had no doubt everyone was feeling what I felt. Seeing those scenes from Devon's past had changed not only Devon, but the rest of us as well.

Devon sat there still sobbing, now bewildered, but still afraid. I couldn't imagine what he was thinking or feeling. The change in his life must have been staggering. He sat there. He was now nothing more than a sixteen-year-old boy. It was as if he'd been sent back in time to his youth, but he was in the present and not the past. He was alone, confused and frightened.

Marshall's eyes met mine across the room and asked the silent question that was in my own mind: *what are we going to do with him?* The answer was not long in coming.

Sean stood and stepped toward Devon. He extended his hand.

"Come with me. I'll show you to your room, and...you're going to need to meet my parents."

Devon took Sean's hand.   He sobbed even harder, but a small, genuine smile formed on his lips.

"I wonder how I'm going to explain this one to Mom and Dad," Sean said, as he passed.

I grinned. How indeed?

Epilogue

Ralph
April 28, 2005

"She has been in there for seven hours," Jordan said and then immediately continued his pacing in the private waiting room.

"That's nothing unusual. Labor can easily take several hours," Jordan's mom said.

"Will you please just sit down?" I asked. "You're wearing out the carpet."

Jordan sat beside me on the loveseat.

"I wonder what's happening in there."

"You can go in, you know."

"No way! She has everyone she needs in there. Sam's mom is with her. Besides, I think Sam is far more comfortable with us out here."

"I'm sure that's true, especially if you paced in there like you do out here," I said.

A nurse stuck her head out the door.

"Samantha would like you to come in now."

Jordan grabbed my hand as we stood. The man who could stand up and sing in front of thousands was trembling.

"Hey," I said.

Jordan turned to look at me. I pulled him close and kissed him on the lips. Jordan smiled. Jordan, Stephanie, and I walked into the birthing room. There lay Sam, her strawberry-blond hair fanned out on the pillow.

"Twins?" Jordan's mom said. Her voice easily rose an octave. She looked accusingly back and forth between Jordan and me. "You didn't tell me?"

"You or anyone else. There's a secret the tabloids didn't get," Jordan said.

We gazed at Sam holding a baby in each of her arms.

"Come in," Samantha said, smiling. "I'd like you to officially meet your sons. Your grandchildren," Sam said, looking at Stephanie.

"They're beautiful," I said. "And so are you Sam."

Jordan and I leaned over and kissed Samantha on the cheek. We just stood there taking it all in for several moments.

Jordan actually had tears in his eyes as he looked at our babies. I held his hand across the bed. The baby on Sam's right, closest to Jordan had blond hair and blue-green eyes. He looked so much like Jordan that I had no doubt Jordan was the father. The other baby, however, had dark hair and eyes the color of my own. He bore a striking resemblance to my baby pictures.

"I take it you've noticed too," Sam said, as she looked at me.

"What?" Jordan asked.

"Could it be? With twins?" I asked.

"They're fraternal twins, not identical twins, as you can see. I asked the doctor and he said it's not impossible. Besides, isn't it obvious? One look should be enough to tell who the biological father is."

"I hate to burst everyone's bubble," Stephanie said, "but you do know that the eye and hair color of babies often changes."

"Not this time," Jordan said.

I gazed over at my partner. One look in his eyes told me he knew that to be the truth with absolute certainty. I had no doubt myself as to how he knew.

"Can I hold him?" I asked. Tears were running down my cheeks by this time.

"Men," Sam said, rolling her eyes. "Is it any wonder I'm a lesbian? Of course you can hold him. He's your son."

I carefully picked up our son and held him in my arms. He grasped my little finger with his hand. His own fingers were unbelievably tiny. Jordan picked up our other son and then carefully walked to my side. We stood there looking down at our babies in awe.

My whole life changed as I stood there. I knew things would never be the same again. So many times my parents had said, "When you're a father, you'll understand," and now I knew exactly what they meant. Nothing else mattered any more except those tiny babies that Jordan and I held in our arms.

"Have you made a decision on the names yet?" Stephanie asked.

Sam looked expectantly toward Jordan and me. The three of us had discussed many possibilities. Jordan and I had offered to leave the final decision up to Sam, but she had turned us down. Now, she waited with Stephanie to hear what our children would be called for the rest of their lives.

"Taylor and Mark," Jordan said, gazing at our sons.

Tears truly began to roll from Jordan's eyes then.

We stood there together in that perfect moment in time. I knew that no matter how long I lived that this would be a moment I would always remember. Suddenly, all that I'd experienced seemed a mere preface to my real story. Only now were we beginning Chapter One.

The Gay Youth Chronicles

Listed in suggested reading order

Outfield Menace

Snow Angel

The Nudo Twins

The Soccer Field Is Empty

Someone Is Watching

A Better Place

The Summer of My Discontent

Disastrous Dates & Dream Boys

Just Making Out

Temptation University

Fierce Competition

Scarecrows

Scotty Jackson Died... But Then He Got Better

The Picture of Dorian Gay

Someone Is Killing the Gay Boys of Verona

Keeper of Secrets

Masked Destiny

Do You Know That I Love You

Altered Realities

Dead Het Boys

This Time Around

Phantom World

The Vampire's Heart

Second Star to the Right

The Perfect Boy

The Graymoor Mansion Bed and Breakfast

Shadows of Darkness

Heart of Graymoor

Yesterday's Tomorrow

Boy Trouble

Christmas in Graymoor Mansion

A Boy Toy for Christmas

Also by Mark A. Roeder

Homo for the Holidays

Ancient Prejudice*

*Ancient Prejudice is an early version of *The Soccer Field Is Empty*, which is recommended by the author instead of *Ancient Prejudice*.

Information on Mark's upcoming books can be found at markroeder.com. Those wishing to keep in touch with others who enjoy Mark's novels can join his fan club at http://groups.yahoo.com/group/markaroederfans.

Made in the USA
Middletown, DE
21 December 2022

19963115R00231